KADJ'EL

ADA HAYNES

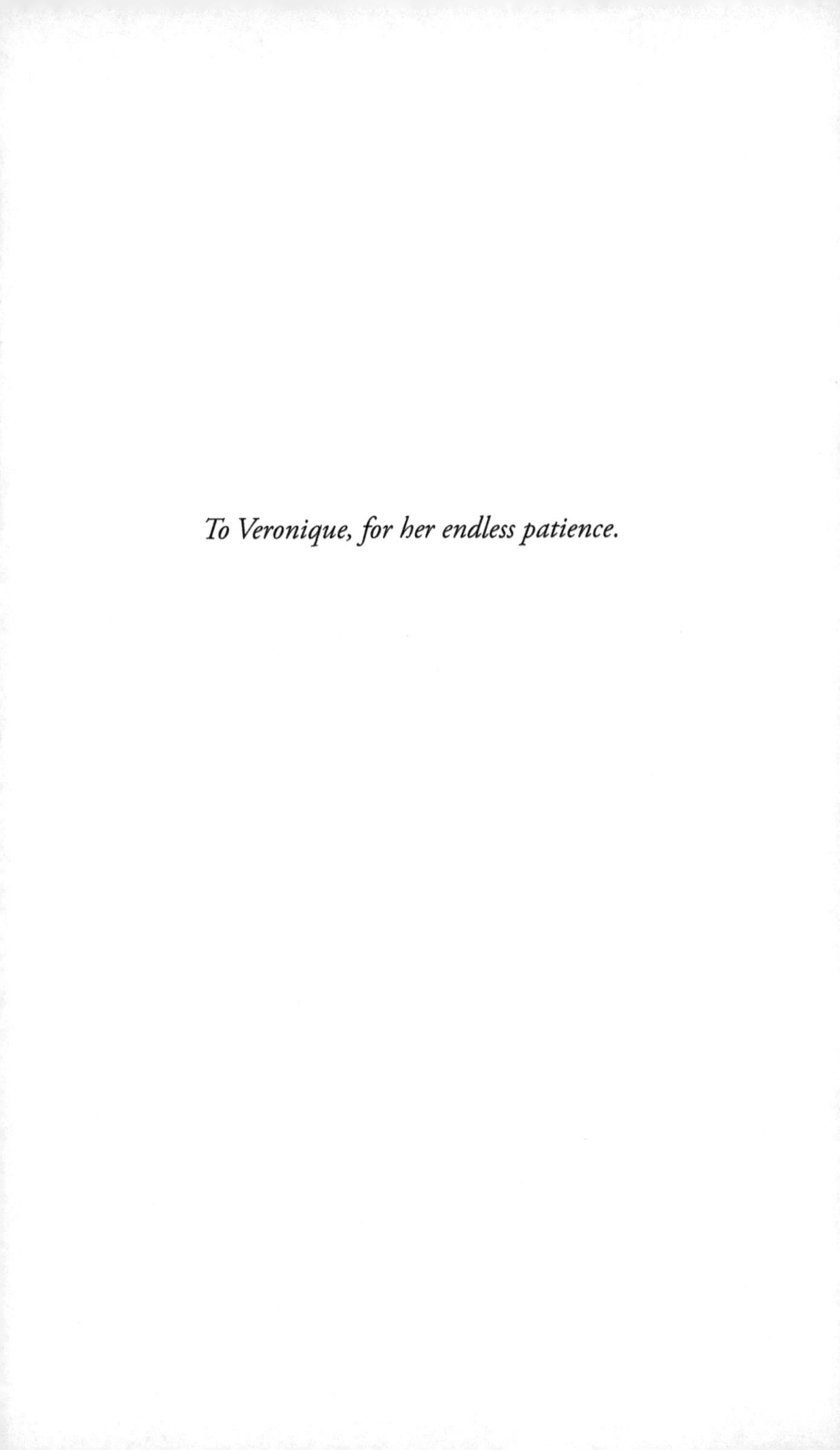

To Veronique, for her endless patience.

1

T HE SILK FELT wonderful under her fingers. She could not help but keep stroking it. How long ago was it that she had worn anything so sensuous? She could not remember.

"Nervous?"

She shrugged, not looking at Jeffrey, not answering.

He lifted his hand to pat her leg, in reassurance, but then probably realized where it was going to land, and replaced it on his own knee.

That brought a smile to her lips, and she nodded. "I should never have let Maire choose this dress for me! It's far too short."

"She's chosen well. I like it. He'll like it."

She caressed the soft tissue covering her, absently. Jeffrey was right, of course, even though his sense of fashion normally tended towards more classic fare, the dress was perfect for what she had in mind. The problem was not the dress. In the past, she had worn far more provocative things. The problem was *her*.

She looked out through the car window. Night was now

falling fast. Street lamps were already redefining the city they illuminated, offering a semblance of security.

Her reflection appeared briefly on the glass window, then vanished, appeared and vanished again. Nothing stable, nothing definite. Like her mind.

There was a time when she would have accomplished her mission without hesitation, straight to the goal—the crazier, the better.

Another time. Another life.

Coming here tonight was a mistake. She was not ready.

Jeffrey knew her too well not to feel her hesitation. "We don't have to go if you've changed your mind, Shona."

She smirked at her reflection in the window. "Bit late for that, don't you think? We are less than ten minutes away from the party. Fate has helped us this time. You don't want to contradict it."

"We can still go home. There'll be other opportunities, I'm certain."

There. She had a choice.

She hated choices. They made her head hurt. They made her want a drink, or…

No.

She turned her head and looked into Jeffrey's concerned face. "I won't chicken out of this."

He nodded, briefly, showing a touch of a smile.

At that moment, their driver slowed down the car. They heard the GPS navigator announce that they had reached their destination.

Jeffrey lowered his window. The head of a young man, probably some kind of security guard, appeared at the opening. After greeting them, the young man asked for their invitation. Jeffrey handed him the document.

She was so tense that she was deaf to the rest of the conversation.

The car started moving forward again. There was no turning back now!

Jeffrey did pat her naked leg this time. "You're going to be all right, girl!"

*

The driver left them at the entrance of the villa, and drove away.

"Is he going to stay nearby?" asked Shona, concerned.

"Yes. Don't worry about it. What do you think of the place?"

Oh! Jeffrey knew her, indeed. She focused her attention on the house they were now approaching, slowly walking on a cement path.

"Mm-hm. That's certainly something else."

What she had so far seen of Zurich houses, she did not really like; they were big, boring concrete blocks, with dull colors and a regiment of unimaginative windows.

This villa was nothing like that. There were four thin rectangular blocks layered one upon another and integrated with the landscape, with picture windows running from one end to the other. Elegant. Modern. Open.

"I like it, Jeffrey. Look at the view on the lake!"

A man, dressed from head to toe in black, suddenly appeared on their left.

"Amazing, isn't it? That's what prompted me to buy the place."

She missed her next step. Had Jeffrey not held her arm firmly under his, she would have fallen.

"I apologize for having startled you, miss."

No one would have surprised her like this in the past.

She managed to put a smile on her face. "No need to. I like your place, Ekbeth!"

She had no doubt about the man's identity. They had prepared this little operation thoroughly. There were only two men at this party who had such thick black hair and mesmerizing green eyes, of that she was certain, and the other one was far younger.

If she had shocked their host with her familiarity, he did not show it. Instead, he gallantly offered her a glass of champagne. "I quite like it myself, miss."

Their fingers touched. She looked into his eyes. "Shona. My name is Shona. No 'miss,' please."

He smiled. "Welcome to my humble home, Shona. I hope you'll enjoy yourself."

Jeffrey accepted his glass and started pulling her away, but she resisted. "I'm sure you have to take care of all your guests tonight, Ekbeth, but I'd really like a tour of the whole place, if you can spare the time."

He hesitated only slightly, then nodded, smoothly. "I'm sure I can accommodate you, Shona. Later."

She stopped resisting Jeffrey. They entered a vast room, already crowded with guests.

*

Ekbeth na Duibhne's parties had a reputation among the jet set. The events were always a bit of a surprise, as they could happen any time, and anywhere. When you got an invitation, Shona understood, you made room in your agenda to attend them. When Ekbeth was entertaining, you could expect the best, in all regards.

True, he was a bit of a mystery. No one really knew much about him, or his family, or even his business. His staff was not talking. Even his former lovers—and rumors said he had had quite a few—were not talking.

What was certain was that he owned one of the most discreet private banks in the world, with its main office based in Zurich, and a very select clientele.

There were rumors that Ekbeth's fortune had been built on money laundering, but that had never been proven. Not that his guests really cared anyway. Counting him as a friend was important to some. Some women hoped for more than friendship. He was probably the most sought-after bachelor this evening.

Shona scanned the room. There were a few potential rivals, but she was certain she had made an impression. Furthermore, she knew the man's biggest secret. Although it was no help for what she intended to do tonight, it would be, in the end, a serious advantage over the other women.

Jeffrey requested her attention by pinching her. "What is your game, girl? He's not the one you are supposed to seduce tonight! Or have you forgotten?"

She took a sip of champagne before answering. Somehow, all her previous nervousness seemed to have disappeared. She was feeling like her old self again, and it was good. Very good. "I have not forgotten, Jeffrey, but I've changed my mind."

Jeffrey was not really surprised, of course. They had been through so much together; he was used to her last minute changes to carefully prepared plans.

Still, he asked, " the ring? Ekbeth does not have it."

She shrugged. "Leave it to me, Jeffrey. I'll figure out something. As usual."

He winced. "Exactly what I was afraid of."

She was the one doing the patting, suddenly, and she was doing it with a huge grin on her face. "Come on, Jeffrey! Have a little bit more faith in me! Now, why don't we do what we promised Maire, and have a professional look at the party? Or were you planning to stay in this corner sipping champagne the whole night?"

He raised a quizzical eyebrow. "After the speech she gave us? No, ma'am. I'm all ready to take notes."

"Good man! Let's start over by the catering! I am starving!"

The buffet was at the other end of the room, and the room was crowded, but with a few deft moves they managed to reach it.

2

"SEEMS LIKE THIS is going to be another of your successes, Cousin! People are enjoying themselves tonight!"

Ekbeth was quite pleased with the party himself, but knew better than to show it.

"Thank Lyas for that, Lyrian! She organized everything, not me!"

His younger cousin smiled. "Ah, of course. Our talented little niece! This is—what— the third event she's organized for you? Where is she, by the way? Knowing her, I would have expected her to be around to ensure the hired staff is doing its job properly."

Ekbeth ignored the sarcasm. "You know as well as I do that Lyas does not like to attend parties—which is a shame, if you ask me. She deserves all the compliments, not me."

Lyrian nodded and raised his glass to their absent niece. For a moment, they silently enjoyed the happy crowd surrounding them.

Lyrian was not the worst member of Ekbeth's family. In fact, Lyrian reminded Ekbeth much of himself, but he was not going to tell the lout that. Same black hair, same green eyes, same height. Lyrian was maybe in better shape than him, as his cousin jogged at least five kilometers every day—something Ekbeth refused even to consider. Travelling around the world to meet his customers was exhausting enough for his taste. But it was more than only physical likeness. Just like Ekbeth, Lyrian was a wizard with figures—a very handy skill when you are trading millions or negotiating loans and commissions on a daily basis. Even their character had many similarities, with one big exception: Lyrian was quick to anger. He would learn better, eventually. At least, Ekbeth hoped so, for Lyrian's sake.

It had already cost Lyrian dearly—his wife, his house and almost his life. He had been lucky that Ekbeth had decided to help him, although that was something they both carefully avoided mentioning. Ekbeth had just happened to need some help with his business and had been glad Lyrian was available at the right time.

"So, Ekbeth. Any potential fun in sight for tonight?"

Ah! This was just so Lyrian! He could not keep his mouth shut for long. But Ekbeth decided to humor him. "Actually, yes."

Lyrian's brows went up in surprise. Normally, Ekbeth just ignored his taunts. "Really? Who is she?"

Ekbeth pointed discreetly with his glass. From where they were, they had a perfect view of the woman. Lyrian whistled his approval. "Very nice! But she's not alone, in case you've not noticed."

"I have, but I don't think he'll mind. I've been watching them, Lyrian. They look to me more like business partners than a couple."

Lyrian observed the woman a bit longer. "You may be right. So what's the plan?"

Ekbeth allowed himself to smile this time. "She's asked to see the rest of the house. I am going to oblige her."

Lyrian feigned shock, and quickly glanced around, looking for someone. Ekbeth knew who and growled, "And I don't care what Kalem thinks of my plan!"

He had nothing against Kalem. The man was just doing his job, protecting him, and he was doing it very well. Sometimes a bit too well.

Lyrian smiled.

"Ah! Then you'd better make a move, Cousin, like, now! Because your best friend the bodyguard is busy with one of his own staff and not looking at you, for once!"

Ekbeth followed Lyrian's stare. Ah, indeed.

"Cover for me, Lyrian. I'd really hate to see Kalem appear at the wrong time."

Lyrian raised his glass. "You owe me, Ekbeth!"

*

Ekbeth took his time crossing the room. He did not want to seem too eager. Plus his other guests wanted to talk to him.

Why did this woman attract him so strongly? He was not sure. She certainly was not the only one who had flirted with him tonight. She was a bit muscular for his taste, and lacked womanly form in the important places. Still, he felt drawn to her. Sure enough, she was showing some very nice legs. He'd always had a weakness for women with long legs on high heels. He also liked her mane of unruly brown hair. With her silky silver dress, she was something of a siren, he thought with amusement.

She felt his approach this time and turned towards him, offering an enticing smile.

"Ekbeth! I almost thought you had forgotten me!"

He bowed slightly, ever the gentleman. "Sorry for having kept you waiting, Shona. Still interested in visiting the house?"

She took the offered arm. "Of course. Are we going upstairs? I'm sure the view is even better from the upper floor."

Then she whispered in his ear. "And much less crowded."

Her partner did not react, did not even seem to have heard them. Apparently, Ekbeth had been right on that account.

Her breath still warm on his ear, Ekbeth guided her towards the lift.

"How decadent, Ekbeth! A lift for such a short trip!"

"But very convenient sometime. The house is big, Shona. I really appreciate being able to go from the garage to my bedroom in less than a minute and at no effort on my part."

There was a security man in front of the lift doors. The man did not ask any questions, and called the lift when he recognized the owner of the place. Ekbeth knew, however, that the guard was going to report his actions as soon as the lift doors closed.

Damn Kalem! Oh, his bodyguard was right, of course. They did not want any guests to start wandering in the private floors uninvited.

Ekbeth could now only hope Lyrian was going to keep his promise.

The cabin started climbing. Her hand moved slightly, caressing his arm. "How much time do we have, Ekbeth?"

He looked at her. She had a nice face. High cheekbones. Large clear grey eyes with long, dark lashes. A full mouth calling for kisses. He touched her lips with the tip of his fingers, playfully. "Enough for what we both have in mind, Shona."

She pouted. "I was not aware you could read minds, Ekbeth."

"You'd be surprised to know how many things I can do that no one is aware of, Shona."

The lift doors opened. Needing only a couple of long strides to get out of the lift, she crossed the main room quickly, towards the huge bay window on the opposite side. "I was right! The view is even better from here."

Ekbeth turned on the light. She turned away from the window, looked around her. "And I like the decoration. Are those real jades? You have quite a collection!"

He simply nodded. No need to pretend, he was quite happy with the place. The soft carpet and the light wooden furniture, as well as the precious yet discreet ornaments, made the room a quiet place to which he always returned with pleasure, even anticipation. And she was indeed right: the view over the lake was fantastic.

He had no regret for having replaced his grandfather's pretentious villa with this one. More than any other place, this was his home.

He observed her as she walked slowly beside the bookshelves that ran all around the walls, displaying some books, but mostly his personal collection of jade sculptures.

Before he could think of a smart comment about her

attitude, she started walking towards him. With purpose. One small gesture and her dress fell to the floor. Except for a very small G-string, and her shoes, she was now stark naked.

She stopped at three paces from him, teasingly. Ekbeth did not respond to the obvious invitation immediately. He took his time studying her.

Her smile grew and she took another step, then another. "Losing time here, Ekbeth! I won't bite, I promise! Or maybe just a little."

He took her in his arms, with a laugh. "Don't you dare!"

They kissed. Her skin was incredibly soft and warm under his hands. Ara! She felt even better than he had expected.

3

J EFFREY WAS IN deep conversation with an older man when she finally came back downstairs, but he immediately noticed her. She walked outside, onto the terrace.

People were staring at her—women with forced smiles on their lips. Everyone seemed to know what had just happened one floor higher.

Maybe she had been a tad too loud, she thought, feeling her cheeks flush a bit. It was all Ekbeth's fault. The man was a wizard. He had found all her sensitive places. She had lost control. Even now, from the top of her toes to the tip of her head, she was still tingling from his lovemaking.

It had been far too long since she had felt so passionately alive. She did not want to dwell on exactly how long, or who it had been. Ekbeth did not deserve any unfair comparison. He had been perfect.

"You were gone a long time!"

She accepted the glass from Jeffrey. "Some things need time!"

"True. And if you are wondering why everyone is staring

at you right now, yes, they too noticed you were gone with Ekbeth upstairs."

She grinned, somehow relieved. "Only that? Good. I thought for a moment they had heard me as well."

He shook his head. "God, no! That would have been really embarrassing! So I guess we can call this a success? Even though you've changed your target at the very last moment?"

She looked at the lake below. Night had always been her favorite time. You could barely make out the landscape, but the moon was full tonight, and it put an eerie light on everything.

"Shona?"

"What? Oh, yes. It was a success. In more aspects than you think. But you'll have to wait to hear the details."

He feigned shock. "I don't want details!"

"Ah! You will want some of them, believe me! How long do you think we have to wait until we can make a polite exit?"

"The owner of the house does not want to show you anything else tonight?"

She shook her head, then caught his sudden grin. "What is your dirty mind thinking, Jeffrey? Ekbeth's bodyguard was expecting us when we came back from the upper floor. The man had some urgent stuff to discuss which could not wait, he said. He just ignored me. Quite insulting actually. But I'm ready to bet that I won't be allowed to approach his boss for the rest of the evening."

Jeffrey's grin only grew. "Clever of him. Yes, I noticed him as well. I think we should postpone leaving until the end of the fireworks. They should start any moment now."

That surprised her. "Fireworks?"

"Yes. On the lake."

"My! I'm so very glad we came tonight, Jeffrey! I wonder how Ekbeth managed this."

"Money, girl. Money opens a lot of doors, even here."

She nodded and sipped from her glass.

"Yes, it is convenient to be rich sometimes."

*

Two hours later, their plane left Zurich airport. For once, she did not complain about the uselessness, to her eyes, of using a private jet, nor the money Jeffrey had to give to arrange a night flight when the airport was officially closed.

She first got rid of her shoes. They were elegant, for sure, but new, and her feet were now hurting like hell. Then she rushed to the toilets. She had to stand and squirm to get to it. It was inserted deeper than she had thought, and it was big. What had she been thinking?

There was a knock on the door. "Are you okay, Shona? You're not sick, are you?"

She cursed, tried another position. "I'm trying to respect your prudery, Jeffrey! Just leave me alone."

She managed to extract the stone at last, with a loud grunt.

"What are you doing in there, Shona?"

Damn the man! She unlocked the door and opened it brusquely. She put the stone under his face. "This is what I was doing! Satisfied?"

Jeffrey looked at the flat circular sculpted piece of jade with a blank look at first, but that did not last long. "Where did this come from?"

"Jeffrey! I know even you can recognize that telling smell! Where else was I supposed to hide it with that dress?"

He shook his head, sternly. "That's not what I'm asking. I mean, where did you take the jade stone from?"

She smiled smugly. "From Ekbeth's safe."

Jeffrey cursed, loudly, before clutching her shoulders and shaking her. "Are you out of your mind? Do you have any idea what you've just done?"

She had expected that reaction, which was the reason she had not told him earlier. "Relax, Jeffrey, we are safe!"

He stopped shaking her, but did not release her shoulders. "Safe? This man, Ekbeth, is very powerful, Shona! And he has connections. Do you think he won't guess who's stolen this from him? And that he'll let it go unpunished?"

She shrugged his hands off and walked calmly to the nearest seat. "But I want him to know who's taken it from him, Jeffrey! Don't you see? We are going to swap it against the Kadj'dur!"

Jeffrey put himself in the seat facing her, still fuming. "One small detail you may have forgotten: Ekbeth is not the owner of the ring! His cousin is!"

She ignored him. "This stone must be worth a lot! He had tons of other valuable jades displayed openly all around the room! But that one was in Ekbeth's safe."

"Why didn't you take one of the others, then? Why go into his safe?"

"Because the rest were too big for me to smuggle away!"

She cleaned the stone with a corner of her dress. "Look at it, Jeffrey! It is ancient, I'm sure! Look at those little decorations! I've never seen anything like this before! Ekbeth will want it back! He'll force his cousin to give us the ring!"

"Or he'll find us, take the stone and kill us!"

She shook her head. "Him? He's not the kind!"

"You are really underestimating the man, Shona! If not him, his bodyguard! Who is a nasty piece to handle from the reports I've seen, believe me!"

He sighed, took his head in his hands. "It was a perfect plan, Shona! Go to the party, seduce Lyrian Farrill, eventually discover where the ring was and discreetly take it from him! Why do you always have to complicate the simpler plans? And at the same time put our lives in jeopardy?"

She had never seen such a blue tinge in jade before. Truly an admirable piece. Yeshe would have loved it.

"Stop the drama, Jeffrey! Ekbeth is not going to kill us! We are going to wait a week or two, then send him a little note."

"And where are you planning to make the swap? How?"

"We'll find the perfect solution in the coming weeks, I'm sure! Now, are you not going to compliment me for having snapped up this little beauty?"

He looked, right now, more like he could strangle her. "Compliment? I still don't know how you managed this magic, Shona, but I know this was child's play for you. So—no, sorry—no compliment!"

He was slowly recovering from the shock, she could see. He extended his hand toward her. "May I?"

She handed the piece of jade over to him. He examined it closely. "It is indeed beautiful, and ancient."

He wanted to return the stone to her but she shook her head. "You keep it. In our safe at the Castle. Until we figure out a plan!"

"But you're coming with me back to the Castle, aren't you?"

She sighed. "I wish. Unfortunately, I promised Maire to

help with one of her projects. Something to do with checking the quality of a rock group, if I got it correctly. I have to go to London."

He nodded, then suddenly grinned. "And what are you going to tell Maire about this evening, tell? She is going to be mad at you!"

Shona winced. Not that she hadn't thought of that already. "She won't, as long as you don't spill it out to her! She sent us to make a little investigation. That's just what we did!"

"Ah! She won't buy it! She knows of our plan. And I'm sure some of the guests tonight are her customers. If not me, someone will tell her."

"Her customers won't make the connection between Maire and me."

"But they'll certainly gossip about the woman who left the party for a full hour in Ekbeth's company!"

Then his eyes went huge. "The invitation, Shona! Ekbeth is going to find out through the invitation what happened and go to Maire."

Damn! Jeffrey was right, of course. It was too late to give the stone back now. It had seemed the perfect plan at the time, but she was not so sure anymore.

She needed to warn Maire. Her friend was not going to take that bit of news calmly. The thought certainly gave her a headache.

Bad choice again.

"I'll figure out something, Jeffrey."

4

S TANDING CLOSE TO the windows of his private
rooms, Ekbeth looked at the view outside. The exquisite beauty of the lake beneath him and the surrounding mountains was normally a sure way to soothe whatever
mood he was in.

Not today though. Right now, it only brought the memory of Shona standing at this very spot. And what she had
done to him.

Outwardly, he was showing his usual self, confident and
quiet. Inwardly, he was seething.

She had fooled him. Completely.

Of all the things she could have stolen, she had to take
the Annilis jewels—the very jewels his long-dead ancestor
Taralieni had saved from destruction when all the rest had
been destroyed, so many millennia ago. Those jade pieces
were his people's only link to their glorious and ancient past.
Even in the worst parts of their history, they had never lost
them. Until today.

If only he had brought them back immediately to the
Valley instead of putting them in his safe. He sighed. Ifs were
not going to help him out of this. Getting back the jewels

before the start of the Aras'arisidz was what he had to do. Which gave him less than a week.

It was, in fact a small blessing that he had discovered the theft so quickly. He had wanted to study the jewels before going to work. It was not every day that he had the opportunity to have a close look at the craftsmanship of his long-deceased ancestors.

Not finding the jewels in their box has not raised immediate panic. No, that had started after he had discussed the disappearance with Kalem and his cousin Lyrian. They were the only other ones who had access to the safe. When they both denied having opened it, Ekbeth realized someone else may have had access to the safe. He had no idea how she would have managed that small feat, but there was no other explanation. He himself had given her a perfect opportunity to commit her crime by inviting her upstairs.

Ekbeth suddenly remembered something one of his uncles had once told him, and he winced. Women would be his doom, the old fool had said. He was too soft with them. They were only scheming little devils, and he was blind to the fact.

The context had been different, but nonetheless quite pertinent right now. One hour of pleasure. If he could not get the jewels back in time, Ekbeth was going to pay for this short moment of fun with his life. Literally.

Behind him, reflected in the window, he could see Kalem's men looking for fingerprints all over his favorite room, leaving dark powder traces over his furniture. That angered him at least as much as the theft. The place would never be the same to him now. No matter how thoroughly his cleaning lady worked to put everything back as it was, the memory of what had happened here would remain.

He felt like hitting something. Hard. He walked to Kalem, who was sitting at the table, scanning a long list of names—the guests of yesterday's party. "Have you found her yet?"

Kalem shook his head. "I've run the list twice already. No Shona on it."

Ekbeth frowned. This should not have been possible. They had taken every precaution possible with the invitations.

Kalem did not wait for his comment. "There must be a logical explanation. I will find her, Ekbeth."

"I know you will."

One of Kalem's men approached them. "No fingerprints anywhere, sir."

"Even on the safe?"

The man shook his head.

Kalem cursed, then looked at Ekbeth with a frown. "Your cleaning lady did a thorough job when she cleaned the room after you left it yesterday. Damn, I never thought I would complain about how good the woman is at her job, but today I certainly am."

It was a small comfort to Ekbeth to see he was not the only one angry.

He could not stand the wait anymore. He needed to do something. Anything. There was not much he could do here. As Kalem had reminded him half an hour ago, it was not his job to go after criminals.

"I'm going to the bank, Kalem."

Kalem only nodded and spoke quickly in his ever-present com. Ekbeth walked to the lift. By the time he reached the garage under the house, his driver was waiting for him, along with a security man.

The ride to the center of Zurich was short, but getting out of the villa helped improve his mood. Just a tiny bit. By the time he got out of the car, in front of his main workplace, a discreet house in a quiet street just off the famous Paradeplatz, he was ready to tackle the daily tasks.

He walked directly to his office. Lyrian was nowhere to be seen. Probably meeting a customer somewhere.

His assistant, Orsina, was expecting him, and held out a stack of messages. She had not heard of the theft, of course. For her it was a day as any other. With a sigh, Ekbeth opened his computer, while listening to her.

There were decisions to be made. Kalem was good at his job, despite his grumpiness. Ekbeth had to leave the missing jewel matter to him and concentrate on the finances, earn money for his family. That was his job.

*

When he came back to his home at the end of the day, Ekbeth found Lyrian and Kalem in the dining room, with three other security people. They were all looking at some computer screen, a few pages of paper spread around them. Kalem was staring at the screen, muttering names—names that his people were checking against the documents.

They were so focused on their task that they did not even acknowledge Ekbeth's entrance.

"Evening, gentlemen."

Lyrian returned the greeting and, when Ekbeth was near enough, whispered, "They are going through the security tapes."

Ekbeth frowned. There were no security tapes in his

private rooms. He had insisted. He did not care what Kalem's point of view was. Had the man disobeyed him?

Lyrian smiled. "Not what you think, Ekbeth. This one is the camera at the entrance. They are checking the guests' arrivals against the guest list."

Ekbeth was even more confused. "Why?"

Lyrian pointed at the papers.

"As you well know, all the guests received a personal invitation. Kalem had the invitations counted this morning. No extra piece of cardboard. Actually, we're missing a few. Which makes sense. Not everyone could come, and they don't always think of telling us. Kalem has now checked that. All the invitations are accounted for. We have them, or their owner has it because he or she did not come yesterday. Then Kalem checked all the names on the invitations we have. All of them were on the list!"

Ekbeth started to understand. "I thought the man charged with checking the invitations had a device with the guests' pictures to check their ID?"

"Correct. And they've interviewed him. He can't remember any anomalies. But there was no name linked to the pictures. The man scanned the invitation, the pictures were appearing on his screen and he just checked if the faces match. That was your decision to protect your guests' identity."

Ekbeth looked at the computer screen. "I never thought this would be a problem. So, what is Kalem doing now?"

"Matching the guest list to the faces again. Looking for the mistake. This man has an impressive memory, I must say. I could not name half of the people we were watching, though some of them are very familiar, but Kalem just says the name as soon as he sees the face!"

Ekbeth had to smile at that. "He'd probably give you their birthdates and addresses if you asked him. He is very good at his job, Lyrian. Did you spend the whole afternoon here? I thought you were meeting that man in Paris today?"

Lyrian nodded. "Correct. The deal is done. I just arrived a few minutes before you, in fact."

He paused briefly then shook his head. "The more I think about this, Ekbeth, the less sense it makes to me. How can she have opened the safe without leaving fingerprints all over it! You said she was left alone ten minutes max! Even with the safe combination, which I can't believe she had, it's an awful short time to open the safe, empty it and close it again!"

Ekbeth agreed. Shona had been quick to clean herself up and put her scant clothes back on, but he had not left her alone that long. She had been waiting on the sofa by the window when he returned to the main room. The safe was located on the other side of the room.

He had tried to remember whether she had seemed out of breath then, but he was not sure.

"Something else does not make sense, Lyrian. How many people knew I had those jewels in the safe? They were there only since yesterday morning!"

Lyrian frowned. "Well, the three of us and a few members of the staff. But surely you don't..."

"No. All the staff has been working here for our family for years. I trust their honesty. So her knowing I had the jewels in that safe is something that really puzzles me."

He was watching the screen from afar. There had been

almost five hundreds guests yesterday. Kalem was going to be busy for some time.

He sighed. "Not a word of this to Lyas, Lyrian. She'll never be able to keep the news to herself."

Lyrian looked at him quizzically. "Are you serious? Not telling the rest of the community is going to put you in a lot of trouble if we don't recover the jewels in time."

Ekbeth nodded. "Tell me about it! But telling them now will bring unnecessary delays at a time when we need to be putting all our efforts into catching the thief."

He could only imagine the reaction of the Aramalinyia when she'd hear of it. And she was the most reasonable person of the lot!

No. Keeping this a secret was the best option for now. Besides… "You know, there might be an explanation for the lack of fingerprints."

Lyrian was frowning again. He had not thought that far yet, apparently.

Ekbeth glanced at the security men around Kalem. No one was paying attention to him. He only needed to concentrate a little, and wait to feel the usual tingling in his fingertips. He thrust his hand through the closed panel of a cupboard. His hand moved through the wood as if through water.

When Ekbeth extracted his hand, he had a glass in it. Intact.

Lyrian was shocked. "You don't mean it!"

"But it makes sense, doesn't it! No fingerprints, Lyrian! And you don't need a lot of time to do this!"

"But you have to be As'mir to do that, Ekbeth! She's not part of the community!"

"Are we so sure of that? I can't swear I know all of them, Lyrian! Besides, she could be a rogue one. A descendant of a banished As'mir we've lost trace of. Or an unknown bastard!"

That last one made them both smile. As'mirin were not very fertile. The chance that one of them would have produced a child by accident was very slim. Their amusement did not last long though.

"Does Kalem know of your theory?" Lyrian asked.

"Not yet. Let's try to find out how this woman cheated our security checks first. Then I suppose Kalem will have to make a trip to the Valley to check whether she is part of the community or not."

"But…it makes even less sense, Ekbeth! The jewels are part of the community! Why would someone want to steal them?"

Ekbeth had had plenty of time today to ask himself that question, as well.

"Well, when the Aramalinya decided it was time to get the jewels cleaned up, I was the one who offered to bring them here and use the services of a professional jeweler on this side. Everyone knows I brought them here. Think of the problems I'd get into if the jewels happened to disappear… the perfect opportunity to get rid of me forever, at least as an Akeneires'el. That's also why I'd rather not inform them too quickly of what has happened. If someone of the Valley is behind this, not showing the expected reaction—by this I mean keeping it quiet—might help us to pinpoint him or her faster."

Lyrian had never lived, as Ekbeth did, in the Valley itself, because his father was, in fact, not an As'mir and had lived with his family outside of the Doors. But he had visited often and knew all about the constant intrigues that ran within the small community.

The fact was that, besides being the community banker, Ekbeth was an important figure in the Valley—an Akeneires'el, the head of the Na Duibhnes' family. He had too many enemies to count, even within his own family.

Ekbeth knew Lyrian was jealous of his cousin's status. Sometimes. But probably not today.

5

S HONA WAS DRENCHED when she entered the apartment, but did not care.

She had not been able to sleep since returning from Zurich. Too many things were playing in her head. The only emotional outlet she had found whenever she was in this agitated state—at least an outlet that did not involve drugs or alcohol—was going for a run.

One big advantage of Maire's place was that there was a big park not ten minutes' walk from it.

"Morning, Shona. I thought I heard you come in somewhere this morning, but your bed was empty when I looked, so I was. Wait a sec! You're dripping! Where were you?"

Her best friend, Maire, was staring at her from behind her kitchen table, where she'd been enjoying her first cup of coffee of the day while reading one of her fashion magazines. But, right now, she did not look pleased at all. She frowned with disapproval at Shona's drenched clothes.

Shona knew what was expected of her. She started undressing, trying to keep all the mud and moisture in one spot instead of spreading it across the expensive wooden floor. Seeing the water dripping on her floor, Maire jumped out of her chair. "Let me get you a towel. And some plastic bags to put those clothes into!"

Her quick return with the bags, before leaving once more to fetch a towel, was a sure indication of Maire's priorities. Shona did not comment. She put her clothes and running shoes into the bags, then wrapped herself in the towel, having dried her body as much as possible.

Maire put the bags in the laundry room then came back with her questions. "Where have you been?"

"Running. Have you made enough coffee for two?"

The attempt at diversion did not work. Maire was frowning. "Running? In that weather? And where did you go? There's as much mud under your shoes as water on your clothes!"

"In Kensington."

"The park is closed so early."

This was going somewhere Shona did not like. She walked around Maire and found herself a cup, and some coffee.

Of course, Maire knew her so well that she understood what had happened. "You entered the park when it was closed?"

"Relax, Maire. I kept clear of the palace, and no one tried to arrest me! I needed the run."

Maire's expression made it clear that she thought her friend had much to tell her, but that she also realized there was no point in continuing. "You need a warm shower and some dry clothes. Why don't you do that while I'm making you some breakfast?"

"I'm not hungry. Too many petit-fours yesterday. Coffee is enough."

"Tsk-tsk. Go to the shower! Now! I don't want to have to nurse you when you have pneumonia!"

That was Maire! Always exaggerating! But Shona accommodated her. She walked to the bathroom.

*

She had to admit she was feeling much better and a tiny bit hungry when she came back to the kitchen, warmed by the shower and the comfortable clothes she was now wearing. Until she entered the room again, that is. Maire had her back to her, but Shona heard the closing of the mobile phone in her hand.

Damn! There was no doubt who Maire had been calling. "You were talking to Jeffrey, weren't you?"

Maire did not even try to deny it. She handed her a cup of coffee and nodded slowly.

Shona was not going to get angry about the fact that they discussed her behind her back. Her friends cared for her. She knew they meant well, but it only showed her how little they trust her sanity.

Well, if she could not trust it herself… She sipped her coffee. "Then there's not a lot I have to add I suppose."

"Actually Jeffrey only told me that I'd better ask you how it went."

Shona made a face behind her cup. Damn the man. This was a sure way to get Maire really curious! And not to trust Shona's answers at face value.

She sipped a bit more then put her cup back on the steel table. "It went well. Everything was perfectly arranged, to my point of view. Catering, number of guests, decorations… Hire that girl, she's perfect for the job!"

Maire ticked a perfectly polished nail on the table. Sure

sign she was having trouble keeping her calm. Shona smiled. "Oh, you mean the other part of the plan?"

"Yes! I'm going to hire that girl anyway, because I have already had plenty of opportunities to judge her qualities. But must I remind you that you asked me to go to a workshop to which I did not want to go, only to meet her and manipulate her to apply for a job at my company! And then to arrange for you to assess her abilities through attending one of her events, which, oh wonder, both her uncles were attending—one of which you very much wanted to meet!"

"Okay! Okay! You did help me! I'm very thankful for that, Maire!"

Her friend's fingers were still ticking on the table. "Out with it, Shona! What did happen? You killed one of the guests?"

Shona had to laugh at that. "Nothing that drastic, Maire!"

"So? What happened?"

"Well, I seduced one of the uncles, but not the one I was originally planning to seduce. Then we had a bit of sex together."

Maire raised an eyebrow. "Jeffrey is mad at you because of that? He knows you as well as I do. This could be expected!"

"He's mad at me because I stole something from that uncle!"

The ticking stopped. Maire needed one long minute before she was able to utter, "You're telling me you've stolen something from…what's his name?"

"Ekbeth na Duibhne. Yes, the bank owner himself. And, before you ask, yes it is something very valuable, or at least we think so, Jeffrey and I."

Shona had expected Maire's next move from the

moment she'd started telling her about yesterday evening. Maire's anger was always very controlled.

Maire put her cup of coffee so hard on the steel table that Shona cringed. Well, not always that controlled.

"Are you completely out of your mind, Shona! Have you any idea what is going to happen now?"

Shona met her glare. "I'm going to ask for the Kadj'dur in exchange of the jade stone I've stolen. That's what is going to happen now!"

"That's not what's going to happen, Shona! What's going to happen is that Ekbeth will find out how you've come by that invitation, then there will be hell to pay for his niece, and for me! The man is powerful! One word from him and I can lose my company. After all the hard work I've done to get where I am now!"

"You are dramatizing, Maire! He's not the kind to take it out on innocents!"

"Ah! How sure are you of that? Plus, I'm not innocent in that story, Shona! That's the whole problem!"

She stopped for a moment, inhaled and exhaled a few times, then shook her head.

"Consequences, Shona! How many times will I have to repeat this to you! Think of the consequences before acting! Damn it! Where are you going?"

Shona had had enough. Two sermons in such a short time about her lack of common sense were enough! Yes, she was crazy! But both her friends knew that already—there was no need to rub it in!

"I'm going to leave you alone! At least you won't have to lie when they ask you where I am!"

Maire suddenly grabbed her by the arms and pushed her

against the wall. Shona almost fought back. She stopped herself just in time. This was a friend—an angry friend, but a friend nonetheless. Someone she did not want to harm.

Maire read something on her face, though, because she released her. Shona saw the hint of fear. That hurt her more than all the previous anger. Maire was her friend yet was afraid of her. Nevertheless, Maire had a nasty undertone when she finally uttered, "Go then! Your acts have put me and others in danger, and your reaction is to fly away from your responsibilities towards us. So typical of you!"

Damn the woman!

Freed, Shona reached the door in no time. Maire was already coming after her.

"Damn you! Come back, Shona! I'm sorry! You can't go back out there in this weather! You're not even wearing shoes!"

But Shona closed the door firmly behind her. It was still pouring, but she did not care!

The rain hid her tears. She was hurting so much inside!

She started walking.

6

KALEM WAS LOOKING as though he could drop dead from exhaustion any instant. Forty-eight hours with barely any sleep, and little food, would do that to a man. Ekbeth could not complain about the lack of dedication of his bodyguard, but that did not make his news any easier to accept.

"Are you certain, Kalem?"

"Yes. The Von Dietem confirmed to me that they called off the invitation, because someone in their family died unexpectedly, and that they returned the paper document per post as requested…by Miss Alyasini herself. Then I checked the database used during the party and found the pictures of our culprits under the name of Von Dietem. Our IT expert took a look at the database. Miss Alyasini was the one who uploaded the pictures."

"Could someone have used her login and pretended to be her?"

Kalem shook his head. "Of course, but she would have to have given it to that someone. I checked."

Ekbeth turned his chair towards the window. "This is a bit unexpected."

Lyrian, who had until now listened to the conversation without any comment, jerked.

"That's the understatement of the century, Cousin! Little mousy Lyas plotting behind your back? Getting someone to steal the Annilis jewels? I've always considered her your best ally! Has she been fooling us all this time?"

Kalem nodded. "Looks like it, Lyrian."

Ekbeth closed his eyes and pinched his nose. "There must be another explanation, Kalem. Lyas did not need a professional thief to get to the jewels. First of all, she probably did not know the jewels were in the safe. And even if she did, she knows the safe combination."

Kalem was listening to him, but his expression was not softening. "Why alter the database then? And let two perfect strangers attend this party?"

Ekbeth shook his head. "This does not make sense. But why don't we ask her?"

Lyrian and Kalem were now frowning at him.

"I thought you did not want to involve her in this, Cousin? If we are wrong on this…"

"Leave this to me."

He opened his agenda, did a quick check, and grabbed his mobile phone.

*

Lyas was definitely hiding something, decided Ekbeth. He could feel her uneasiness.

Sometimes he wished he was able to read thoughts, not only strong emotions, like the pure blood As'mirin had reputedly been able to do. It would have been really convenient right now.

Their dinner in a select restaurant of Paris was reaching

its end and so far, he had not been able to ask anything about her strange behavior, nor had she been forthcoming.

He pretended to inspect the color of his dessert wine in order to look at her.

His niece had turned into a lovely girl over time—tall, slender, long black hair, fair skin, and the typical Na Duibhnes' green eyes, though a paler shade than his. Her mother had been a beauty and Alyasini had inherited most of it.

She had just turned twenty, had just finished her studies cum laude.

She was a very shy person by nature, and that was probably her only weakness. For the rest, he was quite proud of her. He loved her. He trusted her. After all, he had more or less replaced her parents since she was five.

Her treason, if it was really so, was therefore even more hurtful.

"Penny for your thoughts, Uncle?"

He looked at her. "Pardon?"

She managed a tiny smile, while fidgeting with her napkin. "You seemed absent for a moment. And you still have not told me why the sudden invitation to this place?"

He put his glass down on the table. Carefully. "I just happen to know this is one of your favorite places, and I wanted to thank you properly for the time you've spent on the party organization."

She blushed. "You liked it?"

Ekbeth had to laugh. "Everyone liked it, Lyas! Have you not read the thank-you notes from the guests? Someone with a lot more experience than you would not have done better."

At that, she reddened three shades darker. Which was unusual, even for her.

He waited a bit, but as she was visibly not going to comment, he finally asked, "Anything you have to tell me, Lyas?"

This time she became so red, he knew he had her. He took her hand and forced her to look at him. "I'm not going to eat you, Lyas. And we are alone. What is it?"

It took her almost five full minutes to blurt it out. "I've found a job, Uncle."

He released her hand. Not exactly what he had been expecting, but he recovered quickly. "So! That is indeed a bit of news! Want to develop a bit on it? Where is it?"

She was still flushed, but now that she had said it, she could not keep her enthusiasm any longer. Her eyes were bright, making her even lovelier. "It's an event company in London, Uncle. I met their manager at a workshop last month. I'd heard of her before, but I would never have dreamed to meet her in person! And she complimented me for my efforts at the workshop. Told me there was a job available for me at her place any time if I wanted to. It was a difficult decision to take, Uncle. But I decided to apply."

Ekbeth managed not to smile. Knowing her, she probably had not slept well in the meantime. "And she's kept her promise? Hired you?"

Lyas nodded. "She called me this morning. The pay is even more than I would have dreamed of!"

Ekbeth was glad for her. This was obviously something really important for Lyas. He had not seen her that excited for a long time. That probably was why she had not doubted the job proposal. Why would she? She was perfect for the job. She was a wonder at event organizations.

But his little niece was normally not so naïve. Shy, but not naïve. Their family had taken care of that. Still, he did not want to disappoint her, as the offer seemed genuine, and Lyas really wanted the job.

Kalem was going to find out what really happened without needing to uncover what Lyas had done with his invitations, he decided. She was apparently not going to admit anything about it right now, and he had enough to further his investigation. He just needed one bit of extra info.

He raised his glass in a toast to her. "To your new job, Lyas! When are you starting?"

She joined him in toasting. "After the Aras'arisidz. You don't mind me working, Uncle?"

"Of course not! I wish the rest of the family were following your example for once. Become a bit more financially independent. Can you tell me more about this company, or is it so secret? What's its name?"

She smiled. "'Just Ask' That's the name of the company. Very exclusive, Uncle. Maire Kincaid is the best! I heard even the Queen's staff ask for her advice. I will learn a lot from her!"

Ekbeth knew enough. He listened politely to the rest of his niece's conversation, but as soon as they parted, he called Kalem.

"Maire Kincaid. She has a company in London, 'Just Ask.' Find her address."

7

A LOUD BANGING ON the door. Shona ignored it. She was trying to concentrate on her current task.

Damn, too short! She gave it another try. It was not much better.

She turned her head, trying to look at the back of her head.

Mmh. She just had to admit it. She was making a mess of it.

"Shona! I know you're in there! Open the door!"

The banging and shouting finally got to her.

A last look at herself. She made a face. It was really ugly. But she unlocked the tiny bathroom door, opened it and faced Debbie, the Refuge worker. Debbie's first reaction was obvious relief. Too many of her charges were attempting suicide and a locked door was usually not a good thing.

Her relief was soon replaced by perplexity. "Oh my! What have you done to your hair? What did you use?"

Shona handed the pair of scissors over. Debbie absently took them, then took Shona by the arm and brought her near the window. The inspection produced a giggle from Debbie.

Shona cringed. "That bad, huh?"

Debbie faced her again, still a huge grin on her face. "There's not even a word for what it looks like, Shona! What were you trying to do?"

Right now Shona was not sure of what had gone through her mind. She had just seen the pair of scissors downstairs, in the kitchen, and got a sudden urge to cut her hair short.

But she was not going to say that to Debbie. Telling would only get the woman concerned, and probably would involve a visit to a counsellor. Shona had seen enough of those lately.

She shrugged. "I just wanted to cut my hair short. It's hot in here."

Debbie pinched her lips. She probably recognized a lie when she heard one. But after a short moment of reflection, she obviously decided not to pursue the questioning. "Okay. You're lucky we have Rose in the house. She is good with a pair of scissors. Let's see if she can do something to fix your own attempt. Because I don't think that you want to stay like this. Or do you?"

Shona shook her head, then followed Debbie obediently.

That woman's patience was amazing—that was all Shona could think, and not for the first time.

*

Two days ago, after Shona had run away from Maire's place, the pouring rain and her hurting naked feet had at some point forced her to get out of her frantic desperation.

She needed to rest and think. But without money, except the odd pence she'd found in her pockets, pubs were not an option. And the shops were closed. Running out of options, she entered a telephone box. Not the best place to rest, but at least she was dry there. Among the sex ads, she spotted the sticker encouraging abused women to call the National Domestic Violence Helpline. Offering a safe place.

She only hesitated a minute. This was a bit of a stretch, of course. She would have to lie to get refuge. She knew she should go back to Maire's place. Maire would probably bicker a bit, but she had never let her down.

Still, Shona finally took the phone receiver and placed the call. Lying proved quite easy. She just had to tell things she had actually experienced, but only not that recently, and to pretend confusion. Hell! *That* she was not pretending— she was confused!

Two hours later, she rang the doorbell of a safe house. Debbie was expecting her. A single look at her face, her drenched clothes and bare feet had been enough. Shona had been admitted. No questions asked. A room for herself. Dry clothes. Some warm food. Just what she had needed.

She had kept much to herself during the past two days. Only coming into the shared kitchen when she felt really ravenous. If there was another woman in the kitchen, she just ignored her and fixed some sandwiches and a drink before going back to her room.

If there was a woman with children, Shona just went back to her room and tried later.

She was not strong enough yet. Talking to unknown adults was enough of a challenge. Ekbeth's party had been a test. She had managed it, no matter what Jeffrey and Maire thought about it. Children, though, brought back her worst nightmares. Reminded her of her loss. She just could not face any of them yet.

Keeping to her room had brought Debbie to her. Debbie did not push for answers, but did have some questions.

Obviously she wanted to help Shona. Shona did not have to pretend that part either, of being in need of help. She did not get mad. She just started crying when the questioning became too oppressive.

So Debbie stopped asking questions. But she kept an eye on Shona—just as Maire and Jeffrey did. Only Debbie was different. She was not aware of Shona's past. She was not afraid of Shona. She only saw her as another victim, though there was no pity in her.

Shona was glad she had found that place. She knew, of course, that she could not stay forever. She had never been one to chicken out of trouble. But the pause was welcome.

*

Rose was a very small woman. Debbie and Shona found her praying next to a self-created altar in her room. But she interrupted her prayers as soon as she saw her visitors, and smiled at them welcomingly.

Shona had rarely seen such a warm smile. Then she noticed the burns on the woman's arm. She did not ask. She did not need to. She had borne a few of those marks on her skin as well, a long time ago.

"Rose, this is Shona. Shona is visibly not cut out for becoming a hairdresser, as you can see. I was hoping you could try to salvage her latest attempt."

The smile never wavered. Rose offered a chair to Shona. Then, after Shona had installed herself on the decrepit straw chair, Rose examined Shona's head for a moment, before giving her verdict, in heavily accented English. "It will be short. But I can do something."

Debbie nodded. "Good! I'll leave it to you then."

Rose proved to be well equipped. She produced a very

sharp razor. It took all Shona had not to run out of the room. She closed her eyes, but she could not hide her tension.

"I won't hurt you, Shona."

"I know, Rose. I just have trouble with cutting objects, especially when I'm not handling them myself. Just ignore me. I'll manage."

Rose did not ask questions. She started working, humming to herself while working. It had a soothing effect. Shona felt herself relaxing bit by bit.

"So. I think I can't do more than that. Have a look!"

Shona's hair was now reduced to a short crop. But it looked fine. She thanked Rose.

The small woman shook her head. "No thanks. Want a cup of tea?"

Why not? The least Shona could do was to show a little politeness.

8

THE 'JUST ASK' office was located in a quiet part of London. One of the most expensive parts, reflected Ekbeth, while studying the simple red stone two-story building. His own London-based apartment was just two streets away from there. The irony of the fact was not lost on him.

He felt Kalem's impatience, though his bodyguard did not say anything. Ekbeth knew how exasperated the man was. If he had allowed Kalem to handle this his way, they would already have the jewels back. So Kalem thought, at least. However, Ekbeth personally thought this required more subtlety than Kalem was capable of, and had insisted on meeting this Maire Kincaid himself. This had created some delay, as Ekbeth had not been able to find a space in his agenda before this morning.

Yes, Kalem was irritated, but he knew who was the boss and kept his thoughts to himself.

Ekbeth looked at his watch. He only had one hour to handle this. And three more days to get his hands on the jewels. Enough lost time.

He started walking towards the office entrance. Kalem

followed behind him. The door was answered by a small blonde girl, who viewed them with some puzzlement.

Ekbeth produced his most charming smile. "Good morning. Would it be possible to see Ms. Kincaid?"

He was submitted to a quick inspection. The girl visibly recognized a potential customer, but still did not let them in. "Do you have an appointment, sir? Because, if so, I'm afraid I'm not aware of it."

"I had no time to schedule this. I'm not often in London, but I'd really like to discuss a little project with Ms. Kincaid. Can you please tell her Ekbeth na Duibhne wishes to see her?"

She recognized the name, apparently, and opened the door to let them in.

The entrance hall was painted in white, with marble floor and stucco decorations on the ceiling. Simple and expensive.

"If you can wait in the next room for a moment, sir. I'll check with Ms. Kincaid."

Ekbeth nodded and walked inside another room, this one with silk wallpaper and a view onto a neatly arranged garden. Kalem pretended to concentrate on one of the rose bushes.

"Mr. Na Duibhne? This is an unexpected surprise. What can I do for you?"

Ekbeth had not heard the woman enter the room, which was surprising as the small Eurasian woman was wearing stilettos. Apparently she had managed to master the trick of moving without making noise. He shook himself mentally. He was not there for this kind of nonsense.

He extended his hand. "Ms. Kincaid, I suppose."

She nodded. He sensed the guarded hesitation behind her smile. He also noticed the blonde girl behind the door. "Is there a place where we can talk in private? I don't have much time, but the matter I want to discuss with you is quite confidential—the reason I came in person instead of calling."

Maire Kincaid hesitated just a moment before agreeing. She led them to a meeting room on the second floor and closed the door carefully behind her.

She offered them coffee, then placed herself in a plush seat before saying, "I don't think you're here because of my hiring of your niece, Alyasini, Mr. Na Duibhne."

Ekbeth shook his head. "Not directly, no. Though I must say I don't really care for the way you've misused my niece's eagerness, miss."

She managed a smile, somehow, which told a lot about her as Ekbeth was sensing her panic. Oh yes, this woman was involved, no doubt about it.

"The job offer is genuine, sir. Your niece is very talented and I'm very glad she's agreed to work for me."

"Is Shona also one of your employees?"

Maire Kincaid's smile did not waver, but the panic went just a notch higher in her head. "I don't understand…"

Ekbeth sighed. "Miss Kincaid, I'm expected for an important meeting in less than one hour. Can we please stop the pretending? I know my niece arranged for two people to come to my party last Saturday. Because she wanted to show you what she could do, I suppose. The little problem is one of these two people stole something from me. Something I want back. Now."

He had barely raised his voice on that last word, but she

blanched a tiny bit. A reaction, at last. But her voice was still steady when she answered, "I don't have it—whatever she's stolen from you."

Well, at least, Maire Kincaid was not denying his suspicions. He allowed himself to relax just a tiny bit. "But you know where it is?"

She pursed her lips just a tiny bit, then left her chair and made a move towards the door. Kalem put himself smoothly on her path.

She looked at Ekbeth. "I need to make a phone call. Believe me, I want this ridiculous situation solved as much as you do."

Ekbeth nodded and Kalem made a side step. She went outside of the room.

"She's going to call the police, Akeneires'el."

"I don't think so, Kalem. Why would she? I've not threatened her or anything. Let's be glad she did not deny her involvement in this mess, Kalem. "

Maire Kincaid came back five minutes later, a phone in her hand. "Someone is going to bring the stolen object here, sir. He should be here in four hours and will give it back to you. Is this okay with you?"

Ekbeth nodded curtly.

She started talking in the phone again, but it was not in English so he did not listen. She finally closed the phone and took her place again in her seat. "I offer my deepest apologies for what had happened, sir. It was never the intention to steal anything from you during the party. But then, the damn girl never sticks to plans."

This time, he could clearly hear some irritation in her

voice. He had to ask. "A plan? So attending the party was not only about my niece's work, was it?"

She shook her head, but did not offer more, so Ekbeth pushed further. "Just out of curiosity, what was the original plan?"

That brought the first genuine broad smile on her face. "Ah. Well, I suppose I can tell you that. She was supposed to seduce your cousin. At least that's what I understood."

Not really the answer he had expected. "My cousin? You mean Lyrian?"

Maire Kincaid nodded. "Yes. Even that part, she changed her mind about at the very last moment. As I said, she never sticks to plans."

He was confused. If the plan had never been to steal anything, just seduce someone, he was a more obvious choice. Why Lyrian? And why had she changed her mind?

Then Maire Kincaid added, "Please, just forget about this whole mess after we've given you your possession back, Mr. Na Duibhne. We'll keep Shona in check. You won't hear of us anymore, I promise."

That was also his dearest wish. But there was the small matter of how Shona had managed to steal the jewels. If she was As'mir… "I want to talk to Shona once more, Miss Kincaid. Can you arrange that?"

She looked at him for a long time, as if trying to read his mind. Then shook her head.

"You don't want to meet her again, sir. Believe me. Unless you're looking for real trouble."

At that he grunted. "She's already brought enough trouble as it is right now."

Maire Kincaid smiled, sadly this time. "Oh, this is nothing. Really nothing."

Her mobile phone gave a little sound. She looked at it and apologized. "I have to leave. A customer is expecting me. Wedding. You can stay here if you want. I'll have my assistant get you whatever you need."

Ekbeth shook his head. "I have to leave as well, but Kalem here is staying. He will come with you."

She eyed the bodyguard warily. "This is not necessary. The stolen goods are really underway. I'm not trying to run away, I can assure you."

"Probably not, but then, I can't take chances."

Ekbeth turned to Kalem. "Whatever happens, Kalem, I expect you to behave. Take the jewels back to the safe. We'll talk tonight unless something arise."

Kalem just nodded.

Ekbeth looked at his watch and hurried off. He was going to be late.

9

SOMEHOW, ROSE SUCCEEDED where Debbie and all the counsellors had failed.

Sharing a cup of tea was a bit awkward because neither of them was talking. Until Shona noticed how Rose was discreetly scratching at her burns, which prompted her to speak.

"Have you tried vinegar?"

Her question received only a blank stare. Shona pointed at the burns. "On those. Vinegar compresses. It helps."

"Really?"

"Yes. Let me fix one for you."

Shona found what she needed in the kitchen—some facial tissues and vinegar. She poured some vinegar on the tissues and handed them to Rose, who looked at Shona questioningly.

"You just have to put it on the burns."

"Is it going to hurt?"

"Nope. I swear."

Rose placed the tissue carefully on the worst part of the burns. Instantly, her eyes were shining with relief.

"Wow! It does help! How do you know about this?"

Shona hesitated, biting her lip, but then decided there was no harm to admit a few things.

"An old woman taught me that. I've used it more times than I can think of."

Rose kept silent for a moment, and then asked, "Why did you cut your hair, Shona?"

"Massacre, you mean?"

Rose smiled. "If you want. You don't have to answer that if you don't want to."

Shona thought for a moment. It had been an impulsive thing, but she knew where the impulse came from. Saying it, though, was difficult.

"I was thinking about things I don't want to think of. I just needed to do something. Anything to get those thoughts out of my head."

Rose stared inside her cup, then, out of nowhere, she started laughing and shook her head. "You are crazy, you know."

From anyone else, Shona might have taken offense at this remark. But not from this tiny woman, who so far had been utterly pleasant. She returned the laugh, though not as merrily. "You're correct—officially crazy. Everyone would tell you that."

Rose's face took on a more serious expression. "Are those thoughts that bad, Shona?"

Shona frowned. How could she express in words what she was feeling inside every time she thought of Yeshe or her babies? It was… hurting.

She looked at Rose's burns. "Did you hurt when this was done to you, Rose?"

Rose looked at Shona as if she was *really* crazy. "Of course I hurt! I was screaming my head off!"

"Well, those thoughts inside me—it's the same. I used to scream. A lot. And cry. But that did not make them go away or lessen the hurt. So I just try to avoid them nowadays." Shona passed her hand through her short hair. "And that's what happens."

Rose put her hand on Shona's. "A piece of advice from another old woman, Shona. Avoidance is not helping."

Rose showed her arms, her burns. "My husband is a violent drunkard. I have been finding excuses for his behavior for many years. We moved to England last year. I thought it would be better. It got worse. Still I was excusing him. Until he took the iron and started hitting me with it."

She put her arms around herself. "Suddenly I realized what a fool I had been all those years. I left him." She looked straight at Shona. "But before that, I told him why I was leaving him. He was more or less sober when I did that. And you know what?—he listened to me! Something I was not even dreaming of."

"He could have beaten you again, or even killed you! That was very brave of you!"

Rose nodded. "Yes. But I had reached the point where I did not care anymore. It was either confront him, or accept that I must keep suffering this miserable existence for my remaining years."

Shona sighed. "It's not the same, Rose."

"It's exactly the same, Shona! Those thoughts are making you miserable! This time, it was your hair. What are you going to destroy next time?"

Damn! The woman had no idea how correct she was.

Shona had made a promise to Yeshe and it was the last thing that linked them, so she was doing her best, but the temptation was getting worse and worse by the day.

One single little shot… and her problems would be gone. Forever.

Only, every time a little voice in her head stopped her. Told her she had to be strong, that her time had not come yet. Yes, she had some damn strong survival instincts.

She shook her head. Looked at the other woman with a grim face. "That bit of advice sucks, Rose. If I let them in my head, I'll get crazy for sure!"

"How is the saying…? You have to accept what you can't change! Confront your fears. Maybe you'll discover it was not so bad after all."

*

Shona thought a lot about this conversation for the rest of the day. She could not sleep that night.

By morning she had made a decision.

Debbie was a bit surprised to hear Shona was leaving. "So soon? Do you have anywhere to go?"

"Yes. I can't tell how thankful I am for your hospitality, Debbie."

"Just doing my job, Shona. Well, if you're sure— take care."

Shona took the time to say 'bye to Rose. The woman hugged her.

"You're following my advice?"

"Yes. I hope to see you again, Rose."

"Who knows?"

Shona first went back to Maire's place. She had no key

but the lodger knew her and didn't hesitate to lend her his master key.

She took a long shower and put on some clothes.

Going to Bhutan was not something you could get ready for in a minute. She needed to arrange the flights, check whether she was still registered as a Bhutanese citizen or needed a visa. So she called Jeffrey Matheson.

He had bad news for her. Told her that Ekbeth had appeared on Maire's office doorstep this morning, and that someone was underway right now to bring the jade stone to Ekbeth's bodyguard. "And I don't want to hear whether you agree on this or not, Shona. This was a bad move and you know it. It's going to complicate the mission enough already as it is."

Shona's mind went blank for a moment. The mission. Damn. She had forgotten about it.

"Shona?" Jeffrey's voice was insistent on the other side of the phone.

"Yes, of course, you're right. Is Maire okay?"

"Seemed so to me when she called me. She has some experience with dealing with your messes, after all."

Okay, so Jeffrey was still mad at her. She hung up.

Rose was right. Avoiding problems was definitely not solving them. But the way her friends kept rubbing in her mistakes was damn annoying.

She ignored the ringing of the phone.

She did not need Jeffrey to solve all her problems, she decided. She at least now had her passport and her credit cards back. She just needed to go somewhere else until she could arrange her trip to Bhutan. She walked to her room, switched on the radio and started packing, while humming along with the song that was playing.

She did not hear the front door opening, but she certainly heard the arguing.

Maire and two men. One, she was pretty sure was one of Jeffrey's staff. As for the other…

"That was all my boss gave me!"

"It can't be. It's a set! This is just the main piece! Where is the rest?"

"Gentlemen! We are going to call Jeffrey and check this…"

There was a silence, then Maire called out to her. "Shona? Are you here?"

There was not much point pretending otherwise, was there? Shona dropped her duffel bag and left her room.

She had been right about Jeffrey's man. The other she recognized as well. Ekbeth's bodyguard.

Maire was staring at her, as if in shock. "What happened to your hair?"

Oh yes, the hair. Shona had quite forgotten about it. "A little accident with a pair of scissors. It'll grow back. What's wrong?"

Ekbeth's bodyguard growled, "Where are the rest of the jewels?"

"Excuse me?"

He showed the jade stone that she had stolen. "I've been waiting for four hours for someone to bring this. But that's only part of what was in the safe. Where is the rest?"

Shona's mind went blank. The rest? She had only taken that piece!

She met Maire's eyes. This was bad. Really bad. She just

had no idea what the man was talking about. He was not going to accept that for an answer, of course.

The best thing she could do was to make a run for it. She peeked to her right. The front door was closed, but that was no problem.

The bodyguard was just two steps from her and his expression was not promising, so it was now or never. She kicked him between the legs and used his momentary pain to run, ignoring Maire's scream to come back.

The door was near. Almost there… She closed her eyes and immediately felt the familiar tingling. She had never used her gift while running before as far as she could remember, but, hell, this was an emergency, and what worked walking should work just as well at a faster level.

It did work. She felt the subtle change around her. Like she was walking through a water curtain. Then she was free, safely on the other side.

She had gathered too much speed. She miscalculated how far the stairs were and made one step too many. Her foot suddenly only met thin air, and there was nothing she could do to stop herself. She fell downwards and hit the floor below with a loud thump.

There was no time to get on her feet again. The next moment, the bodyguard was on her, shaking her and shouting, "Nice try! Where are the jewels? Answer me!"

She managed to give him a nasty kick under the chin, but it was not enough to free her. The first blow hit her on the side of her head. The second slammed her against the wall.

She lost consciousness.

10

T HE MEETING HAD been boring as hell, so Ekbeth
was glad when it ended. A bit of fresh air was needed,
then there would be a lengthy dinner.

This was not his favorite part of the job, but networking
the other Swiss bankers was somehow a compulsory activity.
A perfect opportunity to grab useful information and exert
influence on the lesser members of the group.

He checked his mobile phone. Seventy missed calls?
From the same unknown number.

That made him frown. Anyone so desperate to reach
him knew he had better chance to do that faster through
his assistant.

The phone rang as he was trying to see whether
any messages had been left. That number again. He
answered. "Ekbeth."

"Thank God! Finally! Ekbeth, you have to stop
your bodyguard!"

He did not recognize the man's voice. "Who are you?"

"Jeffrey Matheson. I was attending your party with
Shona last week. Your bodyguard has no idea, Ekbeth. You
have to stop him before it's too late."

"I don't get it."

The man on the other side of the line was irritated. "Your bodyguard has disappeared with Shona, Ekbeth. I know where they are—in your house in Zurich. I'm on my way there. But I still have an hour before I reach your place. I understood something is amiss…"

"Damn right, something is amiss! The woman stole some jewels from my safe!"

"I gave back the stone, as promised, Ekbeth. Maire told me there should have been more than the one stone I had, but I swear that's all Shona gave me."

Ekbeth started to understand the situation and he groaned. "Where is the rest, then?"

"Only one person knows that, and that's Shona. But your bodyguard won't get any answers out of her by torturing her. She's tough. She won't talk. Knowing her, she is probably going to provoke him to hit her harder."

Ekbeth could not help but ask. "Why would she do that?"

Matheson hesitated before answering. "She has a death wish. She made a promise not to take her life, and so far, she's kept it, but if someone is willing to help her…"

Ekbeth was suddenly in a hurry to go back home. "I'll meet you there, then."

"Don't inject her with any drugs! She's violently allergic."

Ekbeth closed the phone. What kind of people did this Matheson think they were?

Kalem was not the nicest man in the world, but one thing was certain, he was no trained torturer. But his blows… they could be enough.

Damn, damn, damn.

Ekbeth hurried back inside the meeting room. He apologized for not attending the dinner, then found a quiet place from which to be transferred to his house. Driving back home was going to take too much time.

*

All was quiet when he appeared in his living room. No one was in sight. But he knew where to find Kalem.

He hurried to the basement.

When Ekbeth had bought the place, Kalem had insisted that a specific room be soundproofed—mainly because he was a fan of loud motors and wanted to be able to practice his hobby without getting complaints from Ekbeth, or the neighbors.

But it was also the perfect place to conduct interrogations if needed. Not that they had ever used it for that purpose till now.

Ekbeth opened the door. He needed only a glance to evaluate the situation. The room was not well lit, but he could see there were only two people present. Kalem and his victim, who was bound and on her knees, with her head pressed under water.

Matheson had been right on one thing: she had managed to provoke Kalem to lose his usual professional calm. He was almost frothing at the mouth with rage, staring at Ekbeth, defying him silently.

"We need her alive, Kalem. I'm not sure she can hold her breath that long!"

The words were enough to break the spell. Kalem took Shona's head out of the water. It was none too late, from the way she was coughing water.

Ekbeth approached them. Even in the darkness of the room, he could see nasty bruises on her face.

"You have to keep out of this, Ekbeth."

Ekbeth remained impassive. The frustration in Kalem's voice gave a clear indication of the degree of success he was having. Still Ekbeth asked, "Has she told you anything yet?"

Kalem gritted his teeth.

No, then. Well, at least, she was still alive. Shona was now looking straight at him—jaws clenched, eyes burning with hate. No enticing smile on her lips, today.

"Hello, Shona. You may be interested to know help is on its way. Your friend Matheson called me."

That did not seem to please her, but she kept silent.

Ekbeth turned to Kalem. "This is not getting us anywhere. Let's wait for Matheson and see what he has to say. We can always use her as leverage, if needed."

Kalem took a step back, releasing his hold on Shona. She slumped to the ground.

"She's definitely As'mir, Ekbeth. I saw her walk through a closed door."

Ekbeth eyed her. That was not at all good news.

"Well, we can do something about that, before letting her alone in the room, can't we? But no more hitting or anything else for now, Kalem. I'll wait for you upstairs."

*

Matheson did not come alone. He had three men with him, and they were not lawyers. "Where is she?"

Ekbeth allowed them to enter his house. "She's okay, Matheson. Maybe a few contusions, but I'm sure she'll get over it if she's as tough as you say. Let's discuss…first, I'd really like to know what this is about. Maire Kincaid told me the stealing was never intended."

Matheson visibly wanted to see Shona, but he decided to humor Ekbeth first. "Indeed, it was not."

Ekbeth offered the men the sofa and sat in a chair. "Well, your friend had been particularly lucky in her impulsive choice. The jewels she's taken have more value than you can imagine. If I don't bring them back to their legitimate keeper in the next two days, this will cost me my life, and it probably won't stop there. So I'd appreciate some help here. Kalem has given me the main piece. But you have no idea as to where the rest is?"

Matheson shook his head. "Only she knows it."

"According to Kalem, she can't remember."

Matheson groaned at that and shook his head. "I was afraid of that. God, this is such a mess!"

"That's the understatement of the year. But let's do this step by step. Why don't you explain to me why you two came here in the first place? According again to Maire Kincaid, Shona was supposed to seduce my cousin. I don't think it was just because she'd fallen for his charms. Why?"

Matheson hesitated again, but finally reached a decision. "Shona is very good in what she does. She has a reputation among some people—for getting the most impossible things to happen. Someone recently asked for her help. For two things: stealing a jade ring from your cousin, and getting a letter delivered to someone."

Ah, of course! Ekbeth should have thought of this. The Kadj'dur. That was about the only thing of value Lyrian still possessed. Not as valuable as the Annilis jewels, but the Kadj'dur, the jade ring Shona was apparently supposed to steal, was just as famous within the As'mir community. Especially among his direct family.

He concentrated on the second part of the deal. "A letter?"

"Yes. Shona has had it for some time now. I understood she was supposed to deliver it herself, but the girl is suspicious. She was hoping to convince you to deliver it. That's why it was so important for us to meet both of you. That party was the perfect opportunity."

"So you manipulated my niece to get an invitation."

Matheson allowed himself a thin smile. "Actually, there was not a lot of manipulation needed."

Indeed. Ekbeth closed his eyes and thought. There were still gaps in the story—to which As'mirin family Shona belonged, for example. Though that letter might be a clue. If she was expecting him to help, this could mean the letter was for someone of the Valley, and if she was reluctant to go there, she could only belong to one family. A descendant of a banished As'mir would never have had access to the place.

"Tell me, is Shona related to the McLeans—the Scottish family that lives on that tiny island near Skye?"

Matheson looked at him blankly. "You should ask her."

So the answer was probably yes. This complicated the matter only further.

"Good idea—I will. But let's return to our main subject. So her mission was to find a ring and give someone a letter. Instead of that she stole something else, lost three quarters of it and can't remember where it is. A mess indeed. So, what do you propose?"

Matheson relaxed slightly. He had probably not expected

so much cooperation from Ekbeth, but he was quickly adapting to the situation.

"Let me talk to her. First, I'll check whether she really does not remember what she's done with the rest of the jewels. If that's the case, I'd suggest bringing her back to the floor where the safe is and ask her to reenact the theft. That may help. She'll remember eventually, especially now we are in this house. Hopefully, not too late for you."

Ekbeth admitted this was the best course of action.

"Ah. And what about the ring and the letter?"

Matheson shrugged. "I'd say, let's forget about them. I'll be glad to get her out of this relatively unscathed."

Ekbeth thought about this, for a long moment. "You are very loyal to her, Matheson."

The other man just shrugged. "Just doing my job. I was hired to keep an eye on her. But she never listens. She tends to follow her intuition a bit too often, and most of the time, the result is quite disastrous. For everyone."

"Why not just leave her to it then?"

Matheson smiled. "Oh, it's always interesting to watch her save the situation. Sometimes against amazing odds. You would not believe me, but most of the time, she does not even need my help. She really has a way of turning the odds in her favor. Vastly entertaining!"

Ekbeth was not finding any fun in the current situation, that for sure. But he did not have better alternative than what Matheson was offering. Not with so little time left.

"You go and talk to Shona. Convince her it's in her best interest to remember. Fast! And I want to see the letter."

Matheson hesitated. "Why?"

Ekbeth was hoping to find out who had given Shona

her mission through the document, but he lied about his motives.

"I will deliver it as a token of my good will. Or an incentive. I need those jewels back. The ring is not mine to give, but I can certainly help deliver a letter."

Matheson nodded. "Let me talk to her first."

11

SHONA WAS VAGUELY conscious of no longer being alone in the room. They had come back. But she did not care. Concentrating on her body, trying to ignore the radiating pain, especially the one in her left side, was all she could do right now. The bastard had cracked a few ribs when he had beaten her. Her right wrist was sprained as well, though that was a consequence of her spectacular escape attempt at Maire's place.

Every centimeter of her body was hurting. It could have been worse. Nothing major was broken. If needed, she could probably stand and walk, although she was happy to just lie on the floor right now.

"My, my, look at yourself!"

She recognized the voice and groaned. The last thing she needed right now was Jeffrey's sarcasm. She felt his hand on her and recoiled.

He insisted. There was no sarcasm anymore in his next words. "Why do you put yourself through this all the time, Shona?"

They both knew the answer to this question, of course.

"Have you given her any drugs?"

She recognized Ekbeth's voice when he answered, "Just something to prevent her from leaving the house."

"I told you not to give her anything! Her body does not respond well to drugs. You could have killed her."

"Well, she's still alive, isn't she? Apart from blocking her special abilities, it was a test to confirm our suspicions. Though seeing her walking through a door, as Kalem did, is proof enough for me. I hate to admit it, but we have more in common than I like. This drug is inoffensive for us, but a non As'mir would get very sick if he was drinking some of it."

"As'mir?"

"That's how we call ourselves. So, what do we do with her?"

"She needs some care."

Shona stopped listening. She had just tried to move a leg and the pain distracted her.

*

They had moved her somewhere else. A bright place. Jeffrey had taken care of her, cleaned her, bandaged her ribs and helped her get into new, clean clothes. She was now resting on a comfortable sofa.

"Do you want something to drink, Shona?" It was Ekbeth's voice.

She forced her eyes open and saw him holding a glass of water. She was quite thirsty, no matter how much water Kalem's little torture session had forced her to drink.

She nodded and tried to sit. Her ribs reminded her immediately this was a very bad idea.

Ekbeth tried to help, but this caused Shona to scream. "Don't!"

Her voice came out croaked. Screaming tended to do that to voices. She inhaled a few times, deeply, to regain some control. "Don't touch me, Ekbeth."

"Would some extra pillows help?"

This was a good idea. She clenched her teeth while two men were helping with the pillows, and finally she was comfortable enough to be able to hold and drink from the glass herself.

Jeffrey re-entered the room just at that moment. He was holding Keremli's letter. She recognized the document immediately. He had told her he was going to the plane to pick it up, she remembered. The letter was supposed to be in her room, at the Castle.

Trust Jeffrey to always think ahead, she reflected.

He gave it directly to Ekbeth, without consulting her. She did not care. After all, it had been the original plan to give it to him.

She just said, "You have to promise you won't open this envelope, Ekbeth."

Ekbeth frowned when he read the name written on the envelope.

Shona knew what the elegant and totally exotic alphabet meant, as well as who the addressee was. So she understood his reaction.

He looked at her. "I would not dare open the mail of our Aramalinyia, Shona. Even though I have to admit I am curious about the identity of the writer. This way of writing is a bit old-fashioned nowadays. We are not using so many points on the 'nyi' letter anymore, for example."

Shona did not answer the implicit question. "Are you going to deliver it yourself?"

"No. That won't be necessary, Shona. But she'll get it, don't worry."

One instant the letter was in his hand. The next it was not.

"Nice trick, Ekbeth."

"Indeed. But it's not much more complicated than putting your hand through a wall or walking through a door. So, any insight as to what happened to the jewels so far, Shona?"

She looked around her and recognized the place. The shelves filled with beautiful jade sculptures were enough indication. Ekbeth's private floor. They had brought her there to trigger her memory, she realized.

But it was no use. She just could not remember.

Oh, she could remember how she had felt after the sex. Exhilarated. And every detail of what they had done to each other. The pleasure of it. And that she had not been able to resist the temptation of putting her hands through his safe. The idea of swapping the stone for the ring had come later. She had just wanted to prove to herself that she was still able to do it.

And she had. But she had felt dizzy after extracting her hands from the steel door. She'd heard Ekbeth opening the bathroom door just at that moment. So she had acted without thinking. She could only remember having put the stone in the only cavity she could think of. Nothing else.

"Those jewels are important to you, Ekbeth?"

"Not only to me, Shona. You should know that."

"But I don't. Oh, I know who you are and I certainly was told about the Valley when I was a child. But I've never been there myself. And I certainly never heard of those jewels."

Ekbeth got close to her and whispered, "You should at

least know better than to discuss the Valley so openly. It is a secret."

She wanted to laugh, but her ribs reminded her that this was not such a good idea.

"For someone who was referring to the As'mirin so freely a moment ago, that's rich! I'm sure no one in this house is unaware of your famous secret, Ekbeth. Those people have been working for you for years. They must be used to seeing you appear and disappear as if by magic. I had to explain a few things to Matheson when we started working together. Otherwise he would have freaked out!"

"Actually, girl, I did freak out!" Matheson chimed in.

She smiled at Matheson, then returned her attention to Ekbeth. "What is so special about this stone, Ekbeth?"

He only hesitated slightly before answering.

"Not only the stone. The whole set. We call the set the Annilis jewels. They are very ancient. The only thing we have kept of the first civilization before the apocalypse."

She was not sure what he was referring to exactly, and he saw that, because he added, "That means more than ten thousand years old, Shona."

Wow! She kept her voice neutral. "Interesting."

He nodded. "Indeed. I brought them here to get the set cleaned before the Aras'arisidz. Do you know what I'm referring to?"

That at least she had heard of. From her own brother. A long time ago.

She nodded. "Your Goddess Ara's thanks, which are celebrated every ten years. Is this going to happen soon?"

"The ceremony starts at nightfall, in two days. Hence the urgency in getting them back, as they are part of the fourth day celebrations. So, you do know a few things about your heritage, Shona."

Heritage. She hated that word. "I'm not interested in claiming that so-called heritage, Ekbeth."

"Still you belong to a family, willing or not."

"My real family has rejected me. Maire and Jeffrey are my family now."

She could not help but sound slightly bitter when she said that. But Ekbeth misinterpreted her words. He had no clue of what she was referring to, of course.

"I can imagine not even the McLeans would be proud of having an official thief among them."

She hissed at that. "I'm not a McLean, Ekbeth. And they're certainly not my friends either."

Then she cursed loudly. Damn those ribs!

Ekbeth frowned. "Is it that painful? I could give you something to lessen the pain…"

She gritted her teeth. "How considerate of you! I'll survive. Now, if you could leave me alone, I'd be able to work at remembering."

She felt something resting on her chest. It was light, but she was quite sensitive to any change of weight right now. She was sure it had not been there a second earlier.

She looked and saw that a blue piece of paper was now on her chest. Ekbeth picked it up, opened it and frowned while reading. "Damn!"

"What is it, Ekbeth?"

"The Aramalinyia's answer to your letter. She wants to see you. Now."

He left the room.

Shona was still getting over the news when Ekbeth returned with a pile of clothes and a woman.

"See me? But…"

"Yes, that means I have to send you to the Valley. Kalem will go with you. Don't discuss the missing jewels with anyone there! No one is aware of the fact in the Valley yet. And please do behave. You don't want to antagonize the Aramalinyia."

Shona felt a light panic. "I don't want to go, Ekbeth! You can't force me!"

Jeffrey added, "This is not what we agreed on."

Ekbeth nodded his head. "True. But that woman's words are law in the Valley. I can't ignore her request."

He stared at her. "Can you walk?"

"No. Stand is already asking too much of me."

If she had hoped lying would offer her a delay, she was soon disappointed.

"I'll get Nukri, that's our Caller, to transfer you to the main hall of the Aramalinyia's house. A bit unusual, but they should accept this if I explain the situation to them."

She frowned. "The situation? Are you going to tell them you've tortured me? Because that'll sure attract questions."

"What torture? You fell down the staircase!"

The man was thinking of everything.

"You speak some As'mir?" he asked.

Again she lied. "No."

"Mmh…I think the Aramalinyia speaks some English. Otherwise Kalem will translate. Now, we can't let you go there with those clothes. The Aramalinyia is a stickler to proper attire, and by this I mean As'mir ones. Those are my niece's, but they should be fine for you. My cleaning lady is going to help you put them on."

Shona panicked. There was no way she was going to the Valley, to that old woman. And with Kalem of all people!

She concentrated really hard. She knew As'mirin were doing it all the time, but she had never had any proper training. She had done it before, but it had never been easy. If she thought of a place hard enough she could actually get there as if through magic. Most of the time, she would be fainting from exhaustion immediately after, but this was a desperate situation. She had to get out of here!

But it did not work. She tried harder but the familiar tingling sensation was just not there. Then she remembered what Ekbeth had said. The drug they had forced down her throat earlier. It was blocking her abilities.

She could not transfer herself out of this and, physically, she was never going to reach any further than this room door, if that.

She looked accusingly at Ekbeth. "Bastard!"

She did not like his smile at all. He was too happy with himself, right now! She had to admit it—she could not do much right now, other than obey the Aramalinyia's order.

Jeffrey helped her stand and then, with the woman's help, got her undressed and dressed again.

Ekbeth was looking absently at the process.

"While the drug prevents you to use your special talents, any As'mir holding you can get you transferred with him. That's how Kalem is going to bring you to Kse'Annilis, our city. Now, any idea why the Aramalinyia wants to see you?"

Shona shook her head. She knew Keremli had asked her to bring the letter herself. That was, perhaps, the reason. If

Keremli had written about her in the letter, the old woman was probably curious to meet her.

The cleaning lady had just finished draping the loose robe around her. The tissue was amazingly soft against her skin. Pity it was so cumbersome. And black.

Kalem entered the room. Shona and he exchanged mutually wary glances. Ekbeth did not seem to notice. He explained to Kalem the latest development, and what he wanted.

In As'mir, which Shona was not supposed to understand.

Then he turned towards Shona. "I hope the Aramalinyia won't keep you long. See you later, Shona! Think of the jewels!"

Kalem grabbed her right arm. Hard. This time she allowed herself to panic. She did not want to go to the Valley! "Wait!"

But a sense of dislocation she recognized too well told her she was too late.

Willing or not, she was going to meet the old woman.

12

THE SUN WAS setting above the lake and neither Shona nor Kalem had returned yet.

Matheson had accepted Ekbeth's offer to share his dinner, but Ekbeth could see the man was growing impatient.

Only, there was nothing they could do but wait.

"This place they've gone to, where is it?" Matheson asked.

Ekbeth shook his head. "I'm not allowed to tell you, Matheson."

Then he noticed the mobile phone in the other man's hand. He could recognize a map on the display screen. "Is this how you knew she was in my house? Did you put a tracking device on her?"

Matheson pinched his lips, and curtly nodded.

Ekbeth was curious. "Is that not a bit extreme?"

"If you had been around her as long as I have, Ekbeth, you'd do exactly the same. The girl is troubled; she can disappear for days at time, leaving us to worry about her whereabouts. Being able to track at least her location has been a big help. I wish we had thought of this earlier, in fact."

"Ah. That death wish of hers?"

Matheson nodded, with a sorrowful expression. "That. Or when someone like you is determined to harm her."

Ekbeth ignored that last part. He pointed to the mobile phone. "You won't be able to track her where she is now."

Matheson sighed. "I realize that. I really hope your bodyguard is not using that fact for persisting in his torture."

Ekbeth shook his head and was about to reply when Kalem appeared in the room, out of nowhere. Without Shona.

Kalem's face was ashen. That fact worried Ekbeth more than the absence of the woman. In all the years Kalem had been working for him, Ekbeth had never seen him look so perturbed.

Kalem bowed so low before him that his head almost touched the floor. "I've some bad news, Akeneires'el."

Matheson was on his feet. "Where is she?"

Kalem did not look at either of them as he said, "The Aramalinyia refused to let me participate in her conversation with the thief. But after two hours I asked one of the servants what was happening behind the doors." He shook his head. "All I was told is that she's been sent to our ancestors for judgment."

Ekbeth inhaled sharply. He certainly had not foreseen this.

Matheson was furious. "I knew I could not trust you! You've killed her!"

Ekbeth shook his head vehemently, but the other man did not believe him. "Sending someone to his ancestors has only one meaning to me, Ekbeth! You've killed her."

"We use the expression differently. It is a test, Matheson."

Ekbeth hesitated a few seconds. This was not something

he should discuss with this man but, then, he also needed to quiet him. There were three armed people waiting outside and while Ekbeth was certain Kalem and his own men could handle them, he'd rather avoid bloodshed if he could.

"I can try to explain but I'm not sure you will understand."

At that, Matheson produced a thin smile. "I've been around a woman who can walk through walls for years. It now seems she's not the only one able to do this. I'm open to believe anything you'll tell me."

Ekbeth looked thoughtfully at Kalem for a moment and then made a decision. "Very well. Think of our dead ancestors as ghosts. Ghosts we can communicate with, if needed."

Matheson sat back slowly. "Go on."

"Shona shares our blood, but is not officially part of our community. She told us herself she's never been to our own place before. Under normal circumstances, she'd always have a right to visit it. But ours is a very close community."

Kalem snorted at that. Ekbeth smiled briefly, in response. "Or rather, acceptance as an outsider is difficult, no matter what your birthright. One way to gain it is to put oneself through what we called the Oyyads'erel. If you manage it, you gain a lot of prestige in the eyes of our people. In fact, you become pretty untouchable."

Matheson was suspicious. "And what happens during that test?"

"You go and meet our ancestors, at least your soul does, and they decide whether you're worthy of being integrated in the community."

"And if that's not the case?"

"Then you don't come back. And, yes, that means you die."

Matheson's lips became very thin. "So I was right."

Ekbeth shook his head. "As far as I can remember, most people survive the test."

"Sure. That's why your bodyguard is so cool about it. Shona is not 'most people' I don't think you're so-called ancestors will judge her favorably. Most people don't."

"Why did she ask to pass the test, then?"

Kalem intervened. "She didn't, Akeneires'el. The servant told me they were already making the preparation while waiting for us. Whoever wrote the letter requested that the woman be put through the test and the Aramalinyia obliged him, or her."

Matheson cursed. Ekbeth inquired, "Who wrote that letter, Matheson?"

The other man shook his head. "Can't tell. I don't get it. I would expect her to be the last person to want to harm Shona. It does not make sense."

So, it was a woman who was behind this. And someone the Aramalinyia respected enough to perform a ceremony that would be quite taxing to her energy. Some use of drugs was involved, as well—not something Matheson needed to know—but the Aramalinyia had to send the soul of the Oyyad to the ancestors herself. And she would be using energy that she needed for the upcoming ceremonies.

The Aramalinyia was not so young anymore. And while she was fair, she was not known to favor anyone. Most intriguing.

And there was the small issue of the Kadj'dur. The jade ring had been thought lost for a long time. Ekbeth tried to remember the details. One of his ancestors had lost it, but he could not remember which one. They had found it again less than ten years ago—in very curious circumstances, but nobody cared about circumstances. The important fact was that the ring was back.

It was not as prestigious as the Annilis jewels, nothing was, but it had almost as much symbolic and emotional value. It marked the end of an era and the start of a new one. It was the last jewel created by a full blood As'mir before their people had been exterminated, and, as such, was cherished by their half-blood descendants.

But although the Annilis jewels were normally safeguarded behind strong walls and rarely displayed, the Kadj'dur had been used as the Na Duibhnes' Akeneires'elin's wedding ring. That is, until it had been lost.

After it had again been found, Ekbeth had allowed his cousin Lyrian to offer it to his own wife, to the rest of his family's outrage. Perhaps not a good thing, as Lyrian's wedding had been an unlucky one, while the ring was supposed to bring luck. Ekbeth knew some family members thought this was because the ring had not been worn by the rightful person. Superstition.

One of his uncles or another member of his family regularly asked him to claim the ring back. So far, he had always refused. Apparently, someone had decided to take a more direct approach herself.

But what was the link with Shona and the Oyyads'erel? Why the letter? Ekbeth shook his head. He was certain he would get the solution to this puzzle at some point of time.

Shona and the Oyyads'erel.

This was a damn inconvenience. Kalem was right to be

unhappy about it. They could not communicate with Shona as long as she was being tested. Every hour her soul was out there, was one hour less to find the jewels back in time.

If she did not wake up before the beginning of the Aras'arisidz, the Valley would be closed and Ekbeth would have to explain why he did not have the jewels with him. Worse, unless she died, Ekbeth would have to support the full blame for having lost the jewels—because their ancestors would already have judged her for that.

Damn!

They still had two full days before the ceremony. He had to keep believing he was going to solve this in time.

And if not, maybe, maybe she would remember what she'd done with the jewels and that might be enough to save him. It would require a lot of skillful manipulation on his part, but he might have a chance there.

Of course, there was also the small possibility that she would never wake up. He did not want to think about it.

"There's something else, Akeneires'el."

Ekbeth frowned at his bodyguard. More bad news? What could be worse than Shona being unavailable for the coming hours?

"The McLeans are in the city and they intend to participate in the ceremonies."

Ekbeth groaned. He was starting to develop a serious headache. That was indeed bad news. And, in light of Shona's theft, suspicious. He had not believed her when she said she hated the McLeans.

Ekbeth closed his eyes for a moment.

The McLeans had been avoiding the Valley for the past thirty years. The Na Duibhnes' feud with the McLeans belonged to the past, as far as he was concerned. More than thirty years had passed since his brother's fiancée had left him to marry the son of Duncan McLean. But his family thought differently. Of course.

"I suppose some of my uncles want to talk to me urgently?"

Kalem nodded.

Ekbeth was going to have to come down hard on some of his uncles' attitude, before they did something stupid. He would probably have to use all the weight of his title on this.

And he was going to have to speak to Duncan McLean as well. He was aware that the man hated him just as much as some members of his own family—if not more, though for different reasons.

Great!

"Anything else?"

Kalem hesitated.

"Out with it, Kalem."

"There are two more things, Akeneires'el. I did manage to speak to the Aramalinyia, though I now wish I hadn't. She said she did not believe the story of her Oyyad falling in the stairs and that she won't stand for her people being beaten again, no matter if it's ordered by an Akeneires'el himself."

Kalem bowed again after saying that. "I'm sorry for having put you in more trouble, Akeneires'el."

Indeed. Admitting Kalem had acted without orders would put the bodyguard in even worse trouble, though. Ekbeth gritted his teeth.

"And? What's the second bit?"

This time, Kalem really hesitated. Ekbeth waited.

"The Aramalinyia gave me a message for you,

Akeneires'el. She told it to me because she knew you would probably pretend not to have seen it if she had written it. Her words, not mine."

Kalem breathed in deeply.

"She said that if the Oyyad is accepted by the Ke'As'mirin, you are to marry her."

Ekbeth ignored Matheson's reaction, barely registering the man was on his feet again.

So, that was the reason Kalem was so upset by his latest visit to the Valley. Ekbeth was in shock but anger soon replaced it.

What was the Aramalinyia thinking? There was no way in hell he was going to marry Shona!

13

S HONA WAS TOTALLY confused. One instant, she'd
been drinking tea with the old woman who was the
Aramalinyia and thinking the conversation was not
going so badly. She had behaved well, drunk her tea politely
and answered the questions as openly as she could, while
thinking of what she would do to Keremli for that confrontation when she saw the other old woman again.

The next, she'd found herself alone, in a clearing, sur-
rounded by trees so tall that she could not even see their tops.

What was happening to her?

She stood up. And realized her ribs were not hurting
anymore. She looked at her hands carefully. If she held them
in direct sunlight, she could actually see through them.

Impossible!

There was only one explanation to this. The old woman
had drugged her! And that drug had somehow sent her spirit
form here.

She did not panic. She had had worse trips before. And
had always reconnected with her body.

Greetings, Oyyad!

This time she jumped from fright. She had never heard

them approach her, but where there had only been trees an instant before, she was now encircled by beings of the strangest kind: abnormally tall, though full of grace and ethereally diaphanous, as if the sun's rays shone through them.

Who were they?

A disembodied giggle answered that thought. *We are the ghosts of your ancestors, Oyyad.*

Ghosts? She did not believe in…

Oh my! She suddenly realized who they were. Her father had told stories about them when she was little. The Ke'As'mirin, the ghosts of the dead As'mirin, the protectors of the Valley.

Shona began to panic slightly. Her father's stories about those beings were half forgotten, but she could well remember she had not liked them. What did she have to do to leave this nightmare? Before they harmed her.

Do not fear us, Oyyad! Welcome. I am Taralieni, the eldest of the elders.

Shona stifled a scream. From out of nowhere, a being had appeared in front of her. It was so near that she could clearly distinguish the being's facial features, the almond-shaped eyes, the straight nose, the pointed ears and the full lips smiling ironically at her.

This had to be a dream, right? This being looked like…

Yes. We are elves, which is the name humans gave us. In our tongue, we call ourselves As'mirin, the children of Ara, the mother goddess of Earth.

The first moment of surprise had passed. So her father's tales had been true, after all? She had some elf blood in her veins! She had never believed that part, despite her special talents! It was just too fantastic to be true!

But now, faced with this, she had to believe it.

Thousands of questions were coming to Shona's mind. Weren't elves supposed to be immortal? And if Ekbeth and the others from Kse'Annilis were those ghosts' descendants, why did they not show the same features? Surely, their genes had to be purer than hers?

But, foremost, why had Shona been brought to them?

So many questions, Oyyad, to which you, who share our heritage, should know the answers.

Shona's panic only grew when anger filled her mind and the circle of beings drew closer, as if to annihilate her, she thought.

The one facing her raised a hand.

Why so much surprise, friends? She was sent to us for a purpose. She's an Oyyad. I shall answer your curiosity, woman of the Keh Niriel, before we start the Oyyads'erel.

A small room replaced the forest. Shona inhaled sharply. The change had been brutal. Again it changed. Now she was on the top floor of a skyscraper. Its walls were made of glass and the panorama was breathtakingly astonishing: a whole city of light was stretched limitlessly under her feet.

This was Annilis, our capital, our pride, the city of lights, built even before the first human civilizations. Here lived our people, granted long life and beauty, as well as clever minds. We thought ourselves the equals of Ara, and she punished us for it.

The city seemed to explode before Shona's eyes, transforming now, in an instant, into a desert before shifting once more to a volcano crater filled with water.

So few of us survived. Only those who had expected the cataclysm and taken refuge in this place. In the years preceding our fall, we gathered as much knowledge as we could, in books and people. It was a lot. But still, our loss was terrible. Of the original hundred thousands of Families, a scant hundred survived. So many of the people have died—dear friends, sisters and brothers. We are still grieving for them.

For years we lived alone here, transmitting our knowledge to our children, trying to bring back our ancient splendor. Then the humans came.

Bitterness filled Shona's mind. Once more, the being calling itself Taralieni raised its hand.

Pride, again, and arrogance were our doom. Humans found us in the woods, our favorite shelter. At first, we ignored them. We were far more advanced, why should we have bothered to interact? Until they started bringing down our trees and reducing our habitat. We then went to them and tried to forge alliances, promising knowledge in exchange for protection. How stupid of us. Humans accepted our gifts greedily, but soon discovered we knew much more than we gave them. They asked for more. When we refused, the wars began. And, for all our science and superiority, we lost.

Images rapidly flashed before Shona's eyes. The barbarians, for such were the humans the elves had fought, must have been impressed by the sight of As'mirin in armor. Yet what could thousands of As'mirin do against five times their number?

Before all was lost, our people took a drastic decision. Understand, Oyyad, we are not immortals, as the human lore says. We were granted long lives, at least three times longer than a human's. But when we are slain or when our mortal coil gets too old to sustain our spirit, we leave it behind.

Ara then presented us with a choice: to join her or to remain as a protector of our descendants on this Earth. I was one of the first who chose to protect. We were granted special gifts for our decision, such as the ability to temporarily disappear a being or an object from sight. But we were not skilled enough to hide a whole section of the land from human eyes. It took no less than three hundred sacrifices to accomplish this task. Ara was not pleased, but finally yielded to our decision. And, for a time, it seemed our descendants were at last protected against all harm.

The next vision was nauseating. Horribly mutilated corpses wherever Shona laid her eyes. She thought she was now witnessing the sacrifices of which the being had spoken, and then the shining armor of the assailants came to her attention. This was a much more recent event.

Twice, we had suffered huge losses. The third catastrophe of our history almost annihilated what remained of us. We, Ke'Asmirin, the protectors, could do nothing to prevent it and it is our shame, for we are responsible for it. Some of us were not vigilant enough in their watch and let humans find their way through the veil to our hidden land. We couldn't send them back to the Other Side but were reluctant to kill them, because most of them had never been looking for us in the first place. They had just lost themselves through the Veil.

After much debating, we decided to grant them land outside of our Forest. Our descendants built impressive stone doors around the Valley as a reminder of a boundary the humans were forbidden to trespass without our leave, and we, the protectors, stretched our powers to increase the size of our land.

All were happy for some time. Trade took place, and soon enough marriages between humans and Asmirin. Those unions were blessed with children, for, though we are two different species, we are similar enough biologically.

Proud and arrogant are the Asmirin. Ambitious, jealous

and greedy, the humans. One of the human community chiefs, or As'ran as they called themselves, wanted the power over the Valley for himself. He deceived us, learned too many secrets, and thus managed to enter Kse'Annilis with a strong army. He showed no pity: every single As'mir he or his men could find, they killed.

And, as if it had happened yesterday, Shona could feel the frustration and the rage of the beings surrounding her. So many dead!

We could not stop him, for this man had learned how to protect himself and his followers against us. We could not protect our descendants; such was our confusion at his acts. When we at last regained some strength, it was almost too late: only two, we could save, sending them to the Other Side, out of reach of the Murderer. One is your ancestor, Esul Keh Niriel. He married a local woman, took her name and founded the line of the McLeans on the Other Side. The other was a mere child, Nefer Keh Jariel, and she, as well, survived among the humans, grew up, found unsuspected allies, came back to the Valley, and after many more bloody battles, prevailed against the Murderer.

A last image, of a beautiful elfish woman, with hair black as the raven and eyes green as emeralds. Then Shona's awareness was brought back to the forest clearing and the circle of ghosts.

Nefer Keh Jariel and Esul Keh Niriel were the last of our blood. Esul decided to stay outside of the Valley. Nefer wed an Irishman she'd brought back from the Other Side, and changed her name to Na Duibhne. Then she looked for the remnants of our race, the descendants of the human-As'mir unions. She found a few, and invited them to the Valley and Kse'Annilis. Those, and their children, we now protect.

For all the good it did to them, thought Shona too fast.

Curiously, her sarcasm was only met with resigned sighs.

We agree. Much was lost, and more will be lost if they do not change. Our descendants, diminished as they are, fear us and won't listen to our advice. What can we do, Oyyad?

That word again. "What's an Oyyad?"

One of us who has strayed out of our community, asked for forgiveness and returned to us. We, the Ke'Asmirin, are the ones who'll decide to accept or reject your request.

The circle moved nearer to her.

"Request? I've never requested anything! I was tricked into this!"

Too late, Oyyad. We have lost enough time. Open your mind to us and fear not: we were living beings once, too. We understand.

It was the only warning she got. The forest around her dissolved and she found herself facing her oldest memory.

It was not long before she started screaming.

14

G OING TO KSE'ANNILIS was quite a simple operation.

You could do the transfer yourself, with a bit of training and a lot of concentration. It was just a lot more arduous than going through a wall. For one thing, you needed a firm vision of your destination in your head.

Most of the As'mirin would rather let someone else move them through the Veil separating their world from what they called the Other Side. The Caller was the second most important person of the community, their link to the rest of the world.

You only had to concentrate and summon the Caller with your mind, then think of your destination. You only felt the slightest dizziness and before you knew, you were somewhere else.

In the main hall of the Caller's home, in that particular case.

The abrupt change of sight could play havoc with one's brain, so much so that most people closed their eyes before summoning the Caller and only reopened them when the dizziness was gone. Ekbeth and Kalem, though, used this talent so often that they were not even standing still while going through the process.

"Welcome, Akeneires'el."

Ekbeth returned the greeting to the older man facing him, the Caller, sitting in a comfortable chair in the middle of his hall.

"Same to you, Nukri na Liom. Are we late?"

The Caller shook his head.

"Not yet, but you are the last ones."

Kalem left them immediately. He was to warn the servants the Akeneires'el had arrived, though Ekbeth was pretty sure the Caller had already taken care of this.

Ekbeth and Nukri na Liom exchanged a few particularly polite words before Ekbeth left and walked outside the Caller's home, which probably had the best view of the Valley. At his feet was Kse'Annilis, the city of the As'mirin, and the Valley, the best-kept secret on the planet Earth, just a step away from what everyone would call the reality.

How this was done was beyond his knowledge. Night had fallen and it was pitch dark around him already, but Ekbeth did not need daylight to know what was surrounding him. He was born in this place, had spent many years here, but he still felt awe every time he came back.

The Valley was named in many of the As'mirin legends. It was said to be the place where everything had begun. The name of the place was, in fact, not correct. This was not a valley. It was an extinct volcano crater—extinct for so many millennia that it had filled with water and over time its sharp tall edges had eroded to almost nothing.

A deep forest of oaks, chestnuts, pines and other trees, for which he never had found the time to learn the names, covered both sides of the crater. The last city of the As'mirin had been built on the inside flank. It required good physical condition to be able to climb from the Lake to the Caller's house on the ridge. And a good sense of orientation, too, as the houses were built one upon another and linked by small stairways that were deceptively similar.

Getting lost was really easy. Nowadays, most As'mirin just asked to be transferred from one point to the other.

There was no road through the forest. There used to be, their entrance marked by gigantic stone doors, but no one had used them in centuries. Visitors were just transferred into the city or out of it.

The very limit of this secret place extended further than the Valley's forest, though. Beyond the trees, you could make out the skyline of high snowy mountains. Between the edge of the forest and the mountains lived the Aiarz'in, a name designating all the people living on this Side, but outside of the Valley, beyond the Doors—mostly descendants of humans who had arrived in this place by accident, when that had still been possible. A few As'mirin descendants lived here as well, like his own cousin Lyrian Farrill—that is, before the idiot had tried to kill his wife and got himself banished.

The As'mirin considered themselves privileged to be able to live in the Valley. But the Aiarz'in life was not so bad. To Ekbeth's point of view, it was far better. There was good farmland, space enough for everyone, and the liberty to do pretty much whatever they wanted.

They even had their own Callers, distant cousins of the Na Lioms' family. They are not as good as the Valley Callers, the As'mirin tended to assert arrogantly, but it was mainly because the Aiarz'in were not misusing their Callers' special abilities as much as the As'mirin. Less demand made them just a tad slower than Nukri, in Ekbeth's experience. But Nukri had once told him he probably would not be able to cope with the job if not for the occasional support of those cousins.

What Ekbeth envied in the Aiarz'in the most was that they had been authorized to import almost all the technologies from the Other Side. Even cars.

Ekbeth looked once more around him.

Well, cars were not needed here, but any other piece of useful technology was not something that was going to happen in Kse'Annilis any time soon. To say that As'mirin were conservative did not even come close. "Human" (a word which was an insult among some of his people) innovations were simply forbidden within the Valley. The As'mirin had been a great civilization once, they had invented impressive technologies long before the humans could eat anything other than what they could kill or collect. What the As'mirin had not discovered, then, was simply not needed.

They imported their food from the Aiarz'in farms, as no one in the Valley would have dared cut down a tree to create farmland. But that was pretty much the extent of most As'mirin contact with the outside world.

That rejection of anything foreign applied to human beings as well. Ekbeth himself conducted a lot of business with the Aiarz'in when he was not on the Other side. But it was expected of him to conduct those transactions on Aiarz'in territory—certainly not to let them come into the Valley. Outsiders were not welcome. There were some exceptions, of course—the main one being when an As'mir brought a wife from outside the Valley.

The irony of the fact was not totally lost on him.

He did not want to think of the Aramalinyia's latest decision. It had been difficult enough already to convince Matheson this was not a joke and that, no, Ekbeth was not happy about this at all, but he would not have any choice and neither would Shona.

Matheson had left Zurich this morning with more warnings and death threats.

As if Ekbeth needed them.

He began walking down the steep stairs. He was not as lazy as most of his family. He had learned his way through the place. Everywhere he could see the preparations that had been made for the coming celebration. Some houses had been freshly painted. New lamps had been installed. And the stairs had been cleaned up. They were not as slippery as he remembered from his last visit.

For months he had been complaining to the High Council about that. No one cared. But during the Aras'arisidz, no transfers were allowed. So, suddenly, cleaning the streets had become a priority.

Well, he was certainly glad for the improvement. And at this hour, he had pretty much the place to himself. That was, until he entered the Na Duibhnes' house, his house. There was a small group of old men installed in the entrance hall. They noticed him as soon as he entered the room. Ekbeth recognized his uncle Es'ael among them. Great.

"Ekbeth! Finally! You have to do something about the McLeans! They have to leave!"

Just as he had expected. Ekbeth briefly closed his eyes and prepared for the battle.

"You're not going to do anything against the McLeans,

Es'ael! Their blood is as As'mir as ours and, as far as I know, the High Council has not banished them. They are entitled to participate in the Aras'arisidz if they wish!"

"They were not banished because of your father's weakness! If he had listened to us then, there would have been no McLean left to laugh at us today!"

Why was his family so bloodthirsty? The McLeans had paid for the mistake of a single member of their family dearly enough.

"I won't discuss it! My father made the right choice at the time. And now I am the Akeneires'el here, not you! The McLeans are to be left alone! If anyone dares to disobey this order, I'll personally vote for his banishment from the Valley, is that clear?"

He did not wait for their answer. He was as angry as they were by now. Using his title to obtain their obedience was the easiest way to stop their complaints and he hated it, but, on the other hand, it spared him hours of futile arguing.

"I have to prepare for the ceremony. If you'll excuse me."

Es'ael put himself in front of him, preventing his escape. "Not so fast. Why has your bodyguard brought that woman to the Aramalinyia? Who is she?"

Ekbeth gritted his teeth. "I'm sure the Aramalinyia or one of her servants has answered that question."

"Only that she's being tested. An Oyyad! That's something we haven't seen in a long time. But who is she?"

Apparently the Aramalinyia had not communicated her decision to the rest of the community yet. A small blessing. There might still be some hope he could make her change her mind. Though there was almost no chance that this would happen.

Ekbeth tried to smile. "I don't know. I was just asked to bring the woman."

Another uncle pointed at the box Ekbeth was carrying under his arm. "Are those the Annilis jewels?"

"Yes. And now, I really have to go and dress. Es'ael?"

The old fool let him walk away this time.

Ekbeth was glad none of them had asked to see the content of the box, as it was almost empty.

He only had the one piece to show.

Bringing the box and pretending all was well was just delaying his fate. Ekbeth still did not know why he was doing that. Once the Valley was closed—and that was going to happen in the next half hour—there was nothing he could do to avoid the inevitable punishment. Because one thing was certain: the remainder of the jewels was on the wrong side of the Veil.

He put the box in his study, in a special hole in the wall only he was supposed to know about, then rushed to his bedroom, where his servants and his clothes for the ceremony were waiting for him.

The past two days he had had plenty of time to think about what was worse: having to marry Shona or being killed for having lost the community most precious treasure.

He had not yet made up his mind.

*

As he had feared, he was the last one to enter the open space by the Lake they called their temple, but he was not too late. Still, the members of his family were glaring at him. He had disgraced them, but he could not care less.

Thankfully, talking was not allowed within the temple compound, which suited Ekbeth perfectly because his family would have to wait patiently until the end of the ceremony to air their grievances.

He looked lazily at the assembly.

All the As'mir community was present tonight. The Aras'arisidz, their tribute to the Goddess Ara, took place only every ten years and lasted two weeks. Each day was dedicated to a particular aspect of their life, with its own rites and festivities. The two first nights were devoted to prayers with a day of fasting in between, their thanks to Ara for her protection. Only then would they truly begin to celebrate. There would not be much sleep, but a lot of dancing, eating and drinking. It was fun, which explained why nobody, however young or old, wanted to miss it.

Someone managed to get Ekbeth's attention by pinching his arm through the several layers of his clothes. It had to be Es'ael, of course. Talking might be forbidden, but there were no rules against gesturing, and his uncle was now doing that, pointing with his finger to the opposite corner of the place.

The servants had lit the place so brightly that Ekbeth had to squint to see anything that far. He saw what his uncle was pointing to.

The McLeans were placed just opposite Ekbeth's family. That was another reason for the Na Duibhnes to be angry.

An acolyte struck the gong. Ekbeth firmly held the extra layers of his tiki, his outer coat, and proceeded ceremoniously to the center of the temple. There he joined the other Akeneires'elin, heads of the As'mirin families. They were no more than thirty in total, and he was the youngest.

The social structure of the As'mirin was in itself quite simple, an inheritance of the past. The population was divided in families, easily recognizable by one's hair color.

Within that clan, a few were chosen to form a Council. The family Council made decisions for everything that concerned the family. They elected an Akeneires'el, a sort of Head Administrator but also their representative at the High Council. The High Council was thus a meeting of all the families. It was rarely called for, as ancestral rulings were almost never discussed.

Only one person had more influence and power than the High Council: the Aramalinyia, the chosen of their Goddess Ara. Always a woman, whose word was law—a woman who now silently appeared in the middle of the Akeneires'elin circle, as if to reinforce her importance.

She lifted her arms majestically above her. The gong reverberated again. As if a well-rehearsed act, all the assembly kneeled.

Another gong.

The prayers began.

15

THE FIRST THING Shona felt when she was finally allowed to return into her physical body was the sharp pain coursing throughout her body. The ribs hurt the worst, but she also had cramps everywhere, as though she'd stayed in one position for far too long.

Even breathing proved hurtful. She forced herself to breathe in deeply. Once. Twice.

Something moved on her right side, but she kept her eyes closed.

Another breath. And another. She tried to move her toes and her fingers. The pain of doing this brought tears to her eyes, but she kept trying. Eventually her extremities started to respond.

That was it. One step at a time.

"I think she's awake. Look she's moving her fingers."

Shona cringed. The voice was far too loud for her ears. Thankfully, another person was there who was more care- ful. Shona felt fingers touching her brow, then her wrist, the sprained one. But the touch was so light, she did not care. And the person whispered when she talked to her. "Oyyad?"

Oh yes, that was her, Shona thought.

She made a big effort to open her eyes. She was seeing

everything triple at first, but eventually, her eyes focused. Two women were bent over her. One with flashy blue hair, young, the other with light violet hair, and more mature.

That took her back. What was this?

The violet haired one put a feather light hand on Shona's brow.

"Do not fear. We mean no harm. You gave us a fright, you know? It's been a time since someone has gone through the Oyyads'erel. You were gone far much longer than we expected. Are you thirsty? Hungry? I would not be surprised if you are famished after three days."

Hungry? Three days? It did not make sense. Right now, she mostly felt nauseated.

"You're a bit warm. And your eyes are feverish. I see you have difficulty moving. How is your head? Can you move it?"

Shona moved her head slightly side to side. She gritted her teeth.

"Mm-hm," the older woman said, "I think something for the pain would help."

No! Shona was too weak to speak. But she managed to grasp the woman's wrist. That got her attention. Shona shook her head, forcefully. And damn it if her head was play-ing bells inside. She had to get the message through.

The woman seemed surprised. "No? But…"

Shona kept shaking her head. Then tried… "Allergies."

It sounded all wrong to her, but the woman apparently understood. "Ah! I see. Well, I suppose a cold cloth on your brow would at least help a bit."

Shona let go of the woman. A few movements and she was drained of all energy.

She closed her eyes.

16

THE SOUND OF the gong was supposed to keep the As'mirin awake, but instead it was lulling Ekbeth to sleep. He was so tired! He only succeeded in alternating standing and kneeling by sheer willpower. No Akeneires'el had ever fainted during a religious ceremony. He did not want to be the first.

Kneeling once more, he swore silently: the rest of the community had been preparing for this night for months. He had not only been busy with his own activities, but had also cumulated a number of sleepless nights because of Shona and the jewels. He wanted his bed badly.

At last, the first light of dawn touched the temple and a final gong marked the end of the first night of prayers. He knelt a final time, touching the ground with his head, holding the position for a few seconds, then the first night of prayers was over. They were free to go until sunset.

Ekbeth knew he had survived the worst of it. Now, he would be able to get some sleep and the second night would be easier. But before going to bed, he had a few things to do. One of them was avoiding his family as much as possible. He sighed soundlessly, looking around him, at the As'mirin community slowly dissolving out of the temple, noticing how some carefully ignored others.

Feuds, conflicts, complex intrigues. Kse'Annilis was a nest of snakes ready to bite one other to death at the first occasion. He briefly closed his eyes, trying to control the anger he felt every time he was confronted with this fact. This was not how it was supposed to be. There were so few of them left, not even five thousand, of which one tenth was his own family. They were an old civilization. They should know better and be able to live in harmony together.

His eyes met two of the other Akeneires'elin's and he shuddered. Even at the highest level of the As'mir community, there was dissension. That Duncan McLean hated him, he could understand. It was not entirely personal, nor fair, but Ekbeth's own relatives had brought death and pain to the old man's family. As those relatives were now dead, it was understandable that the hate had been transferred to Ekbeth.

But Keryl na Ghorm? The man was older than Ekbeth's father, thin as a rod, and always scolding. The Na Ghorm had become Ekbeth's worst opponent during the rare meetings of the High Council. He simply opposed anything Ekbeth proposed. As Ekbeth did not back down, their verbal fights had become famous in the whole community.

Thankfully, the rest of the Council did not always take the Na Ghorm's side, but Ekbeth could still count his victories on his fingers. It was exhausting. There had to be a reason for this attitude, but Ekbeth still had to find it.

The primary outcome of this dissension was that most of the very much needed reforms were not happening. A second result—to Ekbeth's eyes far worse—was that the Na

Duibhnes' and Na Ghorms' families were not talking to each other anymore.

And this was only one example of the troubled relationships within the community. Each family had at least one issue with another. And then there were the internal problems.

Ekbeth ignored the small group of uncles who were glaring at him from one corner of the temple and resolutely walked away from them.

*

First, Ekbeth checked on Shona. Maybe not his best idea, considering the Aramalinyia's plan, but the woman was their only hope to ever recover the Annilis jewels. If he knew where they were, at least, he might be allowed to live after all. Besides, he did not wish her dead, no matter what. Not really.

The Aramalinyia's house was next to the temple. The only place partially built over the Lake, it was a splendor of architecture that could best be compared to a Venetian palazzo, with its complex arched windows and shadowed ornamented balconies. It was painted white, the neutral color, and even so early in the morning the sun made it painfully bright to sore eyes.

He hurried inside. One of the Aramalinyia's servants brought him to Shona. She was in a small room next to the main hall of the Aramalinyia. Shona was lying on the bed, so still that he wondered for a moment whether she was breathing. Her skin had a nasty greyish tinge. But, when he was near enough, he saw her chest moving slowly up and down. Up and down.

"How is she?"

The servant shook his head. "Not well. She passed the test. She woke briefly after dawn. But the Oyyads'erel has taken too long. We are concerned for her health."

Ekbeth wanted to ask some more questions about her chances of survival, but a loud roaring voice interrupted them. The servant frowned and left the room. Ekbeth followed him.

He had recognized the voice. Duncan McLean had always been loud when angry. But he had met his equal in the Aramalinyia.

When Ekbeth entered the main hall, he found the petite old woman on her feet, face to face with the much taller Akeneires'el of the McLeans thanks to the ornate platform on which her seat was placed. Although her voice was not as loud as McLean's, her anger was just as clearly audible.

"You will do as I say!"

Duncan McLean's face was as red as his scarlet tunic. "She's a criminal, Aramalinyia! A murderer! Even her own mother turned her back on her! I don't want her in my family!"

The Aramalinyia took a step back, but her expression remained stern. "The Ke'As'mirin have judged her and let her live. I was told she's changed her ways. Everyone deserves a second chance, Duncan McLean. We'll give her that."

"Fiona told you this, didn't she? She's always reproached me for what I did."

"Your sister has nothing to do with this. Someone else, not of your family, asked me to help the woman. And yes, that person also told me of Shona's past. I consulted the Goddess. Ara told me to put the woman through the

Oyyads'erel. Ara told me she has plans for her. To the good of this community."

Duncan McLean snorted loudly at that. Ekbeth managed to hide his smile.

The Aramalinyia was their Goddess Ara's voice. A Goddess whose existence no As'mir doubted. Ara had ways to make herself heard. Speaking through her representative was only one of them. But the Goddess had been silent for so long that nowadays people were a bit dubious when the Aramalinyia said she was speaking the Goddess's will, thinking it was just a way for the woman to impose her will on stubborn people.

Though no one was foolish enough to say it out loud, of course.

The Aramalinyia put herself back in her comfortable seat, and sighed loudly.

"Enough stubbornness, Akeneires'el of the McLeans! You have done a lot of wrong to this woman and her family. It is my right to punish you for that if I wish. Don't forget it! Instead, I am honoring your family in presenting her to the Ke'As'mirin! And you will acknowledge her during the naming ceremony! Am I clear?"

Duncan McLean grumbled something Ekbeth did not catch. But then the Aramalinyia noticed Ekbeth. "Ah! Another of my Akeneires'elin. Come, come, Ekbeth na Duibhne! I'm glad to see you."

Ekbeth walked to the platform and bowed deeply before her.

"Are you bringing complaints to me as well?"

The challenge was unmistakable.

Ekbeth had hoped to be able to speak to the old woman

and make her change her mind about the wedding. But he killed the idea. Now was not a good time. Not when she was still so angry. "No complaints, Aramalinyia. I just overheard the Akeneires'el of the McLeans screams and was curious about them."

She nodded curtly. "Good. I hope you got my message?"

Damn! He missed a perfect opportunity and they both knew it. He just bowed again.

"Good. I know you're not happy about it, but this, again, is the Goddess's will. Now, Akeneires'elin, I'm an old woman and I need to rest. I'll see you tonight."

Dismissed, both men left the room and the building.

Ekbeth was still digesting what he had just heard. "So, she's a McLean? She told me that she was not!"

Duncan McLean looked at him suspiciously. "Are you behind all this, Ekbeth?"

Ekbeth shook his head. "No, someone else is. Shona came to me and asked me to bring a letter written by some mysterious person to the Aramalinyia, that's all. I never met her before. Is Shona really a murderer?"

Duncan's frown only increased. "Why do you want to know? What is she to you?"

Ekbeth looked around him. There were too many ears around them. "I'd rather not discuss this in the open. At least as long as the Aramalinyia has not made it official."

The old man visibly wanted to know more, but he too knew his ways around the As'mirin. He finally shrugged and raised his hand in an invitation. "Come along to the McLeans' place. We'll be able to talk there."

The invitation was unexpected. And Ekbeth knew it was going to generate more gossip than the confrontation between Duncan McLean and the Aramalinyia. The McLeans hated the Na Duibhnes and the Na Duibhnes hated the McLeans. They did not speak to each other. They certainly did not invite each other to their respective homes. It was a well-known fact. And all this because, thirty years ago, the betrothed of Kas'el, Ekbeth's brother, had chosen to leave him for one of the McLeans' sons.

At the time, Ekbeth had already been spending most of his time on the Other Side. He had just started his finance studies in an exclusive business school. But he had been there when Arkeri, Kas'el's betrothed, had told them the news, just before she left the Na Duibhnes' house.

Ekbeth vividly remembered everything she had accused Kas'el of—the forcing on her of unnatural acts, the beatings.

Ekbeth had not believed her at the time. None of the Na Duibhnes had. Why would Kas'el do that? They were not even married yet, and Arkeri was from a wealthy Aiarz'i family—a family that was also an important financial partner. Sure, this would have been an arranged marriage, not a love match, but still, Kas'el knew he had to show respect to his future wife. For the sake of the community.

The only thing Ekbeth had thought then was that the woman was lying to get rid of his brother. And Ekbeth had been as angered as the rest of the Na Duibhnes by the false accusations.

He had been, at the time, as determined as his uncle Es'ael to get the whole McLeans' clan banished out of the Valley in retribution. He had been as outraged as Es'ael by the fact that the then Akeneires'el of the Na Duibhnes, Kas'el and Ekbeth's father, had refused to bring this before the High Council.

He could remember how virulent he had been in arguing with his father about this.

Ekbeth shook his head. He knew better nowadays. They all knew now what a monster his brother had been under his pleasant mask. In the end, Kas'el had been punished for all his crimes.

Small consolation this had been for some of his victims, the ones who had survived him. Arkeri and her husband, Alasdair McLean, had been dead for years by that time. A car accident. The McLeans had accused Kas'el of having killed them, but nothing could be proven.

Ekbeth sighed. This was the past. Something both families would be better to forget.

But it was not the way of the As'mirin. The Na Duibhnes were too proud to make amends on behalf of a family member, no matter how bad his conduct had been. The McLeans, Duncan especially, still hated the Na Duibhnes for not making restitution.

Today, Duncan McLean was offering an opening to a possible reconciliation and damn if Ekbeth was going to reject it.

He bowed slightly to the older man and opened his arm. "After you."

*

All the buildings of Kse'Annilis were badly in need of repair. But the McLeans' house looked even more on the verge of collapse than any other. This was not so surprising when you knew it had been left empty for thirty years.

No matter how convinced the McLeans had been of Arkeri's innocence, they had avoided the Valley all those years. Because no one could prevent an assassination attempt, and Duncan had known some of the Na Duibhnes would not hesitate to at least give it a try.

Ekbeth carefully went up the entrance stairs and around the entrance door, as it was so worn out that it could not fully open. The main hall was not in much better state, but it was obvious someone had tried to clean it up.

Duncan brought him to what apparently used to be a dining room. The whole McLean family was there. As it was a fast day, this choice surprised him a bit, until he noticed the mattresses on the floor. Apparently, the room was the safest one in the house and they had all decided to stay in there.

The hostility was palpable when they recognized him, but, after one sign of their leader, they returned their attention to their own activities.

Duncan McLean offered him a chair and sat himself opposite to him.

One of the McLeans challenged Ekbeth. "What's brought you here, Lad? It's a bit late for apologies."

Ekbeth managed to remain stoic. The man who had spoken was older than he, but to be called a lad, like a young teenager…? And that deadly irony in the voice! He had had plenty of practice with that in his own family, though. And he knew the man. "No apologies, Kieran. Duncan invited me."

Everyone looked at the older man, and he snorted. "True, but don't gloat about it. I will never forgive your brother, Ekbeth. He killed my son and his wife. And we both know he was the one to steal Sally from us. I can only praise Ara that he didn't kill her and we have her back."

Ah—another of his brother's crimes. There was the kidnapping of Sarah-Lysliana as a baby as well, of course.

Alasdair and Arkeri's second child. One of Kas'el's crimes, of which Ekbeth really did not want to be reminded.

Ekbeth had sworn never to speak of it. He alone knew Kas'el had had every intention of harming that baby. Thankfully, Ekbeth and their other brother, Arkel, had discovered this and taken her from the monster before it was too late. They should have returned the baby to its parents. But Arkel had been against it. He had feared their brother would only kidnap the baby again. So they had found a foster family for her and had kept the fact that the baby was alive a secret. Ekbeth still thought it had been a mistake, but, well, at the time, he had not been the Akeneires'el. Arkel had been.

Ekbeth bowed his head. "Ara be praised."

A loud snort answered him. Ekbeth realized Sarah-Lysliana McLean was sitting just next to him. The woman had the fierce temper of the McLeans.

Fate had led her to meet and fall in love with his cousin Lyrian. Lyrian had visited him quite often, bringing his wife with him. Ekbeth had liked the young woman from the beginning. They had been almost friends in the past. He had always known who she really was, of course. He had, after all, given the baby to her foster parents himself. Still, he liked her and she seemed to enjoy his company. But that was before…before she discovered who she really was, and the circumstances behind it. Before she decided to return to her family on the Other Side. Before Lyrian tried to kill her.

It suited Ekbeth fine that she kept her current thoughts to a snort.

Duncan McLean as well, apparently. "Let's leave that discussion for another day. What is Shona to you, Ekbeth?"

"My question first. Is she a murderer?"

Duncan McLean scowled when he said, "That's what I heard. That woman has a very bad reputation, Ekbeth. If only half of what I've heard is true, you would think twice about staying alone in the same room with her. I don't want her in my clan and I don't care what the Aramalinyia thinks about this!"

The statement was so forceful that Ekbeth knew there was more to it than Duncan McLean was saying. He needed to know more.

"Admit it—you won't win that round, Duncan. The Aramalinyia is going to bring her to the Lake and name her. Then you won't be able to reject her anymore!"

The old man's eyes narrowed to a split. "And you find this vastly amusing, for sure! Damn it! Wait until my ancestors hear of it! They are going to howl for days!"

At last, Ekbeth partially understood what was going on.

The Callers were able to transfer more than merely people from one place to the other. They also transferred anything that person was wearing, and, by extension, what he or she was holding, be it another person or an inanimate object. They were even able to transfer an inanimate object alone, if two callers were at the each end of the Call.

What they could not bring back to the Valley though was the Soul of a dead As'mir.

Most of the McLean family members had died in the Valley, but more than a few had died on the Other Side, in Scotland. Which meant that the errant soul was not offered Ara's choice and stayed in the world of the living for eternity.

The McLeans' castle was full of ghosts. Literally. Ghosts

who, as far as Ekbeth could remember, expressed their opinion quite loudly.

Ekbeth had to smile. "I'd love to hear why they would be so outraged. Let me guess. A Scottish feud with her Clan?"

"Exactly! You don't want to hear the details. Suffice it to say that one of her ancestors refused to marry her betrothed and went off with a big chunk of our treasure. When her father finally found her again, she was married to a powerful laird, so there was nothing he could do to bring her back. And needless to say, we never recovered the gold."

So, thieving was apparently an inherited gene.

"And when exactly did this happen?"

Duncan McLean sighed. "Can't remember the exact date, but somewhere in the fourteenth century AD, I think."

Ekbeth had been prepared, but not enough. "That was six hundred years ago!"

"So what? The broad went away with our money! And defied her laird! He has cursed her descendants! So do we. There is nothing to forgive!"

The McLeans were ten times worse than his own family, as far as feuding was concerned! Still, he needed their help. So he tried to be his most charming self when he said, "Well, she's still family, willing or not. I think one of you should be next to her bed right now, instead of hiding in here."

At that Duncan spat on the floor. This was going to take time.

"He's right, Gramp. I think I'll go."

Sarah-Lysliana's intervention was as unexpected, as welcome. Duncan glared furiously at his grandchild. "I forbid you to go, Sally!"

She smiled at him. "Ekbeth is right, Gramp. The

Aramalinyia has been clear about her will. That woman is part of our family, whether you want it or not. I'm actually curious to meet her."

Ekbeth jumped to his feet. "Well, I think I'll leave…"

Duncan McLean stopped him. "You did not answer my question, Ekbeth. What is she to you?"

Ekbeth sighed. "The Aramalinyia has decided I am to marry Shona."

The whole room was very silent suddenly. And Duncan McLean's face was showing more pity than anger now.

It was more than Ekbeth could bear.

He left the McLeans' house, walking to his own place, his bed. Though he already knew sleep was not expecting him.

A murderer. Of all things…

17

T HE NEXT TIME Shona woke up, night had fallen. Or someone had managed to darken the room. And there was something cold and moist on her head.

She had dreamed of images of her childhood, which normally made her sad. But right now she felt a bit better. Her limbs were not so heavy anymore. And her mouth did not feel so dry.

"Oyyad?"

Damn! Were they ever to let her alone?

She managed to turn her head. She could not make out the woman in the darkness of the room, but she was sure this was not the same person she had seen earlier.

As though reading her mind, the woman spoke. "They've gone to the temple, Oyyad. For the second night of prayers. I volunteered to stay with you. How are you feeling?"

Shattered. That was the only thing Shona could think of. Physically and psychically.

"I have some broth for you if you feel like eating. We are not supposed to eat before the end of the night, but the doctor said we could make an exception for you. Would you like some?"

Shona suddenly felt how thirsty she was. So she nodded, but then realized the woman could not see her movements in the dark.

She croaked a "yes."

Clothes ruffled. At last alone. Even if probably not for long. She breathed deeply. Her ribs were still hurting, but less so than earlier.

Three days! She had probably spent that time in bed! Which somehow had been good for the physical pain. But what had happened in that clearing… She wished she could forget what the Ke'As'mirin had put her through.

Tears began slowly to flow along her cheeks. Only a few days ago, she'd been ready to follow Rose's advice. Confront her past. She now knew how foolish the idea was.

The Ke'As'mirin had forced her mind open and dissected memory after memory. It had been pure torture. Shona had been confronted with a recent past that Keremli had done her best to erase. But that had not been the worst. No. The worst had been the happy memories, her childhood before her father's death, the time with Yeshe and Sonam.

She had lost so much!

"Oyyad?" The woman had come back, Shona realized. She felt like screaming. She wanted to be left alone! With her pain. Instead she dried her face and tried to sit. The woman instantly came to her help, putting some pillows behind her back to support her.

Then she put a tray on Shona's knees. "Do you need some help with the broth?"

Shona wished she could say no, but her hands were shaking badly. Her first attempt was disastrous. So she handed the spoon to the woman and let herself be fed.

The broth was delicious. And exactly what she needed. After several spoonsful, she realized she should not accept the food. There might be more drugs added to it. But then, she did not really have a choice. She needed the strength only food could provide. And she was just too weak right now to seek out her own meals.

"Oyyad? The Aramalinyia wants to know. Did the Ke'As'mirin give you a name?"

Shona frowned, not sure she'd understood correctly. A name? Then it came back to her. Those bloody ghosts had indeed said something before releasing her.

"Kimiel. I think they said Kimiel."

A pause. Then the woman brought the spoon back to Shona's lips.

"Is it important?"

A few spoonsful of broth passed her lips before she got an answer.

"That's the name they've given you, Oyyad. After the ceremony at the Lake, that's the name we'll give you from now on."

Shona only heard one thing. "What! That torture is not done yet?"

She heard a sigh. "Oyyad! You've put yourself through the worst part of it. Really! The Lake ceremony is just a formality."

"What happens?"

The woman told her. It did sound rather innocent. A sort of baptism. "The Lake is where Ara lives. Or so we think. Putting yourself in the water is entering into contact with her. But it's a formality really. Ara trusts our ancestors' wisdom."

What a load of bullshit. But the woman was kind, so Shona did not challenge her explanations.

Then she remembered. "I need to speak to Ekbeth."

Another pause.

"The Akeneires'el of the Na Duibhnes is at the temple right now. But I'll let him know. Do you want more broth?"

Shona was a bit confused by the long title. But then she remembered some explanations Keremli had given her. Ekbeth was merely a banker outside the Valley, albeit a powerful one, but here, he was top in the Valley hierarchy!

Not someone you referred to by using his first name.

Shona smiled—maybe for the first time since she came out of her spiritual experience.

"Oyyad?"

What did she want? Oh yes. "No thanks. It was very good, and I really appreciate your help. But I can't take more right now."

She yawned. Incredible! She'd been sleeping three days and still felt tired!

Damn! They'd put a sleeping drug in that broth! She knew she should not have trusted them!

She barely felt it when they put her back in a sleeping position.

Thankfully this time there was no dream.

18

"UNCLE? I NEED to talk to you."

Ekbeth managed not to show his exasperation. The second day of prayer had just ended, the Na Duibhnes' servants were waiting for him to check the last details of the coming event and, already, he was interrupted in his progress towards his house.

But it was his niece Alyasini who requested his attention this time.

He managed a smile. "I'm listening, Lyas."

She looked nervously around her. "Not here, Uncle. In my rooms."

More problems?

They entered the house together and he followed his niece to her own place, which was at the very far end inside the crater wall. So typical of her. As the daughter of the previous Akeneires'el, she could have asked for the second best view if she had wanted. But no—that was not her style.

The place was not so bad. When they had built Kse'Annilis, their ancestors had mastered some amazing technologies, one of them enabling them to capture and perpetually re-use sunlight. Sadly, this technology had been lost, but it was still functioning in the old buildings. There was no window in Alyasini's room, yet it was lit brightly enough that no lamp was needed. Furthermore, Alyasini had done a very good job at decorating it. The furniture was a mix of traditional and Other Side furniture. He liked it.

Alyasini looked nervously around the room, then locked the door behind them.

"Lyas? What is happening?"

She signaled him to wait, then walked to her own bedroom and opened the door.

Another young woman entered and prostrated herself on the floor before he had time to see her face. Her long white hair was, thankfully, enough for him to know who it was. Only the Callers had such white hair. Even the very old, as the Aramalinyia, kept a subtle hue of their original family hair color. And there were only two Callers left in the Valley.

"Akalabeth! This is a nice surprise! Why so much formality? I'm your uncle, not a god. You can stand."

She obeyed him, slowly coming to a stand. And he had not been mistaken. He had not seen the young woman in months, and, but for the white hair, she looked strikingly like her father, his own brother. Another reminder of Kas'el's numerous crimes. He had raped the girl's mother, Nukri na Liom's only daughter, and had left her so damaged the woman had committed suicide after her daughter's birth.

Akalabeth was officially of the Na Lioms' family, but Ekbeth had always kept an eye on her.

"Ake… Uncle, I have wanted to speak to you for months, but you did not come to the Valley for a long time, and when you were here others prevented me from talking with you.

With the Aras'arisidz happening, they are not so attentive. You're the only one who can still help us and save our lives."

Ekbeth did not ask what she meant by "they." This could wait. But why was she speaking of saving lives? And then the whole story came back to him. How could he have forgotten?

Akalabeth had left the Valley some months ago to live with the man she loved. The whole As'mir community had been in an uproar at the time. Firstly, because, as the only living family member left to Nukri na Liom, she was the only other As'mir who could transfer people and merchandise between the Valley and the rest of the world, and thus was essential to the Valley. Secondly, because the man she had fallen in love with, Sieven, who belonged to one of the poorest Aiarz'in communities , was someone far lower in status than the civilized As'mirin, certainly not worthy of such an honor.

Ekbeth suddenly understood. "Look at me, Kala."

She obeyed. Tears were glistening in her eyes, but this was not what provoked Ekbeth's anger. The light of the room had fooled him, but he could now see the marks left by weeks of malnutrition. The High Council had passed a ban on Sieven's village. Most of the time, this meant not only isolation, but also being deprived of all food, which condemned the inhabitants to a slow death.

Curse the foolishness of all those stupid bastards!

But then he realized something else. "Wait a second. Have you just transferred yourself here from outside the Valley?"

She shook her head, still avoiding looking at him. "I did not transfer myself. Technically I could do it, but my grandfather would feel it. No, I took enough drugs to block my grandfather from guessing where I am and walked here, Uncle. I used one of the old roads. It was not easy because vegetation has covered it, and I had to brave the Ke'As'mirin's anger. But I had to come here, to see you. I managed. It's only a few hours from door to door."

So she had not transferred herself! Still, she had just broken one of Ara's seven rules! No wonder their ancestors were angry with her. No one was supposed to leave or enter the Valley during the Aras'arisidz ritual. Breaking any of Ara's rules meant a very painful death, if you get caught. Only a very desperate fool would do that.

And Akalabeth was not a fool, not that he knew of. She had found an astute way to enter the Valley, hadn't she? Clever of her. So she had to be very desperate.

Well, her hollow cheeks were explanation enough of her state of mind.

He turned towards Alyasini. He understood her nervousness all too well now. "Can you try to grab some food from the kitchen without the uncles noticing, Lyas? Enough for a few persons."

She hesitated, but then nodded and quietly left the room.

Ekbeth's attention turned back to his niece. "How bad is it, Kala?"

Akalabeth kept her face hidden from him, but her voice was quivering. "Two babies died last night. Sieven's mother will probably be next. All those people, they have died or are dying because of me, Uncle. I can't bear it anymore."

She was now silently crying. "I wanted to return from the moment I heard of the High Council ban, Uncle, but the whole village decided against it. They told me that they had known worse, that they could hold out until the harvest. It was indeed not too bad, until someone set the fields on fire and stole our goats. We were left with absolutely nothing.

The surrounding villages are too afraid of the As'mirin and refused to help us. We're reduced to berries and what meat we can hunt. The whole village is slowly starving to death, all because of me. When the first baby died, I came back, Uncle. For nothing."

"What do you mean, nothing?"

"The Council refused to lift the ban and to send food to Sieven's village, even when I promised to stay forever in Kse'Annilis. So I went back to them."

Mercy was not a word often used among the As'mirin.

"You could transfer some food, Kala, use your gift."

She made a strange sound, a strangled laugh. "Sieven's people are proud, Uncle. I did transfer some food, but they refused to eat it, because they had not paid for it. It's stupid of them, I know. But pride is the only thing they have left. We have no money in the village, nothing of worth left to exchange."

"What are you expecting from me exactly, Kala?"

She made a face. "A miracle. I know you were not attending the High Council when they decided on the Ban. There was no Na Duibhne representing you. So technically you could veto their decision."

A miracle indeed! A veto would only induce a new vote. And they would probably vote again for the ban. She knew that as well as he. She also knew about his lack of influence on the High Council.

"It's not going to work, Kala."

She shook her head. "Still we have to try! I can't think of anything else!"

He thought about it for a minute then asked, "If the situation is so bad that you are ready to break one of Ara's rules to see me, Kala, why didn't you come to visit me on the Other Side? Why wait until I come here?"

She shuffled in her seat. "I don't like to go to the Other Side, Uncle."

His little niece was like most As'mirin, after all. Amazing that she was ready to risk her life by breaking rules, but not daring to leave the relative protection of the hidden Valley.

Alyasini returned from her errand, a big plate of food in her hands.

"I could not take more than that without raising suspicion, Kala! I already saw some uncles frowning at me. They probably think I'm having a private party in here! The fools! Let me find a bag for this!"

Alyasini was showing her true side for once. No more shyness.

She looked at him defiantly. "I had to help her, Uncle."

Ekbeth smiled. "That was very well done, Lyas. And I will find a solution to lift the ban. Just give me some time, Akalabeth. For now, I'd suggest you stay here for the next few hours. Eat, rest. There are too many people walking around. After the break of the fast, everyone will only think of sleeping. Then no one will notice you."

Akalabeth was not happy, but admitted it was good advice.

Ekbeth left the room and walked back to the main hall. That's when one of the Aramalinyia's servants brought the message that the Oyyad wanted to talk to him. There was nothing to be done—the servants would have to finish the preparations without him.

Ekbeth hurried to the Aramalinyia's house.

19

THE THIRD TIME Shona awoke in this bed, daylight had come. And again she was not alone. A red-haired girl was half asleep in a comfortable chair next to her bed. She jerked up as soon as Shona started to move.

"Awake?"

Shona needed the bathroom, she realized. Urgently. And she quickly discovered she was still not able to stand on her own. "I'm sorry, but can you please help? I need to pee."

The girl was immediately on her feet. "Sure. But let me find a servant first. I have no clue where the toilets are in this place."

Thankfully, she was not gone for long. And Shona did not even need to leave her bed to relieve herself. It was a bit humiliating, of course, but Shona was past that. She just needed to empty her bladder.

And she had just completed that undertaking when Ekbeth and the Aramalinyia entered the room. The old woman was beaming. "Ah, Oyyad! I'm glad you survived the ordeal. I feared I'd given you a bit too much of the drug at some point, but all is well now."

Shona wanted to give the old woman a piece of her

mind—teach her a lesson about drugging people without their consent. But then she met Ekbeth's eyes, and he shook his head slightly.

Okay, she was going to keep her mouth shut.

"You are all right, aren't you? Three days is a record, as far as an Oyyads'erel is concerned! We were really worried about your health."

Shona waved a hand—unfortunately, the one with the sprained wrist. "Ouch. I'm fine, Aramalinyia. Thing is, your ancestors took their time to reach a decision."

And they had let her relive some very painful episodes of her past a few times. Things she was not particularly proud of, that she normally avoided like the plague. Well, she'd had plenty of time to linger on them this time. Thanks to the bastards.

The Aramalinyia, though, was apparently satisfied. She turned towards Ekbeth. "I'll leave her to you then, Ekbeth, but don't be too long. The others are waiting for us to start the feasting and I'm quite ravenous myself."

Ekbeth bowed, and opened the door to the woman.

The red-haired girl asked, "Want me to leave as well, Ekbeth?"

He nodded. "But don't go too far. I don't want people getting the wrong idea."

The girl laughed, somewhat bitterly. "Ara! Think of the scandal! A McLean and a Na Duibhne! Tsk-tsk! Not that I think even you would want to do anything with her in her state. No offense intended, Shona, but I'm sure you've looked better."

Shona's only reaction was to hiss, "I'm not a McLean!"

That got everyone's attention. The red-haired girl's smile

broadened. "Ah. As enthusiastic about her new status as Gramp is, I'd say! Call yourself whatever you want. You're still family!"

Then she narrowed her eyes. "What is our relationship, actually? Are you an aunt of mine?"

Shona did not want to discuss this, but she felt the girl was not going to let go until she got an answer. "That Gramp… is it Duncan you're referring to?"

The girl nodded. Shona gritted her teeth and did her best to sound casual—or, at least, not too bitter. "Then we are cousins."

She saw the girl's eyes go wide with surprise. Shona prevented more questioning.

"Ask your Gramp if you want to know more. I'm not talking. Ekbeth?"

The girl left. Ekbeth took the only chair in the room and brought it next to her. She could not read his expression. Only that something seemed to trouble him.

"Cheer up, Ekbeth! I did behave with your precious Aramalinyia!"

He nodded.

"So what's the problem?" Shona asked.

"Problem? I have so many problems I don't know where to start! And most of them are related to you. But what about this? You lied to me. Again! You are a McLean! And you speak As'mir!"

Shona cursed. She only realized now that all the recent conversations had been in the Valley language. And she had answered the questions quite fluently.

"I did not lie to you about the McLean part, Ekbeth. No matter what you've heard, they are not my family."

"Then I'm sorry to announce to you that that's going to change tomorrow. The McLean name will be made part of your new name at the ceremony."

"I'm sure Duncan will object to that."

"Actually, he already did. But the Aramalinyia decided. He has no choice."

That bit of news brought mixed feelings in her. Feelings she did not want to linger on too long.

Shona was starting to feel sleepy again. Damn. This time she had not taken anything. But she had to finish this conversation. "I thought you'd want to know about the jewels, Ekbeth."

He was paying attention now. "Did you finally remember?"

She nodded. Yawned. "Under the palm tree next to the safe, Ekbeth. I only took the stone and dropped the rest under the palm tree. I realize it's probably too late to tell you this. The Aras'arisidz has started. But I wanted you to know. Damn! I'm so sleepy!"

She grasped his hand and held on to it. "I'm sorry."

He squeezed her hand. But it did not keep her from falling asleep again.

20

EKBETH STAYED IN Shona's room for a moment after she had fallen asleep, keeping her hand in his. She looked so fragile in that big bed. He just could not be angry with her, no matter how much trouble she had created for him.

Sarah-Lysliana re-entered the room. "She's sleeping again, isn't she?"

He nodded. He let go of Shona's hand and got to his feet, then spontaneously offered his arm to Shona's cousin. "There's no point in you waiting alone for the next time she wakes up. She looks like she going to be out for a few hours. Come to the Na Duibhnes' house with me."

She looked at him as if he was a snake ready to bite her. That made him sad. "I know we've treated you badly, Sarah-Lysliana. My brother, then my cousin… I feel responsible for them. You deserved better. I regret all of it. Sincerely. But don't let the past make you as bitter as your grandfather. Can we make a truce?"

She hesitated—a long time. Then took his arm, as they walked out of the room.

"You're right, Ekbeth. But is your family not going to kill you when they see us enter your house together?"

He smiled. "Nothing that dramatic. Not in front of the whole community. They will add it to the long list of grievances they have against me. I'm not the most popular Akeneires'el, Sarah-Lysliana, but I get used to it."

They were now out of the Aramalinyia's house. The old woman was standing with her servants in the little courtyard in front of her house. She nodded enigmatically when she saw them together and watched as they walked up the stairs of the Na Duibhnes' house. Ekbeth suddenly regretted his action. What if the Aramalinyia suddenly decided Sarah-Lysliana would make a better bride than Shona?

He was still dead set against marrying. And Sarah-Lysliana was an even worse option than Shona. She was half his age. Damn it, he had held her in his arms when she was a baby! Plus, she had suffered too much from the Na Duibhnes. And Lyrian would have his skin, because his cousin still very much loved his ex-wife.

"I can let go of your arm, Ekbeth. I see you have second thoughts about this."

He managed a smile. Sarah-Lysliana was certainly perceptive. He sighed. "Sometimes I hate this place. Every little thing you do has consequences."

She nodded. "There's not much room for spontaneity, indeed. Gramp briefed us for hours before we came here. So many rules—I'm sure I forgot half of them."

"Can I ask you something? The McLeans have missed the last two Aras'arisidz. Why the decision to attend this one?"

She smiled. "I don't believe in hiding, Ekbeth. And

Gramp does listen to me. It took some persuasion, but he finally accepted coming here with the clan. We left only the children behind. And I think the decision was the right one. Sure, there's a lot of hostilities. But no one has tried to kill us—yet."

"Don't expect anything overt, Sarah-Lysliana. Poison is their favorite weapon!"

She nodded. "We've taken some precautions in that regard. I don't regret we've come, Ekbeth! I missed Kse'Annilis! I came here twice with Lyrian when we were married. I fell in love immediately with the city. I think I'd like to live here permanently."

"You? You have your career on the Other Side!"

"Oh, I'm sure I could arrange something. You also share your time between both sides. And you're an Akeneires'el! That must not be always easy, but you seem to manage."

"Ah! I think my family has a very different point of view on this matter. But look at this wall, Sarah-Lysliana! The wall is just like your house. It looks like it's about to collapse. Half of the city is empty. We have not been able to revive the city with as many inhabitants as were here before the Massacre. And no one takes care of the houses!"

She gripped his arm to negotiate a particularly tricky part of the stairs. "I hear you, Ekbeth. It makes me sad as well. This is a wonderful place. I wish I could do something about the decay."

Ekbeth wanted the same. He brought this to every High Council meeting. And insisted on the maintenance of his own house. That did not make him popular either.

As'mirin were lazy. As long as the food was plentiful, and the beds soft, they were not going to care about other things—except intrigues, of course. He had to move cautiously around them. His own mother had been poisoned when he was a child, because she wanted to impose reforms no one wanted. There had been a few attempts against his life, as well. He had learned his lesson. He had become quite good at manipulating people, moving prudently toward his goals, but the changes he managed to obtain were too slow.

In the meantime, they'd reached his house. The Na Duibhnes' house was said to be the oldest house of the city, the first refuge after their capital, Annilis, collapsed. Then it had welcomed everyone, no matter to which family the surviving As'mirin belonged. So it had also become a tradition to have the first meal after the fast in that house.

And it was large enough to contain the whole community, even for a few hours.

From outside, the house they were now entering looked small. But it was a deception. Their ancestors had designed the facade with so many nooks and corners that it appeared to be a stack of houses instead of one. And as the rest of the city had been built on the same model, from afar you had the impression of a village of small houses built one on top of another.

It was a good deception. But as soon as you entered the place you were immediately dwarfed by the immensity of the main hall. At least, it still had that effect on Ekbeth.

The servants had brought the food to the hall, which was now so crowded that the vastness of its size was diminished—as long as you did not raise your head to look up. Running around the hall was a double helix stairway—climbing and climbing. Actually, it was only a four-story house. But the stairs rose gently, so it looked as if the house was higher than it actually was.

The guest rooms all branched off from the main stair. Some of them had a Lake view. Most of them were within the crater wall. His family was fighting bitterly about getting a room with a Lake view, of course. He could not complain. As an Akeneires'el he had a whole suite to himself and his view was only bettered by the Caller's home.

"You are such a lucky bastard, Ekbeth! I had forgotten how fantastic the place was!"

He smiled at Sarah-Lysliana. "Thanks. I suppose. I'm afraid I have to abandon you to your admiration. The Aramalinyia is waiting for me."

"Oh. I'll manage. And Gramp is really frowning at me right now. Better go! It was nice to talk with you, Ekbeth."

Duncan McLean was not the only frowning person in the room. His Es'ael was particularly upset. Ekbeth ignored them. He took the plate of food offered by one of his servants then turned towards the Aramalinyia. The plate was quite heavy, large and filled with the most creatively prepared food imaginable—As'mir style. The presentation was an artistic representation of the forest surrounding the Valley. Ekbeth was sure his cook must have spent the entire year planning the exquisite decoration. Every single morsel on that plate was a marvel in itself. Fluffy trees, miniature sugar flowers, chocolate butterflies, almond paste swans, and even his own favorite, the small deers made of dough and delicately dotted with sugary mixtures.

Ekbeth could feel the cook's eyes on his back, and managed not to smile. He'd better not let the plate fall, or make a fool of himself in any other way, if he wanted to live another night. The cook would never forgive him. Neither would his family.

It was just a tradition. But traditions were important for the community. And it was only the second time he was participating actively in this one. He bowed, managing somehow to keep the plate level. "Welcome to our house, Venerable. Please accept this humble meal."

The Aramalinyia took her time to pick a piece of food off the tray. The whole community was holding its breath.

These moments made him remember all the family members he had lost in the past years: his mother, his father, then his two brothers. He still had some distant relatives in this house, but direct relatives were few nowadays. His cousin Lyrian, banished. His niece Alyasini. That was about it.

The Aramalinyia finally chose a piece of elaborate fruit shaped as a fish. "Thank you for your hospitality, Akeneires'el. Ara will be pleased."

This was the sign everyone had been waiting. They could start eating.

He gave the plate back to the servant.

The Aramalinyia tapped his arm. "Well done, young man. And very brave of you to enter this place with a McLean. Ara will be pleased, indeed."

*

Ekbeth stayed as long as he had to, then managed to leave the hall without anyone noticing. At least he hoped that was the case. He just needed ten minutes. He hurried. If the girl had left Kse'Annilis already.

He had an idea. A bloody brilliant idea! Maybe he was going to survive this Aras'arisidz after all.

Akalabeth was still in Alyasini's room when he entered it.

Her alarm at his entrance, before realizing who it was, quickly turned to suspicion when she saw Ekbeth's intense expression. He tried to relax to reassure her.

"I want to help you, Kala, with lifting the ban. But vetoing the decision is not the solution. There must be something else. I just need time to think of it. In the meantime… you said you have nothing of value to exchange. That's not exactly true."

This time she looked at him, visibly confused.

"Your talent, Kala! Use your talent!"

Her mouth turned in a bitter bend. "I can't ask for money for my gift, Uncle! That's against…"

She suddenly stopped, putting things in perspective. "Of course, compared to what I've just done, asking for money would not be such a big breach of the law. But no one would be willing to pay me, Uncle."

"Not exactly true. I'm ready to offer unlimited supplies of food for your help, believe me. Will your Sieven accept the food if he knows you've done some Call work for it?"

She hesitated, but finally nodded. "He won't be happy, but I think he'll bend. He's getting as desperate as I am, even though he tries to hide it from me."

"Good. It was a very brave thing you did, Kala, to come here. I'm afraid I'm going to ask you to do it a second time…"

She listened carefully.

By the time they had agreed on the plan and the amount of money Ekbeth was to provide for her help, Alyasini had joined them. The Aramalinyia was leaving and his presence was requested.

Akalabeth was a bit more serene when they left her again. Ekbeth had given her an honorable solution to her problem, even though it was not the ideal one.

But maybe some good would come out of this mess after all. Soon he would have the jewels back. That only left the small matter of his wedding to Shona. Maybe the Aramalinyia would change her mind about that. But he'd been around the old woman all his life. His chances were almost nonexistent and he knew it.

21

SHONA WAS BORED, and depressed. Still too weak to stand—she'd tried twice already. Her legs had not let her even get up. But the merciful periods of sleep were getting shorter and shorter. Merciful because she was not dreaming.

Awake, but unable to move, all she could do was think. And that was not a good thing because her thoughts only brought her back to what she had experienced with the Ke'As'mirin. She could set aside the very bad and the very good moments. But the parts they had insisted on, the parts she was not proud of, she could not get those out of her mind.

It had been all about choices. She had decided a long time ago that whatever the result of her choices would be, she would not linger on whether it had been a bad or a good decision. Once taken, it was just too late to change one's mind. You had to assume the consequences. Whatever Maire had to say about it!

The thing was, most of her decisions had been taken under the influence of drugs, be it hash, alcohol or heroin. She had thought herself so clever at the time. Drugs seemed to help the decision-making. Thinking of her past, she had to admit: she was very lucky to be still alive. Because drugs had never helped. They had just pushed her further and further towards hell. And she probably would still be on that road, or dead, if Yeshe had not been there. He had saved her from herself.

She missed him so very much. She had always thought of herself as being so strong. But without him she was failing miserably. Look at the mess she'd put herself into right now!

The door of her room opened and a servant entered with a tray of food in her arms.

Shona sighed. More food.

They were fattening her up for the sacrifice—that was what they were doing!

"I'm not hungry!"

"Maybe not, but you still have to eat! You've lost a lot of weight during the Oyyads'erel, young lady. The Lake is not very far from this room, but you'll need to be able to walk from this room into the water without help tonight. As you refuse all our medicines, the only way to get you on your feet is through food."

Damn! Was the rest of the ceremony tonight already?

She looked at the Aramalinyia, who had entered the room behind the servant.

She was still angry at the woman for having drugged her and sent her to that awful trial.

But on the other side, she was fascinated.

Keremli had told her the Aramalinyia was well above her own two hundreds year old. How could one be so ancient and still have this youthful look? Oh, the hair was white and the skin all wrinkled, but there was an undeniable youthfulness in the dark eyes and on the lipless mouth, and she was certainly not moving across the room like an old person.

The servant put the food tray on Shona's bed, then brought a chair next to it, on which the Aramalinyia sat. "Leave us, Leli. The young Oyyad is now strong enough to help herself from the plates."

The servant bowed and left the room.

The Aramalinyia pushed the tray toward Shona. "Eat!"

Shona was sure the old woman was not going to leave her alone until the tray was empty. With a sigh, she took the spoon and started picking up the food from the nearest bowl.

The As'mir food, as far as she had experienced it, was very elaborate. It was obvious that the cook took pride in the careful mix of ingredients, and especially in the presentation. It reminded her of Japanese food, except that the As'mirin definitely liked their food on the spicy side. She had had some very nasty surprises the first time she had tasted the food neatly arranged in tiny bowls, and had soon learned to avoid everything with a blue tinge. Curiously, the red foods tended to be rather sweet.

It was very confusing for her. Even more for her palate. A bit of warning would have been nice, but she knew better now. She had first ignored the covered bowl in the far corner of the tray. Not anymore. She took the bowl in one hand, uncovered it, and plunged her spoon into it. It was not rice. More like porridge. But the blandness certainly helped with eating the spicier stuff.

The Aramalinyia watched her eating in silence for a

time, then nodded. "I'm glad you passed the Oyyads'erel, Oyyad. You are going to bring much to our community."

Another mistake was to swallow the food too fast. Shona took her time before answering. "The Ancestors did not have your certainty, Aramalinyia. I understood the vote was almost against me coming back among the living."

"Nonsense! You're back, and the name they gave you is a sure indication they share my feeling."

"The name?"

The old woman nodded. "Yes. Kimiel. That's a most unusual name."

Shona feigned indifference. She picked up a favorite red piece of something tasting like chicken—amazing that she already had favorite food—before asking, "What's so unusual about it?"

The Aramalinyia was not fooled, if her smug smile was any indication. "Well, first of all, Kimiel is a man's name. Then the best translation of its etymology would be 'the redeemer.' Knowing what I know from your past, I have to wonder what kind of redemption you're going to bring us."

Shona stopped eating and glared at her. "Keremli should never have told you about me in that letter. Had I known I would never have asked Ekbeth to send it to you!"

The old woman smiled quietly. "I disagree. My old friend Keremli was very right to tell me about you. What the Akeneires'el of the McLeans did to you and your family was unfair. I'm glad I could make it right. Even if only partially. Would your mother and your siblings be willing to come in the Valley if I invite them?"

Shona shook her head. "I doubt it. My mother decided she wanted nothing from the McLeans and the As'mirin in general after Duncan chased us from the Island, and we've grown up with that idea firmly imprinted in our heads. But you better ask them, I have not spoken to any of them in years."

The Aramalinyia sighed. "Just as stubborn as the whole lot! Being the spiritual leader of this community is sometimes such a heavy burden."

Shona did not relent. "And I am not a McLean! You can rename me, but you can't force me to accept them as family!"

There was a bit of anger in the Aramalinyia's voice when she replied. "Yes. You and Duncan have made this very clear." Then she smiled. "But I have thought of a solution. I'll give you the original name of the McLeans. The one they had before your ancestor moved out of the Valley."

Shona could not help wondering why the woman was being so conciliatory. But she supposed she would find out at some point of time.

She resumed her eating. "I suppose Keremli did not only talk about me in that letter?"

"Correct. She wants to come back in the Valley. It's not only my decision, but she'll have my support. And I think that if she brings the Kadj'dur back when bringing her petition to the Akeneires'el of the Na Duibhnes, he will not object either. He's probably the most reasonable man of the whole lot! And she's his great-great-grandmother, after all."

The Aramalinyia rose. "Finish your meal and rest. The servants will come in an hour to start preparing you for tonight."

Then she left the room.

So, Keremli's problem was settled. Shona just had to find the Kadj'dur.

Just.

Dressing seemed to take forever. Shona had somehow managed to leave her bed and stand. Finally. That was all what was required from her. So she closed her eyes and waited. The women were assembling her costume, piece by piece, directly on her.

"Open your eyes, Oyyad. We're done."

At last! When she saw the result of the hours of work in the mirror, Shona hid her reaction well. The dress was composed of thousands squares of thin cloth, all of the purest white, and, though they covered her decently, she could still see her body through them.

She could live with that. What really surprised her were the jewels she was now wearing. Jade. On her arms, each of her fingers, her neck, her ears, and around her waist.

She recognized the central piece that was around her waist. It was the stone she had stolen from Ekbeth! So, the rest was probably all the pieces she must have put under the palm tree. How had he managed to get them back? When the Valley was supposed to be closed to all?

This was not the moment to ask, of course.

She nodded. "Very nice. Those are the Annilis Jewels, aren't they?"

The nearest servant nodded. "You're so lucky to be able to wear them, even if it's only for a short time. This is our most precious treasure, Oyyad. We couldn't put the hair jewels in though—your hair is too short. You would have lost them. Not something you would want to explain to the Community, believe me."

Of that she was aware.

She had expected the Aramalinyia to come and pick her up, but, actually, Duncan McLean entered the room. They glared at each other for a moment.

Duncan McLean broke the silence. "So, you've won. You are now part of my family."

She shook her head. "Not by choice, Seanair."

He hissed. "Don't call me that!"

She had expected that reaction. This had been her pet name for him when she was a child. "Grandfather" in Scottish. Before he rejected her.

It did not hurt her anymore. She did not care anymore what he thought of her.

"I think they are expecting us," she said.

He grumbled something, then turned his back on her and walked outside of the room, her sign that she had to follow him, she supposed. She was glad some servants accompanied them, as she very well knew Duncan would not help her if she faltered now.

She had to concentrate on her steps, and the corridors were quite long, but eventually they came out of the building in which she had spent so many hours and had her first sight of the Lake and the city.

It took her breath away.

The moon was high in the sky, bathing the whole scenery in a silvery light. The Lake on her left side was so vast she could not see the end of it. On her right, behind a few trees, Kse'Annilis.

She was overwhelmed. It was all that her brother and her father had told her about when she'd been a child. The tiny houses with their uncountable arches, loggias, windows, going up and up, to the sky…

This was an enchanting view, but the most spectacular was the crowd amassed in front of her. The whole population was probably there tonight. Pity the light was not good enough to see more than their faces.

Let the Oyyad come to me.

The voice had spoken in her head, much as had happened with the ghosts in the forest. The crowd before her parted, opening her way to the Lake. One of the servants behind her whispered to her, "Go, Oyyad. Don't be afraid. Our people will shed your robe, layer by layer, on your way to the water, so you appear naked before Ara. Then you will be blessed by the Goddess."

Shona was more than thankful for the warning. She was now stronger than a few hours ago, but when the first hands began to grasp and pull at her clothes, she almost lost her balance.

When she finally reached the shore, she was indeed stark naked, except for the jewels. What was she supposed to do now?

The Aramalinyia appeared out of nowhere in front of her, her feet a mere inch above the water.

Come to me Oyyad.

Curse the woman. This was a nice trick, but Shona was not so lucky. She had to enter the water, communicate with the Goddess, and so on. She could not refuse to go with the whole community watching her. The fools would probably push her inside the Lake if she did.

She placed a foot in the Lake and its water was as cold as she expected. Well, the faster, the better. She inhaled deeply and proceeded as fast as possible toward the levitating silhouette of the Aramalinyia. When she reached the old woman, with water up to her waist, Shona was freezing.

The Aramalinyia face was expressionless.

Ara speaks through me tonight. You have been measured by the Ke'As'mirin and judged worthy of joining our community. You have breathed our air, walked our ground and eaten our bread. Drink our water now.

And without more warning, the old woman pushed Shona's head under water. The woman was strong for her age! Shona had to give in.

When she surfaced again, she was sputtering water, which had a terrible metallic taste.

Welcome back, child of Ara. You'll be known as Kimiel Malcolm Keh Niriel among us from now on.

And, as suddenly as she had appeared, the Aramalinyia disappeared, leaving Shona alone in a bloody freezing Lake. All she could do was to return to the shore and the cheering As'mirin.

Some hands helped her out of the water and she was quickly covered in multiple layers of clothes. It took some time before her teeth stopped chattering from the cold.

Duncan McLean was next to her, she realized, but he carefully avoided touching her.

Most of her family's congratulations were just as rigid. The only exception was that cousin she'd met for the first time two days ago. The young woman embraced her and put a kiss on her cheek. "Welcome, Cousin! I hope we'll become good friends."

While Shona tried to think of something to say that was not too inimical, her cousin was replaced by another familiar figure.

Ekbeth presented her with a flower. "Welcome back to the Valley, Kimiel Keh Niriel."

She accepted the present with a warmer smile than the ones she had offered her own family.

Then she turned to the next As'mir, another Akeneires'el, she understood, from his rigid posture.

There was a huge crowd. And they all wanted to congratulate her.

This was going to take forever.

She put a brave smile on her face.

22

EKBETH WAS ENJOYING in his own way the party given in honor of the new Oyyad.

As soon as he had been able to, he had left the temple and the celebrations and found refuge in his study, approving or rejecting purchasing requests from the community. He had not expected to find so many of them, though.

Administration was something the As'mirin had developed to an art, reflected Ekbeth.

That the huge pile of paper in front of him was due to his own stubbornness was something of which he was well aware. He allowed himself a smile while reading the next request.

When he had taken over the responsibilities from his deceased brother, Arkel, as Akeneires'el, he had been horrified by the money spilling. Especially because he personally knew what hard work it was for him to find that money.

The As'mirin community had no economy to speak of. They did not even have a word for it. There was no earning money by working to spend it on consumables, like on the Other Side. No. Here, it was just spending. You wanted something, you asked for it.

It was Ekbeth's responsibility to generate the money needed to cover the related costs.

Ekbeth had no idea how it worked before the destruction of Annilis. After the city was destroyed, the survivors had been left to themselves and had survived by growing their own food. There had been some trading with the humans at some point of time, but very limited. Only after the Valley had been closed to the rest of the world, the insidious economic nightmare had begun. The As'mirin had allowed the lost humans to stay in the Valley on the condition that they would take over the farming work and give a fixed quantity of the harvest to the As'mirin. It worked quite well in good harvesting years, but not so well in lean years. That had led to the revolt of the Aiarz'in and the almost total annihilation of the As'mirin population.

Nefer, Ekbeth's long dead ancestor, the last pure blood As'miri, had made another pact with the Aiarz'in. They would get money for the food they gave.

There was a big flaw in that pact. The money. The As'mirin had no money.

In the first years, they had stripped the emptied houses of their valuable decorations. That was enough for a good century of sustenance. When that source dried up, they gave their own valuables. Then one of Ekbeth's ancestors thought of creating a bank system in the Aiarz'i part.

The As'mirin had thought themselves very clever. Paying the humans with their own money. It had been a clever plan, Ekbeth had to admit. It had been enough for a time. Until the Aiarz'in realized they could create their own bank and keep the money to themselves.

Ekbeth's grandfather had found a solution by opening a

bank in Switzerland, on the Other side. A very discreet but very active bank. When he had taken over the operation there, Ekbeth had soon discovered most of the activities of that bank involved money-laundering.

He could live with that. All the banks were doing it. Maybe not on such a large scale, but it generated a lot of money in commission, which was fine with him.

Lately, though, the money-laundering was not so profitable. Laws were hindering his work. The clients remained, but they, too, had changed. The current criminal generation was expecting more from their bank than simply laundering their money. So Ekbeth had returned to what had been his first work on the Other Side—the trading business.

However, with the recent financial crisis behind them, even trading was becoming a very risky business. Mistakes were just not possible. Mistakes meant he would lose a fortune, with the consequence that his clients would try to kill him, if his family had not beaten them to it. Because it also meant there would be less or no food on the community table.

So Ekbeth had tried to control the problem from the other side as well. To control the spending. It had been an exhausting battle with the High Council, hours and hours of heated discussion. The As'mirin did not want to hear of restriction. They were not interested in the fact that the humans on the other side had exactly the same problem. That the money they were spending per year was enough to cover the needs of a population ten times bigger on the Other Side.

Ekbeth had not backed down. He had insisted. They had tried to take his title of Akeneires'el from him. When that had failed, there had been some serious poisoning attempts. Ekbeth did not want to remember how near he had been to dying during the last one. He owed his life to Kalem's quick reaction and to Bers'el na Saoilcheach's expertise.

Ekbeth had not relented. In the end, he had won. Somehow. Every As'mir family got an allocated budget, based on its size. Anything extra would have to be approved by Ekbeth. Nowadays, they were getting their revenge. Filing money requests had become a new sophisticated activity, Ekbeth understood. The As'mirin had hoped to bury him under their requests, so deeply that he would relent and drop the concept.

Bad luck for them. They were not the only stubborn ones there. That little victory had cost him too much to step back now.

Sometimes, sometimes he wished he was not Akeneires'el. At least, not the one in charge of the community finance. It was an enormous responsibility and he received no thanks for the hours he spent on it.

The running of the Bank on the other Side was taking far too much of his time, even with his cousin Lyrian's help. He was already glad the bank on the Aiarz'i side was running smoothly without him. Good administrators there. And he really did not care that they were humans.

And then, this administrative nightmare here. For which he had no time. He was not spending enough time in the Valley. That was the problem. Time, time… always the same problem. That was something even the As'mirin had no con-trol over.

He signed the request for the reorganization of the main hall lamps, put his personal seal on it, then pick up the next document. Self-pitying was not going to reduce the pile.

"So, that's where you're hiding yourself, Akeneires'el!"

The sudden appearance of the Aramalinyia in front of his desk startled him completely. She must have walked up to his room, but he had not heard her.

"You should be ashamed of yourself, young man! Making me walk up all those stairs at my age!"

Ekbeth was not intimidated, even though he hurried to find a chair for his prestigious guest. "You could have sent for me, Venerable."

She pursed her lips. "I wanted a quiet word with you."

Alarms went off in Ekbeth's head. A quiet word with the Aramalinyia never was a good thing. It was just one step short of an appearance before the High Council, more often than not with an associated punishment.

They had found out about him helping Akalabeth, was all he could think of. That and the fact that he had almost lost the Annilis jewels.

The Aramalinyia studied him for a moment, then asked, "When are you going to ask for Kimiel Keh Niriel's hand?"

Who? Oh yes, Shona. He still had to get used to her new name.

He was careful not to show his relief. The wedding. It was only about the wedding.

So the Aramalinyia was seeing though his poor attempt at delaying the inevitable. He had thought that avoiding the McLeans and the Aramalinyia in the coming days would be enough. That with the Aras'arisidz ceremonies keeping her busy, the Aramalinyia would forget about this, at least momentarily. And after the ceremonies, he could always pretend he had no idea where his intended was.

No such luck, then.

"I thought this could wait a day or two, Aramalinyia. The

Oyyads'erel has almost been too much for her. She can barely stand on her feet."

This was a sound argument, but the Aramalinyia apparently did not agree, because she said, "The girl is much stronger than she looks. She has survived worse than a wedding proposal. I want you to go to the McLeans' place tomorrow and ask for her hand before nightfall."

Then she pursed her lips again. "Don't force me to make this an official statement, Ekbeth. It is Ara's will, but I want you to make the move. The McLeans accepting your request will be seen as an acceptance that the feud has to cease. If I declare you two have to marry, the bad feelings between the two families will still be there."

The Aramalinyia produced a sweet smile. "I know you're not happy about the whole idea, Ekbeth. But you have to trust Ara's judgment on this. Only good will come out of your union. She told me so."

Ekbeth felt trapped. He could not call the Aramalinyia a liar. Not without costly consequences, even if this conversation was private. But how clever of her to misuse the Goddess's name.

He furiously tried to find some good argument, but all he could come up with was, "Is Kimiel aware of Ara's plans for the two of us, Aramalinyia?"

The old woman shook her head.

Ekbeth had feared as much. And he knew better than to ask why Shona had not been informed of her fate yet.

He sighed. "Kimiel may refuse, Aramalinyia. In fact, I'm certain she's going to refuse. She's not used to our customs. On the Other Side…"

The Aramalinyia interrupted him. "I don't care what happens outside Kse'Annilis. She will have to accept."

Ekbeth cringed internally. He still had Matheson's warnings in mind. Don't force the girl to do anything, unless you want to end with a real bloody mess. Ekbeth especially remembered the emphasis the man had put on the word "bloody."

"I don't think the usual punishment will make her change her mind," he argued. "She did not want to come here in the first place. She probably doesn't care about a threat of banishment."

"Ara will find a way to make her accept. I am certain. And have a bit more faith in yourself, Ekbeth. You are the Akeneires'el of the Na Duibhnes, and not too bad looking either. This should appeal to the girl."

Ekbeth made a last attempt. "I overheard McLean, Aramalinyia. The woman is a criminal. Becoming my wife will give her a lot of authority. Something you may not want."

The lips pursed again. "Even I can't oppose the Goddess's will. You also hear me saying everyone deserves a second chance, Ekbeth. Enough! You will marry the girl. Or I'll get *you* banished! How about that?"

That left him speechless.

The Aramalinyia stood. "You have till tomorrow nightfall."

She left him on those words.

Ekbeth was angry. Angry and frustrated. She left him no choice. No choice but to obey.

After all he had done for this community! This was not fair!

Damn it! Damn this conniving woman!

He sent the pile of administrative paper flying across the room.

23

S HONA AWOKE ON an uncomfortable mattress, in a room she did not recognize.

Then the events of the past night came back to her. After the almost drowning in the Lake and the congratulations, there had been a party in her honor. For the first time since she'd arrived, she had had a good view of other As'mirin. And the moment of wonder she had experienced when she had first met the Ke'As'mirin had come back.

There were no pointed ears, here. But all the As'mirin were showing some Elfin traits. Tall, thin, gracious.

She found the different hair colors… punkish. Someone explained to her that hair color told anyone whose family you belonged to, and the family names. Ekbeth was actually quite lucky to have black hair, because the other families' hair would have shocked people on the Other Side.

She loved their clothes, which were so… medieval. Those long flowing robes were maybe not the most convenient to wear, as she had herself discovered when she walked on the stairs of Kse'Annilis, but they gave an undeniable distinction to the wearer. Again, it was explained to her that there was a strict code of colors for your attire, depending on the family to which you belonged. Na Duibhnes were only allowed black. The McLeans, orange or red. The trick was to subtly combine those colors so that they did not clash when the As'mirin were all together, as at the party tonight.

Shona learned more about colors in one evening than in her whole life.

And the jewels! She just needed to get some!

The new age guys on the Other Side had it all wrong. There was no intricate Celtic lace of silver at the ears of the women. Rather, long pendants of jade stone, delicately sculpted. Jade on their necks. Jade on their fingers. Jade in all colors, all sizes and all shapes.

None of it was as old as what she had worn, but those were antiques that had been passed down from one generation to the other.

Yeshe would have loved it here.

She suddenly understood why Ekbeth had a whole wall display of jade statues in his Zurich house. Jade was the As'mir gold.

They called it Kadj'el.

Kadj'el. Kadj'dur… She understood some things better. And she had had fun, real fun, for the first time since… She did not want to remember since when.

She had met and talked to many people. Not everyone was giving her the cold shoulder as the McLean family was. Though Ekbeth's family members had shown some reluctance to talk to her, it was nothing like Duncan's attitude.

She had tasted some drinks, and tried one dance. But her body did not keep up long.

When it had become too much for her, the servants brought her back to the Aramalinyia's house, only to take back all the jade jewels from her and give her some warm and dry clothes.

Then someone had come to take her to another place.

Because she was not a lost As'mir anymore, she understood. She was part of the McLean family, willing or not, and had to live from now on in their house.

The someone who was guiding her up the stairs was not Duncan, thankfully. But her red-haired cousin, Sarah-Lysliana, if Shona had heard her name correctly.

By the time Shona reached her new home, she was too exhausted for conversation.

She accepted a shot of whisky and that was enough to put her out. She could not remember anything else.

Now, daylight was flooding the room. A sure sign it was late. And she was alone in the room. But not alone in the house. She could hear some loud arguing. Probably what had awakened her.

"Ah, awake at last."

She jerked, surprised. She thought she recognized the voice. "Aunt Fiona?"

The other woman came to her, near enough for Shona to be certain. Of course, her great-aunt had gotten old over time, but Shona recognized her nonetheless. Aunt Fiona had been the only one to keep in contact with Shona's mother after Shona's father's death. Shona had always liked the woman. But it had been some time since she had last seen her.

"Aye. Duncan has forbidden us to talk to you, Lass. But I don't care about his orders. Do you want some breakfast?"

Shona felt ravenous. But she also realized she was unable to do more than sit.

Yesterday's ceremony had taxed her energy more than she realized. And the ribs were still hurting.

Aunt Fiona came to her help. The older woman was smaller than she was, but strong. "We are going to the kitchen. We'll have to be careful on the stairs, they're all wobbly, but staying on that mattress won't help you get better. Don't worry. I won't let you down."

Shona nodded and, leaning heavily on her aunt, left the room. The stairs were not far away and, indeed, in a very poor state. Actually, she noticed, when she paid attention to it, that the whole house looked to be on the verge of collapse. There were huge cracks on the ceilings and the walls, and the colors of the paint were severely faded.

It only got worse when she entered what she supposed was the kitchen. Someone had put some cardboard over the windows. As a result, the room was quite dark. But she could smell the decay of some long-forgotten food, and hear the dripping of a faucet.

The McLeans had never been rich, she knew. They were producing just enough money to maintain their little island of an estate, up in the far north of the Highlands. That and feeding the clan. But surely they had enough money to keep that place as well?

In fact, Shona suddenly realized, the place looked like it had been abandoned for a long time. She must have spoken the last thought out loud because Aunt Fiona answered her. "Correct, Lass! Thirty years to be exact! The Na Duibhnes wanted our blood badly after your Alasdair snatched one of the Na Duibhnes' fiancées. You must remember me telling this story to your mother, even though you were still quite young at the time. It was quite a scandal! We did not dare show up here afterwards! Till today! Have a seat! Take that chair! I can't guarantee the others would take your weight, even light as you are. Still fancying that awful beverage in the morning?"

Shona obeyed her aunt. Sat down. The next moment a big bowl of porridge, some toast and a fresh cup of coffee were put in front of her.

"No butter, I'm afraid. We used the last bit of it yesterday, and I still have to find out how to get replenishments."

Shona started to eat. At least this was not going to destroy her stomach like the normal As'mir fare. The porridge was not even bland, because someone had added milk and sugar to it.

She suddenly felt like crying. She forced herself to eat instead. Fiona was no dupe, however. She sat next to Shona and put her hand on Shona's shoulder.

"What Duncan's done to Emily and you children was wrong, Lass. But he's the Laird. We had to accept his decision. I'm glad the Aramalinyia has at last corrected that wrongdoing."

"She forced him to do so, Aunt Fiona. He's made that clear to me. And probably to everyone as well."

The hand squeezed her. "He's a stubborn man that one. He will never admit his mistakes."

Shona nodded, munching on a piece of toast. Better to concentrate on her food than let the familiar old anger get to her.

"Can I ask you something, Lass?"

Shona nodded.

"Is it true?"

Shona smiled bitterly. That particular aunt had never

been listening to gossip, as far as Shona could remember. But listening was different from hearing.

"Is what true, Aunt?"

"That you're going to marry Ekbeth, the Akeneires'el of the Na Duibhnes. To finally settle that feud between our families!"

Shona choked on her toast. So badly that her eyes started running. It took her some time to get over it, and be able to say, "Pardon?"

"Ekbeth told us so two days ago. It was a bit of a shock to us. I may have misunderstood. Sorry."

Well! Shona had certainly not expected that!

Rumors about her were most of the time about drug use, thievery, craziness, danger, eventually about the money she had accumulated over the years… but marriage? She could not help herself, she started chuckling. And with Ekbeth, of all men!

She shook her head. Wait till that bodyguard of his heard about that! She took her cup of coffee. Time to change the topic. "I never heard you talk about Sarah-Lysliana. She's my cousin, isn't she?"

Her Aunt hesitated. "Yes. Alasdair's daughter. She was born after you left home. That's why you probably never heard of her."

Shona forced a smile on her lips. "Left home," indeed. It was one way to put it. But she did not want to discuss her past right now. "Ah, so she's Andrew's sister?"

"Yes. But the girl has not been in our family for long. I told you the Na Duibhnes were not happy about the fiancée changing her mind. Her betrothed especially. He was a sorry piece of shit, forgive my words. A pervert of the worse sort.

Dead now, but he lived long enough to steal the newborn baby girl and was never willing to reveal what he had done with her."

Shona was not sure she wanted to hear this story. It brought too many memories of what had happened to her own babies. But she had to know. "The clan probably thought the baby was dead, then."

"Exactly. So it was a bit of a surprise to us when she entered our hall four years ago. Everyone was glad, of course. Sally really is a nice girl. And a very talented singer. She's producing music records."

Shona did her best to maintain an inexpressive face. It was very hard. Her description of that little cousin could fit her as well. Only she was not entitled to a warm welcome back. As for her singing talent, well… she could only blame herself for what had happened to it.

"She seemed very nice. Is there more coffee?"

Aunt Fiona refilled her cup, looking at her attentively. "I know what's on your mind, girl. But don't be jealous of her. It's not been all rosy for the girl either, Shona. Apart from not having known her own parents, she's been married to Ekbeth's cousin. The man is a brute. He almost killed her."

Ah! A bit of information Shona should have realized she had already. Because she had investigated the Na Duibhnes extensively. And had known Ekbeth's cousin, Lyrian Farrill, had been married once.

She had just not realized it was to a McLean. "Wait a second. If Sally was married to Ekbeth's cousin, it kind of solves the feud between our families? Or am I completely stupid?"

Fiona shook her head. "Not stupid, Lass. I wish it was so. But see, Farrill only married his neighbors' daughter. He was not aware she was a McLean. Nobody was at the time. Besides, Farrill was not living in the Valley. He's related to the Na Duibhnes by his mother, but his father is not As'mir. So it does not count."

"And he tried to kill her when he discovered she was a McLean?"

Aunt Fiona pinched her lips disapprovingly. "No. He actually only found out about us after the separation. No, the man is just a brute. He had no reason to beat her, but he did it nonetheless."

Mmh. That was too easy an explanation. Shona had seen Lyrian. She had also studied him. He was not an easy man. But a woman beater? That was difficult to believe.

She would have to ask her cousin for more information, apparently.

She had just finished her second cup of coffee when Sally entered the kitchen, a gorgeous young man in tow.

"I think this is the worse room of the whole house," Sally said to him. "We've tried to clean it, but that rotting smell is not going away."

The young man walked around the room, with a supple gait. It was difficult to ignore his presence. Even Aunt Fiona was looking admiringly at him, Shona noticed.

He stopped in front of a wall and started touching it. "The smell is stronger here. If I'm not mistaken, there must be a shaft hidden behind this wall. A shaft to the sewage. It clogs easily. We have the same problem in our house. Let's try to find the opening…"

"Najeb! What are you doing here?"

Shona did her best to ignore the newcomer. But the others all turned toward him.

And the young man did not look so sure of himself anymore. "Father…"

Kalem, Ekbeth's favorite bodyguard, growled, "We've been through this before. You're a bodyguard, not a plumber!"

Shona had trouble hiding her amusement. That hunk was Kalem's son?

Cousin Sally put herself between the two men, no matter that she was a full head smaller than them. The girl had some guts, no doubt about it. "I asked for his help, Kalem. He's the only one who knows how to repair anything here."

It was obvious Kalem had trouble with the situation. Still, he managed a short bow to Sally. "Miss McLean. I'm sorry but you'll have to find someone else for this task."

Duncan entered the room at the very instant, scowling. "What's going on here?"

Both Kalem and Najeb bowed to him. Shona concentrated on her cup of coffee. The old bastard did not deserve their respect.

Sally relaxed a tiny bit. "Gramp. Can you please explain to Kalem that we really need his son's help? Even if it's only for an hour?"

If she had hoped Duncan would be of any help, she was to be disappointed.

Duncan's frown deepened. "We don't need the Na Duibhnes' help with our house, Sally."

"But…"

The old man shook his head. "Inviting their Akeneires'el here was already bad enough, though it was my decision. Take your son out of our house, Kalem."

Kalem's face was neutral, but no doubt he was raging at

the not-so-subtle insults to his family, even though Duncan had just agreed with him. He only bowed. "Akeneires'el, I actually come with a message from the Na Duibhnes' Akeneires'el. He'd like to see you and your relative Kimiel."

Duncan grumbled, "If Ekbeth wants to see me, he can come here."

Another short bow from Kalem. "The Akeneires'el thinks his house will be a more appropriate setting."

Shona noticed how both men were carefully ignoring her. Highly irritating. She left her chair and walked to her grandfather, careful not to show her emotions.

"Come now, not so grumpy, Seanair. I'm sure Ekbeth means well. Kalem? Can you show us the way, please?"

Duncan did not seem to hear her. Ekbeth's bodyguard was slightly more responsive. He glared at her, but nodded, before turning his back on her. She then noticed her cousin's expression. It was difficult to read. Was it pity?

Great. Shona had no idea why Ekbeth wanted to talk to her, but she was now pretty certain she was not going to like the conversation.

*

The house of the Na Duibhnes was not so far. Just a few flights of stairs away.

By the time they got there, Shona was out of breath, doing her best not to show it, and totally disoriented. This city was a maze. A crumbling maze, but still a maze.

When entering it, the main hall of the Na Duibhnes' place made her pause. She had not expected such a grand hall, after the rather simple doorway. That stair along the wall! It seemed to go on forever. In comparison with the McLeans' house, this was a palace.

She saw Kalem's smirk at her reaction. But she let it pass.

What was Ekbeth's game, though? Had he asked them to come to impress them?

She kept a perfectly neutral expression. She was impressed, but she would be damned if she was going to show it.

Kalem brought them—more stairs—to a suite of rooms at the very top of the building.

Ekbeth was waiting for them in a cleverly decorated little room, standing next to the window.

"Morning, Duncan. Kimiel."

That name. She would get used to it, eventually. She put a smile on her face. "Morning, Ekbeth."

Ekbeth was looking at her with an expression she found strange. As if he was having trouble with his digestion, or something like that. He was probably still mad at her about what had happened in Zurich, she thought. Why had he asked her to come, then?

"You wanted to see us?"

He nodded, but still did not speak.

Apparently Duncan knew already what the issue was, because he growled. "Get it out, Lad. She won't bite you."

Shona almost laughed. She actually had bitten him already. In a very sensitive place. She crossed Ekbeth's gaze. He was also remembering the moment. She could tell.

He sighed. Then reached for her hands. Looked into her eyes. "Kimiel Keh Niriel. Will you marry me?"

That was unexpected! Even with Aunt Fiona having asked her about it. She was speechless for a minute. He sounded like he meant it. "You are joking, aren't you, Ekbeth?"

He shook his head. Slowly.

She took one step back, extracted her hands from his grip. "Hell, no!"

Then she stormed out of the room before any of them had time to block her way.

24

EKBETH HATED TO have been so correct about Kimiel's expected reaction to his request. She had not even given him time to explain. There was nothing personal in her refusal. He knew it. Maybe, he should have phrased his request a bit less directly, he now realized. From her reaction, she had not expected this at all.

"Hmm. This did not go very well, Lad!"

Ekbeth glared at Duncan McLean, who was still sitting comfortably in his chair.

"I need to convince her to accept, Duncan. A bit of advice would be welcome, instead of sarcasm."

"This is not my idea. Ask the Aramalinyia for help. Not me."

"It may not be your idea, but neither is it mine. You have to help me. She's your kin!"

The old man scowled. "No need to remind me."

Then he left the room.

Damn the man. Ekbeth thought furiously for a moment. But nothing came to his mind.

He had until nightfall, the Aramalinyia had said. Maybe

he should just let her banish him. He was wealthy enough on the Other Side, even without the community fortune.

He looked outside, at the Lake in front of him. Of course, he would miss the place. But he also had a home on the Other Side. A home where he was respected, where he was the one making the decisions, where he was in control of his life.

He sighed. There was just a slight problem. There was no one to take his job over.

His own mistake, mainly. He had troubles trusting his family. Lyrian could have been an option, a difficult one, as he had not grown up in Kse'Annilis as Ekbeth had, but still an option. Only his cousin had got himself banished.

Ekbeth knew leaving the community to their fate would end in a disaster. And the Aramalinyia would probably recognize her mistake too late, if ever.

If it came to that, Ekbeth could always try to make her aware of the danger in which she was placing the community. But that probably would not help. She had never showed any interest in the financial aspect of his responsibilities. And she had also voted for the ban on his niece Akalabeth, when, surely, she could surmise the consequences. No Caller was just as bad as no money for Kse'Annilis.

No, he could not let the community down. No matter how ungrateful they were. It was his responsibility.

"What's going on, Ekbeth? I just saw the Oyyad and Duncan McLean leave our house."

Ekbeth closed his eyes for a moment. Speaking of ungrateful and very annoying As'mirin. A nosy relative. And, of course, it had to be his Es'ael.

Ekbeth turned to face the old man, telling himself for

the hundredth time that Es'ael was not the worst of the lot. For all his irritating, incessant recriminations, Es'ael sometimes surprised Ekbeth by giving sound advice during the family council. Not that Ekbeth was going to tell him that.

Es'ael was resentful. He had been refused the title of Akeneires'el four times by the Council.

The fourth time had been especially painful for the old fool. Ekbeth, as the third son of the Akeneires'el Maher na Duibhne, had never expected to take over the responsibilities of his father. He had studied finance and had helped with the bank management from early on, but Akeneires'el? No, he had not been prepared for that.

No, no one had foreseen that his two older brothers would die so young. Kas'el's death had been inevitable when the extent of his crimes had been discovered. But Arkel… Arkel had been unlucky enough to fall down the stairs one day when he had had a bit too much to drink, and broke his neck.

A stupid accident. But one that had left only Ekbeth as a direct heir of Maher. Well, there had been Alyasini as well, Arkel's daughter. But she had only been five at the time, far too young to inherit the title.

The Akeneires'el title was not hereditary. But it tends to go to the most directly-related family member of the previous Akeneires'el. Es'ael was not even a brother of Maher. He was a cousin of the third degree through his mother. So, to the council's way of viewing the options, Ekbeth had been a better choice.

Ekbeth had accepted the position and was doing his utmost to do the job correctly. Thankfully, the main responsibility, at least—the banking part—he had mastered.

Es'ael just thought he would have done better, of course. And he criticized Ekbeth's decisions at every step of the way.

And right now, expecting an answer to his question, his frown quickly turned into a full scowl. Well, Ekbeth would have to announce the news at some point of time, anyway.

"The Aramalinyia has asked me to propose to the Oyyad, Es'ael. That's the reason why I asked Kimiel Keh Niriel to come here, with her grandfather."

That bit of news took Es'ael completely by surprise, if his stunned expression was any indication. He stammered, "Propose? You mean… you intend to marry her?"

Ekbeth nodded. It did not seem to quiet the old man.

"But… she's a McLean!"

Ekbeth sighed. "Ara's will, Es'ael. According to the Aramalinyia. There's not a lot I can do about this. And I have to at least admit that it would be an honorable way to put an end to our feud with the McLeans. Even though it is not the way I would have chosen if I had had a say in the decision."

Ekbeth had hoped the news would be too much and would prevent further questioning, and was disappointed when Es'ael continued pressing him for information.

"I met the Oyyad in the hall, Ekbeth. She did not seem to me blissfully happy with your proposal."

Ekbeth could only nod. "Shock, mainly. She was not prepared. She'll get over it."

Es'ael snorted loudly. "She'd better. We are actually doing her a great honor in accepting her into our family."

Ekbeth refrained from commenting on that.

Es'ael's next question was not totally surprising. After all, he had a habit of seeing conspiracies everywhere—another reason for not being chosen as Akeneires'el.

"Is this something you've planned with the Aramalinyia behind our back, Ekbeth? Kalem, your own bodyguard, brought Kimiel here. I don't believe that nonsense about a letter. Is she your lover?"

Ekbeth would never qualify a woman he had spent an hour with as a lover. And it was none of this old fool's business.

"Uncle, I did not lie to you. A week before the start of the Aras'arisidz, I had never heard of Kimiel Keh Niriel. And think for a moment. Manipulate the Aramalinyia into this? Really?"

Not that he had not tried it before during the High Council sessions. But the woman was better than anyone at the game, and Es'ael knew it just as well as Ekbeth. Still, the old man did not believe him.

"But surely, the presence of the McLeans, considering this last development, is suspect. We know you've been to their place."

Ekbeth knew very well who the "we" were. He shook his head. "Coincidence, Uncle. True, the Aramalinyia informed me of her wedding plans before the start of the ceremonies. But I'm asked to wed a perfect stranger. Duncan McLean seemed to know the woman. I tried to get some information from him, that's all."

Es'ael's curiosity took over. "And, what did you learn about her?"

Nothing you need to know, you nosy old fool, thought Ekbeth. Certainly not the bit about her being a murderer. But Duncan McLean had been really loud during his confrontation with the Aramalinyia. Es'ael was bound to hear some rumors at some point of time.

But not from him.

"Only that she has an unconventional past. But that could be expected. She's an As'miri. I'm sure you'll manage to ask her about this yourself. After all, she can't go anywhere in the coming days."

That seemed to satisfy the old man for now. Ekbeth was left alone, to his depressing thoughts. No doubt the whole family would be informed of the latest developments within an hour—and the whole community before the end of the day.

He cringed when thinking how Kimiel was going to react to everyone's good wishes and questions. He needed to talk to her first. Explain. But he could not go and look for her himself. That would certainly raise questions from his family, especially if he could not find her. Kalem was not a much better choice—he, also, was too visible.

Ekbeth pondered for a moment.

Ah. Maybe…

He asked a servant to find his niece Alyasini for him. No one was paying attention to his niece, most of the time. She would find Kimiel for him.

25

S HONA WAS HAVING trouble breathing. Her head was too full, as if ready to explode.

She needed to run. Run until her mind was empty.

But that was impossible in this place. There was nowhere to run except the steps going up and down the cliff. She climbed down them, tripping a few times on the tiresome long dress she'd been given. She was exhausted when she reached the bottom step, and her damaged ribs were hurting.

Even her body was betraying her.

She looked desperately around her. All she saw was an inescapable trap.

She was hurting so much inside. She fought the tears. Tears had never helped.

People were staring at her. And she had nowhere to go to evade them.

Someone was talking to her. She screamed, "Leave me alone! Leave me bloody alone!" She ran away. Ran until she found herself in a place so dark she could not even see where the next wall was.

There, there in that darkness, she could let herself go.

Some animal was howling nearby. Howling in pain.

Then she realized she was the one making the noise. She dropped to her knees. Let the tears come at last.

Oh my… she just wanted to die. Forget the pain. Forever.

*

She had no clue how many hours had passed by the time she managed to regain control. The place she was in was still pitch dark. By the musty smell of it, she guessed it was a sort of cellar.

She slowly got back on her feet. Damn. It had been a long time since she had let herself go so badly. Crazy indeed. She did not have panic attacks anymore nowadays. She had herself under control. She snarled. Who was she trying to fool?

She did not even want to think of how she looked right now. She tasted dirt on her lips. Nice.

It was all because of Ekbeth and that stupid wedding proposal, of course. After all the memories the Ke'As'mirin had forced her to face, that had been the last straw. The proposal had been so unexpected! She wondered what had triggered it. Surely not because of that hour of good sex at his place!

She managed a thin smile at the thought. That would be so… "Victorian" was the only word that came to mind.

Anyway, she could not accept the offer. Not so soon after all those memories that the Ke'As'mirin had brought back. She snarled again. She was not going to marry anyone again. Ever.

Oh, Ekbeth was attractive. And intelligent. And rich. And a fantastic lover. And forgiving. He apparently had forgiven her all the trouble she had put him in.

She did not mind having sex with him. Not at all. He had been really good. But marrying him was something else. It was a commitment. The only thing left, maybe, that was sacrosanct to her.

Her commitment was still to Yeshe. Heart and soul. She had to make this clear to Ekbeth, she thought.

And hiding here was not going to help her. Someone would eventually find her. It was better to meet him on her own terms. Explain to him. But first, she supposed, she needed to clean up.

She had no clue how to get out of the room. So she walked straight until she reached a wall, then just walked through it. She ignored the startled face of the man she found in the next room. She just kept walking through the rooms and the walls until she was in the open again.

At least that drug they had given her on the Other Side was not blocking her special talent anymore. She had feared that the effect would be permanent, but it was obviously not the case. Good.

The sun was setting on the other side of the Lake. She paused for a moment to admire the view, and get her bearings.

"Kimiel?"

The young woman's voice sounded uncertain. Shona probably looked a mess, but she had always been good at pretending nothing was wrong. She turned towards the other woman. Recognized her. Alyasini, Ekbeth's niece, who was trying her best not to show her dismay, but failing miserably.

So much for pretending, thought Shona. She looked like a mess. "Yes?"

That had come out a bit harsher than she had intended.

Alyasini took a step back and stammered. "I have been looking for you. My uncle…"

Shona interrupted her. "If it's about that wedding thing, Alyasini, I'm not interested. Can you show me the way to the McLeans' house? I have no clue where it is."

Alyasini quickly nodded and started walking toward the nearest stairs. A bit too readily, thought Shona. Apparently Alyasini had not been happy with her mission, whatever it was, and was all too happy to forget about it.

She told Shona. "Kse'Annilis is a maze. I can lose my way in it and I was born here. But there are some tricks not to lose yourself completely." She unexpectedly smiled at Shona. "Of course, you have to know where you want to go in the first place. This way."

Shona listened to the girl's chat until they reached the McLeans' house. Something vaguely resembling a choir singing greeted them—a very dissonant choir singing.

Alyasini smiled. "Oh, the McLeans are singing to the Goddess again! I never heard them sing, of course, I was not even born when they came here the last time, but I heard of it. One of my aunts said they could make you cry, so beautiful was their chant."

Shona smirked. "I'd rather cry from pain. My, this is really terrible!"

Silence met her words. Damn. She had not noticed that the choir had stopped singing.

Sarah-Lysliana appeared in the corridor and walked toward them. She did not seem angry. In fact, she looked anxious. "Kimiel. I was worried about you. And I need you. Can you please help? Aunt Fiona keeps repeating that you're the one we need. I have some experience with leading groups of musicians, but they were experts—something very different from this group. The voices are right, everyone knows the texts, but I just can't make it work."

She made no comment on Shona's clothes or the dirt with which she was covered. Shona had to give points to her cousin for that.

The last time she had led a choir seemed ages ago. But surely she couldn't do worse than Sarah-Lysliana. Anything to keep her mind off that wedding proposal. She smiled. "Can I clean myself up a bit first?"

*

She closed her eyes and breathed in deeply. Then started singing. Her voice was not as pure as it once had been. Deeper. But it was still strong. She sang alone for a time, then the choir joined in. It was not perfect, but one could not create miracles in two hours. At least they did not need so much direction from her anymore.

She led them through the first part, then Sarah-Lysliana took over. Her cousin had the voice Shona had once had. Maybe even better. Climbing to the higher notes seemed so easy for her. Shona kept her face carefully neutral.

At the agreed cue, she joined the song again. The singing went up and up. And yes, it brought tears to her eyes.

When they finally stopped singing, the silence seemed too much to bear. She reopened her eyes and found Ekbeth in the room, standing next to his niece Alyasini.

Damn. Just when she was just starting to forget about him and his ridiculous proposition. She ignored him and turned towards her cousin. "I think we won't get any better today, Sally."

The young woman nodded, but her expression was

much more relaxed than a few hours earlier. "We would never have managed this without you, Kimiel. Thank you."

Shona noticed that most of the others were looking at her somewhat more favorably than they had the night before. Had the naming ceremony only been yesterday? So much had happened in the meantime.

"And I think it's dinner time," Sarah-Lysliana added. "It's not going to be as fancy as the Aramalinyia's, I'm afraid, but it serves its purpose."

"Dinner will have to wait a bit more, Kimiel," Ekbeth responded. "The Aramalinyia has requested our presence." He offered an arm to Shona.

Shona eyed him warily, but she had promised herself she would talk to him. Delaying would not help. So she accepted his arm and left the house with him.

Night had fallen and she was glad for his support, as walking down the barely lit steps was even trickier than earlier. Still, she did not forget why they were walking towards the Lake.

"What does the old woman want from us now?"

"No idea."

"Don't lie to me, Ekbeth. It is something to do with that ridiculous wedding idea, isn't it?"

He did not answer her, but his grim expression was enough indication. Yeah, he seemed just as enthusiastic as she was about the coming meeting. That wedding proposal has never been his idea, she suddenly realized. That left only one alternative. It made her angry. "The Aramalinyia has no right to force us into this, Ekbeth."

He sighed. "Sadly, she has every right. She's Ara's voice. The Goddess wants us to marry, according to her. And yes,

I'll admit I'm not happy about it either. But try as I might, I can't see how we can get out of this."

Shona furiously considered the situation. At least she now knew why he had proposed, but she was still not going to accept it, Goddess or not.

She almost missed a step again, but he was there to prevent her fall.

"Thanks. Why are you not married yet, anyway, Ekbeth? There are enough women out there who would kill rivals to get that honor!"

He shrugged. "On the Other Side maybe. Only those women are not As'mir. Because of my function, I have to wed an As'mir woman."

"And there's no candidate for the job in the Valley?"

He smiled thinly at that. "For different reasons, no."

He sensed her incredulousness, because he added, "It's nothing personal. More because of my family's reputation. After my mother's death, my father lived his last years with a harem of a sort. My older brother was not as bad, though he was known to cheat on his wife with women outside of the Valley. Then there was my other brother."

Ekbeth paused briefly. "You'll probably hear of him. And, last but not least, there's my cousin Lyrian, who almost beat his ex-wife to death. This is giving a wrong impression."

She kept silent for a moment, digesting the information. "I see. Still, Ekbeth, I'm sure some of the women would take the risk, nevertheless. You are one of the Akeneires'elin!"

"But not one with a lot of influence, I'm afraid."

"You must be joking, Ekbeth! Your family is the biggest of Kse'Annilis. And on the Other Side..."

He shrugged. "What I am on the Other Side does not

concern them. Here, I tend to let people make their own decisions. And this is seen as a weakness."

"Still. There must be someone…someone you'd rather wed than me."

They had reached the bottom of the stairs, she realized. She let go of his arm. The Aramalinyia's house was close now.

"No. I like women, Kimiel. For fun—like that hour we spent together. But I've tried to avoid marriage like the plague."

"Why? Because you're afraid of being as bad as the rest of your family?"

"Maybe. I'm also a busy man, I don't have time for a wife."

Ah. Honesty. She had always liked that in a man. "Is that why you can't keep your mistresses? Because you don't have time for them?"

She heard his amusement when he replied, "I suppose that's one of the reasons. And that I don't propose."

He took her hand. "I know this has come as a shock to you, Kimiel, but please accept. We barely know each other, but we'll find a way to make this work, I'm sure."

She took her hand from his. "I can't do it, Ekbeth. I just can't."

It was fine to chat about this. Saying yes was still not an option for her.

Ekbeth sighed. "So, what is your plan?"

Her mind was empty. All she could come up with was: "We have to tell the Aramalinyia she's making a mistake."

Ekbeth seemed ready to contradict her, but it was too late, they had reached their destination.

They entered the hall of the Aramalinyia's house. A

servant was expecting them, and brought them through the maze of corridors to the main reception room of the Venerable, the very room to which Shona had been brought when she come here the first time, with Kalem.

Not good.

The Venerable was waiting for them behind a desk but she left her chair as soon as she recognized them. "You took your time!"

Ekbeth bowed. "The McLeans were rehearsing, Aramalinyia. I did not want to interrupt."

The old woman immediately looked at Shona, who kept as straight a face as she could. "Mmh. Anyway, I heard you are doubting Ara's wisdom, Kimiel. About marrying Ekbeth."

Shona gritted her teeth. Rumors were spreading as fast here as on the Other Side, she thought. And the distortion was just as bad.

"I'm not doubting anyone's wisdom, Aramalinyia. I just said no."

The old woman simply ignored her. She clapped her hands and some servants brought a huge urn into the room. Shona was puzzled. "What's this?"

Ekbeth was frowning when he answered, "The oracle."

The Aramalinyia took the lid off the urn. It was filled with hundreds of pebbles made from different matters, from precious stones to simple clay.

"The oracle indeed. If you don't believe me, maybe you will believe the stones. You are each to take a pebble from the urn."

This was getting worse and worse! An oracle of all things! But Shona had an idea. "If the oracle is not good, will you let your ridiculous idea of having us married rest at last?"

The Aramalinyia pinched her lips, apparently not pleased by what she was hearing. But she nodded. That was enough for Shona. She plunged her hand in the vase and picked up a pebble randomly. She had almost opened her hand when Ekbeth whispered to her to wait.

He took a pebble as well, and then extended his closed fist next to hers. They opened their hands simultaneously and Ekbeth was the first to gasp loudly when he saw what was in their hands.

The Goddess Ara certainly has a strange sense of humor, was all Shona could think.

Two pieces of jade. Of the exact same color. Ekbeth saw her consternation and whispered, "Doomed indeed. Jade stands for eternal love, Kimiel, in our tradition. And there are only two such pebbles in this urn, it is said."

The Aramalinyia was smiling radiantly. "See! Are you doubting now? So can we announce the ceremony will take place at the end of the Aras'arisidz?"

Shona's mind went totally blank for a minute. She was having another panic attack. White, pure panic. Twice in one day was a record. She could not allow it. She could not allow this farce happen.

She opened her mind as wide as she could. The familiar sensation of dizziness was not as strong as she was used to. But it should be enough. Bad luck if she lost herself in the between worlds! Anything was better than this!

Ekbeth put his hand on her, a horrified expression on his face. She heard him say,

"Kimiel! Don't!"

She stared at Ekbeth. Then called herself out of this nightmare. To the only safe place she could think of.

26

EKBETH COULD NOT believe what had just happened. Kimiel had just broken Ara's rule, in front of the Goddess's representative, of all things. She had called herself out of the Valley in the midst of the Aras'arisidz.

The ground shook under their feet.

He had felt Kimiel's summon of energy. He had guessed what she intended to do. He had tried to stop her. But he was no Caller himself. One second there had been warm solid flesh under his fingers, the next, nothing.

Another ground tremor. Stronger. The Goddess was angry, no doubt about it.

Breaking Ara's rules in such a blatant way meant death. But how could they bring punishment on someone who was not there anymore? Someone they could not Call back either, because the Caller had no memory of a transfer of that person.

Something heavy fell on Ekbeth's head. He looked absently at the white piece of stucco at his feet, and then realized what was happening. The ceiling was falling apart.

The imminent danger brought him out of his stupor.

He looked around him. There were so many people in the room. "Aramalinyia! We have to get out of here!"

The old woman did not seem to even hear him, but her servants did, if their concerned glances toward the ceiling were any indication. They all hurried outside, to the temple.

The Aramalinyia dropped to her knees, whimpering.

From all sides, As'mirin entered the open space of the temple. They had felt the tremors. They now saw their most important lady in shock, unable to answer their urgent questions. They were confused. What was happening?

They heard the abysmal news, of course. There was no way something this terrible could be hushed down. And the community reaction was even worse than Ekbeth could have expected. That blasphemy, that outrage to their Goddess had been committed by a woman they had just accepted back, by an Oyyad.

Ekbeth felt the anger growing around him. But the anger could not find any release. Kimiel Keh Niriel was not here to pay for her crime. Anger turned into rage.

Someone shouted, "The McLeans! The McLeans have to pay for this!"

Fervent shouts answered the words. The next moment the temple was empty, except for Ekbeth, and the Aramalinyia. Even her servants had followed the crowd.

Ekbeth ran to the old woman, and kneeled at her side. "Aramalinyia! They are going to kill innocent people! You have to stop them!"

But the Aramalinyia was not hearing him. She was bent over as if in pain, her eyes closed, mumbling something he could not make out.

Ekbeth turned his attention to the Lake for a moment.

The As'mir lore said that the Lake was where the Goddess lived. At this point, he had nothing to lose. He shouted, "Is this what you want, Ara? That innocents pay for someone else's crime?"

The ground shook violently. As to whether this was a positive or negative answer, Ekbeth had no clue. He made another attempt. "We'll bring Kimiel to you, Ara. I swear this to you. Save the McLeans. They are innocent."

Nothing happened. Behind him, Ekbeth could hear the clamor of the angry mob. They must have reached the McLeans' house by now. What could he do?

An image came to his mind. A clear image. Was it Ara's answer? He had no time to ponder this. This was probably their best shot at preventing carnage. He jumped to his feet and called Kalem with his mind. His bodyguard answered him immediately. They had worked long enough together that the mental link between them had grown as strong as the one they had with Nukri na Liom, the Caller.

Kalem, call all the bodyguards and go to the McLeans' house. Protect them.

The briefest pause and then Kalem confirmed the order. Ekbeth hoped this would be enough. The As'mir bodyguards were the best you could find, even on the Other Side, but they were no more than a hundred, as only the Akeneires'elin and their most direct family were entitled to protection.

A mere hundred against thousands. Ekbeth cringed, but it was his only hope. They were professionals. If Kalem managed to get hold of all of them on such short notice, a hundred of them should at least make the mad crowd pause.

He kneeled again next to the Aramalinyia. He took hold of her shoulders and shook her until she opened her eyes and focused on him. "Aramalinyia, we need you. The community needs you."

She barely whispered, beginning to close her eyes again, "What she's done…"

He shook her again. "We'll have time to discuss Kimiel tomorrow, Aramalinyia. Right now you need to save the McLeans."

She did not seem to understand. He had no time for this. "The community has turned against the McLeans, Aramalinyia. I've sent the bodyguards to protect them, but it won't be enough. You need to address the crowd. Tell them this is not what Ara wants."

She was looking at him with such a vacant expression; he wondered whether she had heard him. This was too much for her, he realized. The Aramalinyia was too old for this. But then, finally, she nodded. "Help me to my feet, Akeneires'el. You're right. I have to stop this madness."

She felt fragile under his arms, but, as they left the temple, she seemed to regain her strength.

Ekbeth had another short mental discussion with Kalem, announcing their arrival, as he and the Aramalinyia climbed the steps to the McLeans' house. They did not come very far before encountering the first angry As'mirin. The ceremonial area near the Lake was the only place large enough to contain the city's entire population, and the narrow streets of Kse'Annilis, which confined the mob's movement, were now a small blessing. Each step to the McLean household could fit only four people—even in a swarming crowd.

He shouted, "Make way for the Aramalinyia!"

Angry faces turned towards them, but the expressions quickly changed when they saw who was with him. The

As'mirin pushed themselves against the walls to let Ekbeth and the Goddess's voice pass.

She looked into each face. They started bowing. She sighed. "Go home, children. This is not what the Goddess wants."

Ekbeth and the Aramalinyia continued moving toward the McLeans' house. The Aramalinyia kept repeating her message. "This is not what the Goddess wants."

The As'mirin responded with agitated muttering, but after a moment of indecision started walking away.

Ekbeth and the old woman finally reached the McLeans' house. Broad giants of men clad in dark metal, who watched the people in front of them with stone faces, blocked the entrance. A bodyguard in armor was an impressive sight. A group of them made your blood freeze with fright.

But Ekbeth noticed only the shattered wooden doors behind the giants. Too late. Kalem had gotten there too late.

Walking alone now, the Aramalinyia approached the entrance and gave her message once more. "Go home."

The people closest to the house were not so easily subdued, though. Ekbeth noticed that some of them were wounded. The bodyguards had apparently not only been keeping a silent guard. He also noticed that most of the wounded were Na Duibhnes. Something else he would have to deal with. Later.

The Aramalinyia's voice rose strongly. "Go home. Justice will be brought; the High Council will meet tomorrow morning. But the McLeans have to be left unharmed. Ara does not wish their death."

Kalem came out of the McLean house at that moment. He, too, was wearing his armor, but his scowling face was very likely what made his nearest opponents take a step back. He growled, "You've heard the Aramalinyia. Enough blood has been spilled here tonight. Go home."

At last, the crowd scattered, if slowly. Kalem bowed deeply and let the Aramalinyia enter the house. Ekbeth walked to him and whispered, "How bad is it?"

Kalem's expression became grim. "Duncan McLean is dead, Akeneires'el. They mostly focused their attack on him. The rest have fared a bit better."

Later, Ekbeth discovered "a bit better" still meant that the rest of the McLeans needed to be brought to the house of the Na Saoilcheachs, the doctors of the community, and receive treatment for their wounds. But entering the house told him enough. It had been in a really bad state when he had come here, only three hours ago, to get Kimiel. But now… it was utterly destroyed.

The Aramalinyia reappeared after a long time. She really looked her age this time, realized Ekbeth.

"Ekbeth. Get these men to protect this place and its inhabitants. I need to think. I'll see you at the Council tomorrow morning."

There was no celebration that night. Ekbeth barely slept. How could a single woman create such havoc? One moment, he had been moved by her voice as she was repeating that song with her family…in the next, total chaos. Matheson had warned him. Still he had not expected this—"bloody" consequences, indeed.

The woman was mad. No doubt about it.

27

S HONA WOKE UP with a start. There was a small monkey sitting on her stomach, very busy with his lice. Where was she?

She tried to get up and, before she knew it, she found herself with her head on the wooden floor and one of her feet still in the hammock in which she had apparently been sleeping. The hammock and the monkey helped her to realize where she was. Keremli's place!

She had fallen so many times off that hammock, that she had no doubt about her location. But what was she doing here? She concentrated. She was supposed to be in the Valley… Then everything came back to her. The oracle. The transfer. My! What had she done?

"Hungry, Shona? I've made some soup."

Keremli was behind her. Shona finally managed to extricate her foot from the hammock and got to her feet. "I hate those things!"

Her friend smiled calmly. "It was more difficult to put you in it than for you to get out of it. Have a seat."

Sitting was on the floor. This was what Shona really

liked about this place—the simplicity of the accommodation. With the exception of the hammock.

Keremli gave her a bowl filled with a thick broth. Shona had learned early on not to ask about the ingredients. Thankfully, a few years of living in Hong Kong had widened her taste for strange foods.

The two women observed each other in silence for a moment.

Keremli was an old woman—probably as old as the Aramalinyia, though her hair was still more gray than white. And they were both as dynamic as most women decades younger. But, while the Aramalinyia lived in relative luxury in that house by the Lake with all the servants and the community standing ready to answer her wishes, Keremli lived very simply, on her own, on the outskirts of a little village in the Malaysian jungle.

The soup was actually quite good. For once. Certainly, Shona could not have done better. Her cooking talents were almost nonexistent.

"You've cut your hair."

Shona smiled behind her bowl. "Someone cut my hair, Keremli. I first massacred it."

Damn. Shona had chewed on something jellylike. She was not going to investigate what it was. She swallowed it as fast as she could.

"How long have I been asleep?"

"Since you arrived. Two days."

Two days? This was the longest time ever that she'd fainted after a transfer.

"I saw those faded bruises on your body and the

bandages around your ribs, Shona. What have you done this time?"

That woman was too clever for her own good. Shona prepared herself for whatever was coming. "The Aramalinyia got your letter, Keremli."

That certainly got the old woman's full attention. Shona did not much care for the shrewd smile Keremli produced. She pointed at her accusingly. "That was a very nasty trick you played on me, Keremli. You knew I did not want to go to the Valley! I found someone to bring your letter. But then the Aramalinyia insisted on seeing me. All because you had to tell her my sad personal story. I was given no choice."

Keremli just ignored her angry tone and clapped her hands in joy. "So you've been in Kse'Annilis! And the Aramalinyia has accepted you in the community! I knew she would listen to me! I'm glad! Your grandfather's mistakes are finally repaired."

Shona scratched her forearm absently, dislodging a spider. "My grandfather, especially, was very furious when he learned he had to accept me back into his family. Still his. And Keremli, a bit of warning from your part would have been much appreciated. Being drugged to meet my supposed ancestors out of the blue was a surprise I could have lived without, as well as having them dissect my every single memory. It hurt, Keremli. Awfully."

Keremli's eyes went huge. "Wait a second. The Aramalinyia put you through the Oyyads'erel?"

Shona nodded. Keremli remained silent for at least five minutes, concentrating on her bowl, before whispering, "She bestowed you a great honor!"

Shona grunted. "An honor I could have done without,

Keremli. I did not want to go to Kse'Annilis, or become an Oyyad!"

It was obvious Keremli was not going to offer any excuses for her trickery. She was too pleased that her plan had worked so well.

"So, our ancestors have judged you good enough to be part of the community! That is a good surprise. They've seen beyond the façade. I would not have expected them to. What is your As'mir name?"

"Ah! I'm not going to tell you that. I find it quite awful. Now, answer this, was it also part of your plan that I be married to your descendant, Ekbeth? Because the Aramalinyia has decided I had to accept that honor as well!"

Keremli gawked. "No! Is she crazy?"

That reaction seemed sincere. Shona ate a few more spoonsful of the soup, before putting the empty bowl on the floor. "My reaction exactly, though probably not for the same reasons. I could not stay, Keremli. I'm sorry. This was the first place that came to my mind."

Her friend's eyes narrowed suspiciously. "What have you done exactly? Wait a second… The Oyyads'erel can only happen during the ceremonies of the Aras'arisidz. Oh my! You have not called yourself out of the Valley in the midst of the festivities, have you?"

"It was that or marrying Ekbeth, Keremli! And we both just agreed this was a bad idea!"

Keremli jumped to her feet and started pacing the living room. Shona had always thought nothing could trouble the serenity of this woman. Well, she had been wrong. Obviously.

"You've broken one of Ara's seven laws! This is a very

grave offense you've committed, Shona. They are going to track you down and bring you back. For punishment!"

Shona sighed. "Great! More punishment! The Oyyads'erel was already bad enough."

Keremli shook her head. "Take this seriously, please. I know you've been through a lot in your life, but... the Oyyads'erel is nothing compared to Ara's trial, believe me! The drug they pour into you induces terrible internal and external physical pains and powerful hallucinations. You suffer so much, it is said, that you welcome death as a blessing."

"Wait a second. How do you know what that drug does? If it kills, how would you know what the victims felt?"

Keremli sighed. "It is in our chronicles. Some survived the trial. Very, very few, though. And none had committed a crime as big as yours. Don't start to hope. You won't survive it."

Shona closed her eyes. That bad! She had known the Valley was closed, of course. But then... "I could not bear it anymore, Keremli. You have no idea how much pressure they were putting on me to accept Ekbeth's proposal."

Keremli chuckled, unexpectedly. "Oh, that I can imagine. I'm actually surprised they asked for your agreement. They certainly never asked mine when my husband was chosen for me."

Shona nodded. "With the consequence that you left the Valley after two years of marriage, preferring banishment to continue living with the man! See! The timing might have been wrong, but I'm better off not accepting this."

"Your timing is not wrong, Shona. It's terrible."

"Yes, I got that part already. It's a bit late to go back there now, anyway, even if I could do that. So what do you think is going to happen next?"

Keremli sat back on the floor and thought. "They'll have to wait the end of the Aras'arisidz to start looking for you. How long does that leave us?"

Shona made a rapid calculation. She had lost track of the time while in the Valley. Which was not surprising, with all that drugging and sleeping. "Six, maybe seven days."

"Mmh. That should be enough. There is a drug, it prevents you from using your As'mirin abilities, but also prevents the Caller from bringing you back to the Valley. It's not difficult to prepare, just a bit lengthy."

Shona nodded. "I know about that drug. Ekbeth made me drink it to prevent me escaping from…" She stopped in mid-sentence, realizing she'd said too much. Damn!

Keremli was observing her with squinted eyes again. "Escaping from where, Shona? Tell me everything! I can't help you if you hide important details from me."

She was right, of course. Still Shona knew the old woman was not going to be pleased by what she was going to tell her.

And she was correct in that.

Keremli took her time to react. And she was very good at hiding her emotions. "I see. I never thought you would make such a mess of my assignment, Shona. Your friends warned me it was too soon. But you sounded so eager to help me! And look what you've done! I'll never be able to return to the Valley now! Even if the Aramalinyia pardons me for having sent you to the Valley and created all this disturbance, Ekbeth will never be willing to lift the banishment when he discovers I'm behind this!"

"Well, you know me. You could have expected this to happen."

"Don't play the innocent on me, please."

At that, Shona only shrugged. "I don't think you'll be blamed for my breaking of Ara's rules, Keremli. The Aramalinyia won't mention you, I'm sure. And Ekbeth is fair, if anything. And I have some good news. We discussed you with the Aramalinyia. She told me she'll make sure Ekbeth accepts you back if you bring back the Kadj'dur."

"And how am I going to recover the ring now, do tell? Because you certainly complicated things for me. Lyrian is going to be even more on his guard than he already was."

Shona thought quickly and had to admit the older woman was right. "Maybe it's time to stop hiding. Forget about getting the ring. Go to Ekbeth and explain to him how his precious cousin cheated you."

Keremli snorted.

Shona had always trouble with Keremli's derision. She exploded. "Damn it, Keremli! Yes, I messed up badly at that party. Seduced the wrong guy, stole from him. I paid for that. Kalem gave me a good trashing, as you've found out. But the rest was not a consequence of my acts! You got me to the Valley! And it was not a fairy tale being there! I was still hurting from Kalem's special treatment, but I was sent to have a chat with the ancestors. And then had no time to get over the experience that people wanted to marry me to a perfect stranger! I may be certified crazy, but that's still asking a lot of me!"

Unexpectedly, Keremli grabbed Shona's shoulders, hard. The old woman still had an amazing force in her hands. "Enough. We've been through this before, Shona. Everything you do has consequences. Everything. Think before acting! And yes, sometimes things happen to you because of others' decisions. Accept it."

Shona looked into the deep green eyes of the old woman for a moment. This was not the first time she was hearing this, and Keremli had not been the only one.

"I can't undo what has happened, Keremli. And I'm not giving up on your mission. I'll find a way to get the ring. Give me some time."

Keremli released her. "You don't have time, girl. You should only concentrate on fleeing the As'mirin's wrath. Forget about the ring."

Then she looked at her with a strange expression. "You didn't do it on purpose, did you, Shona? Annoy the whole As'mirin community enough that they want you dead?"

Shona shook her head. "Of course not. It was more of a spontaneous thing. The Aramalinyia tried to trick me with this oracle, you see."

Keremli's smile turned mischievous. "Ah. This explains that little jade pebble I found in your hand when you appeared here, unconscious. I suppose Ekbeth drew the twin of the stone?"

"How do you know?"

"Ah, just a guess. This was a good omen, you know. It seems unbelievable to me, but the stones have never lied."

"Don't you start! I got the message, okay! Eternal love and everything. That's why I escaped to here!"

Keremli looked at her with intensity. "Condemning yourself to a death worse than a bad wedding by doing so. I haven't spent so much time helping you to see you dead, Shona."

Shona shook her head. "I won't let them catch me. As you said, they will only start chasing me after the end of the Aras'arisidz. That gives us a few days. It may be enough. Enough time for you to prepare the drug, and enough time for me to find a way to get the ring."

Keremli thought for a moment about this, but finally admitted Shona might be right. "And there's one good thing! If you were drugged when you entered the Valley, the Caller has no mental memory of you in his head. He can't call you back forcefully. And that's very good. Because they'll have to look for you in a human way, shall we say. But then Ekbeth is a very powerful man, and this time he'll have the help of the whole community. You said they've found Jeffrey and Maire already. They'll get to your family as well. Then Ekbeth will probably be able to trace you through your financial transactions."

Shona was already thinking of possible actions. "I'm sure Jeffrey will think of a way to get Ekbeth off his and Maire's back. As for my family, Ekbeth will understand fast enough there's no point in menacing them, as they know even less about me than Jeffrey. Can they get to you?"

"Not if I don't contact them. I don't think anyone knows I'm still alive."

"Except Lyrian Farrill and the Aramalinyia."

Keremli pursed her lips. "Right. I forgot about that. I may have to prepare that drug then. To protect myself. Though the probability of them finding me here is minimal. And their caller is probably too young to have a mental memory of me."

Shona nodded. "So, I just need a good hiding place after I've taken care of Lyrian. Can I stay with you?"

"No. Look, don't take this badly, but I know you. One week here, and you'll start spreading trouble out of boredom."

That was true enough. But then where could she go? She only saw one possibility.

"I know where I'm going to hide. A place where I don't need any money, and even if someone tips off Ekbeth and the others, they won't be able to find me there."

Keremli looked at her with attention. "I see. Are you ready to go back to Bhutan, Shona? It's going to be painful."

"I know. But someone convinced me that I should go there, not so long ago. And I won't be alone there. I still have friends—at least I hope I still have some. I do need my passport, though. It is still at Maire's place."

Keremli smiled. "I can help you get back to London. Though if you can transfer yourself out of the Valley while the currents there are so low, you probably don't need my help."

"I'd rather spend twelve hours on a plane than two days in a coma from exhaustion. Okay for the transfer to London, but the rest I'll do the traditional way."

Shona was already planning her next move. "And I need to talk to Jeffrey anyway, warn him and get some cash for the travel. Now, the real question is, how long will I have to hide?"

Keremli sighed. "That's the real trouble, girl. All your life! They will never stop looking for you!"

28

IN THE MORNING, Ekbeth went to the Na Saoilcheachs' house, and visited the McLeans. Duncan's family apparently had suffered less traumatic injuries than their Laird, although the doctors still feared for one of the older women's life.

Then the convocation to the High Council arrived. With a heavy heart, Ekbeth walked down to the High Council house, located opposite the Aramalinyia's house, on the other side of the temple. That building was not built over the water, as hers, but it was otherwise quite similar in architecture to the Aramalinyia's.

Ekbeth could not say he was happy about what was about to happen. If there was one thing he hated, it was condemning someone to a certain death. But there was no alternative. Not after the commotion Kimiel's transfer had created. Not when even their Goddess was showing her anger so blatantly.

He entered the meeting room. Most of the Akeneires'elin were there already, as well as the Aramalinyia. She looked a bit better this morning, Ara be thanked. If the old woman had weakened under the events, Ekbeth could not even think of what would have happened within the community.

Damn Kimiel! Twice, thrice! What had their ancestors thought when they had decided to let her live?

"Am I late?" Sarah-Lysliana McLean had entered the room.

Losing her grandfather had hit her hard, visibly. If Ekbeth could judge by her red-rimmed eyes, she had been crying heavily. He also noticed the bruises on her face and her arm in a sling.

The Aramalinyia stood up. "No, you're not. Are you the new Akeneires'eli of the McLeans, Sarah-Lysliana?"

Sarah-Lysliana snorted, "In my macho family? No. My brother Andrew got the title. There was not even a vote. But someone broke Andrew's legs yesterday. My brother asked me to represent him as it was impractical for him to come here today. I hope this is acceptable."

The Aramalinyia nodded.

Nukri na Liom was the last to enter the room. The servants closed the doors, the Akeneires'elin took their seats.

The decision about what was going to happen to Kimiel Keh Niriel was a short one.

The Aramalinyia dictated it. Find her and bring her here. Ara's trial.

That was expected.

The Aramalinyia sighed and looked at the grave faces around the table. "Now, about what has happened to the McLeans. I must commend the fast reaction of the Akeneires'el of the Na Duibhnes. Without him the life toll would have been much heavier."

The praise drew attention to Ekbeth. And not all of the reactions were of gratitude.

Keryl na Ghorm rose to his feet. "This would have never

happened if he had his family under control. I heard it was a Na Duibhne who killed Duncan McLean."

Ekbeth did his best to remain calm. He had hoped this would not come to discussion during this meeting. But he had also known there was a good chance the Na Ghorm would not pass up such an occasion to humiliate him in front of the whole council.

He lowered his head briefly and then met the other man's stare. "True. Kalem na Seffet told me about this. Only, he can't point to a specific person. There are a few possibilities. He gave me a names list this morning. Names of those he had found in the McLeans' house yesterday. I have every intention to have them punished, but I thought to do this through my family council."

The Na Ghorm snorted. "Too easy. You are protecting them. They laughed at you behind your back, do you know that?"

Ekbeth did not move. "They won't laugh this time."

His tone caused even the old Na Deargh, who tended to spend most of the meetings scribbling on pieces of paper, to pause.

Ekbeth then shrugged and spoke again. "Of course, I can understand you'd rather see this Council decide on the murderer's punishment. But then, how do you propose that we find the culprit?"

The Na Ghorm growled, "Ara's trial."

Ekbeth's brows went up. "All of them? There were more than thirty members of my family in that house. Sure, none of them is innocent, but is that not a bit drastic?"

Ekbeth knew the Na Ghorm's plan. As Akeneires'el, he was responsible for his people. The honorable way would be to submit to the trial himself, in the name of his family. He shook his head. "Of course, if I find the culprit I'll hand him over."

Keryl na Ghorm hit the table with his fists. "Too easy! You should…"

Ekbeth interrupted him. "I know what you expect from me. But I won't do it. I won't stand Ara's trial for those fools. I'll punish them instead. What about yourself? Must I remind you that the Na Duibhnes were not the only people who were found under the McLeans' roof yesterday? Kalem also told me some of your family members were there as well. Not attacking McLeans, apparently. Rather stripping the walls of what was still worth anything."

Accusing the Na Ghorms' family of being filthy thieves sure brought their Akeneires'el to his feet again. But the Aramalinyia was faster than the old fool. "That is enough! Sit down, Keryl."

The Aramalinyia was actually frowning. Keryl na Ghorm obeyed her, but if looks could have killed, Ekbeth would have now been very dead indeed.

The Aramalinyia looked at Sarah-Lysliana. "You represent your family, Sarah-Lysliana. We are very sorry for what happened to all of you yesterday. I would understand if you wanted to have the High Council punish the culprits."

Sarah-Lysliana shook her head. And she looked pointedly at the Na Ghorm when she said, "Enough blood has been spilled. I trust each of you will take steps to ensure that this never happens again. But please, no more death. My cousin Kimiel may have broken Ara's rule, I'm certain she'd never want anyone to die because of her. Neither would my grandfather."

The Aramalinyia asked, "Do you speak for your family in this, Sarah-Lysliana?"

Sarah-Lysliana nodded. "And we will help Ekbeth na Duibhne to look for my cousin on the Other Side."

The Aramalinyia was visibly approving the decisions of the McLeans. "Good. Then I think we can declare this session closed. The Aras'arisidz is still going on. I'd suggest another evening of prayers tonight."

Everyone agreed with this.

The doors were reopened. Ekbeth had another difficult meeting waiting for him. At his own house.

"Ekbeth? Can we talk?"

He waited for Sarah-Lysliana to catch up with him. She looked relieved. "My, this has gone better than I had feared, except for that bickering between you and Keryl na Ghorm. Is it always like this between the two of you?"

"Sadly, yes. Do you want to come to my house, Sarah-Lysliana? It's halfway to your bed at the Na Saoilcheachs, if you're staying there."

She nodded.

They were not walking very fast. Apparently Andrew had not been the only one who had been hit in the legs.

There was a moment of awkward silence between them, then Ekbeth said, "I'm sorry Duncan died yesterday, Sarah-Lysliana."

"Please, call me Sally, Ekbeth. I don't blame you for what has happened. If not for you, the rest of the family and I would probably be dead right now. I can't even blame Kimiel for what she has done, you know."

He raised a brow. That certainly was unexpected.

She sighed. "As a woman, I do understand her reaction. I might have done exactly the same had I been in her position."

Ekbeth had no doubt about what she was referring to. He coughed. "I know you hate my family, Sally…"

That brought an unexpected smile to her lips. "You misunderstood me. There's nothing personal here, Ekbeth! Maybe it's because I did not get your As'mirin upbringing, I sometimes see things differently than most of you. Why did you all have to impose that wedding idea on Kimiel like this? A bit of courtship on your part would probably have helped, Ekbeth, instead of hammering into her that she had no choice. After all, you are good with women, if anything Lyrian told me is true. I'm sure it would not have taken that long to convince her to accept, instead of throwing the event on her like the Aramalinyia was trying to do!"

"I agree. But Ara required the wedding."

"So I heard. But you could have convinced the Aramalinyia to give you more time."

Ekbeth smiled. "I tried. Believe me, I tried. I was warned against pushing choices on Kimiel and I took that advice very seriously. But the Aramalinyia can be stubborn sometimes. She wanted us to be married urgently. She threatened to banish me if I refused to comply. Sadly, she was not prepared for Kimiel's reaction. No one was. Or its consequences. I meant what I said at the Council, Sally. I will have my people punished."

She bravely smiled at him. "As long as you promise not to kill any of them, I won't complain. Let's get back to Kimiel. I understood Nukri na Liom won't be able to call her back into the Valley."

Ekbeth nodded. Noticing how much difficulty she had with the stairs, he stopped for a moment. "Kalem brought her here. For some reason I can't tell you, we had to drug her before that. So Nukri has no memory of her."

Sarah-Lysliana looked at him attentively. "I hear bitterness in your voice, Ekbeth. What has she done to you? I mean, before she came here."

Ekbeth shrugged. "Nothing relevant to our current situation. Did you know something about your cousin of which I am ignorant, Sally?"

"Depends. What do you know?"

Ekbeth shook his head. "Not much, I'm afraid. Duncan called her a murderer. And a criminal. I happen to know she used her As'mir abilities to steal. And that she has at least two very loyal friends, even though they seem to found her exasperating most of the time."

They started climbing the stairs again.

Sarah-Lysliana sighed. "I asked my family about her this morning. No one really knows her either, except Aunt Fiona it would seem, but Aunt Fiona needs to rest, so I could not ask her. Kimiel has been out of our Clan for so long. Though they all have heard of her, it would seem. She's been long thought dead they told me. And she's rumored to be very rich. A cousin had heard there was a problem with drugs, but he could not be specific. Another cousin heard stories of violence. I think the best option is going to be to pay a visit to her family when I'm able to go to the Other Side. But I don't really expect them to welcome me with open arms."

That comment was strange, until Ekbeth remembered the old feud. "Surely, it's not that bad. Not everyone is as stubborn as Duncan McLean."

She slowly nodded, looked away. "You can say that, Ekbeth. I had not heard of that old feud either before you came to our house and Gramp explained it to you. It also looked ridiculous to me. I knew there was something else behind my grandfather's reaction. And Kimiel's. When she told me we were cousins, I was certain I was missing something. But I only heard the rest of the story this morning, and it's even more difficult to accept."

She sighed and looked back at him. "You know, Ekbeth, as a child I often dreamed of my real family. Because I knew very early on that I was adopted. And though I could never fault my adoptive parents for lack of care, I missed real love. I was pretty sure my real parents were the perfect couple, who had probably lost me and were grieving for me…that we would one day be reunited and everything would be perfect."

He kept silent. What was she expecting from him?

Nothing it would seem. She sighed again. "Reality came back hard to me this morning. Have you ever met my Uncle Malcolm, my father's older brother?"

Ekbeth had to think hard. "Maybe. I was still young when he died, I think."

"Yes, indeed. My own father was also still a child when it happened. There was a huge age difference between them. It was forbidden to say Malcolm's name in Duncan's presence. So I never heard of my uncle till this morning. Unbelievable!"

"Duncan must have suffered a lot with that loss."

Sarah-Lysliana shook her head. "It's not that simple, Ekbeth. It involves that old feud bit. According to my aunts, Malcolm was the romantic of the family. Like Romeo and Juliet, he fell in love with the wrong woman, a distant cousin. Yes, a descendant of that woman who brought such shame to our Clan so many centuries ago. They were in love, and they both thought time had healed the shame. It looked for a while as if they were right. They married and had children. But then Malcolm died suddenly of a heart attack. And then Gramp did something terrible. He did not even wait for the funeral. He denied Malcolm's family their inheritance and threw them out of the Island."

She paused. "I don't think Gramp was so proud of that decision. Otherwise he would have told you of it. But he was certainly stubborn to a fault. Never acknowledged his mistakes. Hence his overreaction when Kimiel arrived in the Valley and he was forced to admit her back in our family."

"Because she's one of Malcolm's descendant?"

"One of his daughters, to be precise."

"So you know her name on the Other Side?"

Sally nodded. "Shona McLeod. And yes, I've noticed the family name as well. Gramp has even denied them that. They've all taken their mother's name back."

Better and better. At least, Ekbeth now knew why Kimiel had been so bitter about the McLeans.

But Sarah-Lysliana was not done with her story.

"The girls have a brother as well, it would seem. A brother who's about your age, so could claim the Lairdship if he wanted, as well as the Akeneires'el title. According to a cousin, the man is a Presbyterian priest, so I don't think he will be interested in our pagan world, but you can imagine that Andrew was not happy to discover that fact either. But anyway, as I said, I'm going to visit Kimiel's family with my brother and make amends. We'll see what we can learn."

They had finally reached the entrance of the Na Duibhnes' house. Ekbeth decided to spare the woman the long stairway to his apartments. He asked a servant to bring chairs and refreshments.

Kalem surprised him by bringing the chairs himself. After some polite exchanges, Kalem joined their conversation.

"So. Any idea at how we are going to find her again?", Ekbeth asked. "Apart from asking her own family?"

Kalem spoke first. "We are going to put some pressure on her friends. Give them no choice but to deliver her to us."

Ekbeth nodded. They would have to talk to Maire Kincaid and Jeffrey Matheson again indeed.

"Or…" Kalem added, "Alyasini is soon going to work for Maire Kincaid. She could spy on them."

That provoked Ekbeth's laugh. "Lyas is probably the worst spy you can think of, Kalem. Besides, the woman might choose not to hire Lyas after our visit."

"Then maybe you should ask the Aramalinyia who had written that letter, Akeneires'el."

Kalem, of course, made a very good point. He himself had thought of it. That mysterious person who had given the so-called mission to Kimiel. They still had no clue about her identity, and this was something he'd really like to know. The only thing Ekbeth knew for sure was that this person was not so young anymore. There had been the old-fashioned writing style on the envelope. And that person had apparently taught As'mir to Kimiel, judging by some quaint expressions Kimiel occasionally used.

And that person was living outside the Valley, he suddenly realized. Probably banned. Otherwise, why would he or she need an intermediary to bring a letter?

Old and banned? How many candidates could there be to this?

"I'll talk to the Aramalinyia, Kalem."

Sally McLean did not seem ready to move. "So, this is our

plan of action. I'll visit her family. You'll concentrate on the Aramalinyia, her friends, and whatever connections she might have. We'll meet when we have more information."

Ekbeth had a sudden thought. "We'll have to involve Lyrian in this, Sally. I can't do this on my own, even with Kalem's help."

She received this idea more serenely than he had feared. "I'm not afraid of Lyrian, Ekbeth. We do see each other from time to time—if only so that he can see his son. As long as you won't let him start on about how sorry he is, we can stay in the same room."

Even Kalem smiled at that. Then his bodyguard reminded Ekbeth that he had another meeting to attend.

"Oh yes, the family Council. Please take your time, Sally. I see you're suffering. I can even arrange a bed for you in the house if you want."

She laughed. "No need. I'll manage to hop back to my bed at the Na Saoilcheachs' house. Don't forget you promised not to kill anyone, Ekbeth."

He bowed to her, and then left.

This was going to be a very grim meeting. He was not expecting a lot of contrition. That was not the As'mir way. But he had every intention to teach them a lesson. He was going to give them a choice. He was just curious to see which option they would choose.

With Kalem trailing him, he resolutely entered the Na Duibhnes' Council room.

29

"BE READY. HE'S coming."

Shona jumped to her feet. It had been a boring wait the past three hours. Searching through Lydian Farrill's four-room apartment had not taken more than an hour, and, apart from condoms in one of the kitchen drawers, she had not found anything unusual or even remotely interesting.

Certainly not the Kadj'dur.

The ring had to be somewhere on this side. Ekbeth had confirmed his cousin still had it, and Farrill no longer had access to the Valley. She just had to find where it was. And as the seduction manoeuver was not going to work anymore, it was time for less subtlety.

She heard the key going into the lock of the entrance door and took a nonchalant pose on the sofa. Lyrian Farrill did not notice her immediately. Obviously tired from a long day at work, she thought.

She purred, "You kept me waiting, Lyrian."

Surprised, he dropped his coat, and turned towards her, recognizing her immediately. "You! How did you get in?"

She smiled. "Guess."

He checked his door, and then growled, "You walked through the door?"

She nodded. "My, you know of me, indeed! But I don't think we've been formally introduced."

His smile was not as friendly as hers. A bit frightening, actually. Not that it daunted her.

"I helped when Kalem and Ekbeth were looking for you," Lyrian said. "And I was at the party, as well. You may have cut your hair and be decently covered this time, but I still know who you are." Then he frowned. "And you should not be there. The Aras'arisidz has not yet ended."

"No it has not, but I still decided I really had had enough of your cousin and all the others, so I left."

"This is not possible…" He apparently realized what had happened because he stopped in mid-sentence and looked at her with astonishment.

Shona nodded. "Indeed. And no need to tell me I broke Ara's rule and this is going to cost me my head. I know that part already."

"Why are you here?" he asked,

Shona stretched her legs. "Good question. Someone asked me to recover something from you. I'm running out of time, so I thought it better to ask you instead of losing time dreaming up complicated plans. Where is the Kadj'dur?"

It did not take him long to make the connection. "Keremli! The old crone sent you!"

Shona nodded. "Indeed. And I'd show a bit more respect to my ancestor, if I were you. Especially after the way you cheated her. She's quite angry with you, you know. But all you have to do is give me the ring back, and I'll leave."

"It's not here."

"I've already discovered that, thank you very much. So, again, where is it?"

Farrill did not answer. Instead, he jumped on her and tried to hit her. She effortlessly blocked his attempt. He was no trained warrior and his approach had been pretty obvious. Unluckily for him, she had spent quite some time over the past few months training with Toshio's men. She had not fully recovered from her experience in the Valley, but it was still child's play for her to evade his fists. She simply had to raise her knee to his most vulnerable place to send him reeling to the floor.

When, despite his pain, he made a second attempt to punch her, he found himself facing the end of a gun.

This was actually fun, she thought. "Lyrian, Lyrian. I told you I had no time to lose. So, tell me."

His face closed up. Mmh. Maybe not that fun.

She picked up her com. "Our target is not cooperative. Time for plan B, guys."

In a moment, her team was inside. They bound Farrill, gagged him, and placed him in an antique leather travel trunk they had brought, securing the lid by fastening its tarnished brass lock and buckling the old leather straps. Shona had found the trunk in the Castle attic some time ago and had always wanted to use it in a kidnapping. This was the perfect occasion.

A few minutes later, Shona closed the door behind her and followed the three men carrying the trunk downstairs.

No one stopped them.

*

They left Farrill in the trunk for another hour after their arrival at the safe place. Then Shona opened the lid herself.

He was not looking so sure of himself after all the time in that cramped space in such an uncomfortable position. She removed the gag, none too gently. "Changed your mind?"

He kept his mouth closed.

She sighed. She had hoped they would not have to go this far. She took one step back and said to her men, "Take him out."

The men pulled Farrill out of the box, and forced him to stand between them. He was squinting. His eyes were probably hurting from the bright neon lights after the hours spent in the dark. And she noticed how shaky his legs were. Cramps.

My, he really was no match for them—and, apparently, not capable of doing a vanishing act on them, as she would have done in his place.

She faced him. "No need to tell you there's no point in screaming for help. Even if you managed to escape us—which won't happen, believe me—the nearest village is a two-hour walk from here. We'll find you before you get there."

At that, at least, he reacted. "Dead I'm of no use to you."

She laughed sadistically and looked straight into his eyes. "I'm pretty sure you're not the only one who knows where the jade ring is, Lyrian. You're just the most obvious choice. So, why don't you stop playing the hero, and tell me what I want to know. I promise I'll give it back to its previous owner."

He shook his head. She gave a tiny nod.

She let the men hit Farrill for ten minutes before ordering them to stop. Then she crouched next to him and gently lifted his head. "Tell me, Lyrian."

He spat blood. One of his eyes was half closed. Still he

shook his head. "I won't tell you. No matter how much pain your dogs inflict on me. You'd better kill me now."

She caressed his chin tenderly. "Pain, Lyrian? This was nothing. Just a beginning. I have far more experience than you with pain. You don't want me to show you what I know. You really don't. Tell me."

He spat again. "Ekbeth will find you and make you pay for this."

She let go of him, and stood again. "He can always try. He won't be the first. I'm not that easy to kill. And I retaliate. Some people have discovered that too late."

She turned to one of the men in her team. They had worked together before. "What do you think?"

He looked grimly at Lyrian's crouched figure, then shrugged. "Five hours. He'll faint. And we need to keep him sane."

She looked again at Farrill. Hesitated only briefly. This was going to be as unpleasant for her as for him. But Farrill had apparently made his decision.

"Do it."

*

It took them six hours.

Farrill was but a shadow of the man they had kidnapped when they finally left him alone. He was whimpering, lying in a protective, fetal position.

But she had her answer. At least, if he had not lied. There was only one way to know.

They left their victim alone and walked to the main room of the apartment that Jeffrey had found for their purpose. They had lied to Lyrian. It was not isolated at all. It was in the heart of Zurich—a new building that was almost completed.

"What do you want to do, Shona?"

"I'd say, let's try it."

The men smiled. Breaking in was something they enjoyed far more than questioning.

"No walking through the walls this time?"

She shook her head. "He gave us the security codes, and we have his keys. I know where his office is. This should not take more than twenty minutes."

One of the men looked back at the door they had just closed, having erased all traces of their presence. "What about him?"

"He's not going to die. We left the light on. That'll bring help faster. Let's go."

They changed clothes first. It had been a gory business. They exited the building by the service stairs.

With their rented car, Ekbeth's bank was just ten minutes away. On their way there she called the pilot and asked him to have the plane ready for departure in one hour.

On the key pad at the front door of the bank she entered the first code. The light turned green. So far, so good. Farrill had not lied. Pity that he had proven so stubborn.

The construction men were going to have a nasty surprise when they arrived at work in a few hours.

30

S ORTING OUT THE McLeans' business took him longer than expected. Ekbeth was only able to return to Zurich two days after the end of the Aras'arisidz. Attending the family councils of the past few days had definitely been an ordeal. But not only for him.

He smirked, remembering the faces of his uncles and cousins. They had certainly been surprised by his decisiveness during those meetings. That was not something they were used to. And he had cut short their protests. That they were used to. But in the past, he cut them off as a way of escaping the situation. This time, he just told them to shut up and gave them a piece of his mind before announcing his decision.

The whole family was doubtlessly going to discuss this new attitude of his in the coming days. They would just have to get used to it. Because he now had every intention of going back to the Valley once a week. And to not tolerate their childish attitude anymore.

Now, if Kalem just could look a little less annoyed by his decision…

As soon as he entered his Zurich villa, Ekbeth headed

for the room he used as an office. It was still early in the afternoon, and, no doubt, tons of emails were awaiting him. It was always like this when he was in the Valley, even though Orsina, his assistant, was sorting them before it hit his mailbox.

Kalem disappeared, probably, Ekbeth thought, to tell the staff they were back, in case they had not yet noticed. Ekbeth took his mobile phone and laptop from the safe—not the same one that Kimiel had put her hand into—and started them up. That was what he missed the most while in the Valley—they had no connection to the outside world, nothing even resembling the Net. He occasionally sneaked his computer inside Kse'Annilis, but it was not really of big use to him without the Internet connection.

Now, he only had to wait for the new messages to come in. In the meantime, he was going to find some coffee—something else he had sorely missed the last two weeks. There was coffee in the Valley, but nothing like the one he enjoyed at his home.

His phone rang just as he was about to leave the room. At the same instant Kalem reappeared with a look on his face that alarmed Ekbeth.

He picked up the phone.

"Sir. Finally! I'm glad you're back!"

His assistant. He frowned. The woman had worked for him for more than twenty years, and he had never heard panic in her voice, no matter what the crisis was. Until now… "Good afternoon, Orsina. How are you?"

"Good. Good. But your cousin, Mr. Farrill…"

Ekbeth walked back to his chair and sat slowly. "What happened to him?"

"Someone kidnapped him four days ago. He was found in a deserted building the next morning. His kidnappers tortured him."

This was even worse than anything Ekbeth could think of. No wonder old Orsina was so upset! "I'm coming to you, Orsina."

"Yes, sir. Of course…wait a second. No! You have to go to your cousin first! He's at the University Hospital. In intensive care. Your driver knows where."

"Have you informed the police?"

"The police informed us, sir. They don't have an explanation yet. They are very puzzled by the event. But really, sir…"

"Yes Orsina. I got the message. I'm on my way to the hospital."

Kalem was impatient to speak as well. "I just heard the news, Akeneires'el! My staff has been investigating. They've found nothing so far. No witness, nothing. But you know what I'm thinking…?"

Ekbeth nodded grimly. "Kimiel."

The driver was waiting for them in the garage. Probably warned by Kalem. Ekbeth prevented Kalem from getting into the car. "No."

"Akeneires'el. I have to come with you."

"There's no point. She's not in Zurich anymore. If Lyrian was found, she probably got whatever she wanted from him. No, I need you to go to London now. Go to Maire Kincaid. Get some answers from this Matheson. Find her."

Kalem was not entirely happy about the order, but he nodded and took a step back.

The car left the garage smoothly. Ekbeth closed his eyes.

There was a remote chance that Kimiel was not involved in this, of course. But Ekbeth tended to agree with Kalem.

His cousin! Why would she kidnap his cousin?

*

The hospital was huge and split into different buildings, so Ekbeth was happy that his driver was able to bring him to the right location and give him precise instructions that helped him find the room quite easily.

He stood at the door, taking in the scene. There was a small group of medical students in white blouses around the bed. And a familiar red-haired woman sitting in a corner of the room. All listening carefully to a lecture given by a professor, while Lyrian lay in the bed, connected to an impressive ensemble of tubes and machinery, moaning incomprehensible words.

Ah, so his cousin's case was worth a lecture, it would seem. Not very reassuring.

Ekbeth entered the room, drawing the attention of the students. Their professor frowned at him. "Who are you?"

Ekbeth approached the bed. The students moved aside. Sarah-Lysliana greeted him with a nod and said, "He is my husband's cousin and also his boss."

Husband? There were too many people present for Ekbeth to get into discussing that bit of information.

Lyrian opened his eyes at this moment and looked at him, but Ekbeth was not sure he was really seeing him. Then Ekbeth noticed how Lyrian's hands were shaking. "What's wrong with him?"

The professor shook his head. "The sedatives we are giving him are not working. He's very agitated."

Ekbeth pointed at the installation. "Is that why there is all this machinery? I was told my cousin has been tortured."

"Oh, there is some physical damage as well—mainly superficial, though. This was obviously the work of an expert. You can inflict a lot of pain without massive damages when you know how to. I'm not saying there is none at all. Most of the skin around his genitals shows severe burns, for example. But we've treated him, and have every confidence he'll fully recover physically. We are much more concerned about the psychological damage."

"Psychological?"

The professor nodded. "I was there when the police brought him in. His kidnappers had broken him, sir. Psychically. I'm used to traumatized victims. I worked in Rwanda after the genocide. This is worse. We could not touch him at first—he would not allow us. We had to literally hold him down to do the first injection of sedatives."

Ekbeth looked at his cousin with horror. Was Kimiel really behind this?

"Will he recover?"

The professor hesitated. "I don't know. We'll have to do some tests. Later. For now he needs to rest. I'd like the sedatives to be more effective, but we can't give him any higher dosage. We'll leave you alone with your cousin. Don't expect much coherence from him yet."

Ekbeth was finally alone with Lyrian and Sarah-Lysliana. He took a chair and sat next to the bed. He still had to get over the shock of this attack on his cousin. This was not supposed to happen. Normally, Lyrian was as well-protected as Ekbeth himself. Ekbeth had an unofficial agreement with Nukri na Liom, one that assured Lyrian would be transferred out of harm if threatened. Unofficial because Lyrian's banish-ment forbade this protection. Thankfully, Nukri had agreed because he understood how important Lyrian was for the community, banished or not.

However, Lyrian had not been protected during the Aras'arisidz. Nukri was out of reach. Ekbeth had to won-der whether Kimiel had been aware of that fact when she pounced on his cousin.

He turned to Sarah-Lysliana. "How long have you been here, Sally?"

"Since yesterday evening. Your secretary left a few mes-sages on my mobile when she could not reach you. I came as soon as I heard what had happened. And, before you ask, I said he was my husband to save a lot of administra-tive complications."

Ekbeth nodded and turned his attention back to his cousin. Lyrian had closed his eyes, but his face was anything but relaxed. Instead it looked grimly determined—maybe in an effort to recover some control of his body. His hands were still shaking very badly.

Ekbeth was also having trouble controlling his emo-tions. Whoever did this to his cousin would die, he decided. He took his cousin's hand. Lyrian tried to pull his hand away. But Ekbeth did not release the grip.

He talked to him, in As'mir. "You're safe, Lyrian. We are here. They won't hurt you anymore. You need to rest!"

Lyrian did not seem to hear him. He was muttering something. Ekbeth tried to understand what he was saying. Just some series of figures. Lyrian was manipulating figures all day long. It could mean anything.

Ekbeth kept talking and holding Lyrian's hand in his until he felt his cousin's body relax. Somehow.

Ekbeth wanted to help him. And there was something he could try. If there was one thing the As'mirin were still good at, it was toxicology. With all the poisoning incidents they regularly endured, there was no other choice but to keep their knowledge up to date. That meant sedatives was also an area of expertise. For Bers'el na Saoilcheach especially. The old man might know of a better solution than that which the hospital was giving Lyrian.

"I need to go to the Valley for a moment, Sally. Will you prevent anyone entering the room while I'm away?"

She nodded, not even asking what his intentions were. She was probably exhausted. This drama happening right after the death of her grandfather was just too much, Ekbeth realized. He tried to comfort her by squeezing her shoulder, then asked Nukri to transfer him back to the Valley he had left not even two hours ago.

Finding Bers'el was not difficult. The old and far too fat As'mir was always in his lab—if such a chaotic collection of test tubes, curiosities and books could be called that. And when he heard what had happened, he immediately accepted the request to help Ekbeth.

What Ekbeth had not expected was that the old As'mir had every intention to go back to the Other Side with Ekbeth.

"I just need my kit."

Ekbeth frowned. "Lyrian is banished from the Valley, Bers'el. I don't want problems because you helped a banished person."

At that the old man laughed. "You've probably heard of

the Hippocratic Oath, Ekbeth. I apply it as well, even though it's a human concept. Meaning I would still help my worst enemy if I had to. We'll just have to keep this to ourselves."

Thirty minutes after Ekbeth had left the hospital room, he returned with the other As'mir. Bers'el na Saoilcheach examined Lyrian, while asking questions neither Sarah-Lysliana nor Ekbeth could really answer.

"We were not there when they found him, Bers'el. And we are no doctors."

"Ah. Who's the professor treating his case?"

Sarah-Lysliana told him. A bright smile appeared on Bers'el's face. "You lucky woman! He's one of the best in his field! You hardly need me here, believe me."

Ekbeth was astonished. "You know this professor?"

"Of course, he was one of my brightest students! I've followed his career with interest."

It was the first time Ekbeth heard Bers'el had ever set a foot out of the Valley and his surprise must have shown because the old man laughed. "Aha! Got you there, didn't I? Now leave it to me! I'm going to find the professor and ask him the questions you could not answer."

Ekbeth had no time to hold the man back. Bers'el was already out of the room. Sarah-Lysliana giggled. "I wonder what the staff is going to think of him with his purple hair and his velvet robes?"

Ekbeth groaned. "My feeling exactly."

He went after the older As'mir. As it was, their concern was not needed. Because Bers'el Na Saoilcheach quickly found the professor, whose acknowledgement of that weird man as a friend apparently reassured the rest of the hospital staff.

"My, Dr. Silk," the professor gushed, "you don't seem any older than the last time I saw you! What are you doing here?"

Ekbeth managed to hide his amusement. Dr. Silk—he? Bers'el did not seem offended by the mispronunciation of his family name. He probably was used to it, Ekbeth supposed.

"I was visiting the City, intending to stay with my friend Ekbeth here, when I heard of what happened to his cousin Lyrian. And you know how good I am with sedatives. I thought I could help."

His former student sobered up and looked at Ekbeth. "Well, I can't discuss the treatment without the family's approval."

Bers'el patted the professor's back. "Since when do you respect protocol? Don't worry; they agree. Right, Ekbeth?"

Ekbeth nodded.

The two others discussed the specifics of Lyrian's case in technical jargon that Ekbeth could not follow. But he stayed nonetheless.

Bers'el rummaged through his heavy bag and extracted a small vial. "Stop injecting him with whatever you are giving him and replace it with a two percent solution of this. It should help. If not, we can increase the dose."

The professor looked suspiciously at the vial. "What's in there?"

Bers'el looked offended. He said, scolding, "Are you doubting me, young man? Don't forget who taught you your job. At least partially. Do as I say!"

Subdued, the professor took the vial and went looking for a nurse to prepare the new infusion. Ekbeth went back to Lyrian's room with Bers'el. Lyrian was still feverishly murmuring his figures.

Suddenly Ekbeth realized what those figures meant: the alarm and security codes of the bank! His cousin had an equal level of security clearance as his. Basically, he had access to every account and transaction. He also had the codes to enter the office building when it was closed for the night.

Ekbeth immediately called his secretary. "Orsina? Can you please ask if anyone entered the building the night my cousin was kidnapped? And it there were some logins in any computers? Call me back."

Ekbeth began pacing in the small room. Maybe Kimiel was not involved in this after all. He did not think she was interested in the bank accounts.

Orsina called him back ten minutes later. "Someone entered the building, but there was no login in the computers. The expert is certain of this."

He ordered all the codes to be changed, and hung up. So, whoever had tortured Lyrian to get the codes was not after virtual money. What else was there? They had no safe. Any valuable was on the Other Side, in the Aiarz'i branch. Ekbeth thought hard about what was there in the Zurich office that might interest thieves. Not much in fact. A few meeting rooms, the trading room, his and Lyrian's offices. It was an old building, with wood panel walls, and some cleverly crafted little niches, where he and Lyrian had placed a few personal possessions, among which…

Oh no! Damn, damn that woman!

Ekbeth called his assistants again. "Orsina? Would you please go to Lyrian's office? There is a Chinese ivory puzzle ball on his desk. You know, those little things with multiple layers of spheres." Orsina did as he asked. "You can see it?

Can you just align the holes on the spheres? Till you see the hollow core? Is there anything inside?"

He waited. Prayed.

After a few moments, Orsina said, "Yes."

So he had been wrong? But then his assistant added, "It's a small jade stone, Sir."

His heart missed a bit. "A stone?"

"Well, more the size of a pebble, really. And it's very smooth."

Ekbeth thanked her and hung up. He was probably the only one, along with Lyrian, who knew where the Kadj'dur had been hidden since Lyrian had divorced his wife.

Matheson had told Ekbeth about Kimiel's mission. And about how tenacious she could be. He had just forgotten to warn his cousin to hide the Kadj'dur in a better place than that little ivory ball.

Ekbeth closed his eyes, trying to contain his anger. The Kadj'dur. Kimiel had tortured his cousin to get hold of the Kadj'dur. Worse, she had replaced the ring with her oracle pebble. He did not need to see the pebble to know what it was.

How dare she provoke him in that way? He was going to find the woman and drag her back to the Valley by the hair. And pour Ara's water himself in her mouth!

31

*S*HE WAS ALL *pain. Breathing was painful, moving was painful. Her tormentor kicked her in the face, viciously. Even screaming was painful.*

"Where is the White Lady?"

She could not answer. Her mouth was full of blood.

Another slap. "Answer!"

She forced her eyes open. She forced herself to look into the face of her tormentor.

Kellerman.

Shona jerked awake, screaming, and heard the soft steps running toward her.

"Are you all right, Madam?"

The stewardess looked concerned, and the other passengers were staring.

Of course not. She was not all right at all! Her heart was pounding so hard that she could hear it.

She forced herself to smile and look at the flight attendant. "Sorry. Bit of a nightmare."

The stewardess relaxed. "Would you like a glass of water?"

Shona nodded.

Damn. She had tried not to fall asleep but had failed miserably. She forced herself to breathe deeply, calmly. It had been a nightmare. Only a nightmare. One she had had every single night since she had returned from Zurich.

Damn Lyrian Farrill. Why did he have to be so stubborn? Seeing him tortured brought back memories she'd rather have forgotten.

She looked at the screen display in front of her. Two hours until the plane landing.

Another reason for her bad dreams—she was not ready for what was waiting for her there. She would never be ready.

"Your water, Madam." She took the glass from the stewardess with thanks.

She should have used Toshio's jet. No one would have been there to witness her weakness. But she did not want to make it too easy for Ekbeth to find her. He was bound to find out Toshio had a private jet and would check the flight log. Of course, knowing she was in Kolkata was not going to be a big help to him, but the fewest clues she gave him, the better. So that meant flying on a commercial airline and frightening a stewardess and a few passengers with her screaming.

Ekbeth had probably found out about the Kadj'dur by now. She wished she could have seen his reaction. But then, remembering Farrill's whimpering body as she had last seen it, it was perhaps better that she could not.

She allowed herself a tiny smile, remembering how she had felt after taking the Kadj'dur out of the ivory puzzle ball. She had had plenty of time to admire her latest acquisition during the flight back to London.

She considered herself quite an expert in jade objects, and this little thing was one of the most exquisite carved rings she had ever seen. She had seen enough of the As'mir decorative art by now to instantly associate the Kadj'dur with it. The pattern appeared to be traditional, intricate Celtic braiding, but inspecting it under a magnifying glass revealed that each little braid was carved with what looked like small flowers and birds. Considering that the ring was not even one inch in width, considerable skill was involved.

It had been difficult to leave it behind, but it was much more secure in the Castle safe. Keremli had certainly sounded satisfied when Shona had called her to tell the news, though the old woman's joy had tempered a bit when Shona had explained how she'd acquired it.

So, that mission was accomplished! It had cost her a lot, she reflected, but she had managed it. Just as she was going to manage whatever awaited her in a few hours.

*

The weather was as bad as she had expected. Sometimes being forewarned did not help. She hated being drenched. Her clothes clung to her body in an uncomfortable and flagrantly revealing way. And there was that permanent smell of mold in the air. Yuck. It was monsoon time in India.

The flight to Calcutta, or Kolkata as it was now called, had been the easiest part, even with the long stopover in Delhi. No one took a second look at her passport at British Customs. A good sign that Ekbeth was not yet home.

And Shona was now in India—with an entry stamp on her passport! The first step of her long trip to the tiny valley in the northeast of Bhutan.

It was not the first time she was travelling to the remote

kingdom from there. There was a bus going daily from Kolkata to Phuentsholing, the only Bhutanese border town that foreigners could use to enter the country by road. She had missed today's departure, but she knew of places to spend the night near to the bus station—important because the bus left around seven in the morning.

The hotel at which she registered had not improved over the years. The weather was rapidly doing its damage in this place. But the staff was just as nice as they had been in the past. Thankfully, though, they did not recognize her name or face. She was not sure she would have been able to answer questions about how the rest of her family was faring.

Other than going out to dinner and to get some provisions for the coming journey, she spent the remainder of that day inside her room. She had always found the city a bit overwhelming—a bit too much for her senses with its vibrant colors, the raucous noises and the constant crowd pressing against her. With Yeshe, she had laughed at her cowardice. Now she just wanted to avoid it.

The bus trip to Phuentsholing was not much better, as far as the mass of people was concerned. The bus was mostly filled with Indian people, hoping for a temporary job in the Dragon country, along with their possessions. There was no room for legs to stretch, even for a moment, and the stops were too short. Also, she had forgotten how nerve-wracking the travel was on that crater-pocketed road. The trip took twenty-six hours—a record slowness due in part to the fact that the bus broke down along the way.

When she finally arrived in sight of the familiar Bhutan Gate, she was exhausted and suffering from an aching back, but she forgot about all of that, and allowed the multitude of emotions evoked by her return to Bhutan to take over.

Despite the eight brightly decorated pillars that supported it, the decorative carving below the intermediate red roof, and the graceful windows that led up to the curves of the final roof, the gate itself was not particularly remarkable. She had seen much more impressive gates in other Far-East countries, especially in China.

But this gate was a symbol for her. Beyond that monumental gate, was her past. She dreaded going beyond it, but she had decided it was time and was ready to go forward.

The administration was not so forthcoming.

She arrived just in time to enter the Customs and Visa Application Office before it closed. The first officer she talked to, just closed her passport and handed it back to her with a piece of paper, explaining in perfect English that foreigners were not given a visa at this desk. She would have to book a tour and apply for a visa through any local travel agency, which should take ten days. Have a nice day.

She pushed her passport back across his desk with a smile, and explained in Dzongkha, the officer's language, that she had been married to a Bhutanese and so had a special status and was granted access to the country without a tourist visa. No, she had no paper to prove it, but the information could probably be found in the foreigners' register that he, no doubt, had in his computer.

This was met with much suspicion. But the officer called his superior, who politely invited her to share a cup of tea. After the greeting formalities, he asked, "Where is your husband?"

There was no point lying. "He's been dead for almost four years now."

"Ah. Why would you want to come back here, then?"

She had expected the question. Bhutan was not really hostile to foreigners, but they did not encourage marriage between Bhutanese and foreigners, with the result that, most of the time, foreigners returned to their country of origin after the Bhutanese spouse's death.

She lowered her eyes. "I want to make a Puja to his memory."

"Surely his family has done that."

She was also Yeshe's family, damn it! No point to say that, though. She had to remain patient. "His family is dead. They are all dead. I'm the only one alive."

That took the officer by surprise. Family in Bhutan tended to be on the extensive side. No one could really be an orphan. There would always be at least a neighbor who would take care of a child in need, and that child would become part of the neighbor's family.

"Are you sure?"

"Quite."

The officer thought for a moment. "This is most unexpected. I will have to check. Do you have your wedding certificate with you?"

She shook her head. "I should have explained. My husband and his family died in a huge fire, with everything they had. Including my marriage certificate."

Again, Shona was met with suspicion.

"Really? Where were you at the time?"

Taken away by monsters…

"I was visiting a friend in Lhuentse. My husband's family

farm is in a secluded place, a three-hour walk from the village. When I came back, it was too late."

The officer was visibly ill at ease with the situation. "Mmh. Lhuentse is very far. It is going to take a long time to check what you are saying. Especially now with the monsoon season. Why didn't you ask for a copy of this certificate at the time?"

"Circumstances. I was not myself, grieving. Then my mother got really ill at the same moment. I had to leave the country in a hurry."

"Still, it was four years ago. Why wait so long for a Puja?"

Shona kept lying. "My mother was very ill until recently. Her illness cost us a lot of money. I have only been able to afford a ticket to Kolkata since last month."

The man was not convinced. Damn. Maybe she should have booked that tour and applied for a visa. It would have cost her only ten days.

She made a last attempt. "The Khenpo of Lhuentse Dzong—he knows me. Maybe you could call him?"

"Uh-uh. Come back tomorrow."

There was nothing else to do other than wait. And knowing the Bhutanese, "tomorrow" probably meant that it would be a week before the senior civil servant would call the Dzong. She just would have to be patient—go to the office every day and politely remind them about her case. Patience was something she had learned from living in this country. It had been that or get crazy.

She found herself a cheap hotel in the neighborhood and borrowed a pile of books from the owner. There was not much else to do except go on the Internet. This was very tempting because Ekbeth was now probably back from the Valley, and she would love to hear the latest news from Jeffrey. But they had agreed contact was out of the question, so she was not going to send any message.

The first thing she did when she entered the small room was to take a shower.

Then she lay down on the narrow bed and gazed at the ceiling. In the next moment, she was sleeping deeply. And blessedly, this time, without nightmares.

32

EKBETH HAD NOT heard the details of what Kalem had done in London. He was still sorting out his emails when he received a phone call from Matheson.

"Tell your bodyguard to stop intimidating Maire Kincaid, Ekbeth. Before she decides to call her husband."

"Then give me Shona McLeod."

A sigh. "Can't do that, and you know it. Anyway, Shona's left the country. I have no clue where the girl is at the moment."

"That's a lie, Matheson. You can trace her on that mobile phone of yours."

"Not anymore. She explained to me that you and everyone in that secret place of yours were going to look for her. I could not take any risk, so I removed the tracking device from her."

Ekbeth cursed softly. He had thought they would manage to get hold of the mobile phone. But then, so had Matheson, of course.

"Has she also told you why we are looking for her, this time?"

"You mean, apart from the fact that she hurt your

cousin? Yes, she has. Though I already knew about it. You tried to impose a wedding on her. I did warn you. You should have listened to me."

Ekbeth growled, "You were there when Kalem told me the news. It was not my decision. Neither is it only my decision to track her and bring her back to the Valley for punishment. Though, after what she has done to Lyrian, I can only agree with the sentence. She deserves to die."

There was a small pause on the other side of the line, and then Matheson said, "I understand your feelings, Ekbeth. God knows she drives me crazy as well. Still, I disagree with you. Shona's suffered enough. She deserves happiness. And your cousin should not have been so stupid. I told you that she was a very determined woman when on a mission. Had he just given her the ring instead of playing the tough guy… Anyway, this call is about Maire Kincaid, not Shona. Maire's husband, and, yes, that's my boss, has a lot of influence and could make you very sorry for annoying his wife. Leave the woman alone."

Ekbeth met influential people every hour of the day. He was used to threats. He was not impressed, so he answered, resolutely, "We'll only do that after we've found Shona."

"Then, don't complain about consequences, Ekbeth. You think Shona is bad? Our boss is worse. You don't want him as an enemy."

With this, Matheson hang up.

*

Ekbeth had quite forgotten about the conversation and was enjoying a late lunch on his terrace when his mobile phone rang. Damn, probably his secretary checking on him. Or

Kalem. But it was neither of the two. It was the manager of his Extreme-Orient operations.

"Sir! We need you here urgently. The Chinese are going mad! They want to close their accounts! All of them! Within the hour! And we started getting calls from the Japanese."

What was this now? The Chinese, or more exactly the Triads, had been his best customers for the past decade. He was actually quite proud to have gained their trust.

Them closing their accounts meant a huge loss of cash for the bank—cash they did not currently have available. And if rumors of this got to the other customers… He did not want to think about it.

"I'm coming."

He only then noticed the message pending on the phone. He called his voicemail and listened. He was certain he had never heard the man's voice before. The message was short and to the point: leave Maire Kincaid alone if he wanted to avoid bankruptcy.

Matheson's warning about consequences had not been idle, after all. He had never expected this, though. Who had enough influence on the Triads that they would all decide to close their bank accounts at his order? No name came to his mind.

He looked at the number. A caller from England? He would solve that mystery later.

He needed to call Kalem. And to go to his office in Shanghai.

Ara! What a mess! First Kimiel. Then his cousin. And now, this crisis!

Talk of a nice welcome back from the Valley.

33

I T BECAME A sort of routine during the following weeks. Go to the immigration office in the morning, fighting her way through the very crowded building to one of the civil servants, then ask to see the manager, then wait inside a room which visibly could not handle the daily crowd that came for a visa or other paperwork. Sometimes she managed to see the man, who invariably offered her tea and asked her to come back tomorrow. Sometimes she saw no one.

She could not blame them. The place was busy. Somehow, the brand new computers did not seem to accelerate the process.

Waiting outside was not much better, but sometimes she had to leave the building because the crowd was too much for her nerves. Outside meant a view of badly parked trucks on each side of the road, and, in front of her, buildings that seemed ready to collapse. That was the Indian side of Phuentsholing.

The Bhutanese part was beyond the Gate. She could go there in the afternoon, at least, after the customs office closed. That much had been granted to her. But no further.

She spent most of her afternoons in the so-called park, eating snacks and reading books. Sometime chatting with Bhutanese people. They were invariably surprised to hear her speak Dzongkha. Some of them insisted on speaking English. But others were more than happy to let her practice her language skills. To avert any questions about her private life, she told them that she had been teaching English in a high school in Thimphu, the capital, for some years now. Though she got asked many questions anyway. Bhutanese were terribly curious, and very open about sexual relationships. She even got a few offers. Thankfully, she was used to that from the past and knew how to deter them with grace.

Evenings were spent in the Indian part—mostly in her hotel room.

After almost one month she was starting to grow impatient. She had read all the borrowed books, and the hotel room was getting too small for her liking. She was pretty sure that she had seen a cockroach a day or two ago on the wall, though the owner assured her it was impossible.

It came to the point that she had to resist her claustrophobia before entering the immigration office. She was having serious thoughts about breaking into the office at night and stamping her passport herself, and had started planning the break-in when the miracle happened.

There was a brand new car waiting in front of the immigration office that morning. Covered with dust, certainly, but still very new.

A civil servant was waiting for her when she entered the building and ushered to the small office of the Senior Civil Servant, who was attending to his guests. Important guests.

The Senior Civil Servant even bowed to her! That was unusual.

"Shona-la. These people have come to attest your claim is legitimate. If you have your passport with you, we'll arrange the stamps while you drink your tea. And you will go with them in their car."

She could not believe it! Finally!

She turned towards the guests. She did not recognize the man sitting on the left, but the red silk scarf around his body and his sword were indication enough that this was somebody important. Bhutanese used the scarf, called kabney in their language, to distinguish their rank. Yellow was for the king and the head abbot. Red was for someone with a high level in the administration.

But her attention was more on the second man. Because she knew him. And she suddenly regretted not having spent more time getting dressed this morning. She was not even wearing a kira, the national costume—just some old pair of jeans and a tee-shirt that had seen better days. Damn!

She bowed deeply before the Abbot of the Lhuentse Dzong, murmuring the long conventions of greeting. She felt the man place something soft around her neck—a white khata. With his hands on her shoulders, he prompted her to rise.

"I'm glad to see you again, Shona-la. We thought you dead."

She was about to answer him when she took a good look at the third man and recognized him. She could not help but stare... and stare...

This was just... impossible! The man had a nasty scar across his face and his hair had grayed considerably since she'd seen him last, but that smile! She would recognize it anywhere!

She extended her hand towards him, but did not dare touch him.

He took a step towards her. It was true! Someone else had survived the massacre!

She could not help it. She started crying. "Dorje-la. I thought you dead! I'm so very very glad to see you!"

It was too much. She did not care what the other men would think. She took another step forward and hugged her brother-in-law.

This was worth all the long weeks of waiting.

34

CALLING BACK KALEM from London and making an apologetic call to Maire Kincaid had been enough to stop his Chinese customers from wanting to close their accounts. But it had almost been too late, because, by then, all his other customers had heard of the Chinese customers' decision and wanted to do the same.

It had taken three weeks of heavy traveling and innumerable meetings with his customers, his colleagues on the trade floor, and the various federal banking authorities to quiet the worries and get the situation back to normal.

Ekbeth was exhausted. He could not remember when his last meal had been. He was not the only one. Everyone working for his bank was exhausted. And he had not gone to the Valley once in the whole time. Had not even thought about going there.

He ordered his chief accountant to give a generous bonus to everyone, and then headed for his home dominating the Zurich Lake. He did not enjoy the view that day. He ate whatever his cook had prepared for him, and collapsed on his bed shortly afterwards.

He slept twenty-four hours in a row. When he woke

up and went downstairs to get another meal, he found his cousin Lyrian in the kitchen. This, at least, was good news. Ekbeth had not had time to check on his cousin, but Sally's frequent reports had not been very promising. He had not expected to see Lyrian out of the hospital so soon.

Ekbeth walked to the coffee machine and poured himself a cup. "So they let you out at last?"

Lyrian smiled sadly. "This morning."

The two men drank in silence for a moment.

"How are you, Lyrian?"

Another long silence. Ekbeth observed Lyrian. This was not his cousin anymore. The old Lyrian would have paced the room while screaming his anger at what had happened to him.

Finally, Lyrian spoke. "I can't even explain how I feel, Ekbeth. I thought I could handle anything. That woman and her friends showed me how wrong I was. I can't remember half of what they did to me, you know. Only that it hurt, and I could not control the pain, or get my mouth to shut up. But you know what the worst part is?" Ekbeth shook his head. "When they left me. I was too far gone to realize I was alone, except that I was not hearing their voices anymore. You can't even imagine what I felt when the medical team finally arrived. I really thought they had left me to die and that no one was going to be worrying about my absence for the next two days, as it was a weekend—not even you, as you were unreachable."

Lyrian had started to cry, probably without realizing it. Ekbeth did not really know how to react to so much distress. Finally, he took his cousin in his arms and waited for the crisis to pass.

Wiping the tears away, Lyrian stammered, "And then… at the hospital… I realized… I'm not better than them, Ekbeth."

Ekbeth hushed him. "What they did to you was wrong, Lyrian. But we'll find Kimiel and she'll pay for everything. You're nothing like her."

His cousin shook his head. "No, I'm not. I'm worse! Oh, don't get me wrong: I hate the woman! I hope Ara will make her suffer a thousands times what she's done to me. But – and I hate to admit this- she had a reason for torturing me. Look at what I've done to my wife! I almost killed her! And I don't even have an excuse for it."

Ekbeth knew perfectly what Lyrian was referring to. The beating his cousin had given his then wife Sarah-Lysliana when she had announced to him that she wanted a divorce. It had been a very close call for her, indeed.

They had discussed this before. Lyrian had never been able to explain exactly why he had beaten her. The only explanation they could agree on was Lyrian's As'mir upbringing. Divorce was allowed outside Kse'Annilis, but the As'mirin would not even consider it. That was why Lyrian had taken the news so badly. Too much pride.

Ekbeth's personal theory was that his cousin had panicked. Lyrian loved his wife deeply. He probably could not even imagine living without her. And they had a son. But he had not been able to make Sarah-Lysliana change her mind. So he had over-reacted and let instincts take over.

The consequences were that Lyrian had not only lost his wife, but had also been banished from the Valley. They had discussed this many times. Lyrian had never shown any contrition. Until today.

Lyrian was shaking under Ekbeth's grip. "I was so full of myself, Ekbeth! It was only about me. I gave her everything. She could not leave me! The shame of it. And the emptiness I had inside of me. It was hurting so much inside me that I had to take it out on someone. I didn't even care about her reasons for leaving me. "

Ekbeth thought for a moment. He had not been directly involved in that story, so had never really asked himself why Sarah-Lysliana wanted to leave her husband, but suddenly he realized he knew the answer. It was probably when Sally had discovered her real family was the McLeans, and that she was living with one of their enemies.

She must have panicked as well. She'd been very young at the time, in her mid-twenties. Talking would probably have been better, but she must have been afraid of her husband's reaction. And Lyrian's reaction to her decision had been all wrong.

Ekbeth was not going to try to placate Lyrian with the probable truth, as he saw it. It was certainly not going to be helpful right now. Just let him blame himself a bit more.

"Have you ever asked her that, Lyrian? The reason? Afterwards?"

His cousin shook his head. "I'm such an ass!"

Ekbeth patted him. "Then, I would do that next time I see her, Cousin. And, though I still don't understand why she would see you, Sarah-Lysliana apparently still cares a bit for you. She was at the hospital, next to your bed, from the beginning."

Lyrian nodded. "So I was told. She was gone when I regained consciousness. I will ask her... In the meantime, do you mind if I stay here for a while? I just can't return to my apartment."

Ekbeth understood the decision perfectly and his house felt rather empty at the moment. "You're welcome to stay as long as you want."

Lyrian looked a bit better after hearing that. Ekbeth let go of him. They returned to their seats.

Lyrian sighed. "I'll never be able to forget, Ekbeth. Even when I'm not sleeping, I keep hearing this voice in my head. "Where is the Kadj'dur? Where is the Kadj'dur?" And that I told her. And all the security codes. But physically, I had no reason to stay in the hospital any longer and lying on a bed all day long without doing anything was not helping. So I'm going to resume work tomorrow."

Ekbeth wished he could refuse Lyrian's offer. His cousin was obviously still badly shaken. But Ekbeth needed to concentrate on other issues than his bank right now.

He joked, "Things are under control now. You'll have an easy job."

Lyrian made a face. "I know. I'm sorry I was not there to help you with this crisis, Ekbeth."

Ekbeth shrugged. "You were fighting your own crisis. No blame there."

Lyrian looked at him for a moment then asked, "At least, it'll give you more time to find that bitch and bring her to her fate. Any idea where she is?"

Ekbeth shook his head. "Nope. Kalem has been working on it more than I until now. But he reports regularly. He is using all his contacts on both sides to track her down, but so far we can't find anything on her."

Lyrian nodded. "And the Chinese connection?"

"Still trying to figure it out. I have a phone number, but I'd rather know first who I am up against before meeting the man. We know it's Maire Kincaid's husband, but Kalem can't find any further information there. Not for lack of trying. It's just a big administrative hush-hush. So we are trying through our Chinese customers, but you know how things go there. They are not talking. Wei, our local director, is trying to get information, but he has to step very carefully. I suppose we'll get some answers at some point in time. I just hope that it'll be soon."

"Ah! The Aramalinyia is getting impatient?"

Ekbeth frowned. "Well, as she's refusing to help with telling us who wrote the letter, or even consult the banishment archives, I certainly hope she'll avoid complaining."

Lyrian was surprised. "Why is she refusing?"

Ekbeth shrugged. "I suppose she's decided to protect the letter writer. Whoever that is. There's nothing I can do here. I hate to ask you this, Lyrian, but can you remember them telling you who had asked for the Kadj'dur?"

Lyrian quickly shook his head. Ekbeth had not expected any other response.

"If not the Aramalinyia," Ekbeth continued, "I still expect a High Council meeting when I go to the Valley. The other Akeneires'elin will want to know what I've been doing all this time."

"Just tell them the truth. Those lazy bastards have the easy part! None of them has moved a finger to help you save the bank, or try to find Kimiel so far. Am I right about that?"

Ekbeth had to smile. "Not completely. The McLeans have helped us quite a lot. They have been visiting Kimiel's family."

"Family?"

Ekbeth's smile turned bitter. "Yes. Quite decent people from what Andrew McLean has told me. I have not met them myself, but Kalem has. Even he says there's no point putting too much pressure there. Her folks have no idea where she is. Kimiel told me her family rejected her. We now realize how true that was. Haven't seen or heard of her in years, they told us. We put some listening devices at various places in their homes and hope she'll contact them."

Lyrian nodded. "And her friends? Matheson and Maire Kincaid?"

"Ah! You've seen what putting pressure on them has done. This has backfired badly on us!"

"But, surely, Kalem could put some mikes there as well? At the woman's place and at her work?"

"Nope. Well, to be more correct, Kalem managed to place a few of them. But they were discovered faster than anyone would have expected. Kalem is a bit sensitive on that particular point, by the way. Don't mention it."

Lyrian showed a hint of a smile for the first time since they started discussing. "Did Alyasini start her work with Maire Kincaid?"

"No. I argue with her about it, but she does not want to see Maire Kincaid anymore. I find it a pity. But I suppose she'll find another job eventually."

Lyrian thought for a moment. "So, in short, we have nothing. Yet."

Ekbeth nodded, looking into his empty cup, as if the answer was to be found at the bottom of it.

"And have you tried to trace her through the financial world?" Lyrian asked.

Ekbeth shook his head. "I did not have time yet. This required a lot of paperwork, and extensive research. So far, I have had other priorities."

"Ah. But I'm here to help now, Cousin."

"Yes. We may find something there. Though it's going to be complicated, as we have no clue where her money might be."

Lyrian's face was grim. "This means getting access to her family and her friends' bank accounts, hoping to find a transfer linked to her accounts."

"Exactly. You need a team of experts to do that. And, believe me, I've asked too much of my personnel right now."

Lyrian looked gravely at him. "Ekbeth! They would go through fire for you! And I want the woman punished! Let me discuss this with them."

Ekbeth nodded his consent. It would certainly be great if Lyrian could concentrate on that part of the job.

He sighed. "Kimiel. I found it such a strange name! What a redemption she's been inflicting, indeed! And in such a short time! More events in a few days than we've experienced in the past year."

Lyrian nodded. "You can say that! And, I hate to say, we are not in control here. What's going to happen next? A bit of forewarning would be nice!"

Ekbeth put down his coffee cup and rose. "We'll find her and Ara will punish her, that's what going to happen. What I am going to do now is go to the Valley. I've delayed it too long. Time to check on how my renegade family members are coping with their punishment."

Lyrian laughed this time. "Oh yes. Bers'el told me about it! Did you really make them restore the McLeans' house?

And under Najeb's supervision?" Ekbeth nodded. "Ara! They must hate you for that!"

"Kalem is not too happy with me either. He does not want me to encourage his son with this building hobby. But, I gave those fools a choice: helping restore the McLeans' house or being banished from the Valley. For once, they are being useful. I'm sure they will thank me at some point of time."

They both smiled, knowing that would never happen in a million years.

35

THE SILENCE AROUND her was frightening. There was not even a whisper of wind to hear. If she remained perfectly still and closed her eyes, as she was doing right now, it felt as if she was alone in the world.

She breathed in deeply. Once, twice. The air was humid, and cold. She fought the urge to cough. Smiled instead. And reopened her eyes.

Her smile dissolved. The moment of perfection was gone.

This place had once been her home. There were so many happy memories associated to this secluded valley, which was only accessible on foot, with the nearest road thirty minutes of gentle climbing away.

At the time, she had never really paid that much attention to the trees clinging to the surrounding mountains, or even the little stream running through the clearing. No. She had only seen the house Yeshe and she had been living in most of the year, with their two yaks—those damned beasts that always refused to obey her—and, later, Sonam. And little Cholkye, for a short time.

She only had to close her eyes to see the place as it had then been. It had been anything but silent! Even when there was no visitor, a rare exception, there had been no silence in this place. Yeshe had built a sort of water mill to help him with his jade sculpture work. The creaking of the wooden wheel on its axle had been a constant companion to their days.

And the nights… She fought the tears. The nights in Yeshe's arms had been magical.

All was gone now. There was almost no trace left of their house, except for a few stones still standing from the lower floor walls.

Burned to the ground.

She could remember that, as well. The flames in the night, vivid yellow in the surrounding dark, the suffocating smell, the unbearable pain. And the men who were holding her, looking at the scenery, indifferent. The bastards who had inflicted so much pain in so little time. Destroyed everything she held dear. For nothing. Because they had not managed to get what they had been ordered to steal.

She walked among the ruins of what had been her home. She hesitantly touched one of the stones on a crumbled wall. It fell to the ground.

"I wish Yeshe had given them the Lady, Dorje-la," she said softly.

Her brother-in-law shook his head. He had been silently following her till now, respecting her need for privacy. He looked as grim as she. "They would still have killed all of us afterwards, Shona-la."

Dorje was right, of course. They had had plenty of warnings that no one would survive the soldiers' visit. From the moment the attackers had entered the house, they had treated their hostages as if they were little better than animals ready to be butchered.

Yeshe had been the only one to know the whereabouts of the Lady, the little jade sculpture the attackers wanted. The piece was normally in their home, but fate had willed that Yeshe had lent it to someone or hidden it somewhere without anyone else's knowledge. It had not been the first time, but their attackers were not aware of that. They had been most unhappy to discover this fact.

Something else they had not counted on was that Yeshe's whole family would be present that night. Forty people in total, children and old people included. Four times the number of attackers. Only, the Bhutanese were no match for those men. They had no rifles and the attack had taken them by surprise, when everyone was asleep, and also, some of them, a little drunk.

The soldiers had beaten Yeshe. Shona had been forced to watch. Then they had beaten her. Then someone else, and another. Even the little ones. Even her newborn baby.

She closed her eyes. It was all so vivid in her mind. They had put a gun to the tiny head. She had begged Yeshe to tell them. He had simply shaken his head.

The echo of the shot still rang in her head. That and her screaming. The rest was a blur. There had been moments of lucidity, though. Yeshe had endured further torture. They had broken his fingers one by one. Still, he refused to talk. In the end, she had done the only thing she could do to release him from the pain.

Remembering, Shona touched another stone of the wall. It was if what had taken place here four years ago had just happened.

The soldiers had been furious when they discovered that Yeshe was dead.

Dorje had lost his wife and their three children in the ensuing massacre and the fire. As well as every other member of his direct family. Shona was still not entirely sure how he had survived the ordeal. Their aggressors had checked thoroughly that everyone was dead before setting fire to the house.

They had only taken her because they thought she knew the location of the little statue. Brought her out of Bhutan. Tortured her somewhere else. Then given her to other torturers when it became obvious she had no answers for them.

She did not want to think of this period—the few moments she could still remember, at least—because most of it was another long blur of pain.

"I should have died with them, Dorje-la."

He nodded, and put a hand on her shoulder. "But your karma has decided otherwise. Shona-la. Accept it."

She let herself breathe out, and brushed away the tears from her face.

"You are brave, Shona-la," Dorje said tenderly. "But it's okay to cry."

She turned towards him, shook her head, but was unable to speak. There was so much hurt in her right now.

Her brother-in-law took her in his arms. He was a bit smaller that she was, but his strong embrace was a comfort. She clung to him, and wept for a long time.

*

Slowed down by the monsoon season and the muddy roads the rains created, it had taken them a week to get from Phuentsholing to Lhuentse, even with the four-wheel drive of the Dasho's car. That had given Shona plenty of time to get used to the idea that someone else had survived the ordeal. She had had many questions for Dorje, most of which he had not been able to answer. He could not remember much of that night—only that he had wandered in the mountains for days afterwards, lost, until someone had found him and brought him back to civilization, more dead than alive, where good doctors took care of him.

The Dasho, the civil administrator who had brought the Abbott and Dorje, had also had some questions for her,—mainly where she had been during all this time. She had not lied about it—at least, those parts she still remembered.

When then finally reached Lhuentse, she asked the Khenpo to organize a puja for her dead husband and his family. The holy man refused the money she offered. The ceremony had lasted two days, but took one week of preparation, during which she stayed with Dorje at the home of some of his friends. The Dzong, the Buddhist temple and administrative center, which dominated the village of Lhuentse, was closed to women during the night.

Attending the prayers during the ceremony had lulled her into a sort of peace within herself. The blessing of the Khenpo had marked the end of the puja. Then she had headed to Khoma, where Dorje lived, partly by car, mostly on foot. The village was famous in all the country for its beautiful textiles, but it was still terribly remote. No wonder almost no tourists came so far, although Shona found that a pity. This would soon change, she thought, because a solid bridge was now being built that would allow cars to reach the city; right now, the only way in was on foot.

Dorje was a master weaver. Shona was staying with him

and his new family. He had remarried two years ago, and he had a lovely baby son. She was glad for him, but seeing that little baby had been difficult. Dorje had noticed it. His wife, as well, but it was difficult to protect her from that particular pain in such a small space. Shona put a brave face on it, accepting the baby's presence for the sake of her hosts.

She told herself that if she could suffer the daily fare of *ema datse*, a terribly spicy dish made primarily from peppers, which was the national fare of Bhutan, she could survive anything. Her stomach did not agree with that reasoning. She suffered from stomach cramps much of the day, and nothing seemed to help. She found herself vomiting her meals out more often than not. She continued to eat the peppers as if nothing was wrong.

Dorje and his wife were busy most of the day with their weaving. Shona gave it a try. Most people in the village learned to weave at a very early age, with the result that most of them were experts by the time they reached their twenties. Shona made a mess of it. She had never been good at any kind of domestic work. She could barely help with the cooking of meals, however simple the task seemed.

She also tried teaching English to the children. She was terrible at it. Seeing the children every day, their little faces so full of attention, caused her too much pain. She had not lasted a week.

It was much more fun practicing archery, the Bhutanese sport, with the local team. Normally a strictly male activity, they made an exception for her. As she did not know any of the men with whom she competed, this was an indication that Dorje had spoken well of her. She could not participate in competitions with the other villages, as the men did, but archery, nevertheless, filled her days.

Time was a relative concept in Bhutan. She had lost count of how many days she had been in Bhutan before Dorje asked her, gently, if she would like to visit her former home, the one she had shared with Yeshe. It would be a two-day journey, and he had time for that right now. She dreaded the confrontation that was waiting for her there, but knew she would have to go to the place eventually. So she agreed.

*

She was glad that Dorje had been able to go with her. If not for him, she would probably never have found the courage to confront the pain of returning to her old home.

They were given a lift in a truck on the way back, and were now walking the last few miles back to the village. Their path crossed that of a few other villagers and some visitors, all carrying big balls of wrapped cloths on their backs. Greetings were exchanged, and introductions made, which made the journey to their destination, Dorje's house, twice as long.

"It's busy today, Dorje-la," Shona said.

"Yes. We had a lot of orders recently, with the new promotions in Thimphu and all. That Internet thing is increasing our profit. When it works, at least."

Shona smiled. Bhutan was really a world apart. So backwards in some aspects, but fast integrating modern technologies, such as the Internet. When one kept in mind that Bhutanese television programs had only appeared little more than ten years ago, it was amazing how fast those people were integrating the changes.

She had to think of the As'mirin valley at that moment

and smirked. Ah! No television there for sure! She wondered briefly what Ekbeth was doing right now, but stopped the thought quickly. She was not interested in the man, or anything As'mir.

Bhutan was her home. Not that other secluded place.

When they entered Dorje's house at last, an old monk was expecting them. According to Dorje's wife, Pema, the man had been waiting for Shona since the day before. Shona was surprised to recognize the lama. She had seen him many times before the fire, when Yeshe and she were stopping by the Lhuentse Dzong on their trips. He had been Yeshe's first art teacher.

"I missed you at the Lhuentse Dzong, Tsering Rinpoche."

The old man smiled his toothless smile. He was not that old, but dentists were only now beginning their prevention campaigns here.

"I am staying in the Singye Dzong nowadays. I am glad to see you, Shona-la. The news of your return has reached us and I've come to see you."

Shona was a bit ashamed. The Singye Dzong was a long trek for such a holy man.

Dorje offered some tea and some betel, another Bhutanese specialty of which Shona was not really a fan. Tsering Rinpoche drank the tea and ignored the betel. Then he took out a small package from beneath his monk robes.

"I have come to bring you back something Buddha put under my protection a long time ago, Shona-la."

Shona recognized the package immediately. She took it with trembling hands. "How...?" was all she could manage.

The old monk nodded. "I always wanted to paint the Lady on a thangka. Yeshe-la lent the sculpture to me at my request. Unfortunately, he died before I could finish the painting. And I did not know what to do with it. Until I heard you were back."

Shona unwrapped the parcel with unsteady hands. The oh-so-familiar little piece of jade emerged from among the folds of cloth. Exactly as she remembered it. This was Yeshe's masterpiece: The Lady. Expensive white jade, carved in the shape of a woman with elfin grace and abnormally long hair, yet wearing Bhutanese clothes. A curious combination of oriental and western art.

Yeshe's present to her for the birth of Sonam, their son.

The sculpture so many people had died for, the sculpture Yeshe had given his life for.

Shona understood his decision now. Yeshe knew they would not survive the soldiers' interrogation. He knew, too, that the brutes would also attack the Dzong and massacre the monks if they had the slightest idea the statue was there. It was another isolated place—easy to attack.

She caressed the jade. So smooth. So warm under her fingers.

Tsering Rinpoche sighed. "I never managed to capture that beauty on the thangka. Yeshe was truly gifted."

Shona nodded. Then she wrapped the cloth around the statue again.

Going back to her former home had been difficult. Seeing this statue so shortly afterwards was just too much. She felt more like screaming in pain than crying this time, though. No matter how much she had treasured that piece of jade, it was now so strongly linked to terrible memories that she had no idea what to do with it. Except, perhaps, to smash it to pieces. To break the curse.

And perhaps to send the pieces to Kellerman. Oh, how much she would have liked to smash the statue in his face.

However, the statue was all she had left of Yeshe's love. And she had promised Toshio no harm would come to Kellerman.

She bowed to the old monk. "Thank you for your visit, Rinpoche."

By the time the visitor left their house the following morning, Shona had decided one thing. She needed to tell the news to Jeffrey as soon as possible. Get his advice.

Hopefully, the Internet connection of the village would be stable today.

36

BECAUSE OF HIS work, Ekbeth had to travel a lot. He was constantly asking Nukri na Liom to transfer him from one spot to another, to save time. His employees wondered how he managed to be in four different spots around the world in the same day. Over the years, he had heard some interesting theories.

His customers were not aware of that fact, though, and, for that reason, he had acquired apartments all around the world in the main financial locations, close to his offices. Orsina took care that the places were ready for his visits and never asked questions. Bless the woman.

Right now he was in Shanghai, one of his favorite cities. Ekbeth's apartment had a fantastic view over the river Huangpu and the Bund, the most touristic part of the city, with its last century international landmarks.

Oh, the city was huge, polluted, a monstrosity of urban anarchy. Tall skyscrapers were being built everywhere. But it was worth walking beyond the modern main streets, where you could still see signs of its former splendor. And everyone seemed to be busy restoring the shabby parts to their former glory.

Ekbeth had to cross the river to visit his customers, and there was always a traffic jam along the way, but it was a slight inconvenience for what he received in return. He certainly missed Hong Kong, but could understand why the Triads had moved their headquarters to Shanghai. Even more than Beijing, it was here that things were happening in modern China.

He walked to his office, a short distance away from his apartment. His manager for the Extreme-Orient business was expecting him.

Recruiting for his bank was always a delicate task. He needed people who were not afraid to overlook some financial regulations—although not to the extent of trying to fill their pockets with the bank or its customers' money—and to be artful in the bending of the rules. The last thing Ekbeth wanted was a close inspection of his accounts by the local authorities. In the specific case of the Shanghai branch, his director needed also to be able to work with the Triads, be aware of the nebulous connections between the groups, yet not forget who was in charge—Ekbeth, not the Chinese mafia.

Currently, Ekbeth was very pleased with this particular manager. Wei fit the job perfectly.

They had not found Kimiel yet. Still had no clue where she could be. But Wei's patient probing among their customers had finally brought results. One of them was apparently ready to give some information. Finally—after weeks of waiting.

Ekbeth and Wei first spent a few hours discussing the current business of the bank, and then took the company car to go and meet this customer. For this encounter, Kalem joined them. His bodyguard looked like a shadow of his former self. Not finding Kimiel was not good for his health. Ekbeth would have preferred that his bodyguard rest, but he needed him right now.

Being able to read his customers' strong emotions had proven really helpful over time. Certainly, it had saved his life once or twice. But the Chinese customers' reactions were sometimes undecipherable to him. He was not so good at reading their signals. He had made a few mistakes in the past. Dangerous mistakes. One time, his customer had been perfectly calm in one second; in the next, Ekbeth was facing a gun, without knowing what had gone wrong. Not that this was really dangerous to him. Short of being taken totally by surprise, such as by an unsuspected bomb explosion, no one could really succeed in taking Ekbeth's life. Not when he could be transferred away in a split second.

With time, he had learned to avoid the worst mishaps. And Wei's presence for the translations was helping to smooth the discussions. Kalem's presence was an extra layer of protection, in case Ekbeth got distracted.

Kalem was never distracted when on duty.

Ekbeth looked out the car window at the scenery. Where the driver was taking them right now was one of Shanghai shabbiest areas. Siping Road. The Shanghai Taiwan City tower. Where, if you had the right connections, you could rent or buy anything from a copy of the latest Microsoft software, to a female or a male partner of any age. And weapons, of course.

Ekbeth has learned to live with his choice of customers He kept repeating to himself that criminals did not create the demand, they only provided for it. As long as people would ask for pandas' paws for medicinal purposes, the Triads would kill pandas. Same for the child prostitutes. Business was business.

Alyasini certainly did not share his cynical point of view. As she regularly reminded him.

Ekbeth was curious about Kimiel's opinion, but was not so sure he really wanted to hear it. She had proven she did not really care for others' life.

The car had reached their destination. Kalem went out first.

Today's contact was an old acquaintance. Not the very top of the Triad group he was affiliated with, but close enough. A well-educated man. Polite. As long as you brought good news—which was the case, this time. In the current climate of world financial crisis, Ekbeth was still lending money where most banks had stopped taking risks. And it brought a lot of earned interest.

Wei had told them to wait before discussing Kimiel and the Triads threats. So Ekbeth told his customer about the revenue generated on his latest investment. The man was so pleased by the good news that he invited them for dinner. Ekbeth played his role, enjoyed the excellent food and shared many rounds of Chinese beer with him before he dared show him the picture of Kimiel—taken by his party security cameras.

Handing him the photograph, Ekbeth asked, "Do you know this woman?"

His customer's reaction astonished him. From a heavily inebriated, laughing man, the Chinese man sat straight in his chair, sober. Ekbeth pushed his luck. "So you know her."

His customer comically squinted at him, clearly having trouble seeing him. Too much alcohol. "What is she to you?"

"A huge source of problems."

That brought a smile to the man's lips. "I can imagine. She's been a huge problem for us, as well, in the past."

Then he gave the picture back to Ekbeth. "Not anymore, though. To us, she is dead. Watanabe's girl is dead."

"Watanabe's girl?"

"Yes. We have a profitable partnership with Watanabe. He's a good friend. But the girl… not good."

The man then ordered more beers—a signal that Ekbeth would not get any more information.

Ekbeth was not walking very straight when he finally left the building, and he was starting to develop a headache. The alcohol percentage of the beer was low, but he had had more than was reasonable. Sometimes he had no choice. He had to follow his customer's drinking habits.

That was why Kalem was here.

But he still remembered the name. "Have you ever heard of this Watanabe, Wei?"

His manager was just as drunk as he was, but managed to nod without falling. "I think so. It would explain a lot, actually. Toshio Watanabe has been active in the country for a very long time. He keeps a low profile, but he has relations everywhere. Still, even nowadays."

They took the car to go back to Ekbeth's apartment. The driver would bring Wei home afterwards. "What do you mean, by 'nowadays'?"

"I have to check a few things, but I think I remember someone telling me Watanabe was in jail somewhere in Europe right now."

"What for?"

"Not sure. He does not belong to any Triad as far as I know, but is certainly linked to them. He's an art smuggler. There are big profits to be made there and, not so long ago, the legal system was not really paying attention to the disappearance of its own cultural heritage. That has changed recently. Maybe he's been sentenced for illegal importing of antiquities. I can ask around."

Ekbeth nodded, "Please do, Wei. Check that Toshio Watanabe, Kalem."

That was his last coherent order for the day. Far too many beers.

*

He still had a headache the following morning when he returned to Zurich, where it was still dark.

An aspirin and another shower took care of the head. He opened his laptop and asked the cook to bring breakfast to the study, where he would be able to enjoy the sunrise. It was still awfully early here, but he had had enough sleep for now.

He was not surprised when Kalem joined him. His bodyguard helped himself to some coffee, and waited silently while Ekbeth finished some complicated financial risk calculations.

Ekbeth noticed absently that Kalem was still wearing the same clothes as the night before. "Did you have any sleep Kalem?"

Kalem shrugged.

With a sigh, Ekbeth closed his files and pushed his laptop away. "So, I suppose you've learned some interesting things about Watanabe."

Kalem nodded. "Definitely our man. He has quite a file

at Interpol. Furthermore, he's one of your bank customers. So finding information about him was not that difficult."

"Ah. But nothing about his girl in all that mass of information?"

Hearing that, Kalem gave a thin smile. It was a bit frightening. "Depending which girl you're referring to. Maire Kincaid is his wife. That's filed everywhere. Irritating that I could not find the information earlier. But nothing about Kimiel."

Kalem growled, "Not a damn thing!"

Yes, his bodyguard was definitely getting really frustrated here, thought Ekbeth, but it was understandable. They had been looking for two months now! And the results so far were almost nonexistent.

"Interesting, nonetheless. What have you learned about Watanabe?"

"He's Japanese. In his late fifties. Comes from a long line of aristocrats and samurais. Some close relationship to the Imperial family, apparently. His father was a diplomat, and has spent most of his years with his family in China and other Eastern Asia countries. Young Toshio refused to follow in his father's footsteps. Studied art instead. Not to become an artist, but to sell art. Antiquities, especially. His first customers were his own people. In the eighties, the Japanese were spending all their hard-earned Yens on anything stamped 'ancient.' He's made a very nice profit out of it, if the history of his accounts proves anything. He got himself a reputation for finding the right item for you, no matter what you wanted."

Ekbeth nodded. "Hence the smuggling accusations."

"Exactly. Not everything he sells is on the market at

the time it is desired. But he will still get it for you, as long as you're ready to pay. And from the Interpol information, it's not only smuggling. He's stealing if necessary. Actually, I found some very interesting stories of impossible thefts linked to him."

"Ah. This is where Kimiel could be involved."

"Maybe. Only her name is never mentioned in any of the cases."

Ekbeth thought about this for a moment. "I think the best we can do is meet Watanabe."

Kalem nodded. "Maybe. Wei was right. The man is in jail right now. In the UK. But not for smuggling. For murder."

"Murder? That's a bit… unexpected. Art smuggling and assassins do not make a good combination."

Kalem laughed at him. Ekbeth let it pass. It was maybe the first time in months his bodyguard was genuinely amused, be it at his expense.

"You have such a romantic idea of thieves and smugglers, Akeneires'el! Those people are pirates of the worst sort. Haven't you learned anything from Kimiel's behavior? They don't care about anyone. They would kill their mother to get her pearl necklace if there was a market for it! Watanabe has very dirty hands; make no mistake about this. The only reason he's not been arrested before was because he was covering his traces and because he's very well connected."

"But at some point of time, his connections were not enough anymore?"

Kalem nodded. "UK is not the best place to commit murder if you want to avoid jail sentences. The justice is not as corrupt there as in other places. The evidence left no doubt he had done it."

"What has he done exactly?"

"Killed two men in broad daylight, and in public. Two members of very prominent Thai families, who were in London for a convention, if the file is correct. The families asked for Watanabe's extradition to Thailand, but that was rejected. That probably saved his life."

"Probably his connections' work, Kalem. So you know where he is?"

"Yes. I have to warn you. Watanabe has quite a high profile at Interpol. Even behind bars, he's still active, or so they think. You may not want to be associated with him."

Good point. Ekbeth thought carefully about this.

"Well. He is a customer. I sometimes meet my customers. The worst, I think, that could happen would be that Interpol asks me to freeze his account. I can live with that. Actually I can pretend Interpol asked me to freeze his account. That would teach him a lesson!"

Kalem finished his coffee.

"Please do me a favor, Kalem, and go to bed. This can wait a few hours. I have a full agenda for the rest of the day anyway."

At that point, a voice was heard through the wall.

"Good morning to you, Cousin! Do you really have to start your meetings at five in the morning?"

Lyrian!—who was sleeping in the room next to his study, Ekbeth suddenly remembered. The walls were quite thick, but Lyrian was still having trouble sleeping. Ekbeth knew this and felt sorry for his cousin, but more important than Lyrian's sleep was finding Kimiel and bringing her to justice.

Lyrian staggered in and Ekbeth offered a chair to his cousin. "Sorry, Lyrian. Want a cup of coffee?"

His cousin grunted something incomprehensible but accepted the offer. "I suppose this early discussion is about our favorite woman? Learned anything useful in Shanghai?"

"We're still investigating that. No direct connection, but we may have found her boss. Our contact called her 'Watanabe's girl.' Whatever that means."

Lyrian produced a crooked smile. "Being someone's girl most of the time means only one thing, Ekbeth."

Lyrian was right, of course. And it might have been the reason why Kimiel had been so dead set against marrying him. Not that it mattered anymore.

Ekbeth pondered, "His mistress? It can also means she's simply working for him. As a thief."

Kalem shook his head. "She must be more than that, Ekbeth. Remember Matheson told us he'd been hired to protect her? You can find skilled thieves anywhere. Okay, the fact that she's able to walk through walls makes her unique, but no one is irreplaceable. And I bet she's been as troublesome to Watanabe as to us. Or he would not have hired Matheson to check on her."

Ekbeth did not want to think of this—that she was another man's lover. Jealousy. The feeling was not sitting well with him. He should hate the woman. He would never forgive her for what she had done to his cousin, if nothing else.

But his mind often returned to their first meeting. To that hour together. How good it had felt. How right. Not something he was ever going to admit to anyone, though.

He slowly nodded. "Who knows? We are going to meet

Watanabe, Lyrian. Not that I expect a lot from the discussion, but we have to try."

Lyrian nodded. Ekbeth suddenly realized his cousin was being smug about something. But Lyrian was not forthcoming. He was taking his time, sipping his coffee.

Ekbeth sometimes wanted to slap the arrogant fool. "I'm not going to beg for info, Lyrian. What is it?"

Lyrian grinned. "Shame, I would have loved seeing you on your knees, but all right. While you were enjoying yourself in Shanghai, I was not inactive. I have a bit of news for you as well. Did you know our bank network specialist has some skills in hacking? He offered to try hacking into our friends' networks."

Alarms rang in Ekbeth's mind upon hearing that. Lyrian saw his panic because he raised his hands in a calming gesture. "Don't worry. I only allowed him to hack into Maire Kincaid's work network. And very carefully. We got masses of very boring stuff. Some people have the worst tastes, really. Green Ferraris for the weekend? Anyway, one email proved our probing worth it."

He tapped Ekbeth's laptop with a finger. "In fact, we forwarded it to you yesterday. Strange that you missed it."

Ekbeth was already reopening the computer. Found the message. "Ah. I still had to handle ten urgent things before getting to that one."

"I did put 'Urgent' on it!"

"As the others did. Next time put 'Kimiel.'"

The message was not making any sense. It was written in Chinese.

Lyrian smiled quietly when Ekbeth glared at him. "Maire

Kincaid got quite a lot of personal emails in Chinese. Family and stuff. But what got our interest was the email address."

Ekbeth looked at it. The country code was BT. He had no idea what country it was referring to.

"Bhutan, cousin. BT is the internet code of Bhutan. It's a small kingdom between Tibet and India."

"I know where Bhutan is, Lyrian. I'm not as ignorant of geography as you are. But why is it so interesting?"

"An email from Bhutan in Chinese? A bit of an unusual combination, don't you think? I got it translated. It refers to a white lady that has been found once more, whatever that means. But the signature was the most interesting. My translator told me it's not a real Chinese name, more like a phonetic translation of a Western name. Three guesses at what the name was? Yes! Shona!"

Ekbeth suddenly felt like kissing the fool. At last, some breakthrough!

Lyrian was now grinning widely. "Indeed! And we've traced the email address back to a location."

Kalem was already on his feet.

37

SHONA WAS IN trouble—she was starting to get bored. Not something she was ready to admit. She had never been bored while living in Bhutan before. Life had not been as hectic as she might have preferred, but there was always something going on. One learned to appreciate life at a slower pace. Any chore took a longer time to fulfill, be it because of the need to walk to a particular place to meet someone, or to many places to get the ingredients for a meal. And there was, for everyone, a lack of pressure to finish anything.

She could remember the hours she spent just listening to the pouring rain outside.

Not so long ago.

It was raining today as well. Only it was not the same. The rain was preventing her from going outside, practicing with her bow, or walking to the bridge to see how the construction was progressing.

The sound of the rain, no longer friendly and soothing, had become a hindrance.

She was currently helping Dorje with sorting the last delivery of silk threads by color and preparing them for the weaving. Still, boredom was creeping inside her. She had learned to recognize the signs over time.

"You are troubled, Shona-la."

She looked at Dorje. The man had always been able to decipher her moods. Even better than her husband, his brother.

She sighed. "I don't know what to do anymore, Dorje-la. With my life, I mean."

He observed her for a long time, before saying, "Something will come eventually. You have to be patient. I can only tell you that you have no future as a weaver! Those are two different yellows in your hand!"

She corrected her mistake immediately, laughing. "You are right about this. And I'm trying to be patient. I thought… I don't know what I was hoping for when I came here."

Dorje nodded. "You were hoping to get your old life back. The life you had with Yeshe. But, you know, my brother was not a typical Bhutanese. There was always unrest in his heart. He travelled outside of the country, learned a trade that is not Bhutanese, married a foreigner. Yes, he came back here with you, eventually. But he had no intention of settling here permanently. Remember all those little journeys you were continuously making? This was my brother. You loved him, Shona-la, so you accepted his ways because of that. Made them yours as well. You're not so different from him, as it is. But he's dead now. And our ways are not his. Our ways are not yours either."

Shona stopped what she was doing and looked at him. He was right, she realized.

Bhutan was still Bhutan. But it was not the Bhutan she had experienced with Yeshe.

She put a smile on her lips. "So much wisdom in you, Dorje! You will always amaze me. So tell me. What are my ways? What should I do?"

He shook his head. "Not for me to say."

He paused for a moment, sorted a few more colors, and then added, thoughtfully, "Maybe you should go to the Tsip."

That made her pause. "The astrologer? Why?"

"He can tell you about your future."

Shona's first reaction was to dismiss the advice. She had never believed in astrology, the Bhutanese version of it or any other. She trusted her instincts, and was a firm believer that you could choose your destiny. No matter how screwed her own had proven to be so far.

But then she suddenly remembered something Yeshe had once told her—that he wanted to enjoy every moment he had with her, because an astrologer had once predicted he would not enjoy her love for very long. She had dismissed the words as a joke at the time. Strange that she suddenly remembered them.

She shivered. Maybe it was time to be a bit more flexible about astrology and beliefs. She had nothing to lose, anyway.

"This might be a good idea, Dorje-la. But is the village astrologer a good one? I've heard many people complain about him?"

Dorje laughed. "I've known the man for a long time. And his horoscopes are frighteningly correct. That's the reason people complain about him. Who wants to hear you're going to have a miserable life, and marry the third daughter of a poor family?"

"Ah. Did he make your horoscope as well?"

The man sobered a bit. "Yes. And he did predict I would marry twice. Though he never said why. No one thinks about this. As you know, it is not uncommon for us to have many wives, or to divorce."

Shona was now decided. "I will visit him. When is the best time to go?"

"Not today. Today is a bad day for horoscopes. And we still have plenty of threads to prepare. But tomorrow will be a good day."

She laughed at that. She was not sure he was making this up to keep her working or because of the rain, but she could never get mad at such a gentle man.

*

The following day, she reminded him about the astrologer. Dorje put aside whatever he had intended to do and told her to follow him. The astrologer was travelling around the area, but Dorje knew just where to find him, as usual. That was something about the Bhutanese people that had always amazed her.

Today, they had to go to the Lhuentse Dzong to meet the man. Thankfully, they found a truck to bring them midway. Dorje covered himself with a white kabney, and took care that Shona's rachu—the feminine version of the kabney—was properly in place, before they entered the Dzong.

The astrologer was in a small room on the side, and they were not his only customers, so Shona and Dorje sat in the courtyard and waited for their turn. There, passing monks looked at her with curiosity, as if they had never seen a foreign face before. She always felt conspicuous among so many curious people. She was glad she was not alone.

She liked this place. The whitewashed walls, the

gaily-painted wooden galleries, and the constant murmur of the prayers coming out of the temple. It always had a lulling effect on her.

When her turn came, she entered the small, barely-lit room and sat across from the astrologer, an elderly man with a wise, creased face and wearing voluminous red robes.

She let Dorje explain her case. Not that she had been unable to do that herself, but she suddenly found herself a bit nervous in the presence of this elder. She gave him her birth date and the location, though the man probably had no idea where Scotland was. He took down some books from a shelf and started making complicated calculations, written in sand in a small sandbox placed in front of him on the floor.

The astrologer took his time. Then he looked at her and asked, "Are you pregnant?"

It was an innocent question, she told herself firmly. He had no idea how much it hurt her. "No."

Her answer clearly perplexed him. "Are you sure? You are not so old."

"I can't have children anymore, Tsip."

That brought further consultation of his books and another long calculation. Finally, he told her, "The interpretations in the books are clear. If you were pregnant, you would die giving birth. But you said it is not possible. We may interpret this passage differently. You need to die to be born again, to embrace your new life."

This surprised her for a moment. Die? Not so long ago she'd said to Dorje that she wished she had died with Yeshe and the others that fateful night. But hearing that she needed to die, her deeply ingrained survival instinct kicked in. As it had many times before.

The astrologer saw her reaction. "Death is not the end. You should not be afraid of it. As you know, we Buddhists believe in reincarnation." He tapped on his books. "Though in your specific case, I don't think the interpretation is about reincarnation."

Now, she was totally confused. "How can I die, and still live?"

The astrologer shook his head. "This puzzles me, as well. Maybe we speak of a symbolic death here?"

It just did not make sense to her. "And that new life? Will it be better than my current life?"

"Ah. I cannot say. It depends on when your death happens. I would need to calculate your horoscope again."

Of course.

The man smiled at her. "There is a another omen. You will get some unexpected good news very soon."

Even more perplexing. The finding of the White Lady had been very good news, of a sort. But this was already in the past now.

She thanked the Astrologer and offered him the few Ngultrum, the local currency, she still had.

The way back to Khoma seemed very long.

"This was a strange horoscope, Shona. Maybe it was not such a good day for predictions," was all Dorje had to offer.

*

There was a party going on in one of the neighboring houses that night. The whole village had been invited. Shona had politely declined. She wanted to think more about that strange prediction. But the party was noisy and disturbed her concentration.

She needed to get away from the noise. Only, going out

of the village at night was not a good idea. There was no real danger of wild animals, but the road was treacherous, full of potholes, and very, very dark. Streetlights were something that had yet to come to this remote place.

But, she knew a spot at the back of the village where no noise would reach her, because she'd been there a few times already before. Even in the dark, it was doable, she should be able to get there with only a flashlight.

She walked to the kitchen corner of the house. She had seen Dorje put a flashlight in a drawer this morning—probably after having replaced the batteries. She opened the drawer. Ah. There it was.

Someone grabbed her arm. From behind. Hard. And she felt an only too familiar tingle!

Impossible! How had they…?

Instinct kicked in. She grabbed the first thing her hand could find in the drawer and slashed as hard as she could with it, behind her. A grunt. The hand released her.

When she turned around, ready to hit again, there was no one in the room. No one except her. But she had not dreamed this—the kitchen knife she still held was covered with blood. Someone had been here.

An As'mir! They had found her! How had they been able to trace her? Her mind was thinking furiously. There was only one explanation possible. That email she'd sent to Jeffrey and Maire! Damn! She had been so careful to write it in Cantonese! They should never have found it!

But Keremli had warned her that they would do anything possible to find her!

Shona was a bit mad at herself, now. She was not that good with new technology. They must have found a way to access her friends' mailboxes. Something she had not thought of. Damn! What now?

She was still in Dorje's house, in Bhutan. Apparently the contact had not been long enough to allow the Caller to bring her along.

But they were going to come back for her. Probably with more people, this time. She had no time to lose. She packed her few possessions in a hurry. No time for a note for Dorje. She hoped he would understand.

She grabbed the bloody knife and flashlight, and ran out of the house. She managed to reach the suspension bridge without breaking her neck. There she paused. Running over the bridge was out of question. It was stable but quite slippery, and falling into the water would mean her death, with the Kurichu River swollen by the monsoon rains. She ran anyway, and was relieved when she reached the other bank.

But then, she had to decide where to go. Lhuentse was the best alternative right now. It was only a two-hour walk—even now, without daylight. There, she would find somewhere to spend the rest of the night and think about her next move.

She had just started walking when the flashlight batteries went dead. She had been wrong about the batteries. The rain started again. Damn! Damn! Damn!

As she walked on, more slowly now, she remembered the Astrologer and his predictions. Some good news, indeed! Why had she bothered going to him?

38

EKBETH RUSHED TO the Na Saoilcheachs' house as soon as he heard the news.

Someone prevented him from entering the room where Kalem was. Ekbeth wanted to knock the impudent guard out of the way. Damn it! He had enough of those people who thought they knew better than him.

But then the voice registered. Najeb. Kalem's son.

The young man met his stare calmly. "We have to wait, Akeneires'el. They are still busy in there."

So Ekbeth waited. And waited. He refused offers of food or drink.

Many hours of the night had passed when Erinani na Saoilcheach, their only trained surgeon, and a few others finally came out of the room, with grim faces and blood all over their clothes.

"Is he dead?"

Erinani looked at him with a blank expression, then recognized him and bowed. "Akeneires'el."

"Leave the niceties for later. Kalem?"

"He'll live, Akeneires'el, but it was a close call. The knife, or whatever she used, barely missed the heart and perforated one lung. It was a large blade. Lucky for him that Nukri sent him immediately back to us. Though, to be honest, I'd rather he'd been sent to a hospital on the Other Side."

Erinani na Saoilcheach had in part studied at a medical university on the Other Side, and was often complaining of how medieval their infrastructures were.

"Can I see my father, doctor?"

She nodded in response to Najeb's question. "You too, Akeneires'el. Just don't stand between the door and the bed. We have someone monitoring him—monitoring as in keeping a hand on his pulse. I don't except complications. But I want to have quick access to him if needed. Understood?"

Najeb and Ekbeth nodded.

The smell inside the room was awful. There was a lot of blood on the bed, and brown spots on the wall immediately behind Kalem's head. The two nurses bowed at Ekbeth, and then went on with the cleaning of the mess.

Someone brought them chairs and refreshments. Ekbeth almost barked at the person. Did he really expect him to eat or drink in such a nauseating place? The nurse saw his expression, bowed, and quickly removed the drinks.

The other nurse said, "We can't move him yet, Akeneires'el. He's too weak. Even a transfer could be fatal, the doctor says."

Ekbeth looked at the nurse. Nodded his thanks. Then finally took a good look at Kalem.

The man looked more dead than alive. He must have lost many pints of blood to be so terribly pale. Almost as white as the thick bandage on his chest.

As he knelt next to his father, Najeb's face was equally ashen. "I should have gone with him, Akeneires'el! Why did he have to go there alone?"

Ekbeth felt as bad as Kalem's son. He had told Kalem to rest, but his bodyguard had refused to listen to him. He had gone to that remote place in Bhutan as soon as they had located it on a Google map. Without a plan and exhausted.

The young man was crying, Ekbeth realized. He put a hand on his shoulder. "Kalem is alive, Najeb. Ara be blessed for that."

He could only imagine what was going through the youngster's mind. Najeb and Kalem had often been at odds with each other. Najeb was a trained bodyguard, but his passion was in building. He spent most of his time in the old archives, trying to rediscover the techniques their ancestors had used, or in the houses, attempting to repair the erosion of time. Kalem had often vented his frustration, in front of Ekbeth, about the stubbornness of his son. Too much of the same temperament here.

"Do you want me to go after Kimiel, Akeneires'el?"

The question took Ekbeth by surprise. Kimiel had been the last person on his mind during the past hours. Kalem had been his only concern. He shook his head. "Too late. She's probably gone from that village by now."

They had missed a perfect opportunity here, Ekbeth realized. Scared, the woman was going to be even more difficult to find. She would not repeat the mistake with the email again. Of that he was certain.

Kalem had made physical contact with her, Nukri na Liom had told him. But it had been too short for the Caller to make use of it. Sadly.

Ekbeth took one of the seats. They would find her. They had to. She had broken so many of Ara's laws! Stolen from him and his cousin, left the Valley when it was closed, tortured Lyrian, almost killed Kalem.

All those things, the thefts excepted, were punished by Ara's trial.

Second chances, had said the Aramalinyia. He could excuse Shona for having transferred herself out of the Valley when it was forbidden. Not the rest. Right now, even Ara's trial did not seem enough to Ekbeth. The punishment would only be inflicted on her once. No matter how much suffering she endured before she died, she deserved far worse.

But Ara's trial was their worse punishment. He could only pray she was going to suffer terribly before she died—something he had never before in his life wished on anyone. Even at their most irritating, his family members had never angered him that much.

What was happening with him, lately?

He rose from the chair. "I need to go to the temple, Najeb. Thank Ara for this."

Najeb just nodded.

*

The following morning, Ekbeth returned to Zurich, without a bodyguard. Lyrian was expecting him. "How is he?"

"Kalem regained consciousness this morning. Erinani is optimistic. But he can't talk yet. Too weak. We are not sure what happened exactly."

"What happened is that bloody bitch put a knife in his chest!"

Ekbeth nodded.

Lyrian looked at him incredulously. "I know how forgiving you are, Ekbeth. You always have been. But don't tell me you're forgiving her that as well!"

"I don't. Believe me I don't! I'm just tired. And we've lost her, again."

Lyrian was grim. "Yes. True. But we will find her. Eventually. Sally called, by the way. Told me she may have an idea to catch the woman. But she refused to give me details."

"I'll call her."

Lyrian nodded, then smiled wryly. "I have some more good news, of a sort. I think I've found some of her personal bank accounts. Two of them are at our bank. Like Watanabe's."

"And?"

"Our accounts have been inactive for almost ten years. The others as well, if the information I managed to get is correct. And there's a lot of money in them. About forty millions dollars."

Inactive most of the time meant the account holder was dead. No one would let that much money lie still for so many years. Unless…

"Sally told me there are rumors that Kimiel is rich. She must have another one somewhere. An active one."

"Exactly. Only I can't find it."

"Well, get those that you've found blocked. At least ours. And about Watanabe, it's really time we go and meet him."

Ekbeth took his mobile phone, opened it, started typing a message.

Lyrian asked, "You think Watanabe is the one who called, threatening to bankrupt us through the Triads? I thought they were not allowed mobile phones in jail."

"Money can open a lot of doors, we both know that. If Watanabe does not answer, I'll try to contact Matheson through Maire Kincaid."

He pressed the send button. "There. Now, enough time spent on this problem. How is the bank business going?"

They spent the next few hours discussing the current issues.

Ekbeth got a reply in the middle of the night.

*

The next morning he was waiting at the meeting point in the main hall of Manchester airport, a very nervous Najeb at his side.

"Relax, Najeb. We are just going to talk. There'll be no need for your talents today."

Najeb nodded, but did not relax.

A black limousine pulled up beside them and no other than Jeffrey Matheson opened the back door to invite them in. They exchanged no courtesies.

They rode for some time, in silence. Ekbeth was not really interested in their destination. Eventually they reached a Victorian square building, which was secured by several layers of barbed wire and various guarded posts.

Matheson led them inside. They presented their passports, submitted themselves to a superficial search, and were brought to a visiting room. Najeb positioned himself in one of the room's corners.

Five minutes later, Watanabe arrived.

Ekbeth did not work with a lot of Japanese criminals. He had expected someone a bit like that famous yakuza actor, Takeshi Kitano. A least a few tattoos.

Toshio Watanabe was nothing like that. If he had any tattoos, his clothing covered them. Tall, thin. Very long black hair flowed down his back, with just a few white threads here and there to indicate his age. Yet, despite the long hair, the general picture was certainly not effeminate. Ekbeth thought immediately of those medieval samurai images. The armor was missing, but the effect was the same. A man of power.

Ekbeth bowed. "Watanabe-san. Glad you could receive me on such short notice."

The man cracked a smile, returned the salutation. "My agenda is not as full as yours, Ekbeth na Duibhne. And I was curious about you."

Matheson brought chairs around the table, then opened his suitcase and extracted a thick file, placing it in front of Watanabe, who sat and opened the folder.

"I hope you won't mind me taking care of business while we have this conversation? I don't see Matheson often and he always has tons of documents for me to sign. Please have a seat."

Ekbeth took the offered chair, fighting a sudden desire to laugh at the absurd situation. This was a prison! Not a private salon!

"So, what can I do for you, Ekbeth-san?"

"Helping me find Ki... Shona McLeod would be a nice start."

Watanabe took the pen offered by his employee and started reading the documents in front of him. He shook his head. "I'm afraid this is not possible. I understood you and your community want to harm her. I won't let anyone do her harm. She's under my protection."

There was an audible threat in that calm voice. But amusement as well. Watanabe was not taking him very seriously, apparently.

Ekbeth hid his reaction and said, "Then we have a bit

of a problem. She has harmed people under my protection. I take my duties as seriously as you do."

An evasive gesture of the hand. Watanabe did not even look at him. "Matheson told me. Your cousin. I know how you feel, Ekbeth. Shona has been working for me for a long time. You're not the first one who wants retribution. It has even happened once or twice that I wanted to hurt her myself. The girl is crazy. When on a mission, nothing can stop her. I'm often left with cleaning up her messes. You don't want to know how many times I've had this conversation."

He sighed, said something to Matheson Ekbeth could not understand, and turned a page. "Protecting her is a tiring business. Whatever she has done to you and your family, forget it. Leave her alone before she starts finding you a problem. She tends to solve her problems in a very definitive way."

Ekbeth nodded. "I know. She almost killed my bodyguard two days ago."

The pen stopped moving. Watanabe looked at him. Matheson looked at him. They had not been aware of that fact, Ekbeth realized. That meant they had not heard the news from Kimiel. Maybe Matheson had not lied when he had said he had no clue where the woman was.

At least, he had the two men's attention now.

"Probably no news to you, but we know she is in Bhutan. Or at least was two days ago. My man went there. He came back with an almost fatal knife wound."

Watanabe shrugged, resumed his reading and signing. "*Almost* is the key word, Ekbeth. Did he attack her by surprise?"

"I suppose. I was not there."

"But then, if so, count her reaction as purely defensive. Not as problem solving."

Watanabe hesitated for a second, then added, "Shona has some nasty instinctive reflexes when surprised or pushed in a corner. They have been drilled into her. My doing, I'll admit. Corner her, she'll fight back. Follow my advice. Forget about her."

Ekbeth shook his head. "Not going to happen. I'm afraid we'll continue to look for her, warnings or not. This is not only about my family and me. Matheson must have told you about the Valley, the place Shona and I are both from. She broke one of our laws there."

Matheson growled, "That's because that Aramalinyia of yours, whoever she is, wanted Shona to marry you! I warned you this was a terrible idea."

For the first time, the studied polish of Watanabe's face cracked. But not as Ekbeth had expected. The Japanese laughed heartily. "What? This is a new one. A marriage. Why haven't you told me about this, Jeffrey?"

Matheson mumbled something in Chinese, or something similar. Watanabe considered Ekbeth with attention. "Is this the true reason why you are looking for her? You're still planning to marry her?"

Ekbeth shook his head. "No. She's broken the law. I have to bring her back to the Valley for punishment. And yes, Matheson, this time it's a death sentence."

Watanabe put the pen on the table. He was done with the signing. Matheson put the documents away. There was almost pity in Watanabe's voice when he said, "Maybe better for you, Ekbeth. Her last husband's life ended with her knife across his throat."

Matheson started protesting but Watanabe stopped him with a hand. His tone turned serious. "I am not joking on this, Ekbeth. Once she's decided to get rid of someone, she does it. No second thoughts. And she's terribly efficient."

He looked at Matheson. "Maybe Jeffrey should send you some examples of what I mean. Not about the husband. A few copies of some police reports we happen to have in our house. Don't ask why. And don't involve any official authorities in this. My friends at the Hong Kong police department would not be amused—the police and a few of my current friends."

Ekbeth absently nodded his agreement, ignoring the threat. He was still absorbing the news of Kimiel knifing her husband. He only managed to say, "Your little trick with my bank won't succeed a second time, Watanabe. I have taken precautions against it by now."

"I would expect you to, Ekbeth. But worse things can happen. Shona will only be part of your problem if you persist in this. I suppose that you've discovered why I'm here?"

Ekbeth nodded. Watanabe looked at his nails absently. "I told you I protect what is mine. In case you wonder why, the two men I killed harmed Shona through me. I could not let them live. And I won't hesitate to do it again if needed."

"You're in jail."

Watanabe smiled, in a way that sent chills down Ekbeth's spine.

Someone banged on the door at that moment. Watanabe rose from his chair. "I have to leave, I'm afraid. It was nice to speak to you."

With those last words, the Japanese left the room.

On the ride back to the airport, Ekbeth admitted to

himself that the meeting had not gone well. Of course he had not really expected help. But at least some answers. Instead, he had only received warnings and now had more unsolved puzzles than when he arrived.

He turned to Matheson. "Did she really kill her husband?"

Matheson nodded. He obviously wanted to add something, but his boss's influence kept Matheson's mouth shut. Ekbeth knew he was not going to get any information there either.

He had only one more thing to do. Sally's idea. "Will you at least give Shona a message if she contacts you?"

After a moment of hesitation, Matheson nodded. Ekbeth took the envelop out of his pocket. Matheson shook his head. "I won't be able to give her a written message, Ekbeth. I don't know where she is."

"It is really important, Matheson. Telling it is not enough."

The man sighed and took the letter, put it neatly in his pocket. "As you wish. I'm sorry it has come to that, Ekbeth. Please listen to Mr. Watanabe. Forget about us."

Ekbeth shook his head. "Too late for that."

A short moment later, he and Najeb exited the limousine. Within ten minutes they were back in Zurich. Only then did Najeb relax. Ekbeth managed a smile. "I told you it would go well. Yes, what we heard is worrying, but at least they did not try to kill us."

"And I'm glad you were right, Akeneires'el. Now, do you think this trick with the oracle stone will work?"

"Only one way to know, Najeb. Now we wait."

39

S HONA HAD NOT managed to reach Lhuentse. It was just too dark, and muddy. She had slipped twice on the dangerous road, and the second time had almost fallen into the river. So, as soon as she'd recognized the form of a house along the way, she'd gone there, no matter that it was late and no light was visible.

There were a few cows settled in the lower part of the house. This was a good sign. But the people lived upstairs, on the first floor, and the ladder to reach it was nowhere in sight. She screamed "hello" a few times, hoping to wake the inhabitants, if they could hear her with that pouring rain. The alternative was to sleep with the cattle. Something she'd rather not. The stench down there was sickening.

Someone suddenly appeared above her. A woman by the sound of it, though Shona was not so sure.

"Who are you?"

"A lost traveler. I was hoping to get to Lhuentse tonight but the weather is really too bad and my flashlight is dead. Can I please stay tonight? I don't want to be a bother but the road is dangerous."

She had to wait for the answer. A powerful light

projected in her face suddenly blinded her. "You're a foreigner! Where is your guide?"

Shona gritted her teeth. She was not really in the mood for questions. "I'm not a tourist. I am staying with Dorje the Weaver in Khoma. He's my brother-in-law."

"Then you should know better than to venture on the roads so late."

"I do know. But I have urgent business in Lhuentse. I was hoping to make it before nightfall. My mistake. Can I please come in?"

"What is your business that it can't wait until tomorrow?"

Maybe she should just go on with her walking. That woman was probably alone in there and rightfully suspicious. There had been some strange incidents lately with some gangsters, or at least the Bhutanese version of it, Dorje had told her.

One last try. She needed a convincing lie. "I just heard there's a truck going to Thimphu tomorrow morning. I wanted to give the driver something for one of my friends there. I will leave with daybreak. With a bit of chance, I'll still get to the driver on time."

More silence. But the light finally was turned away from her face and, after some time, pointed instead at the wooden ladder, finally lowered.

Shona climbed it with precaution. The woman had already disappeared inside. Shona entered the main room and started taking her sopping clothes from her equally drenched body.

"Here." The woman was offering her something dry to put on. Shona took it with many thanks. She probably had nothing dry right now among her belongings.

"You are shivering. Do you want some soup? Or Chang?"

The alcohol was really tempting, but she knew the soup would be more beneficial.

She followed her host to the kitchen corner. The woman put on some light, enough that Shona was able to have a good look at her.

Her host was older than Shona had expected. "Have we met before?" she asked. "I spent the past few months in Khoma."

The woman looked at her attentively, then offered her a bowl of soup with rice and chunks of meat, and sat between Shona and the stove. "Maybe. I don't go out much nowadays. Not since my husband died four years ago."

Shona knew what was expected from her. "Died? I'm sorry for your loss."

The woman sighed. "A couple of foreigners came here, unexpectedly, on a night like this one. Some Chinese. My husband tried to prevent them from entering the house. The younger one shot him. I had no choice—I gave them some food and drinks. Then they left. My husband was dead when I got to him."

Shona could not believe her ears. She must have walked past that house at least ten times since her return to Bhutan. Dorje had never told her of this woman. She had forgotten that the Chinese soldiers had stopped on their way out of the country. All that part was a blur. Maybe that awful rain tonight was a blessing, after all. Another witness.

She had to ask. And as the old woman apparently did not recognize her, she tried to remember how she'd looked then. "Was there a woman with these Chinese? A westerner? With long hair? Probably very dirty."

The woman shook her head. "No. But there was a child. A very small one. The poor thing was crying and the soldiers were hitting him. I could not do anything to help him. I was too afraid. He was crying for his mother." She made a small hand sign to ward off demons. "I remember him in my nightmares sometimes. Still now. He had the strangest eyes. Very clear, like yours. But he was Bhutanese. Most strange."

Shona put her soup bowl very slowly on the ground. She did not trust her hands anymore. They were shaking badly. "His name. Do you know this little boy's name?"

Something in her voice alerted the Bhutanese. She was suddenly suspicious again.

"Why?"

"It may have been my son. Sonam." She thought furiously. She needed a story. A plausible story. "My husband and I were living in a remote valley near Singye Dzong. The boy was always exploring the surroundings, as soon as he was able to walk. One day, he did not come back. We looked and looked but we never found him. We thought he was dead."

A photo. She had a photo of them in her bag! She hurried to it and looked into it frantically. The leather satchel in which she kept her passport and other important belongings was almost dry. She emptied the contents of it onto the floor and found the photo almost immediately. She picked it up and showed it to the woman, pointing to the child.

"This was my son. Was it the boy you saw?"

The woman observed the picture for a long time, before giving it back to her. "I'm not sure. It is a long time ago. But maybe. He has the same eye color as you. But what were the Chinese doing in this region? Why would they abduct little boys?"

Why, indeed?

Shona could only think of the worst things. She firmly shut her mind against those thoughts. She took back the picture and replaced it in the satchel with the rest.

"Your husband?" the woman asked.

"He's dead, like yours. I went back to my own country after his death, but decided to hold a puja to his memory and came back for the first time since then. I'm staying with his family."

The woman suddenly touched her. She had carefully avoided any contact till now.

"We've both lost a husband and a child, though mine never lived more than a couple of hours. You can stay here tonight."

*

Shona could not sleep. It was already difficult to feel comfortable on the thin mattress her host had offered her, but it was her thoughts that kept her wide awake. Sonam was alive! All this time! And she had abandoned him to those monsters!

She should have come sooner. She had to find him!

Sadly, the woman had not been able to describe the two Chinese she had fed—only that there was a young one and an old one. This was too little to go on. She needed Toshio. He had the high-placed connections she needed to follow the link from Kellerman to the soldiers, the butchers who had killed her family. The link to her son.

Toshio had refused to help till now. Find ten Chinese soldiers, or mercenaries, who had ever gone for a secret mission in Bhutan? Too little to go on. Too many possibilities. And Toshio did not believe Kellerman was responsible for the massacre of her family.

But he would help her this time, if she managed to convince him Sonam was alive.

Her head was spinning with everything she wanted to do. She had no clue how she was going to convince Toshio without physical evidence, but surely something would come up. Talking to him face to face would help. That meant going back to the UK. Facing the risk of finding another of those damned As'mirin in her way.

She tried to think. It was difficult. She was confused. Elated. Afraid.

She needed some more info on those new technologies. How to send a secured message to Jeffrey. She would probably manage to do that as soon as she got to India. With all those IT students, there must be some tech wizards among them.

Then, get Toshio out of jail. She knew he had killed the two former owners of the pharmaceutical company because of her. And that he was staying in prison as a personal punishment for what he considered his betrayal of her. Of all countries, he had to kill the two bastards in England. Hong Kong, or even China, would have been much simpler for everyone.

But maybe Jeffrey would think of something. She rolled to the other side of the thin mattress.

One of her babies was alive. It was going to take time to find him, but she was not going to let him down. She did not want to think about any more grim alternatives. He was her son. He would find a way to survive. Sonam was alive.

So the astrologer was right in the end.

Very good news indeed.

40

JEFFREY MATHESON WAS undeniably efficient. A very thick package was personally delivered to Ekbeth the morning following his interview with Watanabe. That this had not happened in his Zurich office or home, but in his New York office where he had meetings for the whole day, was proof enough he was not the only one spying on the other party.

Najeb frowned. "How did Matheson know where to find you?"

"Excellent question. Maybe you should have a little discussion with our network administrator in Zurich. The man is supposed to be the best on the market, and he costs me a fortune in refresher courses to keep him at the top—or so he keeps telling me every time we negotiate his salary raise. He thinks he is a good hacker? Clearly, he has found his match."

"Or someone else is leaking the info."

The boy was just as paranoid as his father! He might lack the experience and a real liking for the job, but no doubt he had been well trained. And Ekbeth knew better than to try to persuade Najeb that his staff was above suspicion. His new bodyguard was just doing his job.

"I leave the details to you." He handed the package to Najeb. "Keep this out of sight for the moment. The next meeting is about to start, and I don't want anyone in the room to wonder about it."

Najeb smiled and put the package in the chained suitcase that always accompanied him. The package was the perfect dimension for it. Another detail which had apparently not escaped Matheson's attention.

He was starting to get as paranoid as Kalem.

Ekbeth forced himself to smile and, pushing open the meeting room doors, entered the space, where four managers of a very big American consortium were expecting him. The men needed cash badly, and quickly—cash other banks were refusing, due to the financial crisis. Ekbeth was more or less their last resort. They knew it. He knew it. Still there was no point in humiliating them. Customers were customers. This was why he, the bank owner, was meeting them, rather than only his local manager.

A bit of respect could do no harm. In the end, it was all just a game.

*

Ekbeth spent the whole morning in that meeting. Then had a quick business lunch with his local manager, and another meeting in the afternoon, this time in Miami, with one of his moneylenders. Mainly drug money. Ekbeth had become the man's only banker over the years, which was a considerable risk for the dealer—a fact the man had become especially aware of during what they now called the "Chinese panic day." It had taken considerable time and effort on Ekbeth's part to reassure the man. The first visits had been very tense, but the dealer's trust of Ekbeth was slowly returning. There was no insulting body search today, and only two menacing bodyguards in the room to which they were brought.

Their host was all smiles. Ekbeth sensed no anger emanating from him. He let his guard down a bit.

"Ekbeth. Always glad to see you!" Then the man frowned. "New bodyguard?"

Ekbeth managed an indifferent shrug. "Kalem's son, Don Luis. His father thought the boy was due for some live exercise."

The drug dealer relaxed a little. Stared at Najeb for a long moment. "He does look a bit like his father. So it's how the job is done? From father to son?"

Najeb did not answer. Another point for him, thought Ekbeth. Kalem would have plenty of reasons to be proud of his son, for once.

Ekbeth shrugged again. "Their family has served mine loyally for seven generations, Don Luis. I can't complain."

He waited until their host offered him a seat, then a drink.

Then the serious business started.

*

They managed to get back to Zurich just before midnight, local time. Najeb allowed himself a groan of relief, and untied the suitcase chain from his wrist.

"You did well today, Najeb!"

The young man smiled. "Thank you, Akeneires'el. But I do understand now why my father was always recommending that I eat and drink every time I am given the opportunity when working as a bodyguard. I'm starving!"

Ekbeth laughed. "Ah, wise advice, indeed. I get enough snacks and drinks during the meetings that I tend to skip proper meals. I'm sorry. But I'm sure the cook has something in store for you."

"So, there's no more traveling around today?"

Ekbeth nodded, then added with a mischievous grin, "Depending on how you define "today," though. I do have an afternoon meeting in Shanghai tomorrow."

Najeb did the math, and winced. "So how many hours of sleep can I count on?"

"Enough—don't worry. I don't need you when I go to the office here."

Najeb looked at the suitcase he had just put on the main table of the living room. "And you, Akeneires'el? Are you going to get any food or sleep?"

"Food, definitely. Sleep?" He gestured towards the suitcase. "Depending on how fast I can look into this."

Najeb had probably also heard his father complain about the Akeneires'el's bad sleeping habits, because he did not comment. He left the room with the promise he would ask the cook to bring something.

At last Ekbeth was alone. He had been patient enough. He opened the suitcase, took the package out, and tore open the wrapping paper. The file was in a box, and was very thick.

Ekbeth sat in his favorite chair and started reading.

*

Three hours later, he closed the last folder. He put it carefully back in its box and shoved everything away from him. The words and the pictures he had seen remained imprinted in his brain.

Most of the files were written in Chinese, but the few titles in English had been enough. "Eviscerated." "Died by slow and painful strangulation." "Unsure of victim's identity." "Whole building destroyed in explosion."

And the pictures: bloody red, charcoal black, livid dead flesh. He needed no translation for those.

He just could not believe it. Kimiel was a thief, misusing her As'mirin abilities. Maybe skillful with a knife… but this… this…

He got up from his chair, walked towards the window and out to the terrace beyond.

The cold air calmed his mind a bit.

Duncan McLean had heard rumors about this. The old man had called her a murderer. Watanabe had said the file was built on Kimiel's acts. He had said that she killed her husband. The question was, of course, how much Ekbeth could trust the man. Watanabe had also said he was ready to do anything to protect her.

Faking such files was not a big deal for someone as well connected as he was. Still, if those files were genuine and Kimiel had killed—no, massacred—all those people, then Kalem had been very lucky to survive his encounter with her.

They all had been lucky. There was no way Ekbeth would let the woman approach him again, even stark naked!

Watanabe's file had certainly accomplished its goal. Ekbeth did not want to be responsible for such carnage among his fellow As'mirin. He looked back at the box through the window. So innocent there, next to the untouched meal the cook had brought him a long time ago.

A ticking bomb.

He should bring it to the High Council. But why pollute the other Akeneires'elin minds with such horrors? The woman was condemned to Ara's trial, anyway.

Then he realized something else. This box was Shona's past. The Ke'As'mirin had seen this during the Oyyads'erel. And still let her live. Why? Were they so frustrated at their descendants that they really thought only a psychopath could bring them back on the right path?

Kimiel…the redeemer.

He felt dizzy. He needed sleep. The meeting in Shanghai was not that important, but it still needed his full attention. And he had some administrative work to do in Zurich beforehand. But first, he needed to decide what to do about that box on his table. If not the High Council, maybe inform Najeb. And Lyrian.

And he needed to warn Nukri na Liom. The Caller was prepared for some form of resistance from Shona's side. But certainly not that much violence. Nukri was old. And their only remaining Caller. Essential to the community.

Ekbeth closed his eyes. Called the old man in his mind. Got a very sleepy answer.

It was also very early in the day in the Valley.

Sorry to wake you up, Nukri. But it could not wait. If Kimiel touches the stone and you manage to Call her to the Valley, transfer her immediately to a safe, enclosed place from which she won't be able to escape or contact anyone.

The Caller muttered an agreement and cut the contact.

Ekbeth hoped fervently Nukri would remember the instructions when he woke up.

Maybe Ekbeth would contact him again later, to be on the safe side.

He made a decision about the box. Walked back inside. No one needed to see this.

There was no fireplace in his villa in which to burn all

this paper. This would have been his preferred solution. There was, however, a very efficient paper shredder in his study. Thankfully, his cousin was not sleeping in the Villa tonight or he would have complained about the noise again.

Ekbeth took the box to his study. He had a little less than two hours to get this done, including taking the shreds to the garbage bin.

Najeb would not ask about the box. And if he did, it would probably be too late. Still, Ekbeth had to hurry.

He reopened the box.

41

I N THE END Shona did not even need a tech wizard, or to leave Bhutan. The first mobile phone shop she entered when reaching Thimphu, the Bhutanese capital, was enough.

The shop owner was obviously a big fan of spy stories. He promised that he knew how to call someone without raising suspicion from potential listeners. To prove his point , after asking a few questions, he called Jeffrey on one of the numerous mobile phones he had for sale. After having greeted Jeffrey, affecting a terrible British accent, the man said he was offering his services as an intermediary, that he had numerous Russian beauties on offer—one, especially, called Sonia. That struck a nerve with Shona, but she managed to smile at the man. She could only imagine Jeffrey's reaction. Actually, she was surprised her friend had not already hung up. He had never found this kind of call funny, whether fake or real. The shop owner continued his spiel for some time, and, having given Jeffrey his phone number, hung up.

He turned to Shona with a huge satisfied grin. "Now we wait."

Shona had considerable doubt, but sure enough, one minute later, another mobile phone started ringing. The shop owner answered it with the same phony accent, and handed the phone to Shona. "Keep it under five minutes. And don't use words that might alert the CIA. They are following all the conversations up there."

Shona whispered, "Can I go outside to talk?"

The shop owner grinned. "You really know nothing about those things, do you? Of course you can."

So she stepped outside. "Jeffrey?"

"Good day to you, Shona. Your knack for finding the strangest friends is still very impressive, I must say."

"No names, please."

"This line is secure. Don't worry. Your other friends are not listening. What can I do for you?"

"I need to come home. Discreetly."

"Where are you?"

"Still in Bhutan."

"And you still have your passport?"

"Yes."

"I will call you back in ten minutes."

"Do you need another number?"

"No."

She waited, sharing tea with the shop owner and learning all she needed to know about the dangerous CIA satellite spying. She was very glad when Jeffrey finally called back.

"Can you get to Delhi on your own?"

"Yes."

"Okay. I'll have someone meet you there with a ticket and a fake ID."

"Can't you send the plane?"

"No. Take a paper and write down this number, Shona…"

She wrote the instructions quickly, then tolerated the shop owner for another two minutes before taking her leave.

*

It took her a week to get back to the Castle in England. The place was not really a castle. It was just a huge mansion located in a lot of peaceful, gentle, hilly English countryside. Toshio's home. Currently, only Jeffrey was enjoying the luxury of the place—Jeffrey and Toshio's staff. From time to time, Shona stayed here, too.

Jeffrey welcomed her at the main door, but his embrace was not as warm as she was used to.

"That bad, eh?", she asked.

Jeffrey only nodded, and let her enter the house. "Go and take a bath and put on some fresh clothes, while I get the lunch ready. Then we'll talk."

Shona could not help but grin. "Oh, it's only my smell that bothers you?"

That brought a smile to his lips. "I would say that your last bath was at least two weeks ago!"

"Not too far off. See you later."

She was feeling clean for the first time in weeks when she finally sat at the small veranda table, where lunch was served. She enjoyed every bit of it. Finally, something without rice and those horribly spiced peppers.

"Mmh, grapes! I've missed those!"

"Glad you came back, Shona. And you look good. I was worried about you."

She ate a few grapes before responding. "I have some very good news."

"That email about the White Lady…"

She sighed. "I know. It brought them right to me. Not my cleverest move."

"Yes. Ekbeth told us that Kalem, the bodyguard, went after you, and that you knifed him. He is also mad at you about Farrill. He is very determined to find you now and make you pay."

She shrugged. "He was already very determined to find me before, anyway, and not for a good reason."

"Ekbeth talked to Toshio last week. Just a day before you called, in fact."

She had expected this. She popped a few more grapes in her mouth. "How did Ekbeth find out about him?"

It was Jeffrey's turn to sigh. "A slight miscalculation on my part. Ekbeth's bodyguard had gone to Maire with heavy threats. She called me, and when it became clear that I was unable to stop the threats, she called Toshio. You know how he is. He called his friends to teach Ekbeth a lesson. Only it worked a bit too well."

"What kind of lesson?"

"Toshio asked his friends in China to close their accounts at Ekbeth's bank. Or at least pretend they were willing to do so."

Shona was impressed. "And they accepted?"

"Yes. But Toshio called too many of them. It looked like a real panic on the part of the Chinese, which, in turn, provoked a massive reaction from Ekbeth's other customers."

"Oops. Is Ekbeth ruined?"

"He saved his bank in the end. Found a few of our own accounts in the meantime and froze them. As well as some of yours. Then started asking questions to his Chinese customers. That's how he got Toshio's name. One of them talked. As to how Ekbeth contacted Toshio, that was a mistake on Toshio's part. Toshio used a phone without even hiding the number. He's just as hopeless as you with regard to new technology. Ekbeth simply had to call back and ask for a meeting. But I imagine that Ekbeth would have found a way to contact Toshio anyway. Our boss is really easy to find nowadays."

Pity she had missed the meeting.

"How did it go?"

"Very polite on both sides. Considering you had just knifed Ekbeth's bodyguard. Kalem survived, in case you were wondering. You are losing your touch, girl."

Shona just stared at him, not reacting to his joke.

Jeffrey grinned. "Anyway. We did our best to convince Ekbeth he'd better stop pursuing you."

"And did you manage?"

"Well, Toshio told him a few things about you I'd rather not repeat and I sent him a copy of some police reports you're very familiar with. With a few imaginative additions to make it even gorier. If that does not frighten him enough, I don't know what will."

She was not sure this was good news. Out of context, she could only imagine what Ekbeth's reaction was going to be.

"Before we part company, Ekbeth left a message for you. Do you want to see it?"

A message? "Later. Why couldn't you send the plane to me?"

"Because you wanted to come back discreetly. They are monitoring the few accounts they have not frozen. They spy on us. We spy on them. Very difficult to do anything without their knowledge."

There were no more grapes. She found an apple.

"Your brother also called. Not sure how he found our number, but he seems as resourceful as you when he needs to be. He was very upset. I understood from his ranting that the McLean clan holds you responsible for the Laird Duncan's death."

Duncan? Dead? How was that possible? Later.

"Did Keremli come to pick up the ring?"

"Yes. We had a formal dinner. She really is a nice lady."

"Good. My turn for the news. The White Lady is only part of what I discovered while in Bhutan. Dorje is alive."

Jeffrey's expression remained so bland that she understood this was not a surprise to him. She asked, "You knew this?"

He simply nodded, but pulled back in his chair, putting a little distance between them, apparently expecting a violent reaction.

She was too tired for violence. "Since when?"

"Since before we found you. Actually Dorje was the one to tell Toshio you had survived the ordeal. That you'd been taken away."

She was too tired for violence, but not that exhausted that she could not get really angry. "Why did none of you ever tell me that?"

"Toshio's decision. Please understand. You know how you reacted until recently whenever we talked about Bhutan. Saying that word only got you hysterical. It did not seem such a good idea to tell you someone else had survived. The right moment never seemed to come."

"You could have told me before I left for Bhutan! At least!"

Jeffrey nodded. "I forgot. Sorry."

Shona tried to get a grip on her emotion. "I've just spent almost three months with the man, and he never told me about this!"

Jeffrey shrugged. "Can't blame him. From what Toshio told us when he came back from Bhutan, Dorje was heavily drugged when they met. Dorje might have forgotten about the encounter."

Shona pondered over the news for a moment. Then asked, "Did Dorje also tell Toshio that Sonam was alive."

This time, Jeffrey showed surprise. "No! Sonam? Your son?"

She nodded, before telling how she had come by the information. "He's alive, somewhere. We have to find him."

Jeffrey was doubtful. "It's been four years. Why did they take him in the first place? I don't think…"

Shona interrupted him. "I had plenty of time to wonder about that bit, Jeffrey, and you know I have a very vivid imagination, so spare me yours. I need Toshio to help me find my son, Jeffrey."

"Toshio is in jail. Life sentence."

"Find a way to get him out. We need him out, and in China, not behind those four walls."

Jeffrey thought about this for a minute. "There is no way we can do that discreetly, Shona. Ekbeth or the McLeans are going to find out you're back."

"If they do, so be it. My problem. Concentrate on getting Toshio out and help him find my son for me."

That got her a long stare. "They won't let you come out of that Valley of yours alive, Shona. There's a death sentence waiting for you there. Ekbeth has told us as much."

Shona managed to smile. "I've survived worse odds, Jeffrey. Have a little faith in me. I do plan to see my son again, and not in paradise. And if I die, please promise you'll keep looking for my little boy."

Jeffrey reluctantly promised. Shona allowed herself to relax. Convincing Toshio was not going to be as easy, but she had won the first argument. She smiled. "Now, you were telling me of a message from Ekbeth? Where is it?"

Jeffrey left the veranda to fetch it. Shona enjoyed the few minutes of solitude.

"There's something in the envelope—looks like a stone. But I did not open it."

From the feel of it, Shona guessed what it was even before she opened the envelope and had it in her hand. The oracle pebble. What…?

The next second, she felt the familiar tingle in her whole body. She let go of the pebble… tried to fight the Call.

This time it did not work. She only had time to order Jeffrey to find her son. The next moment, she found herself in total darkness.

She was so dizzy that she fell to her knees, then her stomach revolted. She puked a few times.

When the dizziness faded, she sprang back to her feet and took a tentative step, away from her own vomit. Her foot touched something furry that scurried away with a screech. Rats! She hated rats! She extended her arms in front of her. Met a wall. She followed it with her hands. It formed a large circle around her. Her feet were getting wetter by the minute. Probably some sort of well. But she could not see any opening above her head.

Trapped! She was trapped!

But she was not defeated yet.

She tried to Call herself out of the place. But the person who had brought her there was firmly, energetically, holding her.

Damn! This was just so unfair! She was trapped somewhere in the Valley. Next would be that Ara's trial.

She concentrated. The Valley's Caller was an old man, she'd understood. One of them would have to give in, eventually.

She was not planning to lose. Her son needed her.

42

THE GOOD NEWS reached him in the middle of a particularly difficult meeting. They had her. Finally!

His interlocutor stopped talking, then looked at his lawyer, puzzled. The lawyer took over, addressing Ekbeth. "Can we deduct from this smile that my client gets the extra loan he needs?"

Ekbeth looked at both of them with a severe frown. "No."

He had confused them, but maybe it was not a bad thing. That conversation could have gone on and on for hours. That was always the case with those Italian guys.

"I give you one more week. I may be willing to renegotiate the interest rate then, but I strongly recommend that you have the money you owe me when I come back next week."

"But…"

Ekbeth looked at his watch. "I'm expected somewhere else, gentlemen. See you next week."

Najeb was already at the door, ready to leave. They walked quickly out of the building, where their driver was expecting them.

"Bring us home."

The driver frowned. "I thought…"

"Change of plans."

There was a bad traffic jam. Ekbeth scowled with impatience.

"Akeneires'el?" Najeb said. "You know this customer we just left? He won't be able to pay."

Ekbeth closed his eyes. It had been a long week. "This is what is going to happen, Najeb. Someone is going to give him the loan he desperately needs and he's going to repay me. Then he won't be my responsibility anymore, but that of the other lender. And our customer is going to discover he had better respect his agreements with me, because his new lender is not going to be as amenable as I am."

"Are we talking of the Mafia?"

The boy was learning fast. No need to tell him, though, that Ekbeth was getting a very nice commission out of this reloan business. Najeb deserved to keep a few of his illusions. For now.

The driver finally reached their address. Ekbeth did not even wait to be in his apartment. As soon as the entrance door was closed, he said to Najeb. "I'm going to the Valley. You go to Lyrian to give him the news and those contracts. Ask him to reschedule all the appointments for the next few hours, at least. Then I'm expecting you in the Valley."

Najeb nodded.

Ekbeth concentrated. The familiar dizziness and he was in the Valley. Nukri na Liom's skin was ashen.

"Are you okay, Nukri?"

The older As'mir just nodded, teeth clenched. This was so unlike him.

Ekbeth frowned. "Is Kimiel Keh Niriel trying to Call herself out?"

Nukri nodded, then managed to say, "She has a strong will."

Ekbeth frowned. "Does the Aramalinyia know about this?"

"Yes, but we need to wait until everyone from the community is there and Ara's water has to be collected. We can't hurry the process."

Ekbeth pitied the man. All those tasks needed his Caller skills. On top of the daily routines of moving the As'mirin from one house to the other at their requests, bringing food and drinks everywhere, or anything else the others wanted, Nukri needed to also keep track of what was happening outside of the Valley itself, in case one of the Callers of the Aiarz'in part needed help. No wonder Nukri was exhausted.

It was in moments like this that the community should realize the danger they were putting themselves in by not lifting the ban on Akalabeth, Ekbeth reflected. He did not really have time to think of a solution to his niece's problem. Yet, obviously, sorting out the situation was becoming urgent.

He observed Nukri. Definitely urgent.

"Are any of the callers outside the Valley helping you right now, Nukri?"

The old man nodded. This was good news.

"I'm glad our plan has worked. Where is she?"

"In one of the water collectors under Kse'Annilis. A dry one."

Ekbeth agreed this was a perfect jail. "Who's still to come?"

"The McLeans. They are slow packers. And your bodyguard."

"Well, Najeb should Call any minute now. I will wait for him."

The next minute, the young man was with them.

Ekbeth took him out of the Call room and whispered to him, "Najeb. Kimiel is in one of the water wells, but she's trying to escape. Look at Nukri na Liom. He's not going to hold on much longer. We can't give her the drug to block her abilities. It would also block some of the effects of Ara's water. Can you think of anything else we could do?"

The young man thought about it for a moment. "I think the best is to knock her out. If I hit her hard enough, it should give enough time for the Caller to rest."

Ekbeth frowned. "You're not going there alone!"

"Akeneires'el. I know the danger! If Nukri can restrain her physically for a minute, there's no risk for me."

The boy was right, of course. "Do it then. And, as far as I'm concerned, you may hit her as hard as you want. As long as you don't break her skull!"

Najeb chuckled. "I would not dare! Imagine the scandal if she's dead before Ara's trial!"

Najeb walked back inside the Caller's house, while Ekbeth went down to the Na Duibhnes' house. The cleanliness of the streets during the Aras'arisidz was already a thing of the past. A thick layer of decomposed flowers petals coming from Ara-knows-where covered them! It was dangerously slippery. But he somehow managed to reach his home without falling.

He discovered, upon entering the hall, that he was expected. To his surprise, most of the persons in front of him bowed to him. What was happening?

His uncle Es'ael approached him. "Sorry for having doubted you, Akeneires'el. You managed to capture the law breaker!"

The others nodded their agreement. Respect from

them? That was certainly unexpected. There had been less muttering since he had forced some of them to work in the McLeans' house. But respect?

He certainly did not want the honor of having brought back Kimiel to the Valley to fall entirely on him.

"Sarah-Lysliana McLean is the one you should praise. It was her idea that brought Kimiel back to the Valley. With Nukri na Liom's help. He kept the trap open for her all those days. They deserve the congratulations, not me."

That only brought more nods, if a bit less fervent. Of course, it was not about him only. Bringing her back was going to honor the whole Na Duibhnes' family. Something his uncles probably thought was needed after their embarrassing implication in the mob and the death of Duncan McLean.

Najeb entered the hall at that moment. He only slightly nodded at Ekbeth, then left the building again. He was probably going to his father. Good.

Ekbeth turned to Es'ael. "Do you know when the trial is going to take place?"

"At dusk, the Aramalinyia said."

In less than three hours then. There was not much to be done except wait. He walked to his study. He was sure to find enough paperwork there to keep his mind off what was about to happen.

They had her. They were going to punish her. Somehow, the news was not elating him as much as he had expected.

Just too damn soft hearted, Lyrian would say. How well Lyrian knew him, thought Ekbeth.

*

The whole community was in the temple, facing the

Lake, when the sun touched the peaks of the surrounding mountains.

The last Ara's trial Ekbeth could remember had been the one of his brother Kas'el.

And, as then, there was lingering anger in the air. Definitely hostile. Some people were holding stones in their hands.

The Aramalinyia entered their circle, followed by her servants. One look from her, and the stones disappeared.

"Bring the lawbreaker to Ara's justice."

Ekbeth had more or less expected to see Kimiel appear out of thin air in front of the Aramalinyia. But he had forgotten how important ceremony was to his fellow As'mirin.

Kimiel got the full extent of the ritual. Four bodyguards in armor walked her inside the temple precinct. Najeb was probably one of them, but Ekbeth was not entirely sure as armor covered the guards from head to toe.

And they had shackled her. Heavily. Still the extra weight did not seem to bother her. Her clothes were filthy from her time in the cistern, but she was walking proudly and gracefully, her face carefully neutral, as if she was arriving at a celebration.

Ekbeth tried to read her emotions, but her mind was blank.

When they reached the Aramalinyia, the guards broke their formation, moving from a square surrounding her into a line behind their prisoner. They cut the clothes off her with sharp knives.

Kimiel did not budge. Naked, she kneeled on her own volition. Or so it seemed.

Ekbeth had no doubt that Nukri na Liom was still

ensuring she could not transfer herself out of this. The Caller had probably also forced her to her knees.

The air around her was tingling with suppressed energy. If he could feel it, probably everyone could.

The Aramalinyia approached Kimiel, a small, open vial in her hands. Ara's water. Only it was not innocent water. It was their deadliest poison, which came from a hidden spring, the location of which only the Aramalinyia knew.

Two guards put their hands on Kimiel's shoulders, while a third forced her head backwards and opened her mouth. Kimiel could go nowhere.

"Ara be merciful. Judge this woman in equity."

The liquid was poured, the mouth closed. Maintained closed till the guards were satisfied Kimiel had swallowed. Then the Aramalinyia and the guards took a few steps back, joining the crowd around them.

Kimiel did not scream or writhe on the temple sand. She just collapsed very slowly, and then lay there, not moving.

But they could all hear her laborious breathing. Ekbeth felt his innards shriveling. He could only imagine what she was going through right now.

Suddenly, he felt her emotions, all too clearly. The light touch of cold. Then the fire… burning… burning…

"Uncle? You're okay?"

Alyasini's touch on his arm brought him back to his senses. He looked away from Kimiel for a moment.

"She deserves the punishment."

Ara, there was such venom in his niece's voice! Not something he would have expected from her. Even though he agreed with her words. He nodded. "Yes, she does."

His niece put her hand through his arm and left it there.

He returned his attention to the crouched form in the center of the crowd. There was nothing else to do but wait now. If Ara was indeed merciful, Kimiel would die quickly.

If not, it was going…

Suddenly, unexpectedly, a loud shriek resonated in his head. He fell to his knees, his head between his hands, trying to make it stop.

The shriek just went on… and on.

"Uncle! Uncle! Ekbeth! Someone help him! Please!"

Ekbeth was vaguely aware of people around him. He was just trying to block the scream in his head. All went black around him.

43

SHONA FOUGHT THE drug. They might have forced her to take it, but she was not going to let them win. Nothing worse than what she'd been through before, she kept repeating herself.

But this was worse. Far worse. She felt the fire spreading through her body. She clenched her teeth. She was the fire.

Concentrate! Do it for Sonam!

Oh, so warm! She was burning!

Fight! You are stronger than this!

Water! She needed water! There was water not far from her! If only she could reach it! But she could not move! Breathing was all she could manage. So be it then. Keep breathing! Ignore the fire!

A violent spasm took her breath away. Yes! Another spasm! Puking the damn drug! That would help! Only, she was not puking. She felt a hot liquid between her legs… Great, she was peeing on herself!

Another spasm, heavier. Something moved inside her.

She suddenly realized what was happening! Impossible! It was just impossible!

You are a stubborn one, child! Believe!

That voice inside her head! She ignored it!

How could have she been so stupid? All those weeks, she had attributed all the telltale signs to indigestion! Some stomach cramps indeed! She was pregnant! And right now, she was losing the baby. Another baby. She could not let this happen.

I can help!

She gritted her teeth. Thought loudly, as she was unable to speak. *Then help!*

You have to promise…

Just help!

She felt a cold hand touching her brow, staying there. And slowly, slowly, the fire in her blood receded. Even more slowly, the spasms quieted. Shona allowed herself to breathe. But she did not dare move.

Kimiel Malcolm Keh Niriel. You disappointed me deeply.

Who was that voice inside her head? Not one of those Ke'As'mirin again, eh?

A peal of laughter answered her. *No, not one of my children. I am Ara, child.*

Shona's mind went blank.

Impossible? I did not expect you to be so narrow minded! You did not believe in your heritage before you came here, Kimiel. Yet you met your ancestors! Why would hearing me be impossible?

Shona was shocked. But she had no time to collect herself, as the Goddess continued talking inside her head.

I had such great plans for you, Kimiel Keh Niriel! I asked the Ke'As'mirin to let you live! I chose your name! And how did you thank me? Ignore my oracle! Break my laws, one by one!

Shona felt like laughing. Only she was lacking the

energy. She had expected to die. She had decided to fight till the bitter end. Now, apparently, she was going to live. Only to suffer the sermon of a Goddess!

Fire ran through her again.

Don't you dare mock me!

Oh my! A susceptible Goddess! The fire was hurting again. But Shona could not help it. She was still amused. As suddenly as it started, the fire collapsed. And the voice in her head laughed as well.

That temper of yours will get you killed eventually! Do you respect anything, child?

Shona nodded. She respected plenty of things. People who survived in the most difficult conditions. People who stood their ground even though it may cost them their life. Yeshe's decision…

A sigh.

Yes. Life has not been easy for you so far. You've survived, but at what price?

Shona did not want to answer that. She had accepted what she had become a long time ago.

It's never too late to redeem yourself.

Easier said than done. Her past kept following her. It was not as if she could erase it, was it?

Well, here you could have done that! No one in the community knew about your past! Except my dearest Keremli, but she would have kept her knowledge to herself, because she loves you. Only, you had to blow it! Again, and again!

Damn! Shona hated to admit it, but the Goddess was right. She had botched it. Badly!

Better.

It was quiet in Shona's head for a moment. So long that

Shona thought the conversation had come to its conclusion and she began trying to find enough energy to stand up. But Ara was apparently not done. In the next moment, her voice was back in Shona's head.

For the sake of this little life inside you, I let you live. This time. But no more law breaking! No bloodletting, no thievery, no torturing, no… In short, behave! Make amends to people you've wronged! Don't think you'll escape my wrath if you break your word: my power is not only inside this Valley. I'll find you!

Her word? Shona had not promised anything! And she needed to find Sonam! She knew only one way to get information.

That insufferable fire again! She went back into her crouching position. Okay, she'd gotten the message!

Find another way! And you will marry Ekbeth Maher na Duibhne! I still can't believe you prefer to trust some vague Buddhist predictions above my own oracle!

Definitely touchy there, that Goddess! Marry Ekbeth? She was pretty sure the man hated her with a passion nowadays. She had done her best to make him hate her. As well as Toshio and Jeffrey.

You'll find a way. You are creative. Promise.

She nodded her agreement before Ara thought another demonstration was needed.

Marry Ekbeth?

Of course, there was the little issue about who was the father of that child inside her.

A laugh in her head.

Oh, don't worry; I have taken care of that. He will have no doubt about his paternity. Now, one last thing, then I'll let you shock those lazy children of mine by surviving against all their expectations!

Shona felt an intense heat on her lower back. This time she screamed. It was as if all the heat she had been fighting earlier was suddenly concentrated in the one spot.

Correct in that. Don't ever forget your oath, Kimiel Malcolm Keh Niriel. And if you do, look at the mark I left you. What I give, I can take back. 'Bye now! Behave!

Shona moved, slowly, cautiously. Her whole body was hurting and she wanted to drink gallons and gallons of water.

Had she dreamed all this? A latent pain on her lower back informed her that, nope, it had all been true.

Then she felt the movement in her belly. She finally managed to sit. Put a hand on her stomach. There it was. A faint but somehow familiar move under her fingers. She felt like crying. Looked at the Lake in front of her instead. It was still dark around her, but she could see the water.

She was going to keep her promise. She had two reasons to live from now on.

44

EKBETH WAS RESTING, trying to understand what had happened at the temple, when he heard the news. Kimiel had survived Ara's trial. That was just not possible! He stood up.

"Uncle! You have to rest!"

"I've rested enough, Lyas! Where is she?"

Lyas bit on her lip, but when she saw he had decided to go she relented.

"At the Na Saoilcheachs' house."

Ekbeth got dressed, and they both went to the doctors' house. Ekbeth wanted to see Kimiel with his own eyes. He needed to see her alive to believe the incredible news.

There was quite a crowd around the building. Ekbeth caught some word exchanges while trying to get to the entrance doors. Everyone was just as surprised as he was.

There were a few guards in front of the house—the Aramalinyia had apparently taken no risk this time—but they moved aside to let Ekbeth and Lyas enter. Sometimes being an Akeneires'el had its privileges.

It was less crowded inside the entrance hall, but still crowded enough to make progress difficult. Ekbeth recognized the other Akeneires'elin, with one or two other members of their families. Asking the same questions as the crowd outside: how come Ara had not taken the life of this lawbreaker?

The Aramalinyia, the Goddess's voice, was nowhere to be seen. Ekbeth was preparing to ask about her when Bers'el na Saoilcheach entered the room from the other side and zoomed towards him. "Ekbeth! I was going to send someone for you, but you're already here. Good."

Why was the old man looking for him specifically? Conscious of being the center of attention, Bers'el smiled mysteriously. "If you'd please follow me? This is not for everyone's ears. At least, not yet."

Ekbeth followed him outside of the hall, before anyone could start asking questions. Despite the intensity of the situation, he managed to speak teasingly. "Bers'el! That was really nasty of you! You know they can't bear secrets!"

The old man laughed. "Oh, they'll hear about the news soon enough. Don't worry."

"Has Kimiel really survived? How bad is the damage?"

Bers'el grumbled. "Actually, surprisingly minimal. Some people will think the Aramalinyia diluted the drug. Or replaced it with something less lethal."

"Why would she do that?"

"She didn't, but she knows some people will doubt her and she's asked me to check the remainder of Ara's water that she collected earlier on. There's nothing wrong with it. As concentrated as my previous tests. Though I'm certain my results won't stop the gossips. And that's not why I was look-ing for you. Did you know Kimiel was pregnant?"

That stopped Ekbeth's progress. Lyas, who had

been following them, hissed in shock. "Pregnant? But that means…"

Bers'el nodded gravely. "That we've put that baby through a lot of pain. Indeed. She—it's a baby girl—seems fine, though it's maybe too early to say. She's very active for a fetus of so few months. I have some drugs that can help, but a nurse suggested something else. I was hoping you could help."

Ekbeth was getting over the shock. "Me? Help? How?"

Instead of answering, Bers'el pushed a door and they entered one of the patient rooms. Kimiel was laying on the bed, apparently asleep, apparently unscathed. The Aramalinyia was at her side, one hand on Kimiel's brow, muttering something he could not make out. Ekbeth still did not want to believe it. It was so unfair, was his first thought. Unfair for Lyrian and Kalem.

Bers'el told him, hesitantly, "I think I know what provoked that mental scream and your fainting, Akeneires'el."

Ekbeth knew what Bers'el was about to say and ask him to do. As'mir parents had a strong mental link with their children, even the unborn ones. It would be the final proof.

He needed to know.

He looked at Kimiel's flat stomach. There was nothing to see. Even covered with blankets, it was flat. He put a tentative hand on its surface. Something resonated in his head. Kimiel's face relaxed. Her stomach under his fingers relaxed.

Lyas was the first to react.

"Oh my! That baby is yours, Uncle! She's reacting to you. She was the one screaming for help! And only you could hear it!"

Ekbeth could only imagine what the baby had gone

through. He remembered the screaming in his head. Burning pain. Panic. So small, and already put to the worse suffering any As'mir knew! His daughter.

The Aramalinyia was looking at him, he realized, but her face was carefully neutral.

She asked him in a hushed tone, "Did you know?"

Ekbeth felt like shouting at her. What was she thinking? That he would inflict this torture to an unborn child because of his feelings against her mother?

But she was the Aramalinyia. She had a right to ask. He sighed. "No, I did not. It's not like I've been seeing Kimiel a lot recently, Aramalinyia."

The old woman looked at him for a long moment, as if trying to read his mind, but finally shook her head and got on her feet. "I need to talk to the community. Ara has decided to be merciful, for once. She refused to explain to me why, but I'm sure we'll soon find out her reasons. She must have some. In the meantime, would you mind staying here until Kimiel wakes up? Someone has to keep an eye on her and I don't trust anyone but you at the moment. You and Bers'el, but I need him as a witness that the trial was fair."

Ekbeth nodded and put himself in the chair the Aramalinyia had just vacated. The next moment, he was alone with a sleeping Kimiel, and a tiny heart beating under his fingers. His daughter. He dared not speak, or move, but in his head, thousands of thoughts were coming and going.

Had anyone told him he was soon going to be a father, he would have laughed out loud. He had always been careful to avoid paternity. Not that he did not want children. It had just never seemed the right moment. And most of his mistresses did not want the burden either. A perfect arrangement.

How had it come to that? He knew exactly how it had happened! One hour of fun with this woman! One single hour! His worst decision ever!

Since then, his whole busy but settled life had been totally turned upside down.

Kalem almost killed. His cousin Lyrian psychically unstable. His business almost bankrupt. Duncan McLean, dead. The whole community in uproar.

And himself. Now soon to be a father.

He suddenly started laughing. Those were just too many consequences for a little slip out of his rather boring life routine. It would have been so much simpler if Kimiel had died.

He looked at the woman's face. So innocent looking. At his mercy. He could easily strangle her if he wanted to. It was tempting. No one would reproach him for the act.

Only, she was bearing his child. And the Goddess had decided she was to live.

Why had Ara let her live?

45

SOMEONE WAS HOLDING her down. Shona experienced a short moment of panic. She could not remember how she had landed in that bed or who the man snoring discreetly in the chair at her side was. She tried to move away from him. The snoring stopped. She had awakened him.

"How do you feel, Kimiel?"

She relaxed a bit, recognizing him. Ekbeth! And it came back to her. The Trial, Ara, the baby…

She immediately put a hand on her belly. Searching.

Nothing.

"Our daughter is all right, Kimiel. At least, that's what the doctors are saying."

She frowned. "A daughter? How do you know?"

"The doctors told me. And, we… connect, she and I."

She did not know what to say. The situation was a bit awkward. He probably shared her feeling, because he pushed the chair a little away from her, saying, "I'm sorry, I was not supposed to fall asleep like this, but it has been a long day for me…"

"Where am I?'

"In the Na Saoilcheachs' house. Our hospital. They brought you here after you survived the Trial."

She looked at him with a half smile. "You sound angry, Ekbeth."

He nodded. "You were supposed to die during that trial, Kimiel."

Oh, he hated her, alright. She stretched her legs cautiously. "Well, sorry, but I did not die. Your Goddess had other plans for me. She decided to spare me because of this baby, mainly."

He scowled. He looked really ferocious when he scowled. "Did you know you were pregnant before the trial, Kimiel?"

Her scowl probably matched his, she was so indignant. "What do you take me for, Ekbeth? Do you really think I would have let anyone pour that liquid into me if that was the case? Of course I did not know!"

"You fought the Caller all the way to the temple, Kimiel!"

"Because I did not want to be tried at all! But believe me, no one would have poured anything in me if I had known! I would have told everyone about the baby!"

Clearly, he did not believe her. "You're… what? almost four months pregnant? Surely you've noticed."

She looked at him gravely. "Ekbeth. Believe me. This tiny girl inside me is as important to me as to you. Maybe even more. Some doctors told me three years ago that they had me sterilized. And another confirmed it later. I had indeed all the symptoms, morning sickness and all, but never considered that diagnosis because it was just impossible. Now would you care to explain to me how this miracle has happened?"

His face relaxed a bit. "I don't know. You could ask one of the Na Saoilcheachs. They are the doctors."

Mmh. Not very helpful.

She stretched her legs again. Yawned. Ekbeth was not ready to hear the great news yet, she decided. He was mad at her, and probably still getting over the news of the baby. She decided she would inform him later about Ara's will.

"So, the bad girl has survived," she said. "What happens next?"

He was obviously doing his best to keep his expression neutral. "Nothing. You're free to go."

Good! She was going to go back to the Castle, then, and further her plans to get Toshio out of jail!

She tried to leave the bed. Her head spun when she sat, but she had expected it. Give it a moment, and she should be able to stand.

"What are you doing, Kimiel?"

"You told me I'm free to go, Ekbeth. I'm leaving."

She realized she was not wearing anything. "Where can I find some clothes, Ekbeth?"

"But…"

She tried to stand. She was not going to listen to his arguments. But as soon as she managed to get on her feet, a terrible pain racked her whole body, but mostly around her stomach, forcing her down again. It was so painful that she could not breathe. It was the trial all over again!

"Kimiel! Don't fight it! Breathe! Damn it!"

She vaguely heard a door open, then some shouts. Hands made her lie down again. More shouts. Pain on her face. Someone was slapping her!

She managed to get hold of that person's hand. Then she

squeezed. Hard! She felt how the bones crushed under her fingers… Her lower back erupted in pain.

You promised!

That pain and the voice in her head took her out of her panic attack. She released the hand. Opened her eyes. Met the face of a furious woman with long violet hair, who was holding her wrist as if it had just been broken.

"Next time, Kimiel, I will give you some sedative! I don't care if you're allergic to them or not!"

Shona closed her eyes again. Damn! She had botched it again!

"I'm sorry! I don't know what happened."

The woman was still furious but she explained, "You need to lie down for at least two more days. You may have survived the trial, but Ara's water is still in your body. If we believe the survivors' tales in the Chronicles, it takes about forty-eight hours to be completely eliminated. In the meantime, the best you can do is stay in bed. Moving increases the elimination speed, but with the accompanying pain."

Two days trapped here!

She reopened her eyes and searched for Ekbeth. He was not far away.

"I'm not so free to go, it would seem."

He shook his head. "You did not let me explain."

"Can someone at least send a message to Jeffrey Matheson, Ekbeth? Tell him that I'm alive?"

Ekbeth nodded. "I'll get a message to Matheson. If you give me his number. Now, you rest."

"Wait a minute before you do that, Kimiel Keh Niriel. Akeneires'el? Thank you for keeping watch over Kimiel. If you don't mind, I need to talk to this woman in private."

Shona did not recognize the man's voice. She was fast falling asleep, but made an effort to stay awake. The fattest man she'd ever seen in her life came into view. Her instinct made her move away from him. His weird hair, violet, showing in tufts here and there on his skull, did nothing to make her feel more comfortable.

He smiled at her. "Don't be afraid of me, Kimiel. I only want to have a little discussion with you. And hopefully help."

She managed to utter, "Who are you?"

"Bers'el na Saoilcheach. The poisons expert of the Valley. Now, I happened to hear my cousin Kes'alri saying that you are allergic to sedatives, and that interests me enormously. I like challenges, you see. Would you mind if I conduct some experiments?"

"Experiments" was a word she had learned to loathe. And she suddenly realized that what he had in his hand was a syringe. She hissed, "You're not injecting anything in my blood, bastard."

His smile did not waver at the insult. "Oh. I was not thinking of injecting anything into you. More like taking a blood sample. It should be enough for my studies."

"What do you want to study exactly?"

"How your blood reacts to sedatives. Maybe there's one you're not allergic to."

"I just heard my body is still full of that green poison. Wouldn't it be better to wait until it is gone?"

He shook his head. "I know how to distinguish Ara's water from the rest. A few shakes of the tube normally do the trick."

She still did not trust him. But what harm could a small

donation of blood do? She opened her hand. "Give me that syringe."

He did not ask why. Just handed it over.

Now, Shona had to think. Her veins were not in as bad a state as twelve years ago, but some of them were still pretty much dead. She studied her left arm for a moment, and finally located a vein near her armpit.

Bers'el had a funny expression on his face when she gave him back the full syringe.

"You're using drugs?"

She closed her eyes.

"Kimiel. I'm not going to tell anyone, I swear. But I need to know, for the experiments."

She opened her eyes again. "I was using, Bers'el. Heroin. More or less for fifteen years. But that's some time ago now. Happy?"

He shook his head. "Is this the reason you're allergic to sedatives?"

"No. Drugs have fucked up my body for sure. But dust is not why I'm allergic."

He hesitated, but finally asked something that took her by surprise. "It is true then? That some mad scientist used you as a guinea pig, Kimiel?"

She looked at him for a long time, wondering how he knew this. Finally she asked,

"What gave you this idea?"

"I told you I'm the poison expert here, Kimiel. I am interested in everything related to poisons. Sometimes I talk to our ancestors, the Ke'As'mirin. They can't keep their mouths shut if you know how to flatter them. They told me a bit about you. I know not all the testing on the Other Side is conducted in an ethical way. Especially in Asia, where you apparently lived for some time. I heard of a lab in Thailand, for example. It was closed down two years ago, but I managed to get some reports of their experiments."

She should be afraid, she thought. She was far too weak to fight such an enormous man if he wanted to kill her.

He only patted her arm. "Your secret is safe with me, Kimiel. Between you and me, I never approved of experiments on human beings. Certainly not the way those developers were conducting them."

He left her on those words. Alone, at last.

She did not feel like sleeping anymore now.

This conversation had brought back too many bad memories.

46

EKBETH ASKED NUKRI to transfer him back to his house in Zurich. He hoped to tackle a few urgent tasks before returning to the Valley. He did not feel like working, but if it kept his mind off everything else…

He needed to make some decisions about Kimiel and the baby. But not now. Not when he was still so confused.

Unfortunately, Lyrian was waiting for him. "And? Did she suffer a lot before she died?"

Ekbeth had hoped this conversation would happen later. He shook his head.

Lyrian frowned. "No? You mean she did not suffer?"

"I mean she did not die, Lyrian."

Lyrian exploded. "What?"

Ekbeth put his hand on his cousin's shoulder. "No need to shout. It came to us as a surprise as well. But Ara has decided to let her live, and there's nothing we can do about it."

Lyrian took a step back, out of Ekbeth's grasp, and started pacing the study.

"Nothing? We can kill her when she's back on this side!"

"Lyrian! Ara's trial was her punishment. She survived it. We have to accept it!"

Lyrian stopped pacing and looked at Ekbeth with suspicious eyes. "You're hiding something from me, Cousin. There's more. You wanted that bitch dead as much as I did."

Ekbeth had no subtle way to disclose the news. He sighed. "We discovered during the trial that she's pregnant. And that I'm the baby's father."

That surely silenced Lyrian for a good minute. All he managed to utter was,

"Pregnant?"

Ekbeth nodded. "Certainly puts things in perspective, don't you think?"

Lyrian was puzzled. "Why are you so certain that you are the father? She probably has slept with tons of guys in the meantime!"

Ekbeth just shook his head. "The baby reacted badly at the trial, as you can imagine. It screamed, mentally, loudly. I was the only one to hear it. Then, later, I put my hand on Kimiel's belly and the baby immediately quieted. Is that not evidence enough?"

Lyrian finally whispered. "So what happens now?"

Ekbeth shrugged. "I don't know."

A discreet cough behind him made him realize that Lyrian and he were not the only ones present in the room. He turned around, and frowned.

A very old As'mir woman was sitting in his favorite chair. He knew she was As'mir from her clothes. And that she was very old because of the wrinkles on her face, and the whiteness of her hair, which was probably long but was now assembled in a complicated knot on the top of her head. He was not sure of her eye color, as the light in the room was dim, but he could have sworn they were green. Like his. And Lyrian's.

He had never met the woman before.

"Has anyone ever told you that staring at people is very rude, Ekbeth?"

Ekbeth got over his surprise and bowed to her. "Please accept my apologies if I've offended you. I was a bit surprised to find you here, as no one warned me I had a visitor."

She smiled, if a bit coldly, looking at Lyrian. "Your cousin told me it would be a good idea to surprise you."

Ekbeth realized something was going on between those two. It was not like Lyrian to keep a guest unannounced. And Lyrian looked ill at ease when he introduced their guest. "Cousin, please meet Keremli Yamal na Duibhne."

Ekbeth searched his memory, but could not remember ever having heard her name before. And the only Yamal he knew was…

He finally realized who she was! "You're the banished Akeneires'eli! My… let me see…"

She nodded. "Great-great-grandmother! As well as to this stupid cousin of yours. And before you start trying to guess my age, just think that I'm just a tad younger than the current Aramalinyia, who used to be my best friend."

Ekbeth had to sit on this. "I didn't know you were still alive, Keremli."

She shrugged. "I technically became dead the day the Na Duibhnes' council banished me from the Valley."

He had to ask. "What did you do to get this punishment?"

She laughed, unexpectedly. "I was fed up with my life, many times grandson of mine. Bad wedding as well. One day, I just decided to leave all my obligations behind me and do what I always wanted to do: discover what was behind the Veil."

Ekbeth was puzzled. "You were banished for that?"

She nodded, gravely. "It's all about circumstances, Ekbeth. I left a small baby behind. This is not really well looked upon in our community. I also took a good portion of the family fortune with me, including the Kadj'dur."

Ekbeth had to smile. "I see. I wonder what made the balance tip: the baby or the money. But now I finally know how we lost the Kadj'dur. I must admit I've always wondered about this."

She shook her head. "It was never lost. Not entirely. I spent all the money over the years. It has been a long and very interesting life, one I'm most happy with. But I never lost the Kadj'dur. I always planned to use it to be accepted again in the Valley at some point of time. When I felt it was time."

Ekbeth had to ask, "So, what happened?"

Keremli glared at Lyrian. "What happened is that I put my trust in this cousin of yours! Six years ago, I met him and he promised to help me. He was supposed to ask you to lift the banishment. Allow me to reintegrate into the community. Ask you and the Aramalinyia. I gave him the Kadj'dur, and what did he do with it? Pretended he had found it in a flea market! Used it as a wedding ring for his wife! And ignored me! Kept me at distance from his home!"

Ekbeth looked at his cousin. He did not need to ask if this story was true. Lyrian's face was telling it. And he did not need to ask why either. He knew how frustrated Lyrian had always been about his half As'mir status. Lyrian was allowed to visit the Valley, but the Na Duibhnes family never welcomed him as a full member of the community.

Finding the Kadj'dur again had certainly help improve his status. And Ekbeth had actually allowed Lyrian to use it as his wedding ring. No matter how much anger this had brought from their uncles, because that little ring was the wedding ring of the Akeneires'el of the Na Duibhnes' wife, and had been made and offered to Nefer Keh Jariel.

Some recent events were suddenly making sense.

Ekbeth looked at Keremli, and then at Lyrian, accusing him, "You lied to me. You knew all along Keremli was behind this, Lyrian! Why did you not tell me?"

Lyrian paled and took a step back. "I only discovered the truth when Kimiel kidnapped me to take the Kadj'dur from me, Ekbeth."

He bowed his head. "I'm sorry. I could not tell you about it without telling the whole story. And it did not matter in the end. You found Kimiel without me telling everything."

Ekbeth got control on his anger. He would deal with Lyrian later. He turned to Keremli. "So, Keremli, you are the one who asked Kimiel to give that letter to the Aramalinyia and to steal the Kadj'dur from my cousin?"

She answered this by a question of her own. "Is Kimiel Shona's As'mir name?"

"Yes. Kimiel Malcolm Keh Niriel."

That visibly puzzled the old woman. "Most peculiar name. I understand now why she refused to tell it to me."

"You're not denying you're behind all this, then?"

She startled, and then focused her attention on him again. "What? Oh, of course I'm behind this. See, I had no choice! I want to go back to the Valley."

"You could have come to me directly, Keremli. There was no need to involve someone like her in this."

Keremli did look a bit sheepish at that. "Call it pride, or

whatever, Ekbeth, but I did not want to come to you empty handed. Also, I wanted to help Shona."

"Help? Lyrian fumed. "Does this bitch need any help? She tortured me! She stole from Ekbeth! She almost killed Kalem! If someone needs help here, it's us! Certainly not her."

Keremli's first reaction to Lyrian's tirade was to purse her lips. "I do admit that her methods do not always agree with me. But she does get results. She got that letter to the Aramalinyia and got the Kadj'dur back to me. And it did help her. She's now more the woman she used to be than she was four months ago."

"I curse your decision, Keremli! She tortured me!"

"Well, you deserved far worse for cheating me, grandson!"

Keremli and Lyrian were glaring furiously at each other. Ekbeth was starting to develop a serious headache. "Enough. So, Keremli, if I understood correctly, you want to return to the Valley. I suppose that letter to the Aramalinyia was to ask her permission?"

Keremli nodded. "And to ask her to reintegrate Shona in the community as well. Though that may not have been my brightest idea, I admit. The girl did not want to go, and I should have known better than to trick her into it."

Ekbeth could only agree with that. "The Aramalinyia is on your side apparently. She refused to reveal your identity when we asked who had written the letter. Do you only need my agreement to return to the Valley?"

"Yes. I was only banished by the Na Duibhnes' family, not the High Council."

Ekbeth pondered the news for a moment. To Keremli's irritation.

"Do I need to go on my knees and beg, grandson? I am

an old woman who just wants to finish her days where she was born. I won't be any trouble. I promise."

Ekbeth allowed himself a thin smile. "I certainly hope so. I've had enough trouble from you and your little protégée for the rest of my life."

He sighed. "I want the Na Duibhnes council's authorization before allowing you to come back. It should not take much time, and I have all reasons to think the result will be positive. And no, I won't tell them about Lyrian's or Kimiel's involvement in your return. Things are a bit hot around Kimiel right now. You really don't want to be associated with her. So I won't link you to the return of the Kadj'dur either. But I would very much appreciate if you could give it back to me."

Keremli's eyes narrowed. "Why? Still planning to wed Shona? I must warn you…"

Ekbeth shook his head. "I had enough warnings about her already, Keremli. No need to add to the already long list. Marrying her is off that list for sure. I just want the ring in a safe place."

She looked at him for a long time, and finally nodded.

As it was, she had the Kadj'dur with her. She unfolded her large coat, extracted a small box from one of its numerous pockets and handed it to Ekbeth.

He opened the box. Only a few inches of jade, but so much beauty. So much trouble.

He resolutely closed the box and looked at his ancestor. "Welcome back, Keremli."

47

SHONA WAS PLAYING with the oracle jade pebble. Jeffrey had received her message and sent some belongings when he had heard that she was not to return for a few days. The pebble had been among them. She had no doubt the Goddess had arranged for the little stone to come into her hands again. A not so subtle reminder of her promises.

Shona had lost her faith a long time ago. The god her brother served on the Other Side did not agree with her. Trusting someone blindly, even God, did not agree with her. Her trust had been betrayed too many times. She had learned to rely only on her own strength.

This Ara, though—Shona could not deny her existence, not after what had happened during her trial. It was easy to discount her experience as hallucination. But her lower back was still glowing warm, and that was not merely her imagination. She could feel the heat every time she put her hand on her back.

Shona had to get used to the whole idea of a constant presence watching over her. A Goddess who was not all about forgiveness and turn the other cheek.

Shona rolled the little jade stone from one hand to the other. She had promised to marry Ekbeth. The idea only brought up so many conflicting emotions in her. Grief, anger, pain… fear, mostly.

She was not ready for it. And neither was Ekbeth. He had not been ready prior to her spectacular escape out of Kse'Annilis. Her hurting of people he cared for had not helped improve his frame of mind. He had made that clear enough during their short conversation yesterday.

She sighed. What was she going to do about Ekbeth?

The door of her room opened but she did not care to look up. Many people had visited her in the past hours. But, most of the time, they just looked at her then went away. Some of them were so bold as to approach and touch her. But not one of them was talking to her.

She knew what was happening. The community wanted to make certain they had not been dreaming. That she truly was still alive. Maybe some of them wanted to say something, but there was always a guard in the room—apparently enough to prevent any hostile comments on her having survived the trial.

Now, about Ekbeth, maybe if she considered this as another mission… If it did not involve emotions…

"Are you going to ignore us much longer, Kimiel?"

Oops. That was no casual visitor. She looked up and greeted her visitors. Andrew was frowning. Sarah-Lysliana was smiling. Two more people she had to make amends to as well, she thought.

Sarah-Lysliana crossed the room and sat next to her. "How are you, Kimiel?"

Her cousin's concern sounded real. Not something

Shona would have expected. She shrugged. "I had better days, but then I'm still alive. Can't complain. I heard Duncan is dead. Is it true?"

Andrew nodded, then he growled, "Do you care to hear how it happened?"

Shona was not going let his rancor affect her. "Actually yes. Take a seat, please. I have a feeling this is going to take time."

Andrew ignored the sarcasm, but he did set himself down on a chair. He told her about what had happened after she had so spectacularly transferred herself out of the Valley. The mob. The attack on the McLeans. Duncan's death. Their injuries. And how her favorite aunt Fiona was now bound to a wheelchair for the rest of life.

Her cousin concluded, "And this all happened because of you!"

My, there was so much venom in his voice. She was not sure how to respond, but, apparently, he was not expecting any justification from her.

He nodded somberly. "We had a family council this morning. We are here to inform you that, since the Goddess has decided to spare you, the least we could do was to open our house again to you. Our grandfather was not very welcoming during your last stay. I am the Akeneires'el now, and I say this: you will be welcome under the McLeans' roof, wherever they are, Kimiel Keh Niriel. Here in Kse'Annilis or on the Island, on the Other Side."

Shona kept silent. She had wanted to hear those words so often in the past, so very often. She had cried bitter tears about it. Now... it just seemed too late. But it was a generous offer from the McLeans, especially considering the recent events. She was not going to tell them to go to hell.

Her voice was shivering a bit when she finally answered, "Thanks. Aren't the Island ghosts going to be angry?"

Andrew cracked a tiny smile at that. "Oh, they are angry. We just ignore them. We have extended the invitation to your mother and your siblings, by the way. We think it is time to put a stop to that feud. For good."

Shona nodded, but her mind was somewhere else. On the McLeans' Island to be precise. She could not wait to go back to her early childhood place again.

"Is it true your baby is Ekbeth's?"

Shona snapped out of her thoughts. Looked warily at her cousin. "Yes, and I'm glad he apparently accepts that fact."

Andrew scowled. "For someone so bent on not marrying the man, Kimiel, it was not a very clever move."

"There was no calculation on my part. I never expected a quick hour of sex to result in a baby, Andrew. No matter how good it was. Marriage was certainly not on my mind at the time."

As she spoke, she was very conscious of the jade pebble in her hand. She did not want to discuss this any further. This was, for now at least, a private matter between Ekbeth and her.

Andrew sensed this and soon after took his leave, but his sister stayed. Sarah-Lysliana had questions of her own. "Why did you have to torture Lyrian, Kimiel? The rest, I can more or less find excuses for, but why the torture?"

My, was she going to have to justify all her acts, to everyone, thought Shona?

"I needed the Kadj'dur and I was running out of time."

Sarah-Lysliana paled a bit. "You make it sound like it is nothing to you. Lyrian was deeply hurt, you know. He'll never get over it."

Then he should not have tried to play the hero, was Shona's first thought. But this was not only about Sarah-Lysliana's ex-husband, she realized. Sarah-Lysliana was trying to understand *her*.

She met her cousin's gaze and said, "I don't enjoy hurting people, Sarah-Lysliana. I really don't. I always save hurting as a last resort. This does not make me better than anyone else. I'm not better. When necessary, I don't hesitate and, yes, I've killed people. Not only in self-defense. Sometimes, you don't have a choice. Some people only understand violence as an answer. I was in a hurry but I gave Farrill fair warning. The man should not have been stubborn. I hope this has taught him something and he won't play the same stupid game if he ever finds himself in the same situation again."

She stretched. Damn, she could not wait to be able to escape the place.

"Why do you care about Lyrian's fate anyway, Sally? You should be glad I made him feel what pain meant in the hand of someone else. I know he's mistreated you."

Her cousin shook her head. "He never meant it. Lyrian has always been all extreme reactions. He loved me with a passion. I was his world. How many women can claim to be so lucky in their wedding? I hurt him when I told him I wanted a divorce. All because I was not brave enough to tell him that I'd discovered I was a McLean and that I was afraid of his family's reaction. I should have explained. Together, we would have found a solution. It was stupid of me."

Shona grabbed her cousin by the shoulders. Her back

immediately started hurting, but it was bearable… She ignored the movements in her belly. Shook her cousin instead. "You are indeed stupid! Don't blame yourself for his brutality! Stop this! He almost killed you, Sally! If that's his way to prove his love to you, he doesn't deserve it!"

Sarah-Lysliana paled. Damn, Shona had never been good at this. She let go of Sarah-Lysliana.

"Sorry. It's just… I've heard your story so often, Sally. The excuses. I just can't stand it."

Sarah-Lysliana somehow managed a smile. "You're right. I know. I'm sorry. And I didn't want to discuss Lyrian with you in the first place! I wanted to ask you to help with my next album."

Shona went very still. Sarah-Lysliana did not noticed it. "I found a picture of you some time ago while cleaning Aunt Fiona's bedroom. You, with a guitar, on a podium. And I remembered how well you managed with our choir attempt. I was intrigued, so I asked Aunt Fiona about it."

She looked at Shona with bright eyes. "She told me about your songwriting. I asked your mother about it as well. She told me you had destroyed most of what you ever created, but she still had one single memory. A tape. She refused to let me take it with me, but I was allowed to listen. Shona! You have so much talent! I already knew that when we were rehearsing that choir song together, of course, but I had no idea you were that good with songwriting as well. You have to help me with my album! Please."

Shona's mind was blank. Curse that woman and her nosiness! Couldn't she understand how much pain she was causing by asking that? Sarah-Lysliana apparently realized something was wrong with Shona, because she suddenly put a safe distance between them, visibly frightened.

"Kimiel! It's all right if you don't want to! I understand."

Shona bared her teeth. The bitch understood? Of course not! No one could understand! But before she could answer, her lower back started hurting like hell.

Stop that.

That made Shona pause. Realize what she was doing. Her cousin was no enemy! Not trying to kill her! Just asking for her help! Politely! Shona forced a smile on her lips, and tried to sound unemotional when she said, "See! I'm mad at you but I'm not hurting you. That's the difference between me and Lyrian."

She inhaled deeply. "Sorry for this, Sarah-Lysliana. Your offer took me by surprise. Give me time to think this over, please."

Her cousin left the room in a hurry, without even saying goodbye.

Is this how you keep your promises, child?

Shona told the Goddess to shut up. She hated this place. It only brought out the worst in her. If she stayed any longer, she was definitely going to get crazy. One more day… One more day and she would be allowed to leave Kse'Annilis. And to hell with her promises!

Shona hurled the jade pebble against a wall.

48

EKBETH WAS ANGRY with himself. He needed to discuss some things with Kimiel—about their unborn daughter, mainly—but his agenda had been so full the past two days, he had not managed to find even half an hour to talk to her.

He gritted his teeth. No doubt she had left the Valley. He had forgotten to ask Nukri about it when he had arrived, but he remembered her reaction when he had told her she was free to go, back at the Na Saoilcheachs' house.

He could not blame her for leaving without even saying goodbye. After what she had been put through from the moment she had set foot in Kse'Annilis, she probably did not want to come to the Valley ever again, or see him.

That was going to be a problem. He could always send her some messages through Nukri, he thought. Or call Matheson, now that he had Kimiel's friend's phone number.

He entered his apartment in Kse'Annilis and walked to his bedroom. No servants were expecting him. It was awfully late, but he had had meetings in Los Angeles the whole day. If not for the budget discussions with the Na Dearghs tomorrow morning, he would have stayed on the Other Side.

He looked at the water clock embedded in the main room of his suite and winced.

Very late. This was going to be a short night. Ekbeth entered the bedroom and saw her immediately. Kimiel was not on the Other Side after all. She was still in Kse'Annilis. Actually fast asleep on his own bed. He observed her silently.

Someone had put a blanket on her, but she had to be a fretful sleeper because most of it was pushed away from her, showing most of her body, luckily covered in an As'mir dress. She must have been waiting for him, he realized, and finally fell asleep.

No matter the disarray around her, she really looked so peaceful, almost angelic, when asleep. He could almost forget how much trouble she had brought him when he saw her like this. She mumbled something in her sleep and turned on one side. Her fists started closing and opening, as if she was trying to grab something.

He decided against waking her. He was too tired for a conversation or anything else, and the bed was large enough for the both of them. He undressed quickly and put himself between the bed sheets, at a good distance from her. For all his defaults, Ekbeth's father had ordered a bed large enough to contain all his "wives" and himself in his later years. None of his sons had ever changed it. It was a monstrosity, for sure, but the Akeneires'el's bedroom was so large that the bed somehow fit perfectly.

Ekbeth rarely slept here, preferring his places in the Other Side. Closing his eyes and trying to relax, he reflected that he actually never had brought any women here either. Wrong place…

"Where were you, Ekbeth? I've been waiting for you for ages."

Kimiel. Her voice was still full of sleep, but she crept towards him and poked him.

He mumbled, refusing to open his eyes. "Busy. I have a meeting in less than four hours, Kimiel. I really need the sleep."

She clicked her tongue disapprovingly. "Then you should have come home earlier. I really need to know. How mad at me are you?"

Damn the woman! He opened his eyes and looked at her, though it was difficult to read her expression in the dark room. "What do you mean?"

Her face was just inches from his. "For all I've done before you found me. How mad are you? Do you want to strangle me, Ekbeth? Reduce me to pulp with your fists? Pour some poison in my mouth and watch me slowly die in front of you?"

He grunted, "Right now, all of this… Don't tempt me. I know you have a death wish, but I won't help you end your life."

She paused, and then asked softly, "Ah. Why not?"

He yawned and turned his back on her. She did not poke him this time. She just put her hand between the sheets around him and started caressing him. That certainly got his attention. He growled at her, "I really need the sleep, Kimiel."

He could hear the amusement in her answer. "The faster you answer, the faster I'll be gone."

The woman was impossible. Disengaging himself from her, he sat and clapped his hands. A dim light appeared. She looked around her, seeming impressed. "Nice trick. Another lost technology from our ancestors?"

Ekbeth nodded absently, then lay back on the bed, but he did not close his eyes. He stared at her. She looked fine, he decided. Certainly too fine for someone who had gone through Ara's trial not even two days ago. And she was waiting patiently for his answer, he realized.

He sighed. "Two reasons. First, our Goddess has judged your crimes. Harming you would mean I disagree with her."

Kimiel pursed her lips in a funny way, as if she was mocking him. "I see. She would not like that, I suppose. And the second reason?"

He put his hand on her stomach. "You're bearing our daughter. I think that baby's been put through enough already. Hurting you is hurting her. I won't do it."

She stared at him for a long time, and then said, touching him where his heart was, "Still, you hate me, inside."

He frowned. "What were you expecting? I could excuse your spectacular Call out of the Valley in the midst of Ara's celebration, but Lyrian's torture? Kalem?"

Her expression remained blank. Ekbeth suddenly got a strong suspicion. "Why do you need to know, anyway?"

She told him with a sad smile, "I have bad news, Ekbeth. The Goddess is stubborn. She still wants us to marry."

That bit of news dumbfounded him. "What?"

"You heard me."

The confirmation did not make it any easier to accept. "How do you know?"

She sighed. "She told me."

He could not believe his ears. "The Goddess told you? Ara spoke to you?"

She nodded. "I had to make plenty of promises to live, during the trial. To marry you. To behave. That sort of thing. They were not empty promises. Damn, but she's watching me! Every time I even start to have evil thoughts, my back is burning like hell."

He remembered having seen something new on her that morning at the Na Saoilcheachs' house, when she had tried to leave her bed too early after the trial.

"It's that tattoo on your back? The Goddess put it on you?"

"A tattoo? You don't mean it!"

"Can I see it?"

She froze. He realized she would need to either undress completely, or at least let him see half of her body naked to satisfy his curiosity. As'mir clothes were all in one piece, from head to feet.

He had to grin. "Timid suddenly, Kimiel?"

The taunting was enough. She returned the grin, and removed the dress in one movement, then slowly turned around to show him her back.

He tried to ignore his physical reaction. There it was. He should have paid more attention to the pattern the first time he had seen it.

"What's there, Ekbeth?"

"It's difficult to explain. I can better show you."

Dressed only in one of the bed blankets, he led her to his private bathroom. There were a few mirrors in it. She shook her head. "I never thought you were such a narcissist."

"Inherited from my father, like the bed. I have never found the time to redecorate. Do you see it now?"

"Yes. Damn! She did speak of a mark, but I never thought… It's even bigger than I feared!"

The tattoo, a complicated knot of large black lines, was indeed covering almost all the lower half of her back. And the skin was quite red around it.

"Any idea what this pattern means, Ekbeth?"

At least he could help her with that. "Yes. This sign is also in the main hall of the Aramalinyia's house. It is Ara's mark. No one is certain what it represents, except that it is hers. I suppose that the Goddess meant that you belong to her now, by putting this on you."

He had never heard of such a thing before. The Goddess marking one of her As'mirin. He would have to ask the Aramalinyia the meaning of this, he thought.

Kimiel was not happy, he could see it, but she kept her thoughts to herself this time.

She stared at her back for some time, and then turned her attention back to him.

"Do you believe me, Ekbeth? When I say she wants us to wed?"

He nodded, but immediately after, shook his head. "I can't marry you, Kimiel. Even if you're bearing my child. Even if it's Ara's will. I'm willing to help raise the child, but marrying you is asking too much."

For a second, he thought he could see some hurt in her eyes, but it faded so quickly, he was not sure. She took a step back from him. "I got it. Lyrian. Kalem."

"Not only that. I've seen the files your friend Watanabe has sent me."

Her eyes narrowed to a split. "Toshio should never have

sent you those. Out of context, you probably now think the worst of me."

"But you don't deny it. You killed all those people?"

"Toshio did not tell you why, of course. We were at war with some local triads at the time. It was them or us. I had no choice. Don't think I enjoyed it."

She seemed sincere when she added, "I never enjoyed hurting others, Ekbeth."

That hit a nerve. "Tell that to my cousin."

She shook her head. "He was stubborn. I gave him more than fair warning. He should have believed me."

Ekbeth was so angered by her obvious lack of remorse, he lashed out at her. "And your husband, then? Did you also give him fair warning before you cut his throat?"

Her face lost all color. "Who told you that?"

"Your dear friend, Watanabe. Is it true, Kimiel?"

She shook her head, whispered, "I had no choice. You weren't there. You can't understand."

She walked away from him. He understood immediately what she was about to do. He grabbed her arm. "Don't you dare transfer yourself out on me again, Kimiel! Once was enough."

He felt the Call familiar tingling, and he fought it, fought the nausea as well. He grabbed her other arm, forced her to look at him. "Walking out of situations you don't like seems one of your specialties, Kimiel, but I won't allow it. Not anymore. I'll have Nukri bringing you back here puking all over the place if needed. As you well know, forced calls are not pleasant for the called."

The tingling sensation disappeared. He released her. Her eyes were a bit too bright. Evidently, she was fighting her emotions. Not something he would have expected from her. His tone was a bit gentler when he asked, "So it's true?"

She inhaled deeply, before meeting his eyes.

"Yeshe asked me to do it. Believe me, had I had any other choice, any at all, I would have taken it. He was everything to me. You'll never understand."

Her pain was so obvious, he believed her. Some things were suddenly clearer to him as well. "You're still grieving for him? Is that why you were so dead set against marrying me?"

She only nodded.

"Why didn't you say this then? Surely the Aramalinyia…"

She shook her head. "The Aramalinyia is aware of this, Ekbeth. As is the Goddess. They just don't seem to care a lot about my feelings, or yours, for that matter."

She took another deep breath, seemed to regain some composure. "A lot has happened in the past few months, Ekbeth. As you've discovered, I was hiding from you in Bhutan. That's where my husband was from. Being there reminded me of my promise to him. I promised to go on with my life, no matter what. It's not easy. It'll never be easy. I certainly did not expect to remarry any day. That's how much I miss him."

She looked at him, with a faint smile. "But I made another promise now. The Goddess's will is clear. I'm not saying I'm happy with the news, still not, but if she wants it, I'll marry you."

Ekbeth felt suddenly exhausted. This was not the right moment to discuss this, and he needed to ponder on what he had just learned. He yawned.

Kimiel frowned. "I'm serious, Ekbeth."

"I know you are. Did the Goddess say we had to marry tonight?"

She at least smiled. "No."

Then she became thoughtful. "Actually, she did not mention anything about timing."

"Good. I'm going back to bed, if you don't mind."

She followed him out of the bathroom. "Ekbeth! Don't you see? We don't have to marry immediately. Oh, Ara is going to insist at some point of time, I'm sure, but why don't we use the time in between to learn more about each other?"

Ekbeth winced. "I already know more than enough about you."

She produced a hearty laugh at that. "Only the worst part. I have a good side as well, I promise."

Ekbeth was doubtful and did not try to hide this fact. She did not seem to mind.

He went back to bed, and, without asking, she joined him, her intentions perfectly clear.

He sighed. "Not tonight, Kimiel. I really need to sleep. And you've just been through Ara's Trial! Almost lost the baby."

She pouted. "I'm fine. Sure? I'd love to show you how good I am as a lover, Ekbeth."

The woman was really impossible. He took her hands from him and said, "Modesty is certainly not one of your qualities, I dare say. I already know you're good. I have not forgotten our time at the party."

She purred. "You haven't?"

"You certainly have done your best for me not to forget. Promise me, Kimiel. You'll never hurt any member of my family ever again."

She shook her head. "Can't do that. I'm sure Kalem, if not your cousin, is sharpening his knives to have his revenge."

"Kalem is a professional. He'll not harm you if I tell him not to. Neither will any member of my family. If they disobey, come to me, I'll take care of it."

She went silent for a moment. "You're asking a lot, Ekbeth."

"So are you…"

She relaxed a bit and said, drowsily, "I don't want to hurt anyone anymore, Ekbeth. I'll try not to."

This was not much of a promise. But it was as near an apology he would ever get from her, he realized.

Lyrian was not going to take the news quietly, thought Ekbeth. Neither would Kalem, though his bodyguard had better control his emotions. As for the rest of the family…

As the Aramalinyia said, everyone deserved a second chance. In Kimiel's case, though, it was more a third, or even a fourth chance.

He sighed, and placed his hand on her stomach until he found a small heart beating under his fingers. He was going to give her that chance.

If only for the sake of their daughter.

49

SHONA LOOKED AT Toshio from the corner of his cell, where Nukri had just transferred her. Her friend had his back to her and had not heard her arrive, as all his attention was on some paperwork in front of him.

She considered the best way to announce her presence.

"Writing your memoirs, Toshio? That must be an interesting tale."

He barely reacted. A slight straightening of his back muscles, maybe. But she had been around him for a long time. She had startled him all right.

He stopped whatever he had been doing and turned towards her. "Morning, Shona. Have you learned a new trick, or have you been walking through every wall of the jail until you could find me?"

"New trick. I had some help. Only needed to concentrate on you."

At Ekbeth's suggestion this morning, she had walked up to Nukri na Liom's house and asked the Caller about the Call talent. She had been a bit afraid he would hold a grudge against her for having tried so hard to escape the well before Ara's trial, but the old man had been obliging. She now had a much better understanding of how the transfers worked. He had also trained her to call him if she needed a transfer, and had rewarded her with a small demonstration.

That was how she now found herself in Toshio's cell. This was going to be so much fun!

And now that she was here she decided to approach Toshio with her request herself, instead of relying on Jeffrey. Her mentor looked at his watch. "I'll be called outside in thirty minutes. Fresh air time."

"It should be enough. Fresh air time! You really are pampered here. There was no such thing when I did my time."

He cracked a thin smile. "You were probably too high on dust to notice the difference."

They observed each other in silence for a moment.

Toshio had not changed that much over the years. Her last clear memory of him was almost six years old. They had met in the meantime, but she had then been too much under the influence of the experimental drugs or her treatment drugs to have a clear recollection of him.

She had never visited him in jail before. Hearing steel gates clang when being closed still gave her the jitters. It used to paralyze her. Panic her. Make her want to become invisible. Prepare for pain. Fight the urge to scream.

She had better control over her reactions, nowadays.

She was still pretty angry, however. "Why did you have to tell Ekbeth I killed Yeshe, Toshio?"

Toshio's eyes narrowed. "It was the best way to get him off your back. Why?"

"He's now thinking the worst of me!"

"And since when is what Ekbeth thinks of you

important? The man wants you dead. He doesn't care about your feelings."

"Your news is a bit old, Toshio. Since you've met him, Ekbeth found me and brought me to the Valley, and I survived their punishment. I'm not on the run anymore."

"Good, but that doesn't answer my question. Wait a second… Don't tell me they still want you to marry him!"

Shona shook her head. "They still want to, but we've both decided to disregard their decision, at least for the time being."

Toshio smiled. "That's my girl. So, why do you care?"

Shona sat on his tiny bed, careful not to show any emotion. The baby had just given a kick in her belly. As if the burning of her lower back was not already pain enough, she thought with humor.

She was not planning to tell Toshio, or Jeffrey, about her pregnancy. If he knew, he would prevent her from participating in the search for Sonam. With a bit of luck, he would not notice anything for another month, maybe two, though that would be a stretch.

She needed to set things in motion. "It's complicated, and not the reason I'm here. I've learned some amazing news in Bhutan, Toshio. Dorje survived the massacre, as you already know—and yes, I'm mad that you didn't tell me—but so has Sonam."

Toshio's brows went up. "Your son?"

"Yes. My son is alive somewhere and we need to find him. I think he's in China. You have the connections there. Help me."

After a moment of thinking, he carefully said, "Who told you this? That Sonam is alive."

She told him of her meeting with the old woman. Toshio did not seem convinced. She forced him to meet her eyes. "Toshio. You know me. I have a feeling about this. Sonam is alive."

They locked eyes for a long moment. Toshio sighed. "I see. One of your revelation moments. True, they've most of the time proven right, but there's not much I can do from here."

"You managed to ask your friends to close their accounts at Ekbeth's bank."

He shook his head. "Phone calls won't be enough for this kind of search. I need to be in China. Meet people in person."

She allowed herself a tiny smile. At least he was not fighting the idea of getting out of jail.

"Toshio, I can get you out of here in less than five seconds."

His face tensed. As much as he recognized her special abilities had their usefulness, he had always refused to go through a wall with her. So, doing a whole transfer? Plus, there would be the small problem of Interpol launching a search warrant against him.

"Alternatively, call a lawyer," Shona suggested. "Make him reopen the case. Pay someone who looks a bit like you and is ready to take your place. Fake the evidence."

"This is going to take months of preparation and procedure. I only know one way to get out of here quickly, Shona."

Of course. The art trafficking section of Interpol had been trying to get information out of him for years.

"This is definitely going to put me out of work, Shona,

and some people will be waiting for me outside, especially if I tell on them."

"I'm sure Maire won't complain about you being home more often. You can always start doing some legal work for a change. As for the enemies, you have enough protection. People will think twice before getting at you."

He looked at her, deadly serious. "Still, Shona, is it worth it? We have no concrete evidence Sonam is alive. No idea who the men who took him are. And I know you. I am not going to help you kill half of China to get your son back, Shona."

"We won't need to do that much killing."

Her lower back suddenly started burning. Damn! That Goddess indeed could track her outside of the Valley!

She added hastily, "Actually probably no killing at all. I have a plan."

"I'd really like to hear it. We are talking here of finding ten men among a few billion Chinese, Shona. If they were Chinese. Without anything specific to start on. Not even names."

"I'll explain the details of the plan once you're free. Have faith in me."

They both heard the door unlocking. She was running out of time. "Please, Toshio?"

Another tiny hesitation, then he nodded.

She asked Nukri to transfer her back to the Valley just as the cell door was opening.

She had a few other destinations on her day list. First, going back to Bhutan and Dorje. She had left his house without leaving even a note. He was probably worried. She wanted to check his memory of the attackers against hers.

They had not much to go on, indeed. Every little detail could make a difference.

She had lied to Toshio. She had no plan yet, but she had plenty of time to think of something.

Then, the Castle, the place where Jeffrey was living, to tell him the news about Toshio, and ask for his help with the plan.

Then, her gynecologist. She wanted to be sure the baby was healthy. She did not trust the As'mirin doctors. How could they be so sure of their diagnosis without scans or other modern technology?

And finally, a steak and kidney pie with mashed potatoes at the pub near Maire's apartment. She had craved that dish during her whole stay in Bhutan and she had every intention of satisfying that need as soon as possible.

My, maybe she was going to enjoy being As'mir, after all.

50

EKBETH WAS CONCENTRATING deeply on a report Lyrian was presenting on the latest developments of the Brazilian economy when Kimiel suddenly appeared in the chair next to him. Without speaking, she took his hand, put it on her belly and closed her eyes with obvious relief.

He could not help but smile. "Good morning, Kimiel."

"Morning. That little devil has been dancing the jig all night inside. Bers'el suggested I tried this before anything else."

"Not surprising if the rumors I heard about you are true. Even I don't get transferred that many times a day, Kimiel, and I'm not pregnant. You should slow things down."

She growled, "Stop the sermon now, or I just go back to the Valley. Would you please go on with whatever you were doing and ignore me?"

Ekbeth was finding the situation a bit awkward, but signaled Lyrian to continue. But his cousin obviously could not. He was scowling furiously at Kimiel and the tensed way in which his hands gripped the report document was a sure sign that he barely managed to contain his anger.

Ekbeth sighed, and called for his cousin's attention. "Lyrian?"

Kimiel opened her closed eyes and looked around her. To her credit, she did not mock Lyrian when she finally laid eyes on him. "Morning, Lyrian. I am sorry to interrupt."

Lyrian became very red in the face. A sure sign that Ekbeth had to intervene before his cousin lost control. Again. They had discussed the new situation between Ekbeth and Kimiel. The conversation had gone as badly as Ekbeth had expected, but Lyrian had finally promised he would not hurt her. However, it seemed a real struggle for him to keep his promise right now.

Ekbeth could understand and excuse Lyrian's attitude, and told him, "We can continue the presentation later today, Cousin."

Lyrian had worked long enough with him to understand the message. He stormed out of the room. Kimiel chuckled, "My! He really is mad at me, isn't he?"

"And you're finding this amusing? Are you ever going to apologize to him?"

She shook her head. Ekbeth sighed. "You apologized to me. Why not to Lyrian?"

She put her hand on his and moved it a bit to the right. "Different situation, Ekbeth. Anyway, it probably would not help. As Sarah-Lysliana has told me, your cousin is all for extremes. He'll never forgive me."

She was probably right in that, Ekbeth had to admit. He asked, "Do you ever feel remorse for what you've done?"

"Sometimes. But never for long. What's the point of torturing yourself once the act is done? It's not like you can go back and undo it! I take responsibility for my acts, Ekbeth. Always. And I don't care what others think of me!"

She then moved his hand to the left. "I'm afraid I'll have to interrupt a few of your other meetings in the future, Ekbeth. Unless you manage to tell that girl inside me that she's to listen to me as well."

The abrupt change of conversation topic told him enough. She refused to discuss her past acts any further. He decided to humor her this time.

"Can we agree on some kind of warning then? I have some very nervous customers. They would certainly not appreciate seeing you appear in the middle of our discussion like you just did."

She absently nodded. After some time, she asked, "Have you missed me, Ekbeth?"

He realized a week had gone by since their latest discussion. Oh, he had heard about her, especially of her transfers, but that was not the same.

"I'm afraid I was too busy. You'll probably be happy to know that the Family Council has lifted the banishment of my ancestor, Keremli. We'll announce it tomorrow and probably throw a small party in her honor."

She smiled. "So, you've met her?"

"Yes! The day following your trial, as it is. At last, things make sense. I'd rather that she had come to me directly with her request instead of including you in her schemes, but she's my great-great-grandmother. I suppose, I just have to accept her choices."

"Good. I'm glad, Ekbeth. Keremli has saved me. This was the very least I could do for her."

"Saved you?"

She nodded, but did not elaborate. Information about her past was not going to come from her either. He had tried Keremli, without success. Really frustrating.

Then she surprised him by asking, "So it has all been work and work. I must admit I admire your commitment, Ekbeth. Do you ever stop working?"

"Not much choice here, Kimiel. As you probably know, the tasks were split between the families after the Cataclysm. The Na Duibhnes got the finance part. Outside the Valley and on the Other Side. The Akeneires'el title also makes me responsible for the family administration. Normally, the administrative and banking functions are split. My older brother was the Akeneires'el. I was supposed to share the banking part with my other brother. Only, both of them died."

"So you really have to do everything on your own?"

He almost told her that her sending Lyrian to the hospital for a month by torturing him had not been helpful, but she had clearly stated she did not care about Lyrian. There was no point, then.

"No. I need to generate about fifty million dollars per year to cover the community costs. That's not a small amount of money. I would never be able to do this on my own. I have a whole staff working for me on both sides of the Veil. Only, no one in my family has been trained to lead the business as I have. Being in charge of the finances does not mean my family likes to bother with money. My cousin Lyrian is the only family member who is helping me with the bank, and his work now is limited to the activities on the Other Side as he is banned from the Valley."

He started putting some documents away. "I have another

meeting in half an hour, Kimiel. One you can't attend, I'm sorry."

She shrugged. "I'm feeling better already. I suppose some napping is also due. You take your responsibilities too seriously, Ekbeth. How long do you think you're going to be able to continue like this before burning out?"

He forced himself to relax. Alyasini was regularly asking the same question, and that had become very annoying over time. He did not want to start a discussion about this. He had no time anyway.

"Thanks for your concern, Kimiel, but it's not needed. I manage, so far. Or are you just concerned I won't have enough time for you?"

She shrugged. "You told me you had no time for a wife, Ekbeth. I got the message loud and clear. And, as we are not going to marry any time soon, I can't complain about your whereabouts, can I?

That made him smile, but not for long. "Correct in that. And, as we are discussing whereabouts... I don't want to pry, Kimiel, but where have you been all week?"

"I can't tell you, I'm afraid. But I'm a bit surprised, Ekbeth. Didn't Nukri tell you?"

"The Caller is bound by an oath not to reveal where he transfers people."

"Ah, don't make me laugh! I'm sure enough incentive will make him spill it."

Ekbeth shrugged. "Maybe, but I did not ask."

"Very good of you."

"So, you're not going to tell me?"

She shook her head. Just what he had feared, she was certainly up to no good again. She needed protection. He was glad he had had that decision approved by the family council already.

"Then I have some other news for you, Kimiel. From past experience, I've learned better than to trust you with your own safety. And as you are carrying my daughter…"

She looked at him suspiciously. "You're not going to restrain me to Kse'Annilis, are you, Ekbeth?"

He shook his head.

"Good, because that would have been a very bad idea!"

"I know. No, I want you to have a bodyguard at your side. One of my own family. To protect you and our baby."

She frowned. "I can take care of myself."

He met her gaze squarely.

"This is not negotiable, Kimiel. Unless you tell me what you're up to."

She was furious, he could feel it, but she kept her thoughts to herself. "If the bodyguard tells you about my whereabouts, I'll kill him!"

Next, she was hissing with pain. It worried him, until he saw her put her hands to her lower back. Ah. The Goddess. Shona managed a loud curse, but that was the extent of her anger at the Goddess's reaction to her threats. The pain only started subsiding after she'd loudly promised she would not kill anyone.

Ekbeth tried not to smile, but Shona could easily read his mood. "It's not funny, Ekbeth. But see…" Kimiel gestured to her back. "I have a bodyguard already."

"Is this happening often?"

"Often enough. She takes all my words a bit too seriously."

"Good. Unfortunately, I can't trust the Goddess with this, Kimiel. Not entirely. It's all approved already. Najeb has volunteered. I don't want you to go anywhere without him from now on. If you try to leave without him, or lose him, Nukri will just transfer him to you again."

She looked surprised. "Najeb? Kalem's son?"

"He's not going to put a knife in your back, don't worry. And he's not going to tell me anything about the places you are going, because he's going to swear an oath to protect you, and protecting also involves not talking."

She was still not happy about the idea, as her expression made clear, but after some time, she nodded. "Good, then. When does this start?"

He had not expected the news to be accepted so quickly. She probably was already planning ways to bypass his idea.

He quickly looked at his agenda. "Are you going to rest all the afternoon?"

"Probably."

"Then we could meet at the end of the day. And what about having dinner together?"

She smiled. "Your people are going to gossip, Ekbeth."

"*Our* people are gossiping already, Kimiel. Ignore them."

She stood. "See you later then. I hope that bodyguarding does not extend to your bedroom Ekbeth… or you're going to be very sorry. I don't like public exhibition."

She disappeared out of the room before he could find a good answer. Ekbeth was still chuckling while he walked to his next meeting. That woman was driving him crazy.

He sobered. His next customer was a recently widowed woman. Not that the woman had had much love for her deceased drug baron husband, but they had to keep pretenses. Chuckling was not appropriate.

He inhaled deeply and opened the meeting room door.

51

"HURRY UP, NAJEB! We are late!"

"That's because you woke up so late, Kimiel, and you forgot to tell me we were going somewhere today. Again! I've spent the whole morning in the drains under the Na Dearghs' house. I need to shower."

"Hurry, then! No need to be so smart this early in the morning!"

"It's already one o'clock!" retorted Najeb as he headed for the shower.

"Just shut up and hurry, all right? Otherwise I'll leave without you!"

Her bodyguard ignored her threat, and whistled nonchalantly under the running water. He very well knew that Nukri would refuse to transfer her outside the Valley without him. The Aramalinyia's orders.

She was still mad about that last bit, but she could only blame herself for it. She had promised Ekbeth not to go anywhere without Najeb. And she had regularly forgotten about that promise in the past days. Oath or not, Najeb had complained to Ekbeth.

Ekbeth had at first been angry with her. Understanding

that she had no intention of changing her ways, he had taken a more drastic step. He had gone to the Aramalinyia and asked for her help.

Arguing that she was not cautious enough and that she needed someone to watch over her and her unborn baby had been enough. As'mirin apparently cared a lot about babies. Not something Shona would ever complain about, but in her specific case, she found the extra protection annoying.

Najeb was following her everywhere. And, as Ekbeth had warned her would happen, the few times she had managed to shake him off, he was back at her side less than a minute later. He only left her on her own when she was in the Valley. And that was because he knew the rest of the community was taking over his job of watching out for her.

Very annoying.

Shona heard the shower stop for a minute, but then it started again. Damn Najeb!

She looked around her. It was actually the first time she visited Najeb's place in the Na Duibhnes' house. It was really neat. Something she would have expected from Kalem's son. What was quite surprising, though, was the quantity of human-written books he had, and the drawings and post-cards glued on his walls. Books, postcards, drawings—all about some architectural wonders, ancient and recent.

She was studying a particularly mysterious drawing that filled half of one wall when Najeb finally came out of the bathroom, thankfully fully clothed and ready to go.

"What is that, Najeb?"

"Oh. I tried to draw Kse'Annilis water and sewage systems. It's quite useful when something stops function-ing somewhere."

Hmm. Probably not something his father was aware of.

Then she noticed the small picture under the map. "You should hide this better, Najeb."

He shook his head. "Her father will never come here."

Shona's relationship with Najeb was tumultuous, to say the least, but in the past days, she had heard of his love for the eldest daughter of the Akeneires'el of the Na Liathes—a girl so far up in the complex community hierarchy that Najeb had not even a remote chance of being allowed to talk to her, at least in theory. However, As'leandra seemed to return Najeb's love—something that probably made them both very unhappy.

Shona had met the girl a few times already, but she was avoiding As'leandra Na Liathe whenever she could. The girl had a bad reputation as well. Not for the same reason as Shona, but she preferred keeping her distance just in case the tales she had heard were true.

She looked at her watch. "Damn! We are a full hour late! They have certainly started without us by now!"

She called Nukri na Liom. The next minute, they found themselves in her own bedroom, in the Castle. They hurried to the main reception room. The Castle was not that big, but the architect had built it with so many odd corridors and stairways that it seemed enormous.

"Toshio! I'm sorry… "

Her friend was in deep discussion with Jeffrey and his men, but immediately came to embrace her when she entered the room.

"No need to hurry. We received a message warning us you may be late. We would have waited for you, anyway.

After all, it's all because of your so-called plan that we are here!"

She had sent no message. She glared at Najeb, who managed to keep a straight face. Oh yes, they both could play that little game of annoying each other, when needed.

She smiled at her friend. "I'm glad to have you back here! It was not the same without you… even though Jeffrey and Maire were doing their best!"

He smiled and touched her brow with his lips. "Now, that's not fair for them. I think they've done more than their best for you."

He let her go, and turned his attention towards Najeb. "So, this is the man Jeffrey told me about? Your new bodyguard? I've seen you before."

Najeb bowed slightly. "I was with Ekbeth na Duibhne when he visited you at the jail."

"Oh yes. I remember now. Well, I'm not going to complain that someone is helping us with the job of keeping you under control, Shona. It is a tiring business."

She ignored the comment. "Shall we start?"

Toshio smiled, amused by her attempt at changing the topic of conversation, and nodded his agreement. "We are all curious about your plan, Shona. Gentlemen!"

They all took their place around the long meeting table, Toshio and Shona facing each other. She was very conscious of all the eyes looking at her. She did not mind. She was quite used to getting the crowd's attention, and at least the present group was a friendly one.

Toshio looked around the table, then nodded at her. "So, Shona. You think your son is alive somewhere. You want him back. You told me you have a plan."

He was really not going to make this easy for her. Thankfully, she had a plan of a sort by now. She closed her eyes and when she reopened them ten boxes were stacked along the full length of the table.

No one in the room moved. Too much of Toshio's influence, they had all learned to keep their emotions to themselves. This Calling of objects was a new trick for her—well, to be fair, with a bit of help from Nukri the Caller, but all the people in attendance there had been around her at some point in time and had long accepted that she was able to do weird stuff.

She put a hand on one of the boxes and looked at Toshio, facing her. "These boxes contain all the paperwork of the pharmaceutical company you saved me from. Everything. Printouts of emails, personal diaries of the managers, all administrative records for the last four years before you put an end to their business. Everything."

That certainly got everyone's attention.

Toshio just raised one eyebrow. "How did you manage to get those? I would have expected these documents to be destroyed when we blew up the laboratory."

"What was destroyed were the official records, Toshio. What's in those boxes is the real documentation of the business. It seems huge amounts of money were going in and out this company that nobody wished to be traced, but the owners did keep track of the transactions, maybe with the idea of covering their asses. For that reason, as well, it was not kept in the laboratory. We can thank a clever intermediary Jeffrey found for me for this. The man went to the owners' families. I would have been happy with them allowing us to have a look into the company bank statements, but this is, of course, much better. The families were most cooperative, in the end. I paid whatever money they wanted. Anyway, I hope we can find who got paid for handing me over to them as a guinea pig, because I can't imagine the bastard did not get any money for that."

She uttered those words quietly. Yet resolutely.

"I am convinced there is one person at the center of everything, Toshio. Someone who arranged for the mercenaries to attack my family in Bhutan, who arranged for me to be kept in a Chinese jail for a few months without raising suspicion, and then sold me to the Thai company. I can't imagine that there was more than one decision-maker involved in this."

Toshio frowned. "So, you abandoned your idea that Kellerman is behind this?"

She gritted her teeth. "No. I know he's the one ultimately responsible for everything. You don't believe me, but he was there in that Chinese jail, helping with the interrogations. That fact, and the White Lady, confirms it. Kellerman is behind all this sad business. But, as you've proven to me again and again, we cannot link Kellerman to this Thai Pharmaceutical Company. And I can't imagine him ordering soldiers around. Not refined enough for him. He must have asked someone to solve this for him. For money, or a favor… but no more than one person. The less intermediaries, the safer his secret."

She placed her hand once more on the box. "And this here will help us track the intermediary, and hopefully we'll be able to track the whole chain back to my son from that person."

She saw the glint in Toshio's eyes. She forced a smile on

her lips. "And yes, I hope this will help prove I'm right about Kellerman, as well. But my first priority is Sonam."

She had made her speech. She had to wait for his decision now.

Toshio took his time, but finally nodded. "Good reasoning. I suppose we could look for payments to Chinese people, and then check those people's backgrounds. We may eventually find the bastard, as you said. But what do we do from there? How do you intend to make that intermediary talk? And the others?"

Shona faked an innocent expression. Toshio groaned. "I told you…"

"Relax, Toshio! I have no intention to leave a blood trail after us this time! Especially since we may have to come back for a second interrogation. I'm thinking more of a psychological war. Whoever was involved in this knew me, Toshio. Even if he's aware of what you did to the building in Thailand, he'll think me dead. He's going to have a nasty surprise when he discovers I'm not."

Toshio frowned. "And you think it will be enough to make him talk?"

She kept her expression carefully neutral. "I have learned a few new tricks lately. I'm going to drive him crazy. He's going to see me at every moment of the day, anywhere. Until he confesses his crime. Everyone is superstitious, deep inside. When we have his confession, we move to the next target. I know it might take time, but I don't expect that many intermediaries. And, as you've said, my son has waited four years already. We have time on our side."

It was difficult to keep an impassive face speaking those last words. She wanted to scream that they had to start now and hurry, but emotional arguments had never got her anywhere with Toshio before. There was the small issue of her current pregnancy, of course, but she would find a solution for that as well.

Toshio shook his head. Shona gritted her teeth. "Why?"

He raised his hand, palm open. Damn. She hated when he started counting his arguments.

"First, there is a good reason for having kept the fact you're still alive a secret. Kellerman, if he is behind this, may decide you're a risk he has to get rid of, even though we have no evidence against him, but he is not your only enemy, Shona. The Triads won't be happy to discover you're alive."

"I'm not afraid of Kellerman. As to the Triads, make a deal with them."

"Another deal? I'm asking a lot of favors from them lately. Just for you. But, yes, I might be able to keep them out of this." Toshio raised another finger. "Secondly, how can you be sure your little game will work the way you want? It is too dangerous. I know what you have in mind, but a paranoiac man can still be fast with a gun."

"I'll be faster."

He raised a third finger.

"We can't be sure of that! But then, even if your plan works and our victim blubbers and talks, we have absolutely no guarantee that he will tell the truth! And he will certainly either have fled or expect us with a small army by the time we've discovered that he lied and come back to him!"

Damn!

"Shall I go on?"

She shook her head. She had been so proud of her idea. But Toshio was right, of course! It was not going to work.

She clenched her fists. "I will find Sonam, Toshio."

He nodded. "And I certainly want to help you. These boxes are indeed a good start."

He looked at everyone and no one in particular. "I'm open to suggestions, gentlemen."

There were actually quite a few offers. Some involving physical torture, others prostitutes—none of them really satisfying. Until an unknown feminine voice resonated behind Toshio. Someone who had just entered the room.

"If I may? I think I can help you with your quest, Kimiel."

Everyone quickly turned towards the voice. Some weapons appeared. Toshio's men were professionals, though, and did not shoot.

Shona recognized the newcomer immediately. Najeb's girlfriend. It was hard to miss the bright green hair on her head.

Shona frowned, but before she could ask anything, the young woman stopped her with a gesture. "Hear me out, please."

Toshio turned towards Shona. "You know her?"

Shona nodded. That was enough for the weapons to disappear under the clothing again. Toshio signed the girl to approach. "Why don't you start by introducing yourself?"

The newcomer waited for a chair and only spoke after she was sitting.

"I am As'leandra S'emoel Na Liathe, daughter of the Akeneires'el of the Na Liathes."

Shona had to laugh when she saw the others' reaction. Puzzlement. And it was not only because of the young girl's heavily accented English.

"Those titles don't impress them, As'leandra!" Shona

said. "Let's just say that we share the same heritage, gentlemen. She can also walk through walls and so on. Did Najeb ask you to come here? Where is he, anyway?"

Shona had not even seen him leave the room. He had been right behind her at the beginning of the discussion, but no one had reacted to his disappearance.

The young woman looked sheepishly at her hands. "Najeb did ask me. He's explained your dilemma to me. Asked me if I would consider helping you."

Help? What help could Shona expect from her? Then Shona remembered what she had heard about the girl. "Oh! It is true then?"

As'leandra nodded. "You could master this as well, Kimiel, with the proper training. It's one of our gifts."

"Care to elaborate on that 'Oh', Shona?" Toshio was showing unusual impatience. Shona allowed herself to smile. This might indeed be the perfect solution!

"As'leandra here can read minds, Toshio. At least, that's what I've heard. She will be able to get the information we need by getting inside our target's mind!"

When everyone looked at As'leandra, with reactions ranging from cautious to incredulous, both women just grinned at each other.

"Where is Najeb, As'leandra?"

"Covering for me."

"He won't be able to do that when we're in China."

"If necessary I will have someone else help me during that time."

Toshio acquired their attention by clearing his throat, loudly. "Suppose I believe you. That you can read minds. You don't speak Mandarin or any other Chinese dialect!"

As'leandra shrugged. "I don't need to. That's the beauty of reading people's minds."

"And how do you intend to proceed? Concretely."

She pouted. "I don't know. I must admit I never did this before. I mean, read forced confessions. I suppose you'll have to constrain the victim, somehow, and ask the questions. I will be able to tell you if he's telling the truth or not, and eventually read information he's not willing to say out loud!"

Toshio was silent for a long time. Shona just waited. He finally shook his head, though not as unequivocally as before. "We'll still have the problem that the victim will remember what happened!"

As'leandra answered by a shake of her own head. "No, he won't."

"Because?"

"I'll erase the memory of the event from his head."

She looked at Toshio and Shona, earnestly. "I can really do that, I promise."

Toshio and Shona exchanged a grin, before Shona spoke. "Oh, we already know about that As'mir ability, As'leandra."

That was how Keremli had given Shona her sanity back, though it had certainly been a very long process. But, then, there had been so much in Shona's mind to erase.

Toshio nodded. "This might work. Certainly better than Shona's plan."

He paused, and then looked at As'leandra. "I'm not sure, though, that you plainly realize what you're going to put yourself through. Restraining and asking questions, As'leandra, means torture. No matter how careful we are going to be, there is no point of erasing a memory if the person has broken bones or deep cuts. We're going to inflict severe pain on someone. It's not pretty. And if you are reading that person's mind, I suppose you will share his pain. Are you up to it?"

For a second, Shona was afraid As'leandra was going to let her down, but the young As'mir surprised her by nodding resolutely. "I will help Kimiel. You won't regret it."

Toshio looked at Shona. "I suppose she's referring to you when she says Kimiel?"

Shona just nodded. Toshio's attention returned to As'leandra. "How much do you want for your help?"

This time As'leandra frowned. Clearly, she did not understand the question. Shona had to smile and told her in As'mir, "He is offering you money, As'leandra."

"Oh!" As'leandra shook her head. "I have no need for money. But I will ask a favor from Kimiel in return."

Shona was suddenly wary. She was prepared to do anything to get Sonam back, but lately she had learned the hard way the need to be cautious around As'mirin! Especially that one. As'leandra was known to like experimenting.

She asked, in As'mir, "What do you expect from me, As'leandra?"

To her surprise, the young woman turned bright red and looked at her hands. It was so unlike her, Shona could only think of one explanation.

"Is this about Najeb?"

As'leandra nodded. Shona sighed. "Najeb told me about your situation, but I don't see what I can do for you, As'leandra."

As'leandra kept looking at her hands, but whispered, "I heard Ara is talking to you. Can you please ask her to help us?"

Shona's back become a bit hot. She just had no idea whether this was a good sign or not.

She wanted to warn the young woman to be careful with her wishes. But damn it, she needed her help!

She nodded. "I can certainly do that. I thank you for your offer, As'leandra. Though I will have a serious talk with Najeb about what I meant about keeping his mouth shut! And you'd better not start spreading rumors about what's going to happen either!"

As'leandra shook her head. "I won't, Kimiel. What I offer to do for you is frowned upon by the whole community. It's misusing our gifts. It could bring me before Ara if I'm not careful."

Ara's trial, the girl meant. Shona nodded. "We have an understanding then."

Then Shona turned towards Toshio, switching back to English. "I think we're done for today. Do we have a plan?"

Toshio nodded.

As'leandra was already gone. Toshio frowned. "I'll never get used to this, Shona! It is just not natural!"

"Depending on the point of view! Those people find walking unnatural!"

"I hate to ask, but before we start this long quest, have you asked them if they could help locate your son?"

Shona had, if not directly. Her son was As'mir as well after all, and she was ready to try anything.

"They can't. I can't explain why in detail, but it's not possible."

The first thing she would do after finding Sonam back would be to plunge him herself into the Lake, then ask Nukri to transfer the boy in and out the Valley. That way, Sonam would be as protected as any other As'mir. She would never lose him again.

"We are going to find Sonam, Toshio, and I'll never let him out of my sight again."

"I can imagine. I suppose you want us to start on those files as soon as possible?"

Shona smiled and pushed a box in his direction. "Indeed. Most of it is in English, but we may need some help with the Thai. Thank you for helping me, Toshio. I know you're not convinced Sonam is alive, but I want my son safe."

He reluctantly nodded. "We'll find him, Shona. Dead or alive, we'll find him."

52

T HE WOMAN WAS exasperating. Ekbeth had taken care of her cat and mouse play with Najeb, but she had now found a new way to irritate him.

"Are you having fun, Kimiel? I know I should not have cancelled our dinner yesterday, but…"

She raised a hand, a sign to hold on for a moment. The next moment, a huge sofa appeared in front of her—the living room sofa from his Zurich house, to be precise.

She opened her eyes slowly, and turned towards Nukri na Liom. The old man was staring at Ekbeth, obviously torn between complimenting his pupil and avoiding further escalation of Ekbeth's fury.

Kimiel turned towards Ekbeth and smiled. "Yes, you shouldn't have, but I'm getting used to your busy schedule. I expect you to make it right tonight. What do you think, Ekbeth? Can we swap that horrible striped thing in your main reception room with this? It's so much more comfortable."

He tried to maintain a scowl on his face, but it was suddenly difficult. They had tried both sofas on one of their few evenings together, and indeed that one had been much more appropriate for their experiment of that evening. Not something Nukri needed to know.

"I'd rather not. That vase you moved earlier broke, for your information."

She looked contrite. "Oh, sorry. I found it quite ugly, anyway."

Nukri hid his amusement with a subtle cough, but Ekbeth was not fooled. He knew his relationship with Kimiel was currently a constant source of amusement among the community.

"It was my mother's favorite, Kimiel! I'd very much appreciate if you could leave my furniture alone. Why don't you practice with the McLeans' furniture instead?"

"Well, they don't have much furniture to start with, and I don't know the pieces as well as yours. Nukri told me to practice on familiar objects."

Keeping the fact that they were practically living together a secret was also impossible, especially with her constant not-so-subtle hints. Though "Living together" was a gross exaggeration. They barely managed to cross each other's path to share a meal or talk once or twice per week. What he knew for sure was that she was sleeping in his bed in Kse'Annilis most nights. It was him who had trouble getting there.

Ekbeth had told her that if she wanted to avoid pressure from the Aramalinyia about weddings, they had to be discreet. The Aramalinyia was old fashioned and romantic that way.

Kimiel just ignored his advice. Discretion formed no part of her personality. She was also far too direct. It did not shock Ekbeth that much, but the rest of the community was still adjusting to her ways.

"What do you think, Ekbeth? Do I have a future as a Caller?"

He raised one brow. "Did I miss something? Are you marrying Nukri?"

The old Caller looked offended. "I had no such intention, Ekbeth…"

Kimiel laughed. "Relax, Nukri. Ekbeth was joking. I'm not marrying anyone. That tradition of the family tasks does not make sense to me. Is there really no way for me to become a Caller if I want to?"

Both men shook their heads. Ekbeth explained, "Not in the Valley, at least. I told you already: from the beginning, each family was assigned a task for the whole community. For example, our Family is in charge of the Finances. The Na Dearghs of the supplies. The Na Ghorms of the Library, The Na Saoilcheachs of the Health care. If you're born in that family, for instance, you'll have to learn how to cure people. Bad luck for you if you can't stand the sight of blood."

"Yeah, yeah, you've told me. And the McLeans are in charge of party organizing and any other entertainment. I wonder why my family got the worst part of the cake."

"This was decided after the massacre, Kimiel. The McLeans lived outside the Valley, so they got a task that did not require constant involvement in the day-to-day management of the community."

"No wonder the rest of the community does not look upon the McLeans in a good light. We're just buffoons!"

He cracked a smile. "You certainly are entertaining us at the moment. Today, a try at Calling. What is it going to be tomorrow?"

Kimiel shrugged. "Keremli never needed a Caller to

go from one place to another. Nukri told me anyone could learn to master this gift, if needed. So I gave it a try, under his supervision."

"Fine with me, as long as you leave my furniture alone. And, on another note, the Aramalinyia wants to see us."

Kimiel made a face. "More oracle?"

Ekbeth nodded. He had warned her this would happen, and he had been right. The Aramalinyia was asking at least once a week when they would begin preparations for their wedding. They just kept inventing reasons for not doing so, but their excuses were starting to sound rather thin.

To his own surprise, he was not as opposed to the idea as some weeks ago. They had spent a lot of time together recently, he and Kimiel. He had to admit she could be quite charming when left to her own devices. And she probably was the best lover he had ever had, even though her pregnancy was starting to get in the way.

He was still mad at her, but almost decided to propose to her again. Only she had not given any sign that she had changed her mind yet. And she still refused to confide in him. Vastly irritating.

What they needed was more time. The Aramalinyia just had to be patient.

They said goodbye to Nukri, and started the slow descent towards the Lake. She stepped in some muck that had gathered on the stairs and looked at it with disgust. "Yuck! What is this? Are they ever going to clean the place?"

"Once in ten years only, I'm afraid. I won't let you fall, don't worry."

She took his arm.

"Nukri is an old sweet man. He doesn't complain

much, but I'm sure he feels terribly alone on his own in this big tower all day. He told me about his granddaughter, Akalabeth Kas'el na Liom, but he got a bit emotional when I asked where she was. Does she ever visit?"

"No. She's been banished from Kse'Annilis."

Kimiel frowned. "Banished? Why was she banished?"

"Fell in love with the wrong person."

She stopped, obviously incredulous. "But, Ekbeth, she and Nukri are the last of the Na Lioms, the Caller's family. Nukri is not eternal. He'll die eventually. Who's going to replace him then?"

"Good question. One everyone seems to currently avoid. We are talking of very stubborn people here, Kimiel. They would never admit their mistake. Until it's too late."

"Ah. I see. Unless Nukri marries again and has children."

"I was joking up there, Kimiel. Nukri will not marry again. He's almost as old as the Aramalinyia."

She stepped carefully around another heap of indeterminate garbage, before answering, "I know. I suppose the same rules applies to Najeb and his taste for architecture?"

"More or less. His family originally comes from outside the Valley, with no As'mir connection, and they have been the Na Duibhnes' bodyguards for a long time. Why should they change orientation now? And architecture is the prerogative of the Na Liathes!"

"This sounds hopeless. Can't you change families?"

"The only way inside the Valley is by marriage, but Najeb is bidding too high. The Akeneires'el of the Na Liathes will never be willing to give him his daughter's hand. Oh yes, everyone is aware of their feelings for each other. To the exception of her father, I hope. We just turn a blind eye to it."

He paused. "The only alternative is exile. Outside here, you can become whatever you want. That has been Akalabeth's choice. But not everyone is as courageous. We live a very protected life here. Even the most stupid among us realize it. Turning your back on it is a difficult choice."

Kimiel kept silent for a time.

"You know what, Ekbeth. Something is so very wrong here. Everything happens in secret! You cannot take any initiative in the open. There's always something, a law or a custom, preventing the smallest change. No room for spontaneity! And the punishments are ridiculously harsh. Ara's trial for anyone who dares come against them!"

She suddenly hissed. Ekbeth was not surprised this time. She should have learned better than to insult the Goddess by now.

"What can I say? he said. "It's not that bad! As'mirin believe in traditions."

"What traditions? From what I've seen so far, most of the As'mirin knowledge has been lost over the centuries. You are only living a pretense of a life here, Ekbeth."

He looked quickly around him, hoping no one was overhearing this conversation. The Goddess was not the only one sensitive on this specific issue.

Not that Shona was wrong, though.

"One of the reasons why I don't live here permanently, Kimiel. You're not the only one who's noticed that. I do what I can to change things, Kimiel. As an Akeneires'el, I do have some leverage in this community."

"Too little, Ekbeth. Not what is really needed to save

the As'mirin. Don't tell me you don't see the community is dying."

"True. But the only person who can bring the necessary changes without incurring death is the Aramalinyia. She's a bit more open to new ideas than most of the rest, but only so much." He held two fingers a half-inch from each other to make his point.

"So, everyone has to stay miserable."

"Not everyone is miserable, Kimiel. Most of my family is perfectly happy with their life."

"Oh yeah? I see them more as a nest of snakes that only look for ways to make everyone else's life miserable! Don't tell me they are happy! I've looked at those budget requests on your desk. Ridiculous!"

"Kimiel. I agree… but I was not joking about the death risks. Most of the time, the complaints don't even reach the Councils. Poison is widely used to get rid of trouble makers."

"All that sneakiness makes me sick, Ekbeth. I'm for a more direct approach."

"And we've seen what comes of your approach! I don't plan to kill all the people who annoy me, Kimiel."

"Ekbeth! I'm really not that bad! There are other ways. Have you ever thought of putting the complainers in a position of power? I've understood that it's quite a common management practice on the Other Side."

The advice took him by surprise. He shook his head, puzzled. Why had he never thought of this before?

"Actually, it's not a bad idea. I'll think about it."

They had arrived at the bottom of the stairs and the Aramalinyia's house stood in front of them. "Here we are. What shall we tell her this time?"

SHONA WAS LAZILY stretched on a chaise longue by the pool at Ekbeth's place in Zurich, trying to concentrate on a book, when Najeb came up to her and handed her a phone. It was Toshio.

Reading the administration files had brought up more names than expected. So Toshio had gone to China to check on their suspects. They had both agreed the Triads would collaborate better if she was not present, so she had stayed behind.

It had taken a few weeks but he had managed to bring the list to three potential Chinese suspects. He summarized their profiles.

One was a small local museum director, collector of jade items—actually, a fervent admirer of Yeshe's work. Shona had met him numerous times in the past. She would probably have dismissed him as a suspect, until Toshio informed her that he had a few relatives enrolled in the army. More troubling, Toshio had not been able to find a valid reason as to why the pharmaceutical company made a transfer to his account of more than a million dollars. Maybe it was in payment of a smuggled antique artifact, but Toshio had some doubts. After all, he had a pretty tight control of the Chinese antiquities market. Such a big transaction would not have gone totally unnoticed, at least not by him.

The second suspect was a high-ranking military man himself. The company had sent him money regularly, anonymously. Toshio had discovered that the man had a serious gambling issue, which, to support his weakness, made him open to corruption. Shona thought he was probably their best shot.

The last one was a multimillionaire industrial man, who had businesses spread all over the country. So a lot of connections and influence. His company was producing some of the chemicals needed by the Thai business. The money transfers might have been legitimate there.

Toshio explained, "I selected that one because he's a close business friend of your main suspect, Kellerman. All three have a connection to Kellerman, as a matter of fact."

Shona knew Toshio was testing her. She was actually glad he at least had taken Kellerman into consideration in the search. She did her best to sound casual when she answered, "Good. So who is our best bet from this trio?"

"No clue yet, but we may be able to save some time here. Can you get yourself, Najeb and his girlfriend over to Beijing in less than two hours, with some formal clothes? There is a huge Communist Party event tonight at the Forbidden City and our three men are going to attend. I managed to get some invitations. As you know, I'm not happy to let some people know you're still alive, but I'm sure that seeing your presence will help us to the next step! If the green-haired girl has not lied and can read our potential culprits' minds."

Shona hesitated. She had not seen Toshio for the last

three weeks, and she had avoided going to the Castle as well. Her pregnancy was starting to be very visible, and she still hadn't told him. Going to Beijing was probably going to be her last opportunity to help find her son. She'd better make it count.

"We'll be there. Where do you want to meet?"

"I've booked a few suites at the Grand Hotel. All under my name. Try to be discreet when you arrive. I want to keep you a surprise to our friends."

"Okay. See you in two hours."

Shona hung up and stretched. "Toshio is expecting us in Beijing, Najeb. You, me and As'leandra. Can you please ask her to come here? We are going to an official event in the Forbidden City. You're going to love the Grand Hotel! It's really Old China decadent!"

Najeb did not look so happy by the news, though. "Why are we going there?"

She explained Toshio's plan. It did not lighten his mood. "It's too dangerous, Kimiel. I can't protect you and As'leandra in such a big crowd. If anything happen to either of you…"

"Toshio's men will also be there. You have trained with them; you know how good they are. We can also ask Nukri to keep an eye on us."

Najeb finally nodded his agreement. "I am going to get As'leandra. Oh, can she borrow some clothes from you? I don't think she has anything appropriate for a formal event on this Side."

She had to laugh. "Najeb! As'leandra is at least three inches taller than I am! My dresses won't fit her. In fact, I don't have anything that fits me either. Bring her here, then we'll go do some shopping in town."

While Najeb was away, Shona went back inside the house and called Ekbeth's assistant. The woman was a pearl. She recommended a few boutiques and promised the driver would be ready for them in twenty minutes.

Perfect.

*

As'leandra had probably never worn high heels before, or a gala dress, but it did not show. She looked regal when, under Shona's supervision, she started walking around her bedroom. But she certainly complained a lot about the blond wig Shona had cleverly chosen to place on her head before they came to Beijing. "Do I really have to wear this, Kimiel?"

"Do you really want our hosts to take you for a demon and kill you, As'leandra?"

The younger woman shook her head. "Of course not! But I've seen people with green hair in magazines. It's not so uncommon anymore."

Shona had to laugh. "You'll have to show me those magazines one day, As'leandra. Do you remember the staff reactions at the shops in Zurich? Green hair is not common! Those people have dyed their hair green. And I can assure you none of tonight's party will have green hair."

"Dye!"

Shona grinned. "I take it from your reaction that dying one's hair is also a taboo in the Valley?"

"Of course it is! That's like pretending to be from another family—without their permission!"

As'leandra suddenly started giggling. "I've been so stupid! Whenever I saw the green hair, I always thought a lost relative had created his own family on this Side!"

Shona did not comment. She looked at her own dress

in the mirror. It was shorter, and not clinging to her body like As'leandra's. The clever cut of the fabric dissimulated her bulging belly. With a bit of luck, Toshio would not notice anything.

Toshio was waiting for them with Najeb in the living room of the suite. "Hurray! They are finally ready! Women! I'll never understand why they need so much time to get dressed!"

Shona just ignored him. Najeb for once seemed oblivious of her. He had eyes only for As'leandra.

Then Toshio's eyes narrowed. "Are you…?"

So much for trying to hide things from her friend. She interrupted him. "Yes, I am. But there's no way you're sending me home now that you know it, Toshio."

"Who's the father? Ekbeth?"

"Right again. Can we please go?"

Toshio almost refused. He, too, was far too protective sometimes. But in the end, he ordered four more of his men to come along. It was quite a small army that finally left the hotel.

With As'leandra at her side, Kimiel looked out of the limousine window. Beijing was so different than Shanghai or Hong Kong. Less glamorous, certainly dull in comparison, but it certainly had charms of its own. That applied particularly to the city main attraction, the Forbidden City. She had visited the place a few times earlier, but it looked as if the ancient buildings had recently received a new layer of paint and that, this time, the gold leaf had not been spared. Perhaps it was just an effect of the lighting surrounding the building.

Whatever. It felt as if the old Imperial Palace had recovered its ancient glory, and were it not for the clothes worn by its visitors, you might well have imagined being in the distant past, waiting patiently for the Emperor to show up. All the courtyards were jam-packed with important people.

She had a short moment of panic. Too many people. The noise was so overwhelming she could not hear what Najeb was telling her. The heavy incense the party organization had cleverly burned to cover the food smell made her sneeze.

Toshio offered her his handkerchief. "Are you all right?"

She nodded and looked around her. People were looking at them with curiosity. Toshio was a known figure in this crowd, and their arrival with no less than ten bodyguards had been anything but discreet.

She had a mission to fulfill. She was not alone. No time to panic.

"Look at them, Toshio. They probably all think I'm your mistress!"

"Not all of them, Shona. Some know exactly who you are!"

She played the role that was expected of her. Let Toshio show her around the place, and introduce her to some of his acquaintances. She laughed politely at jokes, and accepted toasts, though she was very careful with the quantity of alcohol she drank. Her role tonight was primarily silent, but they would never get the desired reaction if Toshio or Najeb had to carry her away.

All in all, it was just a game.

Toshio managed to locate one of their potential candidates by himself, but had to ask around for the other two. It took some time, but at least he had been right. All three of them were present tonight.

As'leandra casually approached each of them, then

turned her attention elsewhere. Or so it seemed. The younger woman had explained to Shona how the mind reading worked. According to her it was just a bit like a Caller's work. She had to create a mental link to the person whose thoughts she wanted to read. She did that simply by touching them. Afterwards, it was just a question of staying focused. She had learned to manage that in a crowd when necessary, she told Shona. Shona hoped it was not all banter from the girl's side. They would not have such an ideal occasion a second time.

When Shona was certain As'leandra had linked to the three men, the next step was hers. She needed them to notice her. Recognize her. If they had not already.

In the end, it proved easier than she had thought. There were few foreigners at the party. They were quite easy to notice, with their lighter skin and hair, even among the tall Chinese.

Toshio was accompanying her towards the end of the second internal courtyard when he suddenly stopped, and changed direction.

"What's happening, Toshio?"

"Nothing."

It was so unlike him, she glanced behind her, trying to discover what had provoked his reaction.

It was not a what. It was a who.

She recognized the man and resisted Toshio's hold on her with all her might.

"Shona! Ignore him! Damn it! I would never have asked you to come, had I known he would be here as well! Najeb! We have to take her out of this place! Quickly!"

She was seeing only the man. The man who had provoked so much suffering!

She hissed, "Toshio, let go of me! Don't you see it's the perfect opportunity! Our three suspects are in this courtyard right now. If they are such good friends of Kellerman, they will notice our discussion. Kellerman will be surprised to discover I'm still alive, I'm sure. That will attract their attention. They will recognize me! At least the one who sold me will! And if not, I'm certain Kellerman will try to discuss this nasty surprise with him later."

Toshio stopped pulling her away. He thought for a moment and shook his head.

"You're not up to this, Shona. You're doing your best to hide it, but I know you. You want Kellerman dead. I can't trust you near him."

She managed a smile, with difficulty. "Have a little faith in me, Toshio. I promise I'll behave. I swear I'll behave."

Toshio was still hesitating. Thankfully for her plan, Kellerman had apparently seen them and had decided to come over to them by himself.

"My, if it's not Shona McLeod! It's been a long time! Almost thought you dead. Have you decided to re-associate yourself with Toshio? What has happened to your gifted husband, Yeshe? Did the isolated life get to you, and you decided to leave him?"

Shona almost lost it when he referred to Yeshe so casually. As if he did not know what had happened to the love of her life.

But then she met Toshio's stare, and managed a thin smile. She turned towards Kellerman. The man had not changed much in the past years. Same sandy hair, same clear blue eyes. Average build, strong face, and as suave as ever.

"Herr Kellerman! What a surprise! I was not expecting to meet you here tonight."

His face did not reveal anything. Yes, he had always been good at hiding his emotions. "Neither was I expecting to see you, Shona."

Shona forced herself not to clench her fists. "My husband is dead, Herr Kellerman. My friend Toshio has been most supportive through this difficult time, and indeed we are thinking of restarting our association. What better occasion than tonight's party to reacquaint myself with some of our customers?"

He looked sincerely surprised. "Dead? My, I'm so sorry for your loss. And to think the last time I met him we parted on such bad terms because of that little jade sculpture! My condolences, Shona."

Shona wished she could erase that insincere expression from his face. With acid.

Instead, she bowed her head slightly. "Thank you. I'll certainly be glad to work for you again, Herr Kellerman. You've always been one of our best customers. And you always have the most interesting orders."

There it was! Just a small tic at the corner of his mouth. Careful Shona! He was getting suspicious.

Toshio put a hand on her arm. "Nice to see you, Kellerman. I would have preferred to keep the news a secret a bit longer, but Shona insisted on coming here tonight."

Kellerman relaxed a bit, turned his attention to Toshio.

"And you? I thought you were serving a sentence somewhere in Europe at the moment."

Toshio nodded curtly. "That difficulty has been solved. I'm now ready to start my business again, though I actually never really stopped it. If you'll excuse us, I still have to present Shona to a few of my other customers."

This time, Shona let Toshio take her away. When they were at a good distance, he let go of her arm. "Phew, I must admit I would never have thought you could control yourself so well, Shona."

She shrugged. "I'm not using anymore, Toshio. Makes a big difference, as far as temper is concerned. Though I really feel like screaming and hitting someone right now! What a piece of shit! How can he lie with such a straight face?"

"Experience! And remember, we have no proof he's behind the sad business, Shona. He might be sincere."

She did not react. They had argued too many times on this already.

"Kimiel! I know who did it!"

Forgetting Kellerman for now, Shona turned towards As'leandra. "Who?"

Toshio put himself between the two women. "Don't tell her. Sorry Shona, but I think it's better that you go back to the hotel now. Let us handle the rest."

Shona could not believe her ears.

"You can't do that to me, Toshio. We are talking of the man who sold me to people who tortured me! I want to know!"

"Not while you're still full of murderous thoughts, as you yourself just admitted. Yes, you did impress me with Kellerman. But this is different. We need our main suspect to answer questions—not dead. Please, be reasonable. Go back to the hotel and let us handle the rest."

Shona refused.

He had to have expected that reaction, she later realized, because suddenly everything went black around her.

*

When she regained consciousness, she was lying on Ekbeth's bed in Kse'Annilis, her head hurting. Najeb was sitting beside the bed.

"Did you hit me, Najeb?"

He did not even try to lie. "For your own security, Kimiel. Toshio was right. It was time for you to leave."

"And you left As'leandra alone at the party?"

"Watanabe swore nothing would happen to her. You are my priority, Kimiel. Above all else."

"Nice way to show it. My head is hurting."

"I know. Sorry about that. Who is this Kellerman, Kimiel?"

She let her head fall back on the pillows and closed her eyes. If she was not moving, the pain was a bit more bearable. "You were there during that part of the first meeting with Toshio. We mentioned Kellerman's name a few times."

Najeb had probably heard most of her story from Toshio or Jeffrey, or he had deduced it from what he had overheard, because he asked, "You really think he's the one responsible for the murder of your husband and his family?"

"I don't think he is, Najeb. I'm a hundred percent certain. But he has covered his tracks cleverly. I can't prove anything and he has a lot of power. Much more than Ekbeth. Kellerman's at the head of one of the biggest world consortiums. Untouchable —or so he thinks."

She tried to quiet down. Speak calmly. "I don't care about his power. I want him dead. If not for Toshio, he'd already be dead."

"I see."

She gritted her teeth. "Indeed. When Toshio forbids me to do something, I obey. At least I try. Kellerman has been one of Toshio's best customers for a long time. Toshio is reluctant to lose his orders."

Najeb was silent for a time before he again spoke. "I don't get it, Kimiel. I believe your story, of course, but it sounds so fantastic. I've seen the White Lady at the Castle. Why would Kellerman go to such an extent for a little jade statue? To hire Chinese soldiers or mercenaries, get them into a closed country as Bhutan, track you and kill so many people? Besides the human aspect, it must have cost him far more than the statue's value. Isn't that a bit extreme?"

"I know how it sounds. But you've never interacted with the man. Kellerman is a bastard who thinks everything he lusts after belongs to him. I was there when Yeshe said "no" to Kellerman. The amount offered was very substantial, and Yeshe still refused, and explained why. You should have seen Kellerman's face, Najeb. This is a man who does not take "no" for answer. And he would go as far as needed to get what he wants. This does not only apply to his art collection. He's just as ruthless in business."

"Still, Toshio is not convinced?"

"No, but I hope whatever he is doing tonight to this intermediary is going to change his point of view."

54

EKBETH WAS ATTENDING another family council and doing his best not to yawn. He was just having too little sleep lately. Too little sleep and far too much on his agenda. He sometimes sincerely regretted his decision to involve himself more in the Na Duibhnes' daily life. He had never expected this would be so time-consuming.

Family councils were the worst. They could take hours, without any concrete decisions being made in the end. After the crisis with the McLeans' house, Ekbeth had hoped the mood would change and the council members would be a bit more proactive. After all, the event had allowed him to get rid of three of his worst opponents within the family.

Sadly, it had been wishful thinking. Every single little change he was trying to make in their habits brought an avalanche of protests. Even when he was not proposing changes, they still found something to complain about. His uncle Es'ael, especially, was very creative when it came to complaining. This time it was about the ice quota that Ekbeth had imposed on the cooks last week. At the previous council, it had been all about the insolence the older man had had to suffer from a mere servant.

All the while, as he listened to the nonsense, Ekbeth worried about what was happening at his bank on the Other Side. The stock exchange fluctuations were worrying lately. Of course, he had people who were as able as he was to interpret the tendencies on the Other Side. Lyrian, for example. But he wanted to be there.

The slightest mistake and there would be more spending restrictions in the Valley. He could only imagine what Es'ael's reaction would be if Ekbeth told him that. He was fed up with the constant whining of his family. It was such a waste of time! But what could he do about it? He hated to admit it, but Kimiel was right. He just could not go on like this for ever.

Thinking of her reminded him of her advice about giving the job to the biggest complainer. The thought brought a small smile to his lips. Well, why not, after all? He suddenly realized Es'ael had stopped talking. The old man was frowning at him.

"Do you find this important matter amusing, Akeneires'el?"

Ekbeth shook his head, and tried to control the sarcasm in his voice. "I would not dare. I already told you, I'm afraid the decision was not only mine, but of the Akeneires'elin council. So there's not a lot I can do to change it."

"Have you told them that we, as the most important family of Kse'Annilis, have rights to derogation?"

Ekbeth smiled sweetly. "No, I haven't, because we haven't." He paused for a minute, and then asked, "Do you think you could do a better job than me, Uncle?"

That question certainly got everyone's attention. This was obviously not the reaction they had been expecting.

Until now, Ekbeth had either flatly refused to agree to Es'ael's requests, or, at best, promised to maybe look into them.

Ekbeth elaborated on his question. "At administration, I mean. I must admit it's not my strongest point. I don't have time for it. If you think you can do better than me—and obviously you do, otherwise you wouldn't complain about my poor judgment—I'm more than ready to delegate the responsibility to you. And by this, I also mean that I'll allow you to attend the High Councils when the distribution of our resources comes up for discussion."

Ekbeth had a hard time not grinning when the older man realized what Ekbeth was offering him. The old man stuttered, "You are mocking me!"

"No, I'm not. I'll be honest. Being Akeneires'el and bank manager is a bit too much for me. I don't intend to give away any of the responsibilities, but I'd really like to delegate some of them. Administration, for example. I can give you a budget and we could meet a few hours per month to discuss what your needs are for the coming period."

Es'ael pouted. "A budget! Money! Money is not important!"

Ekbeth reduced him to silence with a stare. "Money is everything, Uncle. It's not because we're not using money within the Valley that we don't need it. No one will deliver food or anything else without a payment for it. You have really no clue how much we are spending per year to feed the community. I can tell you that some cities ten times our size on the Other Side would be happy to have our budget! And sometimes, the prices are ridiculously high, because our suppliers know we are not producing anything here. So we have to either stop or at least strongly reduce our consumption to show them we won't accept their blackmail. Those ice blocks are a perfect example."

"Buying the goods is the work of the Na Dearghs! We just have to make a list of what we need!"

"Wrong! The Na Dearghs are buying goods with the money I allow them to spend. Not from your wish list. I work very closely with them. But to come back to my offer, I'm not asking to replace me and go negotiate prices with the Na Dearghs outside of the Valley. Though I'd really like to get rid of that job as well! No, I just expect you to make realistic lists of goods needed within the family. And check whether we can afford them. Simple arithmetic. Something I've always heard you are very good at, Uncle."

A bit of flattery was never wasted on his relatives. At least it made Es'ael think, instead of arguing with him. After some time, the old man asked, "Can I think about your offer?"

"Of course!"

Then Ekbeth looked at the other Council members. "And I'd be very glad to hear whether any of you wants to help me with some tasks. Any task. I just can't be everywhere at the same time."

They were suddenly all avoiding meeting his eyes. Not that it meant they would not think about it. He sighed. "Good. Any other item to discuss today? No! Then I think it's time to go and enjoy our lunch. Good day to you."

He left his chair. Kalem was immediately at his side. They walked out of the council room toward his rooms on the upper floor.

"That was clever, Akeneires'el"

"What is the saying, Kalem? Necessity is the mother of invention. I was not lying, I can't go on like this for ever."

He looked at his agenda. "Let's grab some lunch. I have another meeting planned in Moscow in an hour."

"Akeneires'el! Father!"

Both men turned to Najeb, who had apparently been waiting for the Council to end to talk to Ekbeth. The young man bowed to him, then to his father.

"Father! I have to ask you a favor. Can you find someone to guard Kimiel Keh Niriel for a little while?"

Kalem frowned. "That's your job."

Najeb produced an unhappy smile. "Correct. But I can't do it, at least not for the coming days."

"Why? I warn you, if that has anything to do with that hobby of yours…"

Najeb interrupted his father. "No. Don't ask details, but Kimiel is on a mission again. A mission involving a lot of travel and dangerous meetings. Yesterday, her boss Watanabe discovered she was pregnant, and he wants her out of the way. He promised he'd take the mission over, but you know her, she's not willing to accept his decision. She does not trust his motivation. So I promised I would keep an eye on Watanabe. That was the only way I could think of preventing her from playing her nasty tricks on me again to evade my surveillance. So, I'm going. In the meantime, someone needs to keep an eye on her."

Ekbeth said, "Wait a second. Watanabe? He's out of jail?"

Najeb just nodded curtly. That was a bit of news neither Kimiel nor Najeb had mentioned earlier, thought Ekbeth.

"Where is she now?"

Najeb said, "Resting on your bed, Akeneires'el. Father?"

Kalem grumbled. "Damned if I'm going to watch over her!"

"I don't ask you to. Just find someone to do so."

Najeb was really troubled, Ekbeth realized. "There's more to it, Najeb? Is she angry with you as well?

Najeb nodded, hesitated but finally said, "I had to knock her out yesterday. To get her out of a dangerous situation. She knows I did it. I'm not sure she'll ever forgive me. Maybe you'll have to make the replacement permanent."

Kalem was still reluctant. "She's safe if she stays here while you're gone, Najeb. She does not need anyone to guard her."

Najeb shook his head. "Father. We are talking of Kimiel Keh Niriel. She won't stay here. She needs someone to watch over her."

Ekbeth understood he had to intervene. Kalem was just being difficult because it was Kimiel they were discussing. And Najeb was right about her being trouble.

"I'll solve this, Najeb. You can go."

Najeb bowed to them then disappeared.

"The boy is really rude! He did not even thank you!"

"No need. Find someone, Kalem. Najeb is right, she's not going to stay here long, and he looked concerned for her security."

"Akeneires'el. I would be continuously concerned about such a woman's security, if she was my charge! She just runs into trouble; that's her way of being!"

Ekbeth had to admit it was not a totally unfair judgment of her, no matter how biased Kalem was towards her.

"Good. I'm going to go and talk to her. Share a quick lunch with her. Solve the bodyguard issue in the meantime, please."

He looked at his watch again. "We leave in half an hour."

55

SHONA WAS PUTTING another cold compress on her brow when she saw Ekbeth approaching her, carrying a small paper bag.

She growled, "Leave me alone."

He just ignored her. He came and sat next to her. "Good day to you too, Kimiel. Here, have some food!"

"I'm not hungry. That bastard of a bodyguard hit me too hard. I probably have a concussion. I don't want to see his face ever again."

"So he's told me. Sure about the food? You're missing something. The cook makes these cookies only once a month, and people have been known to bribe him to get some. Being Akeneires'el does have its privileges. Will you at least try one?"

The man was impossible! He was going to bother her until she gave up. She took the cookie and munched on it. It was indeed very good.

She accepted the offer of a second one. "I'm still going to kill that sneaky bastard!"

Her back started glowing at that. She ignored the pain.

Ekbeth shrugged. "Najeb is only doing his job. He tried to protect you."

She glared at him. "I never asked for the protection in the first place, remember?"

Ekbeth took one of her hands in his. "He only has your best interest in mind, Kimiel. As your friend Watanabe has. As I have."

She threw the cold compress in his face. "He has no rights! This is important to me! I talked to Kellerman and kept my control! Toshio got out of jail to help me! Not to put me aside during our very first opportunity! He has no right!"

Ekbeth's only reaction to this was to offer her another cookie. The man was just impossible!

She suddenly realized she was saying too much. He had no idea who Kellerman was. She managed a weak smile. "I'm ranting—sorry."

He nodded. "Badly. But you've been through a lot lately, Kimiel. And that baby growing in you is probably not helping either. Everyone knows pregnant women have trouble controlling their temper."

She punched him in his arm. Hard. "That's such a stupid thing to say, Ekbeth!"

"Ouch! Point proven."

Ekbeth then looked at his watch and cursed softly. "I really have to go, Kimiel. Another meeting, I'm afraid! I hope we'll be able to finish our conversation later. Here, have the cookies. Do I get a goodbye kiss?"

His kiss certainly helped quiet her anger, if only a bit. She put her hand behind his neck and looked him in the eye. "Don't think some cookies and a kiss are going to solve everything, Ekbeth. I don't believe in fairytales."

He smiled at her in a way that made her hot all over. Then vanished.

Damn! She picked up the bag of cookies. She allowed herself another cookie as a reward. Ekbeth had apparently believed her and Najeb. Not that it had all been lies. She was mad at Najeb. She was still hurting from his blow. But they had both agreed he would be more helpful on the Other Side, protecting As'leandra and helping Toshio and his men. Their main problem was that he was her bodyguard. He was not supposed to go away from her at any time.

So she had come up with this plan: exaggerate her anger, give a few details that would intrigue Ekbeth without telling him much, and insist she hated Najeb. Najeb, on his side, would tell everyone he had to go on a mission for her to prevent her from doing something crazy.

It was not all lies. And it had worked. Najeb was free to go to Toshio and As'leandra.

She still wanted very much to be with them, but she had to be realistic. She would only delay everyone—or, worse, put them at risk. It was better this way. Najeb had promised to report to her every day, hadn't he?

She sighed and left her bed. Walked through the open windows, to the balcony. Watched the city below her. The Lake.

What was she going to do? The wait was surely going to drive her mad. She needed to do something! The only thing that she could think of was how much she wanted to kill Kellerman. Toshio had made her promise to leave the man alone. She wanted to hurt the bastard as badly as he had hurt her. If only he had a family…

Her lower back glowed fiercely. She was getting better at ignoring it.

The only thing that counted to the bastard was his business. Suddenly, she had an idea. A vague idea… Yes, maybe… It would not be breaking her promise…

She had a lot of money. More than even Jeffrey was aware of. It was, of course, not enough to buy Kellerman's company, but maybe enough to knock Kellerman out of his position.

She got on her feet. It was going to take time, but she did not care about time. As long as the bastard was brought down in the end. She also knew she would need some help. Ekbeth was not an option, but he might be able to advise someone.

Her headache was gone. Her head was now buzzing with this idea. She could not wait to start. But Ekbeth was not here. She needed some distraction, something to take her mind off her plan, until she could speak to him.

She looked blankly at the Lake in front of her for a moment. She suddenly remembered Sarah-Lysliana and her offer to write some songs with her. Meeting her cousin probably meant she had to go to the Island in the Highlands. Enter the McLeans' house. A sure way to temper her current enthusiasm, she reflected. But, hell, she would have to go there at some point, anyway! Delaying had never helped before.

She grabbed the cookie bag as if it was a talisman, and left the room, heading for Nukri na Liom's house. She could have called him with her mind, but she still preferred going to his place for the transfers when she could.

An unknown man in a meticulous black uniform was waiting for her behind the door.

Shona sighed. Great. Another guardian angel.

She walked quickly to the Caller's house.

*

The wind almost swept her away.

Shona looked around her. This was the Island, no doubt about it. The landscape was typically Scottish, with its gentle hills covered with fern and heather. What made her certain of the location was the lighthouse on the next island. There was none like it anywhere in the world. Someone had finally taken the time to repaint it.

Another sweep of wind. She could taste the salt on it. And it was as cold as she remembered.

"Kimiel! What a good surprise! Come here! It's not so chilly behind the wall!"

Shona ran towards her cousin. "Sally! What are you doing here?"

Sarah-Lysliana's face was reddened by the wind and her nose was running. Still her eyes were shining. "Listening for inspiration! Who's that with you?"

Shona crouched, as near to the wall as she could. It was indeed a bit better here, but still chilly. Her new bodyguard did not seem to be able to decide what to do, standing like this in the cold.

Shona laughed. "Come over here! Just keep some distance. We'll introduce ourselves later. Sally, you are mad! I'm sure you could find your inspiration in your room, with a good fire in the chimney, and some hot cocoa to drink! You'll only find death here!"

"Good words! I have to write them down!" Sarah-Lysliana extracted a notebook and a pen from her bag and started scribbling furiously.

"What are you doing?"

"Putting your wise words on paper!"

Sarah-Lysliana looked at her notebook for a second then put it back in the knapsack. Next, she extracted a thermos and a cup.

"I can't do anything about the fire, but I certainly can help with the warm cocoa. Want to share?"

Shona had to laugh! That woman was surely as crazy as she was! Well, she was family! What could you expect?

"Yes, please! And I have cookies! The Na Duibhnes' favorites, I was told."

"Perfect!" Sarah-Lysliana handed her a cup of steaming cocoa, with a grin. "Here!"

It was the strangest place to have a snack, Shona thought. Sitting behind a low stone wall with her cousin, sharing food. Yet it was the perfect place, as well. There was a quality to this place she had never been able to find any-where else, she realized.

She'd been only six when her father had died, when she had had to leave the Island. Too young to fully grasp what the place meant to her. But she had yearned for it every sec-ond of the rest of her life. Unconsciously.

The colors seemed more vibrant here. The gold, green and pink of the landscape, the dark bluish-gray of the sea, the whiteness of the sky.

The wind around them blocked all other sounds. The hot chocolate brew warmed her body. This was home! Her birthplace. She had missed it so much!

"Listen to the wind!" Sarah-Lysliana said joyfully. "It's saying things to me! It carries stories within it!"

Shona absently nodded to her cousin's words. They were so true… She frowned. Where had she heard them before?

She remembered, and turned to Sarah-Lysliana accusingly. "You've been reading my diary! The one I left behind when we had to leave the Island. Where did you find it?"

Her cousin did not deny it. "In the attic. Yes, I read it and I'm glad I have. It was very inspiring! I would never have thought of coming here and listening to the wind without your words. You have a marvelous imagination, Kimiel."

Shona shook her head. "I was six when I wrote that, Sarah-Lysliana!"

"Doesn't make it less wise. Are you ready to help me with the songs, Cousin?"

Shona did not ask how her cousin had guessed. There had always been something magical to this place.

She simply nodded.

56

WHEN EKBETH FINALLY managed to come back to Kse'Annilis and to his apartment, he found Kimiel sprawled on thick pillows on the carpet of his study, a bunch of papers surrounding her, a pen in her hand, nodding to herself. In her other hand was a cookie.

A plate had replaced the bag he had given her, and the fact that it was now almost empty indicated she had eaten more than a few of them in the past hours.

"Enjoying yourself, Kimiel?"

She ignored him.

He suddenly realized why. She was listening to some music on an mp3 player.

Ara! If any member of his family, or the community for that matter, saw her with that device… He did not want to think of the repercussions!

"Kimiel!"

She heard him this time. Turned towards him with an inviting smile that almost made him forget everything. "Ekbeth! Still interested in continuing our kissing?"

He kneeled next to her and took the plugs out of her ears. "This is forbidden here!"

Her smile did not wave. "Relax! I've cleared it with Nukri na Liom! He is to make it disappear before anyone enters the room."

"I'm here and the device is also still here!"

The next second it disappeared. Kimiel stretched lazily. "I suppose Nukri does not consider you as an 'anyone'!"

He looked closely at her face. She seemed much more at peace than a few hours ago, when he left her. There were many questions he wanted to ask her, but he did not want to spoil her mood. Not when she seemed so happy.

He pointed at the papers. "Redecorating my room?"

"No. Sorry for the mess, but it was the only room I could find with a carpet. It makes a difference in comfort. I've decided to help my cousin with her next album."

Then she caressed his arms. "But it certainly can wait. Where were we?"

He had to laugh. "Are you always so horny, Kimiel, or is this just pregnancy hormones?"

She moved her hands to his torso. "Bit of both, I suppose. Those damned hormones! Kiss me before I change my mind, will you?"

He was planning to do more than just kissing, when the floor suddenly shook violently under them. A low rumbling noise outside. Then nothing.

Kimiel went very pale. "I know that noise…"

Ekbeth was already on his feet. He rushed towards the balcony. The windows were closed. A huge cloud of dust blocked the familiar view of the Lake outside.

What had happened? He reached for the window lock.

"Ekbeth! Don't!"

He felt Kimiel's arms embrace him. The familiar tingling of a Call. The next moment, he recognized the living room of his Zurich house.

Kimiel dropped to the floor, unconscious. She had done the transfer herself, he realized. He took her in his arms and brought her to the sofa, all the while asking himself why she had done so.

That dust of cloud, where had it come from? The Goddess sometimes shook the ground under their feet, to show her displeasure, but there had never been any dust before. He needed to go back. See what was happening.

He closed his eyes and mentally called Nukri na Liom. No one answered him. That had never happened before. Even when he was sleeping, Nukri would wake up to answer him. Ekbeth tried for another minute, but when no answer came, he lowered himself next to the inert form of Kimiel.

His worst fear had happened. Nukri na Liom was dead. That was the only explanation. And something bad was happening in Kse'Annilis. He needed to be there. They needed him, no doubt.

Only, he was on the wrong side of the Veil, because of Kimiel's uncalled for action. And with no way to get back. He only had one option left. Akalabeth. She was the only other Caller who had ever transferred him. What was he thinking? Akalabeth was banished.

"Ekbeth! I was not expecting…" Lyrian had entered the room, his laptop under his arm—probably to follow the New York Stock Exchange or attend some meeting—but he was now standing in front of Ekbeth, asking, "What happened? My, have you killed her, Ekbeth?"

It took Ekbeth some time to understand the question. "Don't be ridiculous. Kimiel just fainted, Lyrian. I need to go back to the Valley. Can I please trust you with her?"

Lyrian looked horrified at the prospect.

"Please, Lyrian? This is an emergency. And if she wakes up before my return, ensure she doesn't follow me to the Valley."

Lyrian frowned. "Why? What has happened in the Valley?"

"No time… Thanks, Lyrian."

Akalabeth had answered his mental Call immediately. She, too, must have felt something was amiss.

He was now in what had to be the main room of a simple farmhouse. The smell of the cattle nearby was unmistakable. The room was poorly lit with a small fire, which made it difficult to recognize who was in it. Until he noticed a white halo of hair. Akalabeth.

"Uncle? What is happening?"

"I don't know, Kala. Nukri is not responding. I need you to transfer us both to Kse'Annilis. Now."

She took a step back from him. "Uncle! I'm banished!"

"And this is your best opportunity to get the ban lifted. If the fools of the High Council don't lift the ban in return for your help, nothing will."

A male voice, deep, spoke in reply—probably Sieven, Akalabeth's man.

"We just saw a strange cloud above the Valley."

A young boy entered the room screaming something in a dialect with which Ekbeth was not familiar. Judging by the other occupants' reaction, it was not good news.

Akalabeth jumped to her feet.

"Where are you going, Kala?"

"Outside. I can concentrate better outside. You will need more than me for this, Uncle. I'm going to Call the other Callers, organize some help. The boy has received a message from a friend living nearer the Valley. Looks like half of the crater wall forming the Valley has collapsed."

Ekbeth slowly lowered himself to the ground. Half of the crater? This was impossible!

Kimiel had understood what was happening and had tried to bring them both to a safe place, he realized. He would have to ask her how she had known. Later.

First, he had to go back to the Valley. See the extent of the damage, and what could be saved.

*

From their vantage point, the damage did not seem so bad. Certainly not half of the crater—maybe one tenth. There was however a huge gap in the crater wall now.

Unfortunately, the catastrophe had also hit the city. The whole left side of the city had collapsed onto itself. Where moments before houses had stood, there was now only ruins, broken pieces of wall, all covered with mud and vegetation transported there from the other side of the volcano wall.

It had even swept away the Aramalinyia's house.

Ekbeth moved his binoculars towards the top of the city. The Caller's house was apparently still in one piece, but it seemed to have collapsed onto its side. Evidently taking their only Caller with it.

"My grandfather may be dead, or perhaps he's just unconscious, Uncle."

"I hope for the last, Kala."

Lowering her own set of glasses, she turned toward him.

"I saw some people in the temple, Uncle. Watching us. Are you sure you want to do this?"

Ekbeth nodded. He had chosen the safest option when they decided to go to the Valley—transferring boats with the helpers, on the Lake. It was sensible, but he had no doubt about what the community's reaction was going to be. Boats on Ara's Lake! Maneuvered by Aiarz'in! And a banished woman!

Akalabeth gave a signal to everyone. The helpers started rowing towards the temple shore. He was ready for outrage, but he had hoped the urgency of the situation would bring perspective to the As'mirin minds.

From what he was now able to hear, that had been a miscalculation on his part.

"Outrage!"

"Sacrilege!"

"How could you?"

He ordered the boats to stop, then shouted, "I bring help! The Callers are going to help us find the survivors. The healing houses outside the Valley are ready to receive them for treatment."

The outrage continued.

"We don't need their help!"

"You are using *boats* on Ara's water!"

"The Goddess is going to exterminate us all!"

Before Ekbeth could argue that the Goddess would already have reacted to his sacrilege if she had wanted to, a stone hit him. Square in his face. A lucky bastard.

Dizzy, he fell over the side of the boat. Straight into the Lake.

$$57$$

*W*AKE UP!

Shona jerked awake, with a loud gasp. Her mind registered details. The cream-colored leather of the sofa, the faint smell of the polishing wax, the glistening light on glass, fast ticks on a keyboard.

She relaxed. This was Ekbeth's house, in Zurich.

The ticking stopped. She heard someone talk, then the faint scrape of chair legs on the thick carpet.

"Kimiel?"

Lyrian Farrill. He was standing near the dining table, looking at her. She felt groggy.

Why was she here?

Wake up, child. Your help is needed.

Oh yes. Now she remembered. The landslide. Ekbeth going outside. Her calling them out of the danger. Where was Ekbeth? Her back was ablaze with pain.

Will you listen to me?

The Goddess was having one of her moody days, apparently.

I'm not! Your help is needed at the Lake. Lives are at stake.

Shona tried to sit. Her head was spinning. She was too

weak to help with anything right now. This time, her back hurt so fiercely that she had to hiss, "Stop it!"

Lyrian was now at her side, looking concerned, something she would not have expected from him. "Are you okay, Kimiel? Should I call a doctor?"

She could not speak. She just managed to shake her head. Repeated in her head. More firmly. *Stop it.*

The pain lessened. She breathed in, deeply, and then thought, *How can I help, Ara?*

I need a voice. To save lives. Will you help?

I don't have the feeling you give me much choice here. Will it hurt?

A tiny pause. *Yes, it will. I'll protect your child, I promise.*

Shona knew she could not refuse. The Goddess had apparently made the effort to look for her on the Other Side, used her powers to wake her up. It had to be pretty urgent indeed.

She closed her eyes. She was too weak to transfer herself back to Kse'Annilis.

I'll take care of that.

The light surrounding her changed. The smell as well. There was a lot of dust in the air. And people were shouting angrily.

She opened her eyes. She was in the temple, facing the Lake. There were boats on the water, her mind absently registered. That snapped her out of her lethargy. Boats on Ara's Lake!

It's all right. They are bringing help.

Help for what? A stone hit her in the back. Furious, she turned on her heels and glared. My, there was quite a crowd. An angry crowd. They all had stones in their hands. They were shouting. Most of their attention was turned towards the boat passengers.

Shona noticed the blood, the torn clothes. Remembered. Saw. The landslide. Half of the trees surrounding the temple area had been uprooted by what seemed to be just a massive quantity of earth. But then she saw the odd piece of metal sticking out. She saw the remains of what must have been a table. She saw a pale dead foot.

She forced her eyes to look beyond the trees and the mud. The sight petrified her.

My, was Ara responsible for that?

Of course not! I warned your predecessors that digging such deep holes in the crater walls was weakening it. They should have listened.

Shona shook her head. Half of the city was in shambles. Gone forever.

It can be rebuilt, but we need to save lives first.

Of course. There were people trapped under this devastation. They needed to be dug out before it was too late.

Her back hurt again.

You're Asmir! No need to dig. All we need is Callers, and Healers.

Shona nodded, humbled. She had the training of a Caller, of a sort. She could certainly help. Ara was almost tender when she told Shona, *No, child, this is not your role.*

Another stone hit her, on the arm this time. "Hey! Will you stop that?"

"Kill her! She is the reason this happened! Ara should have taken you! She's punishing us now because of you!"

"Yes! Kill her! Kill her!"

The next stone hit her belly. Instinctively, she fell to

the ground and crouched. Offered as small a target as possible. The next stone hit her on the head. She felt blood running on her face. They were about to stone her to death, Shona realized.

She had no clue what to do. She was far too weak to get away from this. Where was Najeb? Where was Ekbeth? Weren't they supposed to protect her?

Allow me.

Shona nodded.

Don't resist me! It might hurt a bit.

"A bit" did not begin to describe it. It was Ara's trial all over again. She was burning, burning. Her body was not hers anymore. She got to her feet. She noticed how the As'mirin were looking at her—awestruck. At least, they were not throwing stones at her anymore.

Her mouth opened. She spoke, but had no idea what, because the words she was uttering were not her words, and she was struggling to ignore the pain. When it finally ceased, she almost fell to the ground.

Don't. It would spoil everything! Now, I suppose a bit of extra show would nail it. Let's see...

Shona opened her eyes. Realized everyone was now staring at her with open mouths.

A rush of wind distracted her. Loud exclamations from the people in boats on the Lake. The tiny boats were approaching fast, on their own volition, if the fear she saw on the passengers' faces was any clue. The boats beached gently on the temple shore.

Ekbeth was the first to come out. He was drenched and his nose was bleeding, but he only had eyes for her.

Later. Just a few more words, child. Then I'll leave you alone.

This time, Shona was prepared. It did not lessen the pain, but she heard her words. Though it was not entirely her voice coming out of her mouth.

"You will accept the help others have provided. You will help them. You have lost enough time. Show me you're worth my protection."

This time, she fell to her knees.

Thank you, child. I won't forget what you've done. You'll be rewarded.

She felt a caress on her face.

The next second, Ekbeth was with her. She noticed how hesitant he was.

A clear voice rose near the shore. "You've heard the Goddess! We have lost enough time. Let's divide this area in zones. Where are the healers?"

Shona stopped listening. She collapsed in Ekbeth's arms, exhausted.

58

E KBETH WAS GRATEFUL that Akalabeth had taken the rescue organization off his hands.

He needed time to recover from what he had just witnessed. The Goddess had spoken through Kimiel!

They had been too far from the temple to hear the words, but he had seen the pale blue glow surrounding her, he had heard the voice. And then that wind, which had brought them to the shore.

The second time the Goddess had spoken through her, he had been near enough to know that it was not Kimiel's voice that had spoken. It had been much deeper, older. Ordering them to open the Valley to external help. Ordering them to start working.

A cynical part of him whispered that anyone could fake voices, but he ignored it. Voices, maybe, but what about the glow surrounding her?

She was now resting in his arms but he hardly dared touch her. The Goddess had used her to bring her message.

"Akeneires'el? Can I examine her?"

Ekbeth released her. Bers'el, surprisingly agile for

someone of his age and girth, took Kimiel from him and lay her down on the Temple sand.

Ekbeth saw the blood on her face, on her arm. The bastards had thrown stones at her!

Bers'el was quick with his examination. "She's okay, Ekbeth. The cuts are not deep."

He cleaned the wounds, and bandaged them. "She needs to rest. Maybe bringing her to the Other Side is the best alternative, as long as she's not alone. Now, let me fix your nose. Stay still."

Not surprisingly, the nose was broken. Bers'el squeezed it to the right. Hard.

"Ow!"

"Sorry. I don't think you wanted to stay with a bent nose the rest of your life."

Next, Bers'el applied a thick adhesive bandage across Ekbeth's nose and gave him a few pills. "It's going to hurt. I would recommend rest, but I know you won't listen. Bring Kimiel to bed, change your clothes, take the pills."

Bers'el got back on his feet. "That was quite a show she gave us, don't you think?"

Ekbeth could only nod.

Kimiel had given him the fright of his life, was all he could think of.

*

It took them two days to extract and treat all the living As'mirin from under the ruins of the left side of Kse'Annilis. The injuries were quite serious, but handled as fast as possible by the Na Saoilcheachs and Aiarz'i doctors.

Extracting the wounded was actually not so much of a problem, certainly not with so many Callers at hand. No, the real problem was the sheer number of casualties. The temple was full of the wounded. It was difficult to walk among them without stepping on a hand or a foot. It was just too much to handle for the medical teams, as well as for those helping with the food distribution and the counting of families.

But they managed, somehow.

Ekbeth busied himself with establishing lists of the city inhabitants. The previous lists were all deeply buried under what had once been the Aramalinyia's house. They needed to know who was missing.

He brought some food to Akalabeth himself. She was kneeling next to a mattress where a familiar figure was lying. Nukri na Liom had survived. Both his legs had been broken by his massive Caller chair falling on top of him when the house toppled to its side, but he was alive. And seeing his grandchild was apparently doing wonders for his health. Kimiel had been right there, Ekbeth thought, the old man had missed Kala sorely.

Akalabeth took the porridge bowl and expressed her thanks.

Ekbeth shook his head. "No, I'm the one who is grateful, Kala. You rescued me from the Lake."

As an urgent response to Ekbeth falling into the water, she had simply called him back into the boat, and it had saved his life. She knew that—as was true of most As'mirin— he had never learned to swim.

"It was not that altruistic, " She gave a thin smile. "I'd rather have them throw stones at you than me."

"Perfectly understandable." Ekbeth smiled in return. "Thanks for all the help you've managed to bring in such a short time. The death toll would have been much higher if we had waited longer."

They both looked at Nukri. His wounds had not been fatal, but the ensuing loss of blood had almost killed him. It had been a very near call, Erinani had told them.

Akalabeth asked, "Speaking of the dead, what are we going to do about them, Uncle?"

Good question. The Callers had only concentrated on the living As'mirin so far. The more gruesome part of their work was yet to start.

They had two options. Bringing the dead bodies out and giving them a proper funeral, or leaving them where they were and never entering that part of Kse'Annilis ever again.

"The High Council has to decide on that. We are meeting tomorrow morning. If we decide to extract them, will you be up to the task, Kala? You're the only one who can do it."

Transferring a living body screaming in pain or for help was not so difficult for any trained Caller. She just had to open her mind and listen. Finding a soulless body needed a Caller's memory of the person when he had been alive. Ekbeth had an almost complete list of the presumed dead. It was far shorter than he had at first feared, but it was still going to be an awful collection job.

Akalabeth nodded. "It's the only decent choice, Uncle. We cannot let the dead be buried there like animals. People need to be able to see their beloved a last time."

Ekbeth sighed. She was right, of course. He got to his feet and squeezed his niece's shoulder. "Finish your meal and get some rest, Kala. The dead can wait until tomorrow to be mourned."

59

FOR FAR TOO long Shona had been kept in the dark about what was happening in Kse'Annilis. One of the Na Saoilcheachs was regularly checking on her, but adamantly refused to answer Shona's questions. There was no sign of Ekbeth. No messages either. The waiting was driving her mad.

For two days, she had done her best to remain calm and to rest, but her patience was running thin. So it came as a good surprise when the doctor, after examining Shona once more, told her she could return to Kse'Annilis. He helped her with the transfer—not to the once familiar Caller's house but to the Temple precincts.

The place was full of people. People cooking, people sleeping, people eating, people talking… Apparently, life was slowly getting back to normal.

The talking stopped as soon as they spotted her. No doubt, they were still dumbstruck by Ara's little show of two days ago.

She asked the nearest As'mir where she could find Ekbeth. He shook his head, carefully avoiding meeting her eyes.

Great. This was not helpful. She walked a bit further. Asking around her, Shona finally managed to find Ekbeth in the High Council meeting room.

A small crowd was gathered in the building corridors, as well, but she somehow managed to reach the stairs and get to the second floor.

The meeting room was impressive. Huge. The walls were wood-paneled, and a deep green carpet covered the floor, but even more stunning was the light. There were no windows and yet the room was lit as if completely open to the outside world.

This was where decisions were made, she realized. While probably full of hushed voices in normal times, the room was now extremely noisy and its central table was covered with papers. Everybody sitting around it looked anxious. They barely acknowledged her entrance.

She walked straight to Ekbeth. He was checking a long list. Probably the missing persons, she thought. "Morning."

He did not look at her, only frowned. "You should be resting on the Other Side, Kimiel."

"I had more rest than any of you, so can't complain. Lyrian was driving me crazy, the way he tried to be solicitous when it's obvious he'd rather strangle me."

Someone brought her a chair. She peeked at the list. "How bad is it?"

He sighed and looked at her, his eyes red with exhaustion. "Actually, I was expecting far worse. It looks like only the facades of the houses went down with the slide. There are not many actual rooms down there. We are still counting the survivors, but I think we've lost no more than fifty people in total."

It was still a lot, for such a small community, but Ekbeth was right. It could have been far worse.

"Good news is that our Caller, Nukri na Liom, is alive. He'll never be able to walk again, but he's alive. And his granddaughter Akalabeth has come to help. Ara bless her—she has been really helpful."

"And the Aramalinyia, Ekbeth. Is she dead? Is that the reason the Goddess needed me to speak to the community?"

At that, Ekbeth's expression sobered. He just nodded.

Shona felt a twinge of sadness. The old woman had been more a bother than anything to her, but still she'd never wished for her death. She knew how important the woman had been to the community.

She noticed Najeb and As'leandra in a corner of the room, in deep conversation above a map. She frowned. What were they doing here? They were supposed to be with Toshio.

Ekbeth put his hand on hers. "We need both of them here now, Shona. I'm sorry but your mission will have to wait."

How much did Ekbeth know? He could only have heard it from Najeb or As'leandra.

Ekbeth unexpectedly grinned and shook his head. She looked at him suspiciously.

"Are you reading my mind? Like As'leandra?"

"No, I don't have her talent. But I am getting better at reading your emotions. They did not betray your secrets, Kimiel. I sent Kalem after his son as soon as the Callers found the time to do something other than saving injured people, and he told me he'd found them with Watanabe. Both of them. What is As'leandra doing with Watanabe for you, Kimiel?"

Shona managed to keep her expression neutral. Sadly she could not do the same with her mind. Ekbeth nodded. "I thought so. Some mind reading. I don't need to know why. It's all right with me, Kimiel. It really is. As long as you don't abuse their talents, which I don't think you're doing right now. But they'll have to stay here for a while. Again, I'm sorry for that."

She was thinking furiously. "I need As'leandra, at least, Ekbeth."

"Kimiel! The girl has just heard her father is dead! Give her some time to grieve, at least! The Na Liathes' house was the worst hit. She's probably going to be the next Akeneires'eli of the Na Liathes—a lot of responsibility for someone so young. Especially in sorrowful times like these."

He pointed at the map Najeb and As'leandra were holding. "The Na Liathes are also responsible for the maintenance of the buildings. She will certainly be glad Najeb can help."

He shook his head. "The only good thing in that whole sad story, maybe, is that with her father now dead, and her becoming the head of her family, she can marry pretty much anyone she likes."

Shona's mind went blank with shock when she heard that. Surely, the Goddess would have not gone so far to answer As'leandra plea?

Her back started hurting.

Of course not! I don't control everything! This landslide was not my doing. S'emoel na Liathe was just at the wrong place at the wrong time!

Shona gritted her teeth until the pain receded. She would have to talk to As'leandra at the earliest occasion.

No doubt the girl was blaming herself. And she needed an update on the progress being made in the search for Sonam.

Ekbeth was now frowning, while looking at her. She patted his arm. "Stop worrying Ekbeth. Toshio will manage without them if I don't have a choice. Now, will you please go rest yourself? At least a few hours? I can certainly take over for you in the meantime."

He shook his head. "Can't. We have a Council in a few minutes. To discuss the urgent decisions that need to be made."

"Can no one replace you?"

"No. One of those decisions will be about lifting the ban on Akalabeth and her family. Then how fast we can assess the stability of the remaining houses. No one dares sleep inside the houses anymore. Then we have to decide what to do with our dead."

Ekbeth went on to explain the choices and Shona realized the horror of the situation. Then she asked, "And the new Aramalinyia? Are you not going to choose a new Aramalinyia?"

He made a strangled sound in his throat upon hearing her question. Something between a laugh and shock.

"What? What did I say?"

He shook his head, a strange smile on his lips. "Kimiel. You are the new Aramalinyia. The Goddess has made her will clear to all when she spoke through you!"

What? This had to be a joke!

Believe it, child. I told you I had plans for you, didn't I? I wish the circumstances were different, though. I was not expecting Pes'almari, your predecessor, to die for at least another ten years. That would have given you time to get used to our traditions.

Shona snorted. She very much doubted she would ever get used to the As'mirin ways. There were so many things she found inacceptable, like the state of the city streets to start with.

Indeed. Well, now, you can do something about it. Remember, your decisions are law from now on.

Had the Goddess gone mad? Putting the fate of all those people in her hands! When she had shown time and time again she made wrong decisions…

Her back grew warm. Oh, of course, the Goddess was going to keep a tight control on her. Perhaps for the first time, Shona was quite happy about that.

Others will help you, as well. This new beginning is going to be a difficult time for you, child. You'll have to attend all the funerals, for a start, and that will remind you of other losses. I know what I'm asking of you, but remember—you're not alone in this. You'll never be.

The sheer immensity of what was expected of her was slowly dawning on Shona. It was not only the funerals. Il was the lives of a few thousand people the Goddess was asking her to take care of.

She started to panic. Still, refusing the position was probably not an option.

Indeed not.

Shona sighed. Well, if it was the Goddess's will…

Don't complain about the consequences, though.

Agreed.

When she focused her attention again on Ekbeth, Shona

realized everyone had stopped talking and was looking at her, most of them with their mouths open.

"What's wrong?"

Ekbeth seemed amused more than anything. He whispered to her, "You are glowing, Kimiel."

Oh damn! Her skin was, indeed, showing that blue tinge again.

That way, no one will ever doubt I am speaking through you.

Shona sighed. Walking around as embodied neon was not her idea of fun, but then, the Goddess was probably not going to leave her any choice on that matter either.

She looked at Ekbeth. "Looks like I don't have any say in the matter. Where do I sit during the High Councils?"

60

T HE SILENCE IN the car was a blessing. There had
been too much noise around them lately. Too much
stress. All the decisions to be made. The complaints.
The funerals.

Above all, the funerals. The past month had been a time
of sorrow for the whole community.

Every family still living in the Valley had lost some
of their members. Three of them had even lost their
Akeneires'el. The only exception was, of course, the McLean
family, but, then, they had not been in the Valley at all when
the crater wall collapsed.

Ekbeth had said farewell to seven members of his family
and had lost count of how many funerals he had attended in
total. And, even though he sometimes managed to forget the
sorrow, the ruins that once were the left side of Kse'Annilis
were a constant reminder of the catastrophe that had hit
the community. Whenever Ekbeth looked in that direction
he felt like crying. They would never be able to reconstruct
their city to its former state.

Most As'mirin still refused to go to their houses to eat
or sleep. They were just living in the Temple, in the open.

And prayed a lot. For Ara's forgiveness. As for him, he was just too exhausted at the end of the day to join them. Besides organizing the funerals, attending to them, and supervising the daily routine of his household, he had to keep track of his bank business on the Other Side. Even with Lyrian's increasing help, he barely managed the deadlines.

Not all the most recent news was bad, though. Akalabeth was now reinstated as a full member of the As'mirin community. She was spending her time between her husband's village and Kse'Annilis, and both remaining members of the Na Liom family seemed happy.

As'leandra and Najeb were openly living together.

And there was a new energy buzzing in the community, as if the landslide had been a much-needed wake-up call to a society that had been half asleep up until then. The budget request pile on Ekbeth's desk had tripled in size, but this time it was not to annoy him—it comprised serious, concrete, improvement projects.

Many of the requisitions were not carefully thought out, so Ekbeth would return the claim to the requestor with a few suggestions. Sometimes, two people had the same idea, and he would then ask them to work together.

The selected projects he submitted to Kimiel.

He sighed, and looked at the woman that was now resting her head against his shoulder in the car as they returned from dinner at a fine restaurant in Zurich on the Other Side. Discovering she was the new Aramalinyia had certainly been a shock to her, but she had recovered amazingly quickly from it. She had immediately started to sit at the daily High Councils, making decisions and giving advice.

It surprised no one that she proved to be nothing like

their former Aramalinyia. In fact, most of her decisions were in total disagreement with her predecessor's. She was also not prone to compromises. She had overruled a few Akeneires'elin's decisions already, and harshly.

But it was obvious to everyone she had the best in mind for the community. And that she was open to radical change—something the previous Aramalinyia had certainly not been. And if a protest was ever raised against her at the Council table, the slight glow of her skin reminded them immediately who she was.

Ekbeth was worried about her. Kimiel kept reassuring him she was fine, but the rings under her eyes were telling a different story—as were the violent moves he felt under his hands on her belly every time they were able to share a bed. She was now well into her sixth month of pregnancy.

As she was not reasonable when in Kse'Annilis, Ekbeth enticed Kimiel to the Other Side as often as possible by treating her to spectacular shows or meals at elegant restaurants around the world, after which, to be sure she received enough rest, he insisted on a good night's sleep at the nearest of his apartments.

Those excursions were their privileged time, during which no one was authorized to bother them. Of course, there was some security. It could not be otherwise. She was too important. But Kalem was doing his best to make it as invisible as possible.

The car turned into the entrance path to his house. She opened her eyes.

Their eyes met, and Ekbeth gave her a guarded smile. He was getting used to her presence at his side.

Love? It was far too early to speak of love between them.

It seemed so long ago, sometimes, but only two months had gone since Ara's trial. He only hoped their fragile truce would hold a few more years.

The driver put the car in the garage. Kimiel get out of the vehicle, and walked directly towards the lift. "And thinking that I once thought it a toy for lazy fatsos! I'm really glad it exists right now!"

He smiled. "Go ahead. I need to discuss something with Kalem."

She shook her head. "Work. Always work. Don't linger too much, Ekbeth, or you're going to miss a lot of fun."

He was shaking his head when the lift door closed behind her. Lately, the "fun" had been limited. They just did not feel like it, either of them. Sorrow, exhaustion, pregnancy… She would probably be asleep by the time he got to bed, no matter how fast he managed to finish his work!

He had just reached Kalem's office, when a loud explosion of glass reverberated through the house. Ekbeth and Kalem immediately looked up. It had come from the second floor. They both rushed towards the stairs.

"Kimiel!"

The main room was still in the dark when they entered it. In the dark, and terribly cold. Kalem switched on the lights. The whole window overlooking Lake Zurich now lay shattered in tiny pieces on the floor. This explained the cold.

"Kimiel?"

They found her behind the sofa. Crouched. Her hands pressed against her heart.

Trying to prevent blood from draining out of her body. Already unconscious.

Kalem was the first to react. He took his jacket off and

gave it to Ekbeth. "Press it against her wound. I'm getting some help!"

Ekbeth mindlessly obeyed. Kalem returned after what seemed to Ekbeth to be an eternity—enough time for Ekbeth to get over the worst of his shock and come to his senses. "It's going to take too much time, Kalem! We should bring her to the Valley!"

"I've Called Erinani and Bers'el na Saoilcheach, Akeneires'el. They should be here anytime now. Let them decide!"

Erinani was there shortly afterwards, with two other Na Saoilcheachs.

She looked at the wound and her face was grim. Ekbeth refused to admit there was no hope. "You saved Kalem, Erinani! You can save her!"

She shook her head. "I told you bringing Kalem to me had been a mistake. This is worse. This looks like a direct hit, a bullet in the heart, Akeneires'el. I'm not good with bullet wounds. I never thought I would have to operate on one. She needs modern equipment for this kind of wound. Monitoring. Blood transfusions."

Bers'el appeared next to her. "And no anesthetics! Those would kill her even surer that the loss of blood."

Erinani and Bers'el looked at each other for a second. The fat Na Saoilcheach asked for a phone. Kalem handed him his, and Bers'el started making calls. In the meantime, Erinani was examining Kimiel, while trying to evaluate, Ekbeth imagined, how serious the loss of blood was.

Bers'el closed the phone. "Let's go. They will have a team ready within three minutes, they promised me."

Ekbeth could only stutter, "Where are you taking her?"

"To the University Hospital. I would not dare a longer transfer. She's already too weak."

The old man put a hand on Ekbeth's shoulder, and forced him to look at him. "We'll do our best, Ekbeth, but don't expect miracles. It is as bad as it looks!"

Both doctors disappeared, along with Kimiel. Leaving a huge puddle of blood behind.

Kalem was talking to him, Ekbeth realized. Telling him the driver had taken the car out again, and was going to bring him to the hospital. Kalem was going to call the police.

Ekbeth nodded and allowed Kalem to assist him into the car.

*

Minutes became hours and, too soon, the first rays of day chased the darkness of the night away.

Ekbeth had been seated, silently, on this plastic chair since the nurse had welcomed him, explaining that his wife was in the hands of their best surgeon and all they had to do now was wait until the team came out of the operating room.

At some point in time, Alyasini and Najeb had joined him. Even Lyrian. But they respected his silence, and sat expectantly next to him.

The reality was slowly dawning on him. Someone has shot Kimiel. Why? How? Those were the two first questions that came to his mind. The how would be for Kalem and his son to answer. He had to admit he did not have the slightest idea about the why. Kimiel had been so damn secretive about her past. He knew she had enemies, but which of them had wanted her dead?

The worst thing that could happen was that she had been shot because of him.

But the most pressing matter for now was whether she was going to survive the ordeal.

She was their Aramalinyia.

She was his woman.

She could not die.

He only had to close his eyes: that puddle of blood on the carpet came immediately to his mind. Funny how you discover how much you care about someone only after they disappeared from your life.

"Mr. Na Duibhne?" A man in green scrubs was addressing him. He looked exhausted, and, if not for the color of his garb, Ekbeth might have taken him for a butcher at the sight of his blood-soaked clothes.

The surgeon was drying his hands on a towel. Ekbeth guessed the truth before the other man even started talking. "I'm really sorry. We've done our best, but the bullet hit the heart, as you know. It stopped four times during our intervention, and the fourth time, there was nothing we could do to make it start again."

Small cries of dismay rose around them. A woman started crying, or was it Najeb?

Ekbeth knew he had to say something. He was only feeling hollowness.

The surgeon made another step towards him. "We've been able to save the baby, though."

Ekbeth had to admit he had forgotten all about the baby in the last hours. "Where is she?"

The surgeon was taken aback. "I'm afraid we can't allow you to see the body yet. We are still stitch…"

"I mean my daughter. Where's the baby?"

"Oh, sorry. We've put her in an incubator, had to, she's

such a tiny thing. She'll need some intensive care in the next weeks, but I think she'll make it all right in the end. She's been responding fantastically to all our tests."

"Can I see her?"

"I'll ask a nurse to bring you there. Please accept my deepest sympathy for your tragedy."

Ekbeth only nodded. He knew the man had done his best, even though it had not been enough.

He went to his daughter. The baby was placed in a glass box, seemingly deep asleep. She looked so tiny and vulnerable in there.

He put his hands on the glass, trying to send reassurance to this little bit of himself through the panel, like he had done so many times recently, on Kimiel's belly.

The baby moved slightly. It was just not the same. This was so wrong! She needed her mother.

He could not handle that responsibility on his own! He could not handle the whole community on his own!

Despair replaced the emptiness inside him. Without really realizing it, he started crying bitter tears.

61

SOMEWHERE AND NOWHERE.

"Where am I?"

You died, child.

"What? It can't be!"

I did not foresee it myself, but it is as it is.

"I can't be dead and talk to you. I was on the Other Side."

You are dear to me. I made an exception and collected your soul on the Other Side. Now…

"I don't want to choose. I did not want to die."

Almost no one welcomes that moment, child, but losing your physical body is part of the cycle. Not so long ago, you'd have welcomed the choice.

"Not anymore. I still need to find my son. There was that baby to be born. The future of Kse'Annilis! You said it yourself—you did not foresee it. It was that bastard, wasn't it? He hired a hit man to bring me down. I should have expected it."

Silence.

"Goddess, you owe me a favor."

Silence.

What you have in mind is not possible.

"I don't believe you. You created the As'mirin, didn't you?"

An eternity of silence.

It will take time.

"I'm not going anywhere. And this time, less tattoos, please."

62

"HERE YOU ARE, Ekbeth! Do you really have to spend every hour of the day in the neonatology ward?"

He recognized the woman's voice and did not look up. That little bundle in his arms was so fragile that he did not dare move for fear of hurting her.

He just said: "She has no mother left, Sally. It's the least I can do to be with her as much as possible."

Sarah-Lysliana came to stand next to him and peered over his shoulder. "She's really a sweet thing! She's grown since the last time I visited. Relax, Ekbeth. She's not going to break."

He shook his head. "Look at her. She's so tiny! I'm not sure I'm ready for fatherhood, Sally."

Sarah-Lysliana put her hand on his shoulder. "You're going to be the best father ever, Ekbeth. See it as an extra dimension of your Akeneires'el's role. You take care of people. You'll take care of her just the same."

He nodded, and allowed himself a proud smile. "The doctor just left. He told me that if she goes on like this I'll be able to take her home next week."

Sarah-Lysliana nodded. "Your little girl has survived Ara's trial while in her mother's womb. I'd say that certainly proves her will to live, don't you think?"

"Certainly."

"Have you finally thought of a name for her?"

He nodded. "Judikali. It was my mother's second name."

Sarah-Lysliana smiled. "Good choice. I like it!"

She looked around her. "So, is this where you're spending all your time nowadays?"

He shook his head. "Not all my time. I still have the bank to run."

"Lyrian told me he's not seeing you in the office a lot lately. And you have not gone to the Valley since Kimiel was killed."

He sighed. "Not true. I go there from time to time, but they don't really need me. I just can't stand the others' looks, Sally, or hearing their false condolences. And I know some still reproach me for not having protected her enough. I mostly work from home."

"And where is that home? I heard you were selling your house in Zurich."

She saw his frown, and quickly added. "I'm not spying on you. Some people are concerned about you, Ekbeth. It's not all false concern."

He looked at his daughter. She was still sleeping, but her fingers were moving. He smiled tenderly at her, and put her back in her cradle.

Sarah-Lysliana was still waiting for an answer, he realized. "I'm staying in a hotel suite lately. Until I've found something else for me and her."

"Mmh! The hotel guests are going to be very happy to hear a crying baby all night!"

He growled, "I can buy the whole place if I want to."

She laughed. "My, how touchy you've become, Ekbeth! I was joking."

He tried to smile.

She nodded. "Better. Now, in case you're wondering, I have come to bring you an invitation, Ekbeth."

That certainly surprised him. "An invitation? I don't think…"

She stopped his refusal with a hand. "We are holding a wake in memory of Kimiel on the Island next week. There will be a Presbyterian service, I'm afraid—her family insisted—but we all thought you should be there as well."

A wake? His mind went blank.

"I don't know… I have to take care of my daughter. And the bank."

She took his arms, and forced him to look at her.

"Ekbeth. Hiding won't lessen the pain. You're not the only one to mourn her. As I said, her mother, brother and sister will come, with their families. They really would like to meet you. Her friends will be there as well. Please come."

Then she looked at the cradle and smiled, if a bit sadly. "And if you want to bring your daughter along, she'll be more than welcome! There are plenty of people who want to meet her!"

Ekbeth shook his head.

She tapped his shoulder. "That's also something you'll have to admit, Ekbeth! You won't be able to hide her forever. She's not yours alone!"

He was well aware of that fact; he knew he was too

protective, but she was all he had left. He did not want to lose her as well.

The McLeans were okay though, he reflected, and Sarah-Lysliana was right: he had been hiding lately.

He made a decision. "I'll come. When is it exactly?"

She gave him all the details and hugged him before leaving. "See you in a week, Ekbeth."

*

The Island.

The freezing wind was enough to dissuade any sane man from settling here. You could not grow anything here, as the layer of soil was too thin, and the few cows the McLeans owned were in constant danger of falling into the sea from the high cliffs.

Ekbeth still had to understand why the McLeans were so attached to this little piece of land. In the Middle Ages, living on that remote chunk of rock made sense, a natural protection against attackers, as long as they were not As'mir. But nowadays? It was so isolated! More than a one-hour boat ride from the mainland.

He tightened the collar of his coat, and started walking briskly towards the castle.

That was another thing he had trouble understanding. Why bother keeping such an impractical medieval building? It was crumbling at every corner, and lacked any modern equipment.

The McLeans were just as bad as the rest of the As'mirin community, was his reasoning, as far as hanging on to traditions was concerned. They were clinging desperately to the past.

The main entrance door opened as soon as he knocked

on it. Andrew McLean himself, dressed in black, as was appropriate on this Side, stood there.

He nodded to Ekbeth. "Welcome. I hope you don't mind that we are wearing the Na Duibhnes' colors, Ekbeth."

Ekbeth heard the slight challenge in the younger man's voice. He smiled. "I live on this side, Andrew. I'm not as narrow-minded as the rest of my family."

Andrew returned the smile and let him enter the building. The entrance hall was not very impressive—rather narrow, which was not surprising as it used to be a defense area—but after a rather steep staircase, Ekbeth entered the main hall, and that was certainly imposing. The McLeans had tried to keep the medieval atmosphere even inside. The ceiling was extremely high, with massive wooden beams across its breadth. The walls were stone, covered with colorful tapestries. There were two monstrous chimneys on either side of the room. The only light came from the small windows set in one of the thick walls.

A huge oaken table filled the middle of the hall, and the family and their guests were standing comfortably around it. It was quite a small gathering.

Sarah-Lysliana came to him as soon as she saw him. "Glad you came, Ekbeth. Let me introduce you to some people."

She led him toward a group of people standing apart from the rest. As they crossed the room, she whispered, "I should have warned you, they are a bit uptight, but, well, you're probably used to their kind."

When they reached the group, she said, "Ekbeth, let me introduce you to Kimiel's family."

She started with Kimiel's mother, Emily, a tall

brown-haired woman with a kind face, then the Reverend Richard McLeod—a priest!—who exhibited the telltale red hair of the McLeans, and his family. Richard and his wife had produced quite a lot of children.

Then… Ekbeth's heart missed a beat. Sarah-Lysliana saw his reaction and touched his arm. "This is Kathleen and her husband Philip Murray. She's Kimiel's sister."

He did not really need that added piece of information. He had thought for a second she was Kimiel.

But when he looked at Kathleen more attentively, he saw some differences. Though with the relatively poor light of the room, his confusion was not surprising. The sisters looked a lot alike.

"This is Ekbeth Maher na Duibhne, Akeneires'el of the Na Duibhnes. He was Kimiel's partner."

They all politely nodded to him, reserved. With Sarah-Lysliana's warning in mind, he was not sure how to react either.

Sarah-Lysliana announced. "We are still waiting for Kimiel's friends to arrive. I heard the boat is underway. Should not take much longer. Do you want something to drink, Ekbeth?"

He declined. She left him among those perfect strangers, and there was an awkward silence while they all looked at each other without really knowing what to say.

Ekbeth was the first to make an attempt. "I wish we'd met earlier, before she was killed. I must admit I've been very curious about you."

Kimiel's mother smiled sadly. "It probably would have been as embarrassing as now, Akeneires'el. We have not seen Shona, or Kimiel, as you seem to call her, for the past twenty-six years. I would not have known what to say to her, or to you."

Twenty-six years? She must have been very young at the time. What had she done to deserve their rejection? They were now on the defensive, so he did not ask details.

He tried to sound friendly instead. "Please, call me Ekbeth. That Akeneires'el title has no meaning outside the Valley."

They seemed to relax a tiny bit.

The reverend even smiled. "I went to the Valley when I was little, you know, with my father Malcolm. During Ara's ceremonies. But it's already forty years ago, I'm afraid. I have rather vague memories of the place."

His sister intervened, offering her first smile. "That can't be true. You kept telling me and Shona about how fantastic it was! We were terribly jealous that we could not come with you that first time."

She suddenly sobered. "And we never had our chance to go. Because our father died and we were thrown off the Island."

She did not sound as bitter about this as Kimiel had been, but judging by the way the whole family hushed her it was still apparently a sensitive subject.

He tried to lighten the mood, even though his choice of topic was far from ideal. "You would be very disappointed if you saw the City right now, Kathleen. I suppose Sally told you about the landslide?"

They all nodded. Richard said, "We are sorry for your losses. I've prayed for the victims."

Ekbeth thanked him. He wanted to tell them the role Kimiel had played in the rescue, but saying to a priest his sister had been possessed by a Goddess, even if for a short moment? He did not think it was such a good idea.

Kimiel's mother asked, "Sally told us Shona was pregnant when she was murdered."

Ekbeth nodded, and was suddenly glad he had prepared for that question. He took his mobile phone out of his pocket. There was no internet connection in that dreadful place of course, but he could at least show them some pictures of Judikali.

"The baby was saved, and, though our daughter was born far too early, she's recovered from the trauma really nicely. Here, look. I took these yesterday."

They all looked eagerly at the few pictures.

Kimiel's mother asked, "What color are her eyes?"

The question was not only out of curiosity, he reflected. Emily wanted to know whether Judikali was a McLean or a Na Duibhne. She was just as bad as his own family, who had been asking the same question every time he saw them.

"It's really too early to say. She does not have much hair either, as you can see. We'll just have to give it a bit more time."

Kathleen asked, prudently, "Would it be possible to see her, later? She's my niece, after all."

Ekbeth nodded. "Of course. I am currently looking for a new house, but you're all more than welcome to visit us."

Richard McLeod intervened. "In this family we are not travelers, Ekbeth. Shona was really an exception to the rule. Always interested in the weirdest things, the more exotic the better. My family and I are living with my mother in a village that is more or less across the Island. If you are visiting the McLeans, you'll also be welcome to come to our place, if only for a few hours."

Richard's wife suddenly asked, "Who's taking care of the baby right now?"

"Judikali, that's our daughter's name, is still in the neonatology department, in very good hands. I visit her every day. I've found the perfect nanny for her, when she is allowed to leave the hospital, which should be any day now."

The woman did not seem to appreciate his decision. "A nurse! That child needs her parents' affection, not a surrogate mother."

She realized her mistake immediately, of course.

Ekbeth kept his face carefully neutral. Sarah-Lysliana had judged them correctly, it would seem. He was suddenly not so sure that seeing these particular relatives on a regular basis was such a good idea.

"Judikali will be very well taken care of, do not worry. Her nurse will never replace her mother, of course, but the woman's come to me with impeccable references. And my daughter still has me. I'm a very busy man, but I've already reduced my activities considerably over the past few months—to everyone's frustration, believe me—to be able to spend more time with her. I'll let no harm come to my little girl. Losing her mother was already hard enough."

Toshio Watanabe entered the hall at that moment, and Kimiel's whole family suddenly became distant again. The attitude puzzled Ekbeth a bit, until he heard one of the children ask in a whisper if this was the criminal who had put his aunt on the wrong path. He was quickly silenced.

That was one way to see it, of course. It was always so easy to blame others for one's acts.

Of course, Ekbeth still knew so little about Kimiel's past. He still had trouble seeing the whole picture in the fragments he had managed to collect during recent months, and he had a strong feeling that, with the disapproval of him that they displayed, Kimiel's family was not going to come forward with the details.

He really needed to talk to Watanabe.

Maire Kincaid was there as well, and Jeffrey Matheson, and Najeb.

Najeb had asked for a leave soon after Kimiel's death, without explaining what he intended to do. Ekbeth had not asked questions. He knew the young man was with Watanabe, trying to complete Kimiel's mission. Whatever it was. He had never found the time to ask Najeb.

Najeb looked tired, and nervous. Not himself. The whole group looked exhausted, he realized, with the exception, perhaps, of Maire Kincaid.

He walked over to them and nodded briefly to Watanabe, then talked to Najeb. "Are you okay, Najeb?"

The young man bowed to him. "Yes, Akeneires'el. We just arrived from China—Jeffrey, Toshio and me. I offered them the use of the Caller's services, but Toshio does not trust it, so we travelled the human way. He has a private jet but it was quite a long trip! That last bit on the boat just finished us off."

Ekbeth smiled. "You could have called yourself out of the situation, Najeb!"

He shook his head. "We have become well acquainted over the past weeks. I found it disrespectful to them."

Ekbeth wanted to ask him what they had been doing

during that time, but Watanabe interrupted him. "We need to talk, Ekbeth. Later."

Ekbeth was only too glad that the two of them agreed on that point. "I have wanted to do that for a long time already, but you never answered my messages."

"I've been busy. Sorry. But all is well now… Except we still don't know who ordered Shona killed."

Indeed, thought Ekbeth. Not for lack of trying on Kalem's part and by the Swiss police forces. The murderer had been a pro. They had not been able to find any trace of the killer, except his bullet, extracted from Kimiel's heart.

He felt a familiar tingling in his back, and when he looked behind him, he discovered As'leandra Na Liathe had appeared in the middle of the Hall.

Ekbeth had to grin when he noticed the open mouths of Kimiel's nephews and nieces. As'leandra was certainly a sight. She had the genetic slenderness of the As'mirin, and with her long dress—green velvet with fine gold-thread embroidery and floor-length sleeves—and her long, green, elaborately coiffed hair, they probably took her for a fairy or some other fantastic creature. She was only missing the wings.

As'leandra blended perfectly with the room's Gothic decorations. She made her brief reverence to everyone, and to no one in particular. "Sorry for being late."

Andrew McLean smiled at her from the other side of the room. "You are just in time, Akeneires'eli. And very welcome. Shall we start?"

Suddenly, the whole room was filled with somber silence. Andrew finally broke it.

"Dear family, dear friends, we are here today to remember Shona, also known in the As'mir Valley as Kimiel, daughter of Malcolm and Emily, sister of Kathleen and Richard, partner of Ekbeth, mother of Judikali. She was taken from this Earth far too early, in a cowardly act. She had had a tumultuous life, had decided to follow a dangerous path, but it does not lessen our pain for her loss."

Ekbeth could not help but think how hypocritical they all were right now—with the exception, perhaps, of Watanabe, Maire Kincaid and Matheson. The McLean family barely knew Kimiel—knew her even less than he had. Her family was pretending to grieve, but admitted openly that they had not seen Kimiel in years.

He kept a straight face. There was no point in saying this. He was, after all, not much better than them in that regard. Her sudden death still brought up an uneasy mix of feelings in him. People thought his voluntary isolation was due to grief. That was only half of it. He did miss her sorely, but the dominant feeling was guilt. Guilt for not having adequately protected her. Guilt for not having had the time to know her better. Guilt for having lost Judikali's mother.

"…The Reverend Richard is now going to pray with us."

For the entire ceremony, Ekbeth stopped listening. Not for lack of respect, but simply because he could not follow one single word of the prayer. Did they really have to do this in Gaelic?

He saw a sudden smile on As'leandra na Liathe's face, standing next to him. Damn the girl, she was probably reading his mind right now. She just nodded slightly, then seemed very interested in her hands.

After the prayers, Andrew invited everyone to go outside. As they exited, Sarah-Lysliana handed each person some flowers. Ekbeth asked her where they were going.

"We've chosen a nice place for a small memory stone for her. It's not far from here."

Well, the Island was not that big in the first place, thought Ekbeth.

In five minutes, they were all standing in the chilling wind, beside a low stone wall, with a view of the sea and an odd lighthouse.

Sarah-Lysliana spoke. "I'm going to miss Kimiel, Shona. A bit more than four months ago, we were sharing a cup of hot cocoa here, while listening to the wind. I know how it sounds, but she wrote once that there are stories carried in this wind, and if you listen very carefully, you'll understand it is true."

She then took a small thermos and emptied the contents on a small square stone at her feet. It made a brown puddle on the stone.

Not blood, told Ekbeth to himself, fighting a sudden queasiness. This was probably hot chocolate.

"I hope you hear us now, Kimiel, wherever your soul is. I hope the wind will carry this to you."

When an As'mir died outside of the Valley, his or her soul was not given Ara's choice. It was doomed to wander forever outside of the Veil. To avoid this fate, tradition prescribed incineration of the body in a favorite place on the Other Side, instead of within the Valley, to create an anchor point for the soul. If the complaints of the many McLean ghosts were any indication, it was not a much better option, but at least their descendants knew where the ghosts were and could, when necessary, still pay homage.

Only, Kimiel had not been an ordinary As'miri, she was their Aramalinyia. So they had brought the soulless body to

Kse'Annilis and performed the cremation rites in front of the Lake. So far, none of them had felt any manifestation of her ghost. But it was still early days.

He approached the stone and read.

Kimiel Malcolm Keh Niriel once was here,
listening to the wind music.

He walked towards Sarah-Lysliana and whispered, "This was a really nice ceremony, Sally. Thanks for the invitation."

"You are most welcome. You know what? I wish she had found time to write those songs for me, Ekbeth. I only got one, in the end, and it's really good. There was a lot of sensitivity under that tough attitude of hers. I'm still busy with the last adjustments, but the CD should come out in three months. Pity she died so soon."

They both looked sadly at the stone.

Yes, Kimiel was gone forever.

63

T HE LUNCH INVITATION at Watanabe's place arrived two days later. Najeb explained to him how to get there and tried to prepare him for a surprise.

Ekbeth was glad for the warning, as he was taken aback as soon as he saw the place. Kalem, at his side, hid his reaction no better.

It was not a house. It was a monstrosity. He had never seen anything like this before. The setting was an impressive acreage of English countryside, and the house was not that big. No, what had surprised him was its style, or rather lack of style. He was not an expert in architecture, but the house looked to him like an experiment turned bad. It was just a bit of everything. A medieval turret in one corner, flanking a classical façade that was interrupted by a Tudor bow window and ended at the other end with a modern steel and glass greenhouse—and that was only one side. The house rambled in all directions. As if the architect had simply gone mad.

It was either that, or the place had been constructed bit by bit, something he very much doubted, as no one in his right mind would have combined so many different styles.

"Welcome to my humble house, Ekbeth!" Watanabe

was expecting him by what Ekbeth supposed was the entrance door.

Ekbeth shook his head. "Humble? There's nothing humble about this place! Is it the reason you murdered two men? To get out of it?"

Watanabe laughed. "It's quite the thing, isn't it? Maire felt in love with it as soon as she saw it. I've grown used to it over time. Come in, please."

Ekbeth soon realized the inside of the house was just as crazily planned as the outside. Near the entrance, three flights of stairs rose, all located on the same side of the hall. He could not see where they led.

"Who built this?"

"A very eccentric man, as you could expect. Eccentric and rich. After his death, none of his heirs wanted anything to do with it. Potential buyers were not really enthusiastic. The house had been on sale for ten years already when we visited it, Maire and I. You'll have to excuse my wife. She's quite busy with her business in London, so it's going to be a men only affair today. You, your bodyguard, Jeffrey and me, I'm afraid."

"I was expecting to see Najeb as well."

Watanabe shook his head. "He's occupied with something else right now. Ah, here we are!"

Ekbeth kept his expression neutral. Watanabe was evidently not much more forthcoming than Kimiel or Matheson. He was giving as little information as possible.

He looked around the room they had just entered. In contrast to the architecture, this was a cozy little place, simply decorated with modern furniture, comfortable armchairs and a low table, and a view onto the gardens from the French windows that was quite charming.

Jeffrey was waiting for them.

"Can I offer you a drink, gentlemen? Lunch will be served in the room next door, but we can start our discussion here."

The armchair Ekbeth sat in was as comfortable as he had expected. It was tempting to let his guard down, forget for a moment the man sitting opposite him was not a friend.

"I'm glad you could find time for this lunch, Ekbeth. I asked to meet you to compare notes on the murder."

Ekbeth asked, "I was expecting you to ask this earlier. Three months have passed since she was killed."

Watanabe shrugged. "I told you, we were busy elsewhere. I was not really anticipating that you would need our help. If you managed to find Shona twice while she was trying to escape from you, I don't think anyone can escape you."

Ekbeth made a face. "Well, not this time. Kalem has been working with the police, but we just don't know who's behind this. Only that the murderer was a hired pro."

"Your house is heavily secured. How was this possible?"

Kalem explained to them. "The shot was fired from one of our neighbors' houses. A neighbor who was away. His security system was shut down. Too far for our cameras to catch anything, but still near enough to have the perfect positioning for the shot. A nearly impossible angle, but still doable for a skilled sniper. The murderer just had to wait for her to walk in front of his weapon."

"So, you are certain she was the intended victim. Not Ekbeth?"

Kalem nodded. "We were not so sure at the beginning,

of course, but there has been no other attempt since then. No, I really think she was the target. As to why? I've checked all the possibilities on our side. With no results. Can you help us with that? I don't need to ask you whether she had enemies—it's more, how many did she have?"

Matheson and Watanabe looked grim.

"More than you can even imagine," Watanabe said. "But many of them are my enemies as well. They would have tried to kill me before her, or send me a warning—at least, that's what we think. No... someone who wanted her dead specifically? Five, maybe six people. I may have missed someone."

"It would help if you could tell us a bit of her past." They reacted to his request as Ekbeth had expected. Distrustfully. He insisted. "We won't solve this without helping each other, Watanabe. We need to know her past!"

Watanabe stared at him for a long moment, and then finally asked softly, "What do you know of her?"

Ekbeth had to think about this. There were some bits Watanabe certainly did not need to hear, like Ara's talks with Kimiel.

"She's of the McLean family, but her own family rejected her. They think you're responsible for what she's become. Lost her father when she was very young. She killed her husband, but was still grieving for him. She worked for you. She was a thief. Also a killer. She was rich. Had some connection to Bhutan, of all places. Beside all of this, for all her toughness, she was not very stable emotionally. At least, I don't think she was."

Watanabe allowed himself to smile at that. "No, she certainly wasn't, but when you hear why, I'm sure you'll be amazed she's not stark raving mad."

He then paused. Took his time. "Did she tell you about her son?"

Ekbeth did not manage to hide his reaction. "A son! She never told me she had a son!"

Watanabe shook his head. "She never told me she was pregnant again either. You always had to find out the facts about her by yourself. Hopefully, before it's too late."

He shifted a bit in his chair. "I suppose she would have told you about Sonam eventually. We both thought the boy was dead, but she recently discovered he was still alive. Or at least, that he might still be alive. I must admit I did not believe her when she announced this news. More than four years had gone since the boy was last seen alive and he was not in a good company. But Shona can be so damn convincing! She convinced me to get out of jail to help her. With or without me, she would have gone after him anyway! And, as I told you, I protect my friends. Trouble is, we had no clue where to find him, except that he was probably in China."

Ekbeth was trying to sound uninterested when asking. "Did you find the boy?"

Watanabe nodded, but there was nothing exultant about his expression.

"I'll spare you the details. We would never have managed it without Najeb and his girlfriend's help. I must admit that that ability of reading minds came in very handy a few times. Anyway, the boy was found last week. We brought him back with us from China before going to the wake."

So, that had been what Najeb and As'leandra had been doing for Kimiel. Not that it was so important anymore. No, he was more concerned with the undertone in Watanabe's voice. "What's wrong with the boy?"

"Wrong? Let's just say his keeper liked the idea of having a human pet. We found Sonam chained in a kennel. He tried to bite me."

Ara! Who would do this to a little boy? "Is the boy going to be okay?"

Watanabe nodded. Grimly. "Eventually."

Kalem suddenly asked, "Is Najeb with him, now?"

"Yes. We brought the boy to a hospital. We had no choice: he's really in poor health, and the doctors still have to examine his psychological state. Still, we can't leave him alone for long. He's refusing food and treatment when it's not coming from us, and will not rest when we're not around. Najeb has taken on the responsibility of guarding him. At least, until we can bring him here."

Watanabe looked at Ekbeth with a hesitant face. "We've been thinking of adopting him, Maire and I."

Ekbeth was too shocked by the news to oppose the decision. "We can decide on this later. I want to meet him. I can understand now is not a good time. But I want to see Sonam at some point in time. If he's her son, he's my daughter's brother, which makes him my responsibility as well."

Watanabe did not seem to find the logic strange. He only nodded, and then said, "Anyway, Sonam apart, I think you've got most of the important elements of her story. As for her family, let them think what they want about me. They don't know the real story, and Shona wanted to keep it so. She never wanted anyone's pity."

A servant came into the room to announce that lunch was ready. So they moved to the next room, which was just as simply decorated as the previous one, and took their places around the table. Ekbeth waited until the first course, a soup of some sort, was served. He did not really pay attention to the food.

Watanabe barely touched his meal. Instead, he told Ekbeth about Kimiel's past.

"I don't know much about her younger years. On the rare occasions when Shona referred to those, she only said that she sometimes had the feeling she would suffocate among her relatives. They were never going anywhere. Her brother got quite religious over the years. This kind of thing. Her only consolation at the time was music, she told me. Have you ever heard her sing?"

Ekbeth nodded. Watanabe continued. "She really had a lovely voice, didn't she? At seventeen, she entered a music school in Glasgow. Was one of the top students there, if what she said is true. I never checked. Problem is, there is a lot of pressure when you perform that well. From your fellow students, from the teachers, from your family. At some point in time, it just became too much for her. And that's where her problems started. She started using drugs. Heroin. From the beginning. She very quickly became an addict. Got expelled from school. Her family refused to help her, threw her out of the house. So here she was, nineteen, living on the street, in need of money to buy some drugs and no reliable source of income."

Another slight pause. "An unfortunate situation. But not an exception. I don't need to tell you what happens in those cases."

Ekbeth shook his head, a bitter taste in his mouth. "Is it how she became a thief?"

Watanabe sighed, hesitated. "Not directly. She never exactly lived on the streets. She had some older friends in

Glasgow. Some freaks who had missed the flower revolution but were big on the idea. They were living together in a squat, sharing the money they were earning and the drugs. Shona was allowed to come and live with them. She told me she only needed to do a few favors to get what she needed."

The plates were taken away, the servant brought the next course.

"Those favors soon brought her into the prostitution circuit. She could not remember that time very well, she told me. I found the social worker's files of this period. The reports are rather sordid. She had more powder than blood in her veins at the time."

He took a bite of his meat, chewed on it for a moment.

Ekbeth asked, "So how did you two meet? Did you have sex with her?"

Watanabe almost spit his food. He tried to hide his reaction behind his napkin, but his eyes were glistening when he answered, "No! I was already married at the time!"

"So what?"

"Ah! I may be a criminal to your eyes, Ekbeth, but I do love my wife. I would never hurt her feelings that way. Besides, Maire'd probably kill me if she ever found out. No… I met Shona in different circumstances. Many things happened to her in the meantime."

Watanabe drank some water, and took a few more bites.

"I don't know when this happened exactly, but one day, so she told me, she just walked through a closed door of her community squat. She was too stoned to realize what she had just done but someone else had seen it. He asked her to repeat it. She slammed into the door. That man kept an eye on her from that moment on. He saw her walk through doors and walls a few times. Always when she was not paying attention, which by then was more often than not. The man was also a drug-user, but he was not as far gone as Shona was, and he was a thief. He saw the opportunity immediately. I've met the man. Briefly. He told me it took some convincing to prove to Shona she was able to walk through obstacles, and that by helping him with his job she could put her body to better use than selling herself for a few pounds a day."

Watanabe gave a brief smile. "The man probably saved her life. He managed to force her to reduce her doses, at least low enough that she was not a zombie anymore. He taught her the fine art of entering a house undetected and to chose the objects they could easily get rid of for some cash. Shona came to the idea of getting into the safes on her own, she told me. According to her, it's actually easier than walking through a door."

Ekbeth did not need that reminder. He was glad Matheson hid his obvious amusement at that. Watanabe did not seem to have noticed anything.

"The Glasgow police arrested her a few times. She had become a bit too confident, left some fingerprints. She finally spent some months in jail. When she came out, she was involved in a big deal. She had met someone who told her about an art dealer in London who had so much valuable stuff in his house he would probably not notice one or two missing pieces. Her contact assured her that—whatever those pieces were—she'd be able to sell them. That's how I met Shona."

Ekbeth was not certain he had followed.

"She sold the stolen goods to you?"

This time both Matheson and Watanabe smiled.

Watanabe shook his head. "No. I was the art dealer she stole from. True, I would probably not have noticed the theft, at least not immediately, except that she had taken two small thirteenth centuries Japanese tea bowls that had been sold the day before for a very high price. I got quite furious when I discovered their disappearance. I have connections. Something Shona's contact forgot to mention to her. My men only needed two days to bring her to me, with the bowls."

His smile turned into a snarl. "She had just shot up a few grams when my men found her. She was barely standing on her feet when we met. Yet, I had no intention to let her live, and she knew it. Even as fucked up as she was, do you think she begged me to spare her?"

Ekbeth did not need the amused glint in Watanabe's eyes to know the answer to the question. He remembered all too well how Shona had reacted when she had been at his mercy.

He shook his head. "Not her. She probably told you that you deserved it."

Toshio nodded, a sad smile on his lips. "Close enough. She told me that she wanted to offer her talents to my benefit, and the theft was just her way to show me how good she was."

Ekbeth chuckled. So typical of her, indeed. "And you accepted?"

Toshio moved his glass slightly. "Not before my men gave her a good thrashing for her insolence, but I must admit I was curious about how she had managed the little feat. My security is very good. So, when she regained consciousness, I asked her to explain herself."

The servant refilled the glasses and offered some dessert,

which everyone declined, before Toshio Watanabe went on with his tale.

"I have seen a lot of strange things in my life. But someone walking through walls like they were not there? I could not believe it. Yet, that girl was doing it, in front of me! As her mentor, I saw the advantages immediately, of course."

Ekbeth nodded. "So, that's how you started working together?"

Watanabe said, "My best idea ever. Understand, I only considered using her special talent as a last resort. I'd rather buy the goods, of just take them if necessary, but sometimes there was no other alternative. It was so simple for her! A few walls, a safe? Nothing was too difficult for her!"

He shook his head. "For ten years, we worked together. I taught her everything she knew about valuable Chinese antiquities. As well as self-defense, because she had a way of putting herself in the worst situations. But she was never really good at it. That's why I hired Jeffrey as her guardian angel at some point in time. Shona and I had agreed on a commission for her work. She was spending most of it on the heroin, but she had a nicely filled saving account when she left me. If not for her drug abuse, and her sometimes quirky moments, she would have been the perfect partner."

Ekbeth asked something else. "And all the people you allegedly killed in the process?"

He had never told Kalem about this, but his bodyguard did not seem surprised.

Watanabe sobered a bit. "That came mainly in our last year of collaboration. Collateral damage. Shona's words, not mine. As long as the Triads were not involved, there were very few victims. Art trafficking was not one of their businesses.

At least, not until they started noticing how much profit we were making. ”

He made a face. “Then, they tried to take over from us. To us, it was as much about protecting our business as our lives. You’ve seen the files Jeffrey sent you. That’s how bloody the war grew at one point. It was a very stressful period, I’ll admit. We could never sleep under the same roof twice. The Triads were losing men and they were really pissed at us. The thing is, Shona had no mercy for anyone trying to stop us, police or triad. She never gave any of them a second chance. Many of her victims made the mistake of underestimating her because she was only a woman, and an addict on top of that. A fatal mistake. Suddenly, she remembered her self-defense training and became very good with knives. Many of her victims realized that too late. Not a lot of them survived the encounter.”

Ekbeth looked at Kalem. His bodyguard was unconsciously touching the ugly scar on his chest. Yes, they had first-hand experience of that specific talent of hers.

“You’re still alive. You won against the Triads? I can’t believe it.”

“Winning is a big word, Ekbeth. It could not go on like this forever. We made a truce, which is still standing to this day.” Toshio smiled. “At that point in the story, her husband, Yeshe, comes into the picture.”

A slight pause. “Yeshe was the only man who ever counted in her life. Again, her words.”

Ekbeth ignored Watanabe’s deliberate provocation. “She told me so herself. Can you tell me about him?”

“He was an artist. From Bhutan, but living the best part of the year in Hong Kong. We met him regularly at gallery openings. He was truly an amazing man. Probably one of the most skilled jade sculptors of his generation. His work still sells for amazing prices. It made him a multi-millionaire, but he never cared for money. Always so quiet, so serene, and just as stubborn as Shona when he had set his mind on something. He knew about Shona and I, about our activities, I mean, and I'm sure someone told him how deadly Shona was. Still, he approached her and started courting her."

Both Matheson and Watanabe smiled at the memory.

"It's still a mystery to us, but she fell for him. They had been having an on-and-off relationship for two years at the time our little war with the Triads culminated. One of the Triads suddenly had the idea to get to us through Yeshe. They paid him a visit, threatened him, destroyed his atelier and many valuable pieces. Shona certainly made them regret the idea, but Yeshe had been badly frightened and he gave an ultimatum to Shona. He basically told her to quit heroin and her criminal activities, and come and live with him, or get out of his life."

Ekbeth knew exactly how Kimiel would have reacted if he had made such an outrageous offer. "And she accepted? I can't believe it! If anything, you can't shrug off years of addiction like that."

Watanabe smiled. "My reaction exactly when she told us her decision. I probably never realized how much she loved the man. She stopped using, something she had been refusing to do for years! Went and lived in Bhutan with him. Not my idea of a paradise, believe me. We thought it would never work. They proved us wrong."

Ekbeth shook his head, amazed. "I just can't believe she accepted!"

"Still, it's true. The timing could not have been better. The Triads were also wary of the war. I offered the truce: they would let me pursue my business; I would give them a percentage of my profit. And Shona was out of the picture from that moment, married and sent off to a distant land, at least for the best part of the year."

So now Ekbeth knew about the man Kimiel was still grieving. It did not explain what had happened to him.

"Yet he's dead. You told me she killed him. When I confronted her, she only told me it involved circumstances that I couldn't understand. Do you know how it happened?"

Watanabe's expression became unexpectedly sour. "Oh yes, I know how it happened. Unfortunately."

All was very still around the table suddenly. Until Watanabe managed to get a grip on his emotions and proceeded with his narration.

"This is what happened. Yeshe and Shona had been married for maybe six, seven years when a big art gallery in Hong Kong asked him to present a retrospective of his work. He accepted. Most of the sculptures were merely lent by their owners, but Yeshe brought a few pieces of his personal collection. The exhibition was a huge success."

Watanabe made a terrible face.

"Success is not always a good thing. It attracts attention. Makes people envious. Shona's memory is… let's say confused, about this period, but of some facts, we are fairly certain of. One morning some armed men arrived at their place in Bhutan. The mercenaries found quite a lot of people, as Shona and Yeshe had been celebrating something with his family. There were a few children in the group. The mercenaries did not care. They tortured everyone, especially Yeshe."

"Why?"

"They were looking for a specific jade sculpture. One they could not find."

Torturing a whole family for a piece of jade? Watanabe saw his reaction, of course, and nodded, grimly. "I know how it sounds. But some people would do anything, really anything, to get to something they crave. I know. I have made quite a lot of money satisfying that craving. I never expected that someone so close to me would one day suffer the folly of such a man."

He shook his head. "Shona was eaten by memories of the suffering of the ones she held dear. She was a tough girl. Very cynical about humankind. But what happened there, in that little valley, was too much, even for her. Her husband, everyone, was tortured before her eyes, and there was nothing she could do about it. Almost nothing."

The servant came again. This time he only offered drinks.

Watanabe was visibly doing his best not to show his emotions, but his clenched fists were indication enough.

"Shona killed Yeshe. She told me she had to kill him. The mercenaries had broken everything that could be broken in him. He would never have been able to work again. Killing him was an act of pity. Yes, she's tough, but the act sure broke her, more than the physical torture the bastards had put her through. As I said, he was everything to her."

Watanabe shook his head. "The soldiers were so furious when they found out Yeshe was dead, they killed the whole family. Killed them, then set fire to the place. They only let Shona live. She had to watch it from beginning to end!"

"Why let her live?"

Watanabe's lips suddenly produced a horrible grimace.

"They were still hoping to get that piece of jade, I suppose. They brought her somewhere and tortured her some more. At some point, they probably realized it was useless, and they handed her over to even worse torturers. When I finally found her, two years ago, she was a wreck."

The conversation was visibly particularly difficult for his host, but Ekbeth had to know.

"What had happened to her?"

Watanabe stared at some point outside. "The mercenaries sold her to a Thai pharmaceutical company. This company has a branch that developed some nasty drugs, which they then sell for a very good price to the military around the world. Drugs that break even the strongest will. The company needed guinea pigs, unofficial ones of course. People like Shona. Officially dead, not missed by anyone."

He clenched his fists. "The doctors I hired told me her years of drug use were probably the only thing that saved her, in the end. It had helped her resist the effects of some of the experimental drug components that had killed others— and fast. It had been a very close call, though. I apparently found her just in time. One or two more tests, and her body would have failed her. Sometimes, I wonder if that would not have been the better option."

Ekbeth tried to ignore the bitterness in those last words. He asked, "How did you find her?"

"Luck, mainly. Yeshe and Shona used to come to our place once a year, to bring his new collection, negotiate the commissions and have a bit of fun in the big city. When we heard nothing of them that year, Maire and I tried to contact them, without success. I decided to go and visit them. Bhutan is not exactly a country you can enter easily, especially the remote part where Yeshe's family was from, but I got in to Lhuentse eventually. My guide found out what had happened, or rather what rumor said had happened. There had been a fire, a whole family killed and only one survivor."

"Shona?"

Watanabe shook his head. "Dorje. Yeshe's older brother. No one knows how he escaped the massacre but he did. He was still in the local hospital when I visited the place. The doctor confirmed the fire accident. His patient had delusions about some demons that had attacked the house and tortured everyone. No one believed that part, but the doctor confided in me that a fire alone could not explain some of Dorje's wounds. I asked to see him. I could have been spared the effort; Dorje was so heavily drugged to keep him quiet that he was barely coherent. Still he seemed to recognize me, even though we had only met twice before. Seeing me made him talk. Or at least try. All in Dzongkha, the Bhutanese language. I could not understand what he was saying, except Shona's name. He kept repeating it. He got so agitated by my lack of reaction that the doctor quickly hustled me out of his room. When I asked the doctor what Dorje was saying, the man just shook his head. Nonsense, he told me. But I insisted, and the doctor finally translated me Dorje's words. That's when I heard the second round of positive news that day. Shona had not died in the fire, according to Dorje. She'd been taken away by the demons."

Ekbeth frowned. "And you believed him—the words of a traumatized man?"

Watanabe nodded. "I wanted to believe him. When it became obvious she was nowhere to be found in Bhutan—they don't have that many foreigners in that country, so it was easy to check—I used every connection I could think of, promised a huge reward for any clue. I wanted to believe."

He closed his eyes for a brief moment. Sighed.

"My patience was rewarded, eventually. Luck, more than anything. It took more than a year. Someone contacted me. Shona, or someone looking a lot like her, was held somewhere in Thailand for some testing. The place was heavily secured. I did not care. I hired some mercenaries and stormed the laboratory. We were almost too late. As I said, Shona was a total wreck when we freed her. She was plain crazy. There was not much hope for recovery. Drugging her was not an option. She had developed a nasty allergy to any sedatives. We had to chain her to the bed. Force-feed her. It was worse than having to watch an animal in a cage! Hopeless.

"I was very tempted to kill her myself, just to deliver her from her suffering. At least until one of my men told us about an old woman living in the Malaysian jungle who had created miracles with cases like Shona before. I met the woman in person before organizing Shona's transfer. Keremli only accepted to treat Shona after meeting her. She first refused because of her old age, but then she changed her mind. She told me Shona was kin, though I did not realize at the time what she meant by that. I discovered it later. For all her strange gifts, it took Keremli more than a year to heal her into a somewhat normal being. I don't know how she did it, but she erased the worst memories. Gave the girl her sanity back—at least most of it."

So! That was what Keremli had done for Kimiel! He should have guessed it himself! She had helped so many As'mirin get over their trauma after the collapse, after all.

Watanabe inhaled deeply, and managed to meet Ekbeth's stare.

"So, that's more or less her story. The rest, you are aware of. I've answered your question. Not sure it will help us discover who's behind Shona's assassination, though."

Kalem was the first to react. "You said she had very few personal enemies."

Watanabe nodded. "I will check them."

Matheson quietly said then, "The only possibility is Kellerman."

Watanabe shook his head. "I already told you, Jeffrey. I don't believe it! Why would he do such a thing?"

Ekbeth had heard that name earlier, he realized. From Kimiel herself. "Who is this Kellerman?"

"Oh, you've probably met him, Ekbeth. He's at the head of a huge international consortium. The headquarters are in Hamburg. Moreover, he's a big jade collector. That's why I think you know him. You probably met at some auctions, if not in a financial setting."

Ekbeth realized Watanabe was right. He knew exactly who the man was. Him? A killer?

"And why do you think he's behind Shona's murder?"

"I don't. Jeffrey here does. Shona has always been certain Kellerman was behind that attack on her family. She remembered an accident during that Jade Exhibition I was telling you about. Kellerman is a huge fan of Yeshe's work and has bought most of his pieces. According to Shona, this time he had set his mind on a specific piece, but Yeshe had made it as a present to Shona for the birth of their son, so would never have sold it. Kellerman apparently made a whole scene about it. Now, incidentally, it was that very piece the soldiers were looking for when they attacked the family."

"You mean, Kellerman ordered a whole family tortured and killed to get a piece of jade?"

"I know how it sounds. We've no solid proof of this. Sure, the man has the means and the influence to get some help from Chinese administration. He certainly could have asked someone to send the soldiers to get the piece of jade."

To kill how many people to get a single jade statue! If true, the man was really sick! And this madness did not reconcile with the Kellerman Ekbeth knew.

Toshio Watanabe apparently shared this view. "Again, I'm not convinced of his culpability, even though recent events might have proven me wrong. If he's behind this, he probably never intended it to be so brutal. Shona has a different point of view on this. Sadly, even if she's right, Kellerman's pretty much untouchable and he knows it. So that's why her murder does not make sense to me. Especially that he ordered it. Why take the risk of being discovered and kill her?"

Ekbeth thought about it. "She must have done something which made him panic, and ordered her execution. But what?"

He suddenly remembered some discussions he had had with Kimiel in the last weeks before her death, during their evenings outside the Valley. It had been about money. Financial transactions. How to take over companies. He had given her the phone number of one of his friends.

Oh my! What had she been doing?

"Ekbeth?"

He looked at Watanabe. "That discussion was not

useless, Watanabe. I think I understand some things better, but I have to check a few other facts. I need your trust for that. Can I have all the bank accounts numbers she would have had access to?"

Watanabe hesitated only slightly, but finally nodded. "What is your plan?"

"I need to look into the transactions she made in the weeks before her death. I may need your help, but, if I'm correct, we will have definite proof that Kellerman is our culprit. Or not."

64

L YRIAN'S OBVIOUS PLEASURE at seeing Ekbeth back at the bank did not last long.

Ekbeth explained to Lyrian what he needed and put the list of accounts on his cousin's desk.

"You are joking, Ekbeth! I really hope you are! There are more than fifty accounts on that list! Couldn't they provide you with the bank statements as well?"

"Well, Matheson is going to do that for the accounts he also has access to. Those are the ones marked in green. But I'm afraid that still leaves twenty of them that we have to start investigating ourselves."

Lyrian took a second, closer look at the list, and groaned, "Those two accounts in Hong Kong belong to a Triad bank, Ekbeth!"

"Ask Wei to help. It is important."

"I may have to ask the help of our internal hacker again to get that info, Ekbeth. You do realize what the consequences are going to be if we get caught?"

Ekbeth nodded. "You'll just have to stress the importance of discretion to the man, Lyrian. It's urgent. I want to know the movements on every one of them."

His cousin looked at him with a pained expression. "At your service, Akeneires'el. May I ask what his lordship is going to do while his servants are risking their lives for him?"

"Ah, sarcasm! That's more like you! Well, I'm going to look for a new home, if you want to know. And take care of my daughter, now that she's finally out of the hospital."

Lyrian moaned, "This is just so unfair! Do you know how many hours per day I have to work to manage the business without you?"

Ekbeth nodded, with a grin. "You're doing very well, Lyrian. I really can't complain."

Lyrian frowned, and looked at him with suspicion. "Oh no! I know where this is going, Ekbeth! I don't want the responsibility!"

Ekbeth's grin only grew. "Bad luck for you then, because the family council has already validated my decision. Not a small feat, you'll admit, knowing that you're banished from the Valley. As of today, you are the bank director on this side."

All of a sudden, Lyrian turned green. "It's just too much work, Ekbeth! I'm not ready for it!"

"Relax, Lyrian. I was not much older than you when I took over, remember? And, contrary to me, you won't have to figure out things from scratch! Besides, who said I was going to leave you alone with the job? I will still help in the coming months, and I hope to find another cousin to assist you. After he or she has been properly trained."

Lyrian was still not convinced. "You can't seriously think of stopping, Ekbeth! You love the job! You were born for it!"

"I thought so, too, but I have other priorities nowadays. My daughter, my family. We will still see a lot of each other—don't worry. You are family as well and we'll have to figure out together how to generate the money to repair Kse'Annilis. I expect that we'll have to meet frequently to discuss our cash positions."

Lyrian sulked for a moment, playing with the document Ekbeth had given him a moment ago. "I want a bodyguard from Kse'Annilis. No way that I'm going to meet your clients without one. The ones we have here are just not good enough."

Ekbeth nodded. "Very good point. I'll ask Kalem to arrange it. Now, about those bank accounts…"

Lyrian looked at the paper. "I'll see what I can do. What do you expect to find there, anyway, Ekbeth?"

Ekbeth was glad for the change of topic. "Kimiel had started asking me a lot of questions about the finance world, in her final weeks. At the time, I just thought she was pretending to be interested in my work."

"Was she asking about something in particular?"

Ekbeth nodded. "OPE's, loans and things like that."

That certainly surprised Lyrian. "You think she was considering taking over a business?"

"She told me she had money to invest, and we both know how true that was. So I gave her a friend's contact. I called him this morning. He was quite open about what they intended to do. She was trying to get a shareholder seat on the board of Kellerman's company."

Lyrian shook his head. "Ara! Did she have any idea who she was playing with? She might have been a criminal, but she was a neophyte as far as complex financial transactions are concerned. The sharks would have eaten her alive!"

Ekbeth nodded. "And maybe that's exactly what happened, Lyrian."

"Oh! I see. I certainly don't miss her, Ekbeth—sorry to say it. The woman was a bitch, no matter what you felt for her. I still hear her voice in my sleep—in nightmares."

Lyrian had told him this a few times before. Ekbeth could not blame him for his reaction. Lyrian had suffered at Kimiel's hand. It did not help Ekbeth in dealing with his loss, though. He left his chair, while pointing at the paper on the desk.

Lyrian grumbled, "Why did she need so many accounts?"

"Watanabe believes in spreading the risks. She's apparently accumulated quite a lot of money between her association with him and her husband's work—money none of them was using, till quite recently. Find those transactions for me."

Then he left the room.

65

S ARAH-LYSLIANA HAD BEEN right. Living with a newborn baby and her nurse in a hotel, albeit a luxury one and a very large suite, was indeed not such a good idea. Judikali was crying a lot, and, if no one had been complaining so far, he personally was starting to find it hugely embarrassing. Hence his efforts to find a suitable house as soon as possible.

He had no idea why the baby cried so much. She only stopped when he was touching her. Taking her in his arms transformed her from a little red shrew into the most angelic baby in the world. As soon as he put her back in the cradle, or handed her back to her nurse, she immediately started wailing again.

The nurse had a perfect explanation for his daughter's attitude. "You are her universe, right now, Ekbeth. She only feels safe with you."

"I understand, but I can't be with her like this all the time, Annabel."

"She'll get over it with time. She'll get used to me and others. Some people suggest to let the baby cry to accelerate the process. I'm sorry, I don't like the idea."

"Neither do I, but there must be something we can do."

"Well, we could try those little baby carriers. It would at least free your arms."

It was a good idea as long as he was staying on this Side and not visiting customers, but, as that had to happen more often than not, the nurse's idea was not practical. He had no intention, either, of taking the baby to the Valley, but he just could not leave Judikali behind like this, for what would be at the very least a few hours.

He suddenly thought of something. He had never been really impressed by the mothering instincts of the As'mir women. They tended to spend more time comparing the beauty of their offspring, or choosing clothes, than really taking care of them. Still, they were mothers and had to know some tricks, like how to put a baby to sleep, and so on.

He walked back to his desk and took out a piece of paper. The women were going to laugh behind his back, and gloat for hours about his inadequacy. For sure. Hopefully, they would also be willing to answer him, eventually.

He wrote a note and sent it to the Valley, to his great-great-grandmother Keremli. She was probably the best option, even though her own attempt at motherhood had been disastrous. Then he returned his attention to the nurse. She had not blinked when the paper had disappeared in front of her. Good for her! His staff had probably warned her about his strange habits.

"Did you have time to look at that property in Dietikon, Annabel?"

The nurse was a bit flustered when she answered, "Ekbeth, really, I told you I would follow you wherever you decide to live. As long as it's in the neighborhood, of course.

My family would not survive it if I had to move to China, or even France."

He smiled. "Agreed. But did you have a look at it? I want your opinion as a professional nurse."

She nodded, blushing a bit. "It's certainly different from your previous house, Ekbeth! Far less modern. We'll have to do something about the stairs when Judikali starts to walk, but it's actually quite baby-safe, I would say."

"Good! Then I'm going to call the real estate agent and make an offer on it."

Judikali woke up at that moment from her nap in his left arm, and opened her mouth widely. Not to wail, it was just a yawn. Ekbeth smiled. Yes, that daughter of his was a little tyrant, but she certainly had stolen his heart. He knew he would go through hell for her. No matter how little she was.

He suddenly chuckled. He had never promised such a thing to any woman before! Certainly not to her mother.

Annabel got on her feet. "She does have a perfect sense of timing—right on the spot for her meal! I'll prepare the bottle."

He was cuddling his little girl, when a piece of paper appeared on the desk in front on him. That was fast! Keremli must have known the answer…

He opened the note. Sadly it was not a reply to his request but a notification that the High Council was to meet in the next hour, and that, this time, all the Akeneires'elin were expected to attend.

He looked at his daughter. "Okay, we just have time to feed you properly. Then I'll be off, for hopefully a very short time. You're going to be a brave girl with Annabel, Judikali. You have to promise daddy!"

She just stared at him, calmly.

*

He was the last one to enter the High Council room. He bowed politely and walked to his seat.

The collapse had brought its changes here, too. He could not remember the last time three Akeneires'elin had been replaced all at once. Perhaps he should not have felt so, but he was glad he was no longer the youngest member of the council. Compared to the young As'leandra Na Liathe, who was quietly talking with her neighbor, he felt ancient. She could not be more than thirty.

As'leandra na Liathe cast a curious glance at him when she saw him enter. The others were not so polite. "That baby is not welcome at the Council, Ekbeth!"

He had been expecting that reaction, and calmly returned the Na Ghorm's glare.

"It was that or not coming. She's not reacting well to my absence, Keryl. I left my accommodation for ten minutes before Nukri transferred me here, and—Ara!—was she loud! Actually you should feel quite honored by her presence as you are the first to see her, even before the Na Duibhnes."

The Na Ghorm grumbled, but the only other woman present in the room besides As'leandra was smiling. "Babies can be such little monsters sometimes. My firstborn certainly required all my attention in the first months. I'm glad I was not the Akeneires'eli of the Na Saoilcheachs then. I say, let her have her mind for once."

The rest of the group nodded their agreement, if reluctantly. Ekbeth relaxed a bit.

The doors were closed.

Traditionally, when the Aramalinyia was not attending the Council, the Na Liathe opened the session.

The Aramalinyia seat was ominously empty at the end of the table.

As'leandra Na Liathe sat rigidly in her chair, as if her height could compensate for her lack of years. Ekbeth repressed a smile. He was no better than the others. He should know better than to judge aptitude on the number of years.

She suddenly looked at him, and he would have sworn her eyes were twinkling. He was certain she was reading his thoughts. It was quite annoying.

She ignored him.

"Akeneires'elin! The servants of our Aramalinyia have summoned the High Council. I'll let their representative speak. Leli?"

A woman, recognizable from her white clothing as an Ara servant, approached the table of the Council with all the arrogance Ekbeth was used to from the women dedicated to the Goddess.

Arrogance well matched around this table.

The Na Ghorm smirked. "So, Ara's made a choice at last?"

The servant raised a brow and superbly ignored the old man.

"Time is nothing to our Goddess. If we had to wait a century for another Aramalinyia, who are we to argue against it?"

Ekbeth had to smile, but he was probably the only one amused by the reprimand. The others were too stiff in their seats now, a sure sign they were all irritated.

He had to admit that not having an Aramalinyia was an inconvenience. Her servants were still celebrating the daily prayers in the temple, but for the rest, pretty much all the important decisions were blocked because Ara's voice was not there to validate them.

The plans for rebuilding the city, for example. The Aramalinyia was also Ara's voice to dispense justice as a last resort. On a less dramatic note, she was the one to perform the naming ceremony, and the weddings.

They could not wait a century.

Even the servant knew that. Almost four months had been a long enough delay.

Ekbeth was as curious as the others to hear the news.

When an Aramalinyia died, and the Goddess had not made the successor's choice obvious, as in Kimiel's case, it was customary for all the As'mirin women to throw a stone with their name on it into the Lake. Then, the community had to wait until one of those stones came out of the water.

"My sisters and I have walked the Lake edge every morning, as is the tradition. Only this morning did we find the Goddess's answer. This is Ara's choice."

The servant put a simple stone on the table before her. A stone with a deeply carved inscription on it. This was a bit unusual. Normally the women only wrote their name with some paint. He was nearer to the stone, so he bent over to read it. He looked at the servant with puzzlement.

Impossible. He had to be mistaken. The servant looked calmly back at him. "I know, Akeneires'el of the Na Duibhnes. I must admit we are as puzzled as you are. My sisters and I have consulted the archives. We could not find a similar case in our whole history."

All regards were now turned to him. Nukri na Liom finally asked, "Whose name is on the stone, Ekbeth?"

"Kimiel's."

Everyone gasped.

"What kind of joke is this? You told us she was dead, Ekbeth! Have you been lying to us?"

Ekbeth tried to remain calm, but he glared at the Na Ghorm. "She is dead! You were there when we cremated her body at the Temple."

The Na Ghorm returned the glare.

"Gentlemen! You will behave in the Council!"

As'leandra na Liathe was looking grimly at the Na Ghorm. "Enough. Now, Leli, we are facing a little mystery. You are certain that stone was not outcast from the water before this morning?"

The servant nodded firmly. "As I said, Akeneires'elin, this is an unprecedented situation. The Goddess has never made such a choice before. We discussed the situation with my sisters before asking the Council to meet. We have no answers yet. Except that maybe someone placed the stone for us to find. Someone other than the Goddess."

Ekbeth was the center of attention again. Thankfully, As'leandra came to his rescue.

"Interesting theory, Leli. We can of course ask the As'mirin. But we also have to consider the following. What if the stone is not lying? What if Kimiel is still alive, somewhere?"

She paused. A bit too long.

The Na Ghorm exploded. "So, she is alive! The Na Duibhne is lying to us all! And you are covering for him! You, the McLean, and you, the Na Liathe! Even the Na Saoilcheach! The filthy whore is alive!"

Suddenly, the whole room was in uproar. The only ones who were still seated were Ekbeth, who was trying to protect his little girl from the turmoil around them, Nukri na

Liom, who could not stand, anyway, since his accident, the Aramalinyia's servant, Leli, and As'leandra na Liathe.

As'leandra looked with annoyance at the scene for a moment, then, when it became clear to her that it could go on for hours, she just said one word: "Sit."

Ekbeth sensed it. They all sensed it. She was playing with their minds. Imposing her will. Suddenly, the room was very, very quiet. And they all obeyed her. It was a bit frightening how easily she could manipulate them.

Nukri na Liom raised a hand. "I've just tried to Call Kimiel Keh Niriel the past five minutes, without any results."

As'leandra shook her head. "Does not prove anything. There can be plenty of explanations for you not being able to Call her."

She looked around her. "I think we have to be a bit more open-minded about this, Akeneires'elin. Yes, we've all seen her dead body. Yet, Kimiel Keh Niriel may be alive. Stranger things have happened before, but you may not know this as few of you ever bother to read the Chronicles. She may be alive. Somewhere. And, I have to stress that point, no one was aware of this before this Council, Keryl na Ghorm. Ekbeth is grieving his partner and he certainly has done his best to solve her murder in the meantime. So no need to point fingers at anyone. We just have to find her."

Then she looked sternly at the Na Ghorm. "And I strongly advise you to remember you're talking of the Aramalinyia next time you call Kimiel a filthy whore, Akeneires'el! The Goddess might take offense, if Kimiel doesn't herself."

66

EKBETH WAS STILL getting over the news when he came back to his hotel suite. He called Annabel and handed Judikali and her new toy over to her.

"My, she's not crying!"

Ekbeth absently nodded. Then he realized the nurse was right. Well, that was at least one of his problems solved.

"Indeed! I was a bit skeptical when my aunt told me to try it, but apparently she was right. Just place the doll next to her when she starts crying. It should do the trick."

Annabel looked at the rag doll with a bit of skepticism. "That's it? A doll?"

"Ah! But a very special doll! I first put it under my clothes. It now wears my smell. I will have to do this a few times again, I suppose, but as you can see, it seems to work!"

He was certainly glad he had met his aunt before the Council had started. He had just had time to grab the doll she offered and place it on his stomach before running to the High Council meeting room.

Annabel smiled. "That was a very clever idea of your aunt, indeed. Now, Miss, let's do a bit more testing. It's time for your meal and your bath. See you later, Ekbeth!"

Annabel had just left the room when Sarah-Lysliana appeared in the middle of it.

Ekbeth hushed her before she could speak. Signaled her to go to the lobby downstairs.

He met her at the bar. "Good day to you, Sally!"

She did not look as if it was a good day for her. Her hair was going in all directions, and her clothes were stained with a suspicious yellow liquid. A smelly one at that. She certainly seemed out of place in this luxury environment.

She noticed his expression, and smiled. "I was just having a try at making cheese when Andrew told me the news, Ekbeth. I had to talk to you! Why couldn't we speak in the room? Was it because of Judikali? Was she sleeping?"

"No. Because of her nurse. She would have heard you—she had only just left the room."

Sarah-Lysliana shook her head. "You will have to explain things to her, Ekbeth! And soon. I expect you're going to have a lot of visitors in the coming hours. Is it true then? Kimiel is alive?"

"As'leandra seemed convinced!"

Sarah-Lysliana made a face. "Damn! I was so pleased with that memory stone! I suppose I'll have to take it away before Kimiel sees it!"

Ekbeth could not help it. He laughed. She grinned a bit sheepishly. "I know. Sorry. It must have been a shock for you, and all I think of is that stupid stone!"

"It's fine, really. Thanks for being here, Sally! I needed to laugh!"

She took his hand. "You're welcome. So, what's the plan?"

He shook his head. "I have no plans. I'm still getting

over the news. I held her dead body in my arms at least twice, Sally. I lit her cremation fire myself. How is this possible?"

"We'll probably discover a logical explanation in the end."

Ekbeth laughed again, shaking his head. "Logical explanation? Sally, we are talking of Kimiel here!"

She grinned. "Right. I almost forgot."

"But you are right, Sarah-Lysliana. There must be some explanation."

As'leandra appeared quietly behind him.

Damn!

"Don't worry, Ekbeth! I was careful to enter the building in a proper human way. And look, human clothes and hidden hair. All checked!"

He realized she was indeed blending nicely into the surroundings. He offered her a seat. He was not surprised when Kalem, Najeb and Lyrian joined them soon after. He sighed. "Wait for me here. I think we would be better off going to Watanabe's place and discussing this with everyone concerned. Can you let him know we are coming, Najeb? In the meantime, I'll warn Annabel I am going to another meeting."

*

They soon found themselves around a table in one of numerous rooms in Watanabe's house. Ekbeth, Sarah-Lysliana, As'leandra, Najeb, Kalem, Lyrian. Watanabe and Matheson. This time, Maire Kincaid was there as well.

Watanabe was frowning. "What's this that you told Jeffrey? You think Shona is alive? I saw her dead body before you took her away to cremate her, Ekbeth."

Ekbeth nodded. "I know how it sounds. I set fire to her funeral pyre myself. Still there are some signs…"

Ekbeth let As'leandra tell their hosts the latest news. The reaction was the same as in the Council. Consternation.

Watanabe was the first to get over it. "So you think she's alive because a stone with her name carved on it appeared on a lake shore? Is this a joke?" All the As'mirin present around the table shook their head.

Watanabe growled, "Please, how naïve do you take me for?"

As'leandra said, "We don't have an explanation for this yet, Toshio, but you have to believe us. She is alive, somewhere, until we can prove it's not the case."

Matheson shook his head. "I can't believe it. She would have contacted us if this was true. She would have told us."

Watanabe looked grim. "But she didn't. I can only say this… is… not… a good sign!"

The two men had had a much longer history of knowing Kimiel than the rest of the people present in the room, but Watanabe had expressed the general feeling.

Ekbeth asked, "What do you think she's up to, this time?"

Watanabe answered with another question. "Did you have time to look into the accounts we gave you? The ones where we have no transaction statements? She may have used them recently."

Ekbeth looked at Lyrian, who shook his head. "I'm still going through the paperwork for most of them. I did look into the ones at our own bank. No movement there, but I was not expecting otherwise. If she's using her own money, and doesn't want us to know she's alive, she certainly won't be using those accounts!"

Matheson said, "I think she's in Germany. In Hamburg. And she's just waiting for the perfect moment to kill Kellerman."

Everyone looked at Matheson. Watanabe thought about this for a moment. "She had almost four months to kill him, Jeffrey. To my knowledge, he's still very much alive. That does not sound like Shona. At all."

"Unless…"

Watanabe glared at Matheson. "Care to elaborate, Jeffrey?"

"You remember what she did to the Triad lord who had threatened Yeshe?"

Both Watanabe and his wife blanched. Maire Kincaid whispered, "She can't do that! Not to his office! It's a huge building! I've seen pictures of it on… Oh, my!"

Matheson nodded quietly. "On our network! Shona has been collecting information on Kellerman for months. It was quite an obsession for her at one point, but I don't think she had been contemplating repeating her worst ever exploit prior to Kellerman hiring someone to kill her. It is a huge building indeed. You need preparation, careful calculation, money, material. Hence the four months."

Watanabe shook his head. "She would at least need the structural plans to do this."

"We had the building schematics as well. Yes, we all know how useless she was with computer software, but she had the passwords to log in remotely. She just needed to find someone to explain to her how this works. I need to check the log. It might be a more solid proof of her existence, if we find something in them."

Ekbeth asked, "Can you tell us what you are talking about, gentlemen? What did Kimiel do to that Triad Lord?"

Jeffrey gritted his teeth. "She asked someone to put a bomb in his office. The whole building blew up. She got fifty persons killed in that explosion."

Watanabe made a face. "It certainly made the other Triad heads think twice about continuing the war. They offered a truce not long after. But she killed a lot of innocent people in that act. She never asked me if I agreed with it either. She just did it."

Watanabe shook his head. "We need to warn them, Jeffrey!"

"I can't just call the building security and tell them to check for a bomb or explosives, Toshio! They will never believe me! Even with the schematics, how would she manage to find the quantity of plastic needed? And to put it in place? We are talking of a skyscraper here!"

Ekbeth had an answer to this. "She's been training with our Caller since after her Trial. I don't think that positioning plastic would be a great difficulty for her, if she has the building plans. I'm not even sure she'd need to spend money on it, if she knows where to find explosives."

Kalem intervened for the first time since his arrival. "I know someone in Hamburg. Not working for Kellerman's company, but at the head of an important security firm. He'll believe me if I tell him I've heard rumors. He'll warn Kellerman's security."

Ekbeth nodded. "Do it then. Now."

Kalem left the room. Watanabe took over the conversation. "If those men find explosives in Kellerman's building, this will be the final proof we needed that Kimiel is alive, but she's going to be mad when she sees her plan falling apart and she'll resort to a more direct solution. Kill Kellerman, preferably in a very public place. She'll want everyone to know the reason behind her act!"

Ekbeth could imagine the scene. The chance that she would survive was very narrow. The chance that he would be able to help her out of the situation if she survived was nil. Except if he transferred her out of jail, but he would need to approach her to do that, he or another As'mir, and he would not be able to do it discreetly. He certainly did not want his name associated to a suicidal killer, even if she was the Aramalinyia.

Kalem came back. "My contact promised to call back within an hour with news."

"Good. So, the question is, how can we prevent her from committing public suicide?"

Matheson looked at Watanabe. "We should kill Kellerman ourselves."

Watanabe shook his head. "I can't do anything without serious evidence, Jeffrey. I already explained this to you. Kellerman has some very close high-level friends in the Triads, among others. Killing him out of the blue would make them very angry. We don't want to get into another survival war."

Both Matheson and Maire Kincaid shook their head.

As'leandra spoke. "We need to find her."

Kalem snarled at her, "Of course we need to find her, Akeneires'eli. Last time, we managed because she made a mistake. A mistake she won't make again. And you've just heard her best friends saying they had no clue she was still alive. That means no known mobile phone number, no email address, not even an address. Yes, we may have a location, but Hamburg is a big city. We'll never find her, or at least not fast enough. We can't Call her either. So how do you propose that we find her exactly?"

As'leandra was taken aback by his reaction, but Sarah-Lysliana snapped back. "No need to be so aggressive, Kalem. True, we have no clue where she is. Why don't we try to solve the problem for the opposite side? She knows where we are! Can we get her attention? Tell her to contact us?"

Watanabe shook his head. "She's not really responsive to messages when she's in such a murderous mood, Sally. I'm sorry."

She showed her stubborn side and continued arguing. "There must be something to which she would react for sure!"

Maire nodded. "Her son, Toshio! We have to tell her we've found Sonam."

That bit of news did not surprise Sarah-Lysliana apparently. Interesting how that woman seemed informed of all the important events. She shook her head. "Too personal. We need something we can put in the news. In the papers, on TV, everywhere."

Maire Kincaid suddenly jumped out of her seat. "I know! I know!" She certainly had everyone's attention now. "We are going to put the White Lady on sale, Toshio! At Sotheby's, or Christies. They'll inform Kellerman! I'm certain Shona is keeping track of his activities! She'll hear of it!"

Watanabe suddenly had a huge grin on his face. "You still have your body armor somewhere, love? Because she's going to come here all knives out and you'll have to tell her it was your idea!"

Matheson nodded. "There's also the risk that she'll just come to the house and take the sculpture from the safe."

Ekbeth was glad that he could at least help with that bit. "You remember that message I gave you when you brought me back to the airport, Matheson? We could use the same trick on the sculpture."

Matheson smiled. "Of course!"

Ekbeth was glad the situation was growing less grim. All this talk of explosives, murder and suicide had made him fear the worst for a while.

He still had to get over the idea that she was still alive, but damn if he was going to lose her a second time in such a short time.

They had a good plan.

First Kimiel.

He would arrange Kellerman's punishment himself. Watanabe was apparently afraid of going after the man. Understandably, if they had no proof to bring him to court. At least not one on this side. Ekbeth did not have such restrictions.

Kalem's phone rang. This time he did not leave the room. It was a very short conversation, and most of the talk was from the other end of the line.

Kalem was grim when he finally hung up. "My friend wants to know how I've come by my information. The security found some plastic in the walls. Not the inoffensive kind, and not a small amount of it. They are evacuating the building. Seems our timing was perfect. The bomb was in place and just needed a fuse."

"In the walls? How did she manage to put it there?" asked Watanabe. Then he looked at the As'mirin present around the table and sighed. "Of course. Nothing worse than opening a safe or walking through the walls for you, I suppose. I'm glad we've found her before it was too late. We have to act quickly. I'd say we have three days. Maire. Call your friends at Sotheby's. Ask them to make a special sale. I'm going to put a few extra things in the lot to convince them it's worth their effort. And insist they have to shut up about the previous owner's name."

"They'll ask for more commission."

"Fine with me. If they link this to us, Kellerman won't bite."

67

MAIRE'S CONTACTS AT Sotheby's were eager to help when she told them they would get fifty percent of the sale price as commission if they managed to organize the sale before the end of the week. They asked when they could see the goods so that they could start preparing the catalogue.

Kalem brought the auction items, with Matheson and a few other security members of Watanabe's team providing additional protection. Just to reinforce the importance of what was entrusted to the auction house.

The experts were certainly impressed by the objects. Though all their interest quickly went to the White Lady.

Ekbeth understood it perfectly. He had had plenty of time to admire the little white jade sculpture. It was perfect. It was unique. It was priceless. Only, it was not his.

Matheson told the expert the sculpture story—how it had been made by Yeshe, the famous Bhutanese jade sculptor, for his wife, and so on. The enthusiasm only grew. They had just the perfect customer in mind, they told Matheson. A big collector of Yeshe's work. With any luck, the artifact would hit the million pound mark.

They took all the pictures they needed, and then the collection left Sotheby's, back to Watanabe's house. They could not take the risk that Kimiel would try to steal the White Lady from the auction house. It was just impossible to keep an eye on the sculpture from inside Sotheby's. Kalem and Najeb took turns next to the safe.

Ekbeth tried to concentrate on the decoration of his new house. He had signed the contract that morning while Kalem was in London.

Luckily, Alyasini offered her help. She was a much better interior decorator than him, anyway.

*

Kimiel did not try to steal the sculpture from the safe. No, she entered the house in the middle of the night and pointed a gun at Watanabe's head, demanding to know what he thought he was doing?

Watanabe, calmly, pressed the alarm button on the small device he had been given by Kalem. Twice to signal she was armed.

Then, as instructed, he tried to talk to her. This time, Kalem took no risk. He was lucky enough that Nukri transferred him to the perfect position for a hit, but the rest was all his doing. He hit Kimiel on the back of her head, hard. She collapsed on the bed. Thankfully, without any shots involved.

That's how Watanabe related it to Ekbeth afterwards. Kalem's version concurred.

Ekbeth was impressed that Watanabe had managed to stay so cool under the threat.

He was not sure he would have been.

"Where is she, now?"

Kalem shrugged. "Watanabe decided to trust your talent as a negotiator. He just warned me to allow her to cool down her wrath first. So I've asked Nukri to send her back into the cistern under the city and given her some of that drug to prevent her from calling herself out of the situation."

"Nukri's going to tell everyone we've found her."

"No. I've explained the situation, Ekbeth. He owes you for having solved Akalabeth's problems to everyone satisfaction. He's going to keep it quiet. She can shout all she wants in the cistern—no one will hear her!"

"Good. How long do you think we should wait?"

"Watanabe advised at least six hours."

"That much?"

Kalem nodded. "She had never pointed a gun at him before, he told me. Even in her worst moments."

"Fair enough. So let's wait, then I'll ask Nukri to transfer me in the cistern."

"Ekbeth! It's not the best place to have a friendly discussion. It's humid, dark and small."

"I can bring some light. Think for a second! I have no place where I can discreetly talk to her. Because I'm pretty sure she's going to scream at me!"

Kalem finally nodded. "We've taken care of the gun, but she's still dangerous without it. I want you to stay in contact with Nukri at all times. And please take some time to talk to Watanabe before you go and meet her. He has experience in dealing with the effects of her crisis, as he calls it."

Ekbeth nodded grimly. "I certainly will."

*

He waited a full day before he asked Nukri to transfer him inside the cistern.

Discussion with Watanabe had been helpful, if not reassuring. It had mainly confirmed that he had to be cautious around her.

The cistern was a really dark place, damp and smelly. He was glad he had thought of bringing a lamp. He could not see her at first, so he raised the lamp above his head and slowly turned around in the cramped space, cursing silently about the layer of filth his feet were currently in.

She moaned and covered her face with her hands when he finally discovered her, curled up against the wall. Kimiel was not a pretty sight. Wild chopped hair. Blood on her face, blood on her hands. She had probably spent some time hitting the stone wall. Still, it was her all right.

His first reaction was to drop the light and take her in his arms.

First, check her state of mind, Watanabe had said.

He crossed his arms, thinking furiously, but could only say, lamely, "I'm still not sure I'm glad you're alive after all, Kimiel. What were you thinking? Pointing a gun at your best friend? A man that has saved your ass twice at least?"

She spit on the ground. "Go to hell, Ekbeth! This is not your problem! Why are you bothering?"

So, still pretty mad. He took a few steps back, until his spine hit the other side of the cistern wall.

"Your friend Matheson made very clear to me that you were my responsibility from now on. So here I am, trying to prevent you from doing something you'll regret later."

She hissed, "Toshio has no right to sell the White Lady! Yeshe sacrificed his life for it! Doesn't that count?"

"Look at me, Kimiel!"

She was used to the light by now. She lowered her hand.

Her face was really not a pretty sight. Covered with blood, mud and dried tears. But her eyes were blazing.

He talked to her sternly. "Did it enter your mind, Kimiel, that Toshio may have announced he was selling the White Lady to get a reaction from you? To hear from you? You, who kept quiet for four months—four months—that you were still alive? We've been grieving for you, Kimiel! We missed you! Why didn't you tell us?"

It slowly dawned on her. He could see it. She hit the ground with both fists. The smelly muck splattered on her face but she did not seem to notice. "I hate you all! A trap! This was a trap!"

"True, but we were a bit desperate to get your attention before you did something stupid. Even more stupid than trying to blow up Kellerman's main office!"

She hit the wall with one hand. Hard. Fresh blood started oozing from her palm.

"You! You were the one who called security! I was almost ready! It took me weeks of preparation!"

She threw a ball of mud at him. He was glad it was only mud.

This was not going well. There was no point in discussing this with her as long as she was still so mad at him.

"Maybe I should leave you here to reflect on your crimes a few more hours, Kimiel. I am not your enemy. Neither is Toshio. We are trying to help."

She shook her head. "You don't understand. That man is evil. He kills to get what he wants! He killed everything I held dear. He killed my husband. He killed my daughters. All this for a little piece of jade! He had no right. I hate him! I want him dead!"

Daughters? He was fairly certain the use of the plural has not been a mistake.

He tried a different approach. "You've killed your fair share of people as well, Shona."

"It's not the same! It was never the same."

He could see tears on her face. Fresh ones. Almost there.

"Daughters, Kimiel? I'm only aware of one daughter, and that's ours. I've discovered a lot about your past recently but Watanabe only told me of your son, Sonam. Who Watanabe found, by the way."

She remained silent for a moment. Probably registering that bit of news.

Then she told him, between her tears. "I never told anyone about Cholkye. No one knew about that pregnancy, apart from Yeshe and his family. We wanted it to be a surprise. I wanted Toshio to become the baby's godfather. She was barely a month old when the soldiers entered our house. She was the reason everyone was at our place. We were celebrating her naming ceremony! So little! She was their first victim. One of the soldiers put a bullet in her head. I had to watch them. Do you have any idea what I felt, Ekbeth? I had to watch them kill my baby!"

Ekbeth fought a sudden nausea. "I understand. Still, you can't hold Kellerman responsible for these men's barbarism."

She looked at him. He wished she had not. He had never seen such hatred in someone's eyes in his whole life, and the light in the cistern was not even that good.

"How convenient that he only pays the executioners, Ekbeth! Are you so accommodating about your own daughter? The killer wanted to call it off until I had given birth, but Kellerman promised to triple the amount if I was killed within one week."

"How do you know that?"

She remained silent for a moment, then said, "I found the bastard who shot me."

Ekbeth decided against asking what had happened to the man. He'd rather not know.

Kimiel moved, uncurled, and put her back against the wall. "The bastard killed me. I died, Ekbeth. The last thing I remember of that night, I felt the baby die within me."

"You still have to explain me how you miraculously rose from your ashes, Kimiel, but in the meantime, I have some news for you. Our daughter is alive, Kimiel."

She stared at him.

"I'm not lying. The ER team managed to save her. I'm sorry for little Cholkye, but you have another daughter who needs you out there, Kimiel, and a son. Don't you think they need your love more than this mad plan of yours to avenge them? "

He heard her choke. She took her head between her hands. Wailed.

This time, he left the light on the ground and walked to her. He took her into his arms. She just curled into his embrace.

"I'm sorry… I'm sorry… I just want him dead. So badly."

"Sssh. I understand, Kimiel. We'll take care of Kellerman. Together."

They stayed embraced in the disgusting mud for a long time. Something crawled around his feet, but Ekbeth managed not to move.

Eventually, she stopped crying. "I want to see them, Ekbeth. Sonam, and my little girl…"

"Now? Do you want to give them nightmares for the rest of their life? Shall I bring a mirror to show you your face?"

She winced. "No, you're right. I may need a bit of cleaning up first."

"Nice to see you so reasonable at last. Let me bring you home."

She nodded. Home was the hotel room in Zurich. Not knowing how long his discussion with Kimiel would take, and since the rag doll had proven its efficiency, Ekbeth and Annabel had agreed Judikali would sleep at the nurse's place for the night.

He and Kimiel had the place to themselves. He let go of Kimiel next to the bathtub and turned the taps on. Then he undressed her. The stay in the cistern had made her clothes filthy beyond recognition. His as well, but that could wait.

"Do you want to keep them?"

She shook her head.

He helped her into the warm water, then washed her gently. Even touching her as he now was did not make the truth any easier to believe. "I thought you dead, Kimiel. Don't ever do that to me again."

She answered in a drowsy voice. "I was dead, Ekbeth, but I was not ready. I reminded the Goddess she owed me a favor. She gave me a new body for this soul."

He had noticed some differences, but somehow his brain had not realized the truth. Ara had given her a new body? That was unheard of. He did not even need to read the Chronicles to be certain it had never happened before in their whole history.

She was really special to the Goddess, he realized.

That's when he noticed the pointed ears. They had been hidden under her hair till now. He touched them hesitantly. Kimiel cringed.

"Yes, I was not very happy with those when I woke up in that body and discovered Ara's little joke, but they are quite easy to cover."

He looked at her back. "There's no tattoo anymore."

"Ah, another of her little jokes… How did you find out I was still alive, Ekbeth?"

He told her about the new Aramalinyia's stone, carved with her name. "Did you put the stone in the Lake, Kimiel?"

She shook her head, and pondered Ekbeth's question. "I think Ara did this. I have been ignoring her orders for too long."

Ekbeth finished washing her. He helped her out of the tub and started drying her.

"Orders?"

She nodded. She was now leaning against him, eyes closed. "She wanted me to return to the Valley. I refused. We had a little discussion."

He bandaged her hands, and put some adhesive bandages on her face. "You are a sight, Kimiel. Why did you have to mutilate yourself like that?"

She shrugged. "I'll heal. So, what do you think of my new body, Ekbeth?"

He could not miss the playful tone in that question. She was unbelievable. Not less than an hour ago, she was all hysterics, and now… "I thought you wanted to see your children first, Kimiel? We'll have to arrange a visit to…"

She turned around in his arms and put a finger on his lips.

"The children can wait another hour, or even till dawn. I did not expect it but I did miss you all those weeks. This new body is all yours, Ekbeth. Heart and soul. Kiss me."

He discovered two things about her that night. How thoroughly new her body was and what she had meant by Ara's little joke about the tattoos.

When she finally fell asleep against him, he was grinning. No one would ever know about the first thing… but my, the tattoos!

It had surprised the hell out of him when he had seen them appear on her skin the first time. He would get used to them eventually, he supposed.

He chuckled. He could not wait to see the community's reaction to this new Kimiel.

68

KIMIEL LOOKED OVER the balcony at Kse'Annilis and the Lake.

This was her home. She did not plan to go anywhere else at least for some years to come. Shona McLeod had died that night in Zurich. She was now fully Kimiel Keh Niriel.

Aramalinyia of the As'mirin of Kse'Annilis. Ara's voice.

She knew most of the As'mirin still had trouble believing her tale. How the Goddess had given her a new body. She could understand that. She had trouble believing it herself. She could still remember when she had opened her eyes as if emerging from a long restful sleep, only to discover this body slightly different than the one she had been used to. It was not only the pointy ears and the tattoos. This body had never been abused by drugs and beatings. It had never fought. It was not ready to fall apart. This was more than a second chance. It was a new birth.

Dead, to be reborn. How true the Bhutanese astrologer had been.

She had woken in the Temple, which, thankfully, was deserted at the time. Her first movements had been a bit awkward, but she soon got the hang of it.

Ara told her she was to stay and assume her Aramalinyia functions again. Kimiel did not think so. She had asked for this new body for one reason only. She had transferred herself to the Other Side. Something else that had come to her much more easily. She had not fainted.

She did not want to remember what had happened next. Oh, Kellerman had become a bit of an obsession all right. She had used the money from one of her secret accounts to hire one of the best computer hackers she could find. They had managed to access Kellerman's private accounts. Trace her killer. What the man had told her before she'd killed him had only reinforced her determination to get rid of Kellerman forever. She was done with niceties.

She could have killed a lot of innocent people, she now realized. She was glad that Ekbeth and Toshio had found her in time and stopped her. Brought her back to her senses.

She looked around her and sighed. She was the Aramalinyia now. There was so much to do. Her lifetime probably would not be enough. Kse'Annilis had to be rebuilt to its ancient glory.

Ekbeth and his cousin were trying to find a way to finance the reconstruction.

As'leandra and Najeb had somehow managed to find the original plans. Najeb was busy experimenting, guided by the ancient books, trying to understand them. She smiled, remembering how his latest experiment had destroyed another house. Its family had been indignant, but she had just told them Najeb had her full support, and this had been enough to pacify their fury.

This was perhaps the only advantage of those tattoos she now wore. Ara's glow had been something, but the tattoos got an even faster reaction. They only became visible when she got emotional—whether angered or overjoyed, but they covered her entire body, even her face. Difficult to miss them. It was enough of a warning to be cautious around her.

She had many reforms in minds. Reforms she could simply have imposed on the community overnight and they would have accepted because of who she was. Ara had to be crazy to have given her so much power over these people. It was frightening sometimes.

Ekbeth had strongly advised her to wait before introducing those reforms to the High Council. Some of them he just told her to forget about.

She was glad to have him. He was her safeguard. Her smile turned warmer. He was her lover, her partner. She looked at the perfect creature nestled in her arms, fast asleep. He was her daughter's father. She kissed the little angel's brow.

From the moment Ekbeth had put Judikali in her arms, Kimiel had had the hardest time to let go of her. She and Ekbeth regularly argued over the right to hold her. There was not going to be another little girl so loved in the world, this side or the other, she had decided. Judikali had suffered enough. Now, there would be only love. Love and protection.

That brought her thoughts to Sonam and her smile turned sad. She had cried bitter tears when she had first seen her son. He had cringed in fear when she had tried to embrace him. He had not recognized her.

Their relationship was a bit better now. She visited him every day, and last week he had started smiling at her. She had hope that he would get better. His doctors were optimistic. Sonam was still young enough to survive this trauma, they had told him. With their good care, he would eventually forget.

The hope did not lessen the guilt. She had abandoned her baby boy to this monster. Najeb had explained to her where he and Toshio had found him. If only she had gone to Bhutan earlier…

She sighed and kissed Judikali again. She could not change the past. Hopefully, Sonam would get better. She could not wait to bring him here with her. She wanted to have her family all around her.

She heard steps behind her, coming in her direction.

"Aramalinyia? We are ready."

She put a last kiss on Judikali's cheek, and put the baby in the cradle. Annabel gave her a little encouraging smile.

It had been a risk to introduce Annabel to the As'mirin world, but Ekbeth and Kimiel had agreed it was best for their daughter to keep the same nurse, so they had carefully started preparing her for the big news. Annabel had reacted to the explanations more calmly than they had expected. She had certainly freaked a little bit after her first transfer, but, all things considered, she had adapted to the new situation wonderfully.

They had someone be with Annabel constantly, so that she did not feel alone. Kimiel made sure that all her questions were answered.

This was one tiny problem taken care of.

And another problem was about to be solved. For good.

After a last look at her sleeping daughter, Kimiel left the room and walked to what was now her own study. Thankfully, Ekbeth's apartment had enough rooms to provide all the needed space for the administration of both her duties and his without reducing the private segment.

She retrieved a small vial from its special compartment,

and Called herself out of the room. She reappeared in the very center of the Temple. The center of all attention.

All the As'mirin were there today, she realized.

As they had been for her own trial.

The irony was not totally lost on her.

She said the words, "Bring the prisoner here."

The guards brought their charge. She met Kellerman's incredulous stare calmly.

He stammered, "You! You are dead!"

She smiled at him. "You should know by now that I'm not easy to kill, Kellerman. Kneel."

The guards forced him down. His eyes were burning with anger. "You are going to pay for this, Shona. I am powerful! I'll destroy you."

She shook her head. Kellerman had apparently repeated those words from the moment Najeb and Kalem had taken him from his cozy villa two days ago. Even a stay in her favorite cistern had apparently not helped hush him up. He would probably never learn.

"You are a human. I am the Aramalinyia, the Goddess's voice. Hear your sentence and repent before it's too late."

He tried to shake the guards' hands off.

"You can't..."

She ignored him, looked at Ekbeth instead. His tiny nod was all the encouragement she needed. She focused on Kellerman again. "Kellerman, you've been brought here today to be judged by our Goddess. Your crimes are many and odious, but she'll been the one to decide whether you should be allowed to keep your miserable life or not."

His eyes were glowing with hate. "This is a farce."

She saw the tattoos appear on her hands, then on her arms. At least the sight shut him up.

She had tried to remain composed. She really had tried. But she had suffered too much because of this man. His hate for her was well met.

She took the vial and opened it. "Undress him."

When the guards were done with their little knife play, Kellerman was white with fear.

Finally, he understood what was about to happen.

She looked into his eyes. "Not a farce. Actually you are probably the first full blood human who has ever been put through Ara's trial, if that is a comfort. Open his mouth!"

The guards obeyed. She poured the liquid into his mouth. She knew that she was now not only showing her tattoos—she was also glowing. Ara was sharing this moment with her and she was glad for it.

"Ara, judge him. And don't be merciful. He does not deserve it."

Kellerman started screaming a few seconds later. He screamed and writhed on the temple sand for a long time. Then he stopped moving.

One of the Na Saoilcheachs confirmed his death. Kimiel closed her eyes. Justice was done, at last.

Yeshe could now rest in peace. Yeshe and all his family.

She felt a hand on her shoulder. Ekbeth. She covered his hand with hers. Shona's life was now truly over. Kimiel would never completely forget her past, of course, but it was time to embrace her new life.

A quiet laugh answered her.

Yes, indeed. Welcome home, child.

THE HUMANS

Toshio Watanabe : Antiquities dealer, Shona's boss
Maire Kincaid : Toshio's wife, Shona's friend
Jeffrey Matheson : Toshio's employee
Yeshe : Shona's first husband, dead
Dorje : Yeshe's older brother
Sonam : Shona's and Yeshe's son
Cholkye : Shona's and Yeshe's daughter, dead
Orsina : Ekbeth's personal assistant

THE AS'MIRIN

Ara : Goddess

The Aramalinyia (Pes'almari) : Ara's voice
Leli : servant

THE NA DUIBHNES (FINANCE)

Ekbeth : Akeneires'el

Arkel : Older brother of Ekbeth, former Akeneires'el, dead

Kas'el : Second brother of Ekbeth, dead

Alyasini : Arkel's daughter

Es'ael : Uncle

Keremli : Ekbeth's and Lyrian's great-great-grandmother

Lyrian Farrill : Ekbeth's cousin, ex-husband of Sarah-Lysliana McLean

Kalem na Seffet : bodyguard

Najeb na Seffet : bodyguard

THE MCLEANS (ENTERTAINMENT)

Duncan: Akeneires'el

Fiona : Duncan's sister

Alasdair : Duncan's second son, dead

Arkeri : Alasdair's wife, dead

Andrew : Alasdair's and Arkeri's son

Sarah-Lysliana : Alasdair's and Arkeri's daughter, ex-wife of Lyrian Farrill

Kieran : relative

(The McLeods)

Malcolm : Duncan's Elder son, dead

Emily: Malcolm's widow

Richard : Malcolm's and Emily's son

Kathleen : Malcolm's and Emily's older daughter
Philip Murray : Kathleen's husband
Shona (Kimiel) : Malcolm's and Emily's younger
    daughter

THE NA LIOMS (CALLERS)

Nukri : Caller
Akalabeth (and Sieven) : Nukri's grand-daughter,
    Kas'el's daughter, Caller

THE NA SAOILCHEACH (DOCTORS)

Erinani : surgeon
Bers'el : expert in toxicology
Kes'alri : doctor

THE NA LIATHES (BUILDINGS)

S'emoel : Akeneires'el
As'leandra : Eldest daughter of S'emoel, mind reader

THE NA GHORMS (LIBRARY)

Keryl : Akeneires'el

THE NA DEARGHS (PROCUREMENT)

Please visit my Facebook page (Ada Haynes' worlds)

or my website (www.writer-adahaynes.com).